BIRTHPLACE

moving into nearness

William S. Wilson

north point press · san francisco · 1982

Copyright © 1982 by William S. Wilson
Printed in the United States of America
Library of Congress Catalogue Card Number: 81-83968
ISBN: 0-86547-068-5

for my children,
Kate, Ara, and Andrew

The accent of deviation in the living thing
That is its life preserved, the effort to be born
Surviving being born, the event of life.

Wallace Stevens

I. correspondence

Dear Octavio,

I am writing this letter on the theory that someday you will return to Primavera to explore your background. I allow myself to hope so, perhaps because I returned to explore my background fifty years or more ago. I have walked, or shambled, up from the isthmus where I was collecting berries for ink, and collecting my thoughts, focusing on the eastward ocean, then turning to focus on the westward sea, until I felt some resolutions, some reconciliations, and even a few resignations. Now I sit at my desk in the postoffice, my bare feet comfortable on the mat I sleep on under the desk, preparing to launch myself into writing this letter for you, to tell you that you were brought to this island, a child about two years of age, in a black-rubber wet suit, by two observative dolphins, Mirador, and another one that has never been given a name. Letters have been arriving addressed to you, and in your absence I have opened those that, because of silverfish, damp spots, or fungus, would soon become unreadable. I am going to copy some of the letters for you here. Also I write to let you know, since Delenda has been dead about thirteen years, and you left us about two years ago, how we have continued to live, and to govern ourselves, and also to tell what I know of your origins, which Oliver and Olivia did not keep secret from you—their letters chronicling events simply did not become due for delivery before you departed. I expect more letters will arrive for you as I write—indeed, one arrived as I was about to sail into this letter, and occasionally some are still being written to you. Olivia writes to you almost every day. I will incorporate the letters that seem appro-

3

priate in this my letter which will be waiting for you when you return to Primavera, the green island sighted by Renaissance sailors from the East, where first we sighted you on the ridges of the blue-grey-green waves upfurling into salty white blossoms, nudged alongside the immense eye of Mirador, the eye that seems a porthole through which we see into her seaworthy impulses, toward her maritime heart. When I took you from Olivia's arms, when she would at last let me hold you, she looking me in the eye and saying one word, "Freedom," you were already weathered and strong, a resilient and flexible, lean and waspwaist boy, built for leaping and vaulting, a salty lad. I thought to myself the words that Orlando, who was fast becoming your father, quoted aloud: "sailing strange seas of thought alone." Now, Octavio, before whom I open our lives as I slice open these letters awaiting your return, I am at last an old greybeard whose eyes still swim with tears when I hear a footstep that might be yours, my lithe grandson. I listen for many footsteps that I will never hear again. Oh where, in what is left of the world, could you be, Octavio? How far could you have gone in that canoe? Sometimes I think I see you enter the postoffice, but I know it isn't you, I would have heard a stir of people gathering about you. Or I think I see Oliver, for I have trouble remembering that he drowned, rushing in to inform me of a delicious, elegant new fact, or to show me a piece of paper he had made. I have been bartering some of his paper, his "poems," for larger quantities of more ordinary paper, so that I can write to you. How can I think of Oliver as our little prince yet make you remember him fondly? Of course you did not know him when he was about your age, as I did, but always, even when you knew him, his beauty was such that it tempted one to believe in something beyond it. And Orlando, as Oliver's cousin, and my son, and custodian of language, would have asked what "prince" could possibly mean, for he required that words precisely designate, wanting words to copy things, even as he was always copying down our words in his notebooks when he was a child, words like *brouhaha* or *immiscible*, words that might come in handy. But he had few words helping to lay Oliver's body out in the grove, building the leafy mound which the Indians and Creoles decorated, individually but collectively, as their individual offerings—discarded objects, sand sculptures, shells, and old gifts from Oliver— constructed the mound which the rats are gnawing at. I try to see the rats as part of the living monument to Oliver, to see the rats as their movements and to see their movements as deflections of light, as Olivia teaches me, yet I resent them and shudder as they scurry about serving their own purposes. Aurelia, as part of my daughter's lifelong attempt to teach me objectivity and scientific relativity, tries to get me to understand, if not to appreciate, the rats and their opportunism. She encourages me to respect the logic of their whiskers and tails and little eyes, and their capacity for breeding, for the rats feed and breed, feed and breed, among the mounds where our dead are lying under heaps of found objects, vines, and an occasional plate of food. I tell Aurelia how I find the cryptophagous rats repulsive, and I can see that she doesn't quite decide for or against the rats which swam ashore from the earliest ships (and some of those ships, *Los navios al través*, were made to be dismantled upon arrival so that neither the slaves brought to slave in the sugar cane fields, nor the rats, could have sailed home, and to step on the threshold of my father's house is to step upon the beam of a slaveship). Aurelia can see that the rats, with their behavior which Oliver, who liked to return a metaphor to its source, called "ratty," threaten the survival of more indigenous species. The rats create imbalances which Aurelia thinks herself obliged to contemplate neutrally, as though we live in a laboratory and are objects of an experiment. She argues that such imbalances are creative disequilibriums, that evolution gains its momentum from succeeding imbalances. Yet in other moods she has been a partisan of clean and healthy island life, and has killed rats when they lived under the houses of the living, or *in* the houses. Aurelia does not regret extinctions as I at my age do, she so confidently expects new living forms to emerge, some novelties. But even if we remain tolerant of the rats, eventually they will have nothing to eat but other rats. Your aunt Aurelia, reluctant to interfere with the imbalances of nature, receives no comfort from Olivia, who reminds Aurelia that in her role of medical engineer she had eliminated the mosquitoes ("About thirty years ago," Aurelia comments, as though she would have second thoughts about doing it now), and Olivia, speaking for herself, says that she sees above the rats oblong bars of silver, a blackish silver, she insists, although once when she used that phrase Oliver said that she had borrowed it from a novel by Joseph Conrad, even if he uncharacteristically couldn't put his finger on the passage. Olivia complained that the following day or week would turn up sources for her best images and ideas, or that at least they would seem like sources to Oliver with his pack-rat memory, trying to drag her back to some purported origin for her most original remarks, while experience showed as even Oliver could see that her sources were all to be found in the future, not in the past, so that Oliver's hindsight diminished her foresight. And she told and told, as verbal as she was visual, that she preferred to go out to the kitchen to talk with Delphine as she cooked because they could begin from the beginning each time (which is almost the opposite of the truth; Olivia chose to overlook the continuity), while her husband Orlando was always in the middle of a story she too often could guess the ending of, and cousin Oliver was quoting a source or analogue for whatever he was saying, as though "Western Literature" would put a foundation under his thoughts when actually he, as she saw it, was putting a foundation under "Western Literature" by using it to think his thoughts. Oliver of course grew up with quotations, for his father used to write them on the walls of Tornata, where Oliver lived much of his childhood with his grandmother. He could, as he said, read the writing on the wall in his childhood, at least until Converse, if that is who it was, set Tornata ablaze. And even after the wreckage of Tornata toppled onto the sand below the cliff, looking like a shipwreck that has become a breakwater as sand built up around it, we could read some of the peculiar quotations visible for years afterward through the windows whose shapes had become what Olivia called "perfect Euclidian catastrophes." She enjoyed prowling around Tornata while Aurelia dug in the cliff for fossils, hoping to read the evidence of fossilized eyes, or at least evidence for emergent photoreceptors. Olivia complained that Aurelia wouldn't notice *her* emergent photoreception, which might be useful evidence in the story of the sources, origins, causes, and evolution of eyesight (but Aurelia, once she had eyes only for Delenda Kinh, seemed to understand Olivia better, even if she couldn't quite believe her). For uncritical understanding Olivia sought Delphine in the kitchen, or in her room in the attic, as Oliver sought the Indians, and as Orlando sought the Creoles, as they all or each sought others not because they — Oliver, Orlando, Olivia, and Aurelia — were not enough for each other, those four, but because they were sometimes too much for each other, each a part which contributed more to the whole the more it at-

7

tempted to be a separate part. The farther their lives and interests had sprawled away from each other, the closer they had grown together again, unwittingly. Separated, they read the same books, listened to the same music, discovered the same words, or found an idea that would be a perfect gift for the others. "Oliver wrote a poem about plows and furrows. I can't believe it. You've been doing this paper on plowing imagery and contradiction in philosophy, and I've been studying the relations between the length and shape of fields and the draft animals used, the ease or difficulty of turning them, and finding these lovely paintings with horses in short fields and oxen in long fields, and here is Olivia experimentally getting the gardeners to plant the vegetable garden without having it plowed up. I wonder what we're thinking." They found their lives most real when they discovered in them correspondences with each other's lives. I could show you the similar sentences they wrote in an essay-writing exercise for Father Converse when he was tutoring them: "To be is to be congruent with," Aurelia; "To be is to refer to," Oliver; "To be is to be reciprocal," Orlando; and, "To be is to be collateral," Olivia, who could make a flat word sparkle with bitterness. Years later, they were still quoting and misquoting each other's sentences, and a few of mine. Facts about the four of them together add up to a larger sum than facts about the four of them individually. They built interrelations into rapport—each so different from the others—and they influenced each other so fluctuatingly that the differences among them were always the same differences, and remained recognizable in spite of apparent peculiarities, and they could and did exchange traits sometimes, as when they first saw Delenda Kinh stand upright, Aurelia, upon seeing him stand vertically in the canoe, was astonished into quoting "The armstrong offspring of the doubled night," although quoting was contrary to her plans for a scientific language, lapsing into a quotation as she saw, enabling us to see, what she had not guessed until that moment she had been looking for, not only a man who seemed like something ever more about to be, awakening into even more believable awakenings, but also a man who was our immediate defense against Kwant and our defense against our defenses against Kwant, and before that day (which because of the falling ash obscuring the sun had never quite been a day) had ended, we had dared defenselessness, emboldened by the sight of that man, Delenda, who drifted from the west to the shore of Umberland, he the first true spring to reach our Primavernal place, as Aurelia said later, sounding more like Olivia than like herself. When Aurelia quoted "doubled night" she did not know that the Indians would regard the night as indeed doubling itself dangerously because the sun was not visible. They were lamenting the confusions in the sky to Kwant when Delenda appeared and made Kwant disappear from Primavera, only to reappear across the isthmus at Umberland, Oliver laughing out the line ruthlessly at his own grandfather, Kwant, "He topsy turvy ding-donged down," as naked Kwant set off running and dingling, naked except for his khaki drawers and for his urine-collection device strapped to his leg and dangling yellowly, the only suffering I ever let myself laugh at, yet it was a regrettable burlesque, for he was my father, he owed us some discretion, but this *opéra bouffe* helped to set the tone for the romance that followed it as Aurelia, still uncharacteristically, for when had she noticed a man since she had dissected one in medical school?, still quoting, this time "Down with arms and up with legs," embarrassed her usually earthy brother Orlando, who seemed to have lost his voice in the excitements, and who stood with the childish expression he cul-

tivated when we were not supposed to disturb him because
he was apt to be a writer and was in fact at that moment
thinking of a story, as I remember him eight years old with
a pad and a pencil, writing down a word now and then that
he had heard Delphine use, and then copying it into his
notebook along with Creole proverbs, even copying Delphine's mock "conjure-woman" warning that he would be
punished for stealing words from poor people, later trying
to tell the men sitting and squatting outside the company
store about the interest of their language, with doubtful
success, and making me feel if not exotic then quaint when
he wrote down my description of a book, that it was "as
dry as church," or my comment on Father Pasquale, that
he was "as cold as charity," he copying down our words as
though a collection of them would add up to something,
but it was the *copying down* that was historically interesting,
not the words and proverbs. As I will copy down for you to
read so many letters written in his hand, the handwriting
of my only son, so familiar to me, indeed so like my own,
that I begin to suspect that handwriting is an inheritable
character. So, Octavio, if your desire to know where you
came from is strong enough to pull you back to Primavera,
then you will receive this letter of letters which will tell you
most of what we know. I have erased some of Oliver's old
verses, and I will search in the Infirmary or if need be in the
ruins of Utterly. I will accept gifts of paper in order to write
this letter. I could use the surplus paper which people
leave on a table stationed along the wall in the postoffice, I
would be welcome to use it, but that paper produces fewer
memories and thoughts than the other papers do. I am
going to tell you who we are as the only answer I can think
of to the question who you are, for wherever you are now
you did once join us, and I want you to know us as we are,
so that you can know the family you were borne into the
midst of, and so that, should you rejoin us, you will join us

as we are. Hence this letter. Which assumes, now that your father is dead, that I have inherited some rights in you, as I once unwillingly but necessarily acquired some rights in your mother, Olivia, whom we bought from two young-sters, Ginevra and I, two sandy, sandy-haired youngsters who looked like children to me, wanting to sell a child they couldn't keep, so we bought her as quickly as we could — what were the alternatives? — while wondering what to do, and then those youngsters whom no one knew — they seemed to have been passing by the island in a boat, they seem to belong to a story of impossible possibilities — they were here and then they were gone. We told ourselves that Aurelia would have another little girl to play with, al-though Olivia said later that Aurelia didn't need a play-mate, she needed a subject to experiment upon, so that Olivia said she became an expert at her first determining and axiomatic metaphor, *experiment*, the hard-earned pain-ful way, from experience, and I suppose that she was the result of an experiment between those sandy-haired youngsters, whom we hurried to rescue the baby from, for the point was not to buy a baby we didn't need but to save a baby who was not wanted, we had to attempt that experi-ment ourselves, and Aurelia would say that we are all ge-netic experiments, at least experiments in the sense of trial and error if not experiment as a repeatable concrete opera-tion, and Olivia said that she was an experiment in what would happen to a child who was experimented upon by a three- or four- or five-year-old medical student named Au-relia, that she knew all too well what a concrete operation was from experience. "I was not diapered as a baby, I was bandaged," which is of course her exaggeration. Aurelia adored her and was always careful, and indeed Olivia ap-parently had not been diapered until we purchased her, and she didn't like it at all. Exaggerations. Olivia com-plained that Kwant did not say, "What are you doing?", he said, "How do you plead?" We knew that Aurelia was only playing with Olivia and never hurt her, although Olivia still claims that she had to sacrifice her bear dolls to Aurelia's operating theater under the veranda, that she let her Pooh Bear have an appendectomy, vividly vivisectional to her animistic baby eyes which performed biopsies on the stuffing from the bear, and that she let Teddy receive an eye transplant of one of the human prosthetic eyes which that anthropologist had used in barter, smuggling it across the veranda past any watchful adult eyes in her vagina, "Oliver's idea," she said in a tone which suggested that it went without saying. Olivia was, and is, happier than she knew, or knows. I feel that I have spent a lifetime telling myself this, and sometimes telling her, to which her response is that it doesn't make her at all happy to be told that someone knows what she is feeling better than she knows herself. I was always frightened by the title of an old essay by Sigmund Freud: "A child is being beaten." Olivia was never beaten. She often spoke like that, with a slight ironic distance, a gap she could not close between herself and the self that was speaking to you. Except with Delphine. Kwant had brought a black servant from Baltimore who couldn't find much to do for the first few years, so she became a nurse to Olivia. Aurelia seemed to regard the term *nurse* as her license to be a doctor. Delphine mediated between doctor and patient. Aurelia would say, "Someday you'll want me to operate on you and I won't, you'll see, you'll be sorry." She was born digging into things. But predicting what Olivia would see was unscientific of her, for Olivia's sight is unpredictable. She was, as Aurelia once said in her only moment of deliberate cruelty, "She was that way when we got her."

Well, dear Octavio, you were a most emphatically rescued and welcomed child, so that I would like to think as I sit here preparing to copy letters for you that I have some motive other than rescue. I probably can't save you from anything but my good intentions. If the sea was your cradle then I was your grandfather in the kinships we fell into on this island, and I worry about presuming too much on the relationship. I would say, What harm can a letter do?, yet I am always learning the power of letters, at least their power in this place Olivia called "the Republic of Letters," where Oliver said that soldiers, if we still had our ten soldiers (Kwant's soldiers in U.S. Army fatigues camouflaged themselves as people within hours after Delenda arrived) would study belleslettristics, not ballistics, and would learn to trace the trajectory of a missive, not a missile, as a letter might fall from the packets hanging in the wooden rafters above my desk and hit someone on the head. Not that we had missiles. One advantage of Kwant's dictatorship is that he approved of nothing much invented after about 1939, so that we were spared modern weaponry, and the soldiers had only a few old rifles and an abandoned U.S. Coast Guard tower to protect our freedom. Still, I can see that I am rescuing the letters, and catching myself at an unfamiliar form of a familiar game of mine, as though I am captain of the lifeboat, delights me sufficiently for me to forget about you somewhat and to get on with the task at hand, here in the peculiar theater of my task, the island postoffice. Your father, Orlando, dead now these two years, here writes to you in a letter that arrived for you only last week, thereby prompting me to start this whole endeavour of going through the mail that has been accumulating for you.

The Loft—Primavera—Huc-Uinkil 10th—Year 16

Dear Octavio,
I have been to my supply closet for paper because I know that my letter will be a long one, and it will be interrupted, and I will use these interruptions patiently because I can-

not look at you without remembering the uses of improbable accidental interruptions. As I write, you sit across the room from me, a child of about five, almost six years of age, playing ferociously, and looking at me occasionally with reproach because I am ignoring you. You gather cat hair, moth wings, and other stuff to give to Oliver when you make paper with him. I caress you, and read aloud to you—will you remember this scene as you read this letter? We are in the loft where I work as a scribe for people who prefer to dictate their letters. You and I are alone here. I have told you that I am writing you a letter. You are playing, or rather you are working at playing. I never quite have your full attention. I read aloud to you the letters I received today. I will copy them here, then give the paper to you to tear up. First a letter to me from your mother, Olivia:

Chan-Uinkil 7th—Year 13

Dear Orlando,
Today is one of those days that I will recognize the face of if ever I see it again. Delenda may have a point about the physiognomy of days. Anyway I suppose that I can scarcely argue with what he sees as the features of a day when I see swatches of light, the lively adventurous distances among the reds and yellows and blues in the sunset, and anyone could have seen what I was seeing until scathing Orlando marched past me in a searing light, a livid glissando from aquamarine to violet-blue, jolting me out of my remote transcendence in the ordinary sunset into a local, albeit nonspectral purple, a domestic shade of silver, and several lustrous shades of grey, which, attempting to manipulate the purple and silver, succeeded only in appearing dismal. Ah, Orlando, I cannot scribble a note to you for this year or next without wondering which of us will be

dead, without remembering what we, so robust, were determined to be and to do and to have, and without thinking that we are never to know quite what happened to us, or to Octavio in the years he lives beyond our years. Therefore so many purples and violets, which alternate merging with each other, and so many silvers and greys, which melt into each other, all dwindle into one lacklustre mauve. I think—and I know what you think, that I overreact, and overwrite—that you should forgive me as soon as you can. You must stop using silence to get the last word with me.

Cheerfully pensive,
Olivia

Octavio, your mother's letters are sometimes difficult for me to read, and painful to copy here, but I wanted you (I want you) to know us as we were, caught as we are in peculiar temporal deflections as I write to you now a letter you will not receive for a decade, so that as I sit in this scene I look back upon it; this scene contains that later scene, you reading my letter, if only as a phantom, although as my goal it is a real goal, and that later scene in which you read this letter preserves this present scene, a legacy. We do, I hope, live for the day, but now our day always contains intimations of the future because of the letters awaiting us. And today feels like the future imagined on some past day because I received also a note from Oliver:

Tornata (the Ruins)—Batzul 4th—Year 8

Dear Orlando,
I am writing to say that I received a letter from you this morning, written to me so long ago, in the year 1, that *annus mirabilis*, that you may have forgotten it. I walked over here to the cliff at Tornata to sit and read it, and to ponder why I walked in this direction rather than take the path toward

the mausoleum. Your letter reminds me that I owe your future, our future, a letter. I want to say, and the words never quite come up comfortably in our conversations, that I am angry, or more precisely, jealous, because I went through that night so many years ago sleeping in the tomb, the year we called 1997 in the old style, sleeping in the tomb like a sleepwalker in the sense that I was never awake to what I was doing or to where I was, and only because when I walk I seem to walk toward the crypt, although I haven't chosen it as my destination, but then as I veer off this way, toward Tornata, I realize my loyalty to my childhood parents who failed me by dying, my loyalty to their failure, which abstracts as loyalty to failure itself, and here I am, rather older now than they were when they died, and rather afraid to walk past them in their crypt as I am afraid to live past them, and succeeding to their confusions, I try to mold their confusions into the words of my verses, but I fail. I feel that I belong to a secret society of one, and that the secret is all too safe with me. As I move, even grow, toward the future which at least contains letters waiting for me from you, Olivia, Aurelia, and various stray friendly creatures on this island, I want to live past the fear of my parents, buried alive and bickering in my flesh on their endless macabre honeymoon. Delphine shook her head and not saying what she was thinking, made do with a canny, or was it uncanny?, observation: "Pardon me, Mr. Oliver, for what I says, but you mother never be dead while you alive." Which leaves me with two riddles: if she is not dead, where is she, and who is buried in that tomb? and why did Delphine act the bandana-head *mammy* with me, slurring her speech? I am writing this letter to you now, when I think that you would not have any idea what I am thinking about, with the perhaps futile hope—does that sound condescending? —that you will be able to help me read my images. Don't I have pain written all over me, or does the memory of the lily-colored clothes I used to wear obscure the inscriptions? This paper, by the way, is made from hibiscus stalks, another mistake. The flowers look so much like the flowers of kenaf that I thought, wrongly, that the pulp might work as well as kenaf. Next time I will try the flowers instead. As Aurelia would say, "Well, you were willing to experiment." Which, translated, means, "Well, you were willing to fail." But I have already done that, and I am not as willing as I might seem, for the general happiness since Delenda arrived, which I share, makes me reluctant to say how unhappy I am that I am not yet a poet.

Fastidiously,
Oliver

I can tear up his letter now, Octavio, for you to add to your collection of stuff to make paper from. I hope that you are learning these words: *kenaf, hibiscus.* I want you to like us, I suppose, and looking back on this scene, a decade hence, I want you to have liked us, but of course at five years of age, or six, you can never know us as we know each other. I am forty-one years old if I can still count correctly, and Oliver is about the same, but I can still see him walking toward me as he did when he was four years old, or eight, or sixteen, even as I can see Olivia in so many eras and modes of her life that sometimes I do not know which temporal plane to focus on. How odd and how painful is the realization that as you grow toward us in number of years you grow away from this era of our still youthful selves, selves which may be intelligible only in this era. I am longing for your understanding and approval, while declining to conceal much. Yet with too much to tell you all at once. And Aurelia writes to me:

Otterly House–Zakilab 20th–Year 8

Dear Orlando,

I haven't lost track of all anniversaries. *The Origin of Species* is 150 years old this year, unless, as some think, we lost or gained a year when we switched calendars. I have sometimes lost track of the days, although Salathiel keeps accurate count in the postoffice. Dear Orlando, I know that you are not the husband to Olivia that Delenda is to me. Be patient. You think me a dry, surgical, and sometimes antiseptic paleontologist who has never quite defined her field of interest. Yet I tell you that I love Delenda fiercely as I see in him, in his visible bones, the history of survival and of weaponry. His teeth, which he bares for me sometimes when he is making faces to show me the faces of the months in his Mayan calendar—as when he tries to look like a jaguar with its tongue sticking out—his teeth are fangs when he is showing me the face of an era, otherwise they are part of a smile that reminds me that there must once have been a first smile, and a first counter-smile. Delenda's arms, which are so strong that they are armaments; his skin, burned in endurance of the flaming sun to shining black-brown; his eyes so vulnerable that I understand why his face is a fortification of high cheekbones—I always feel that I have put myself in danger just as I see that I have put myself beyond danger because all ancient threats are summed up and surpassed in the fortress-face of him who declines to threaten me. Who smiles. Who makes me feel, when he smiles, and when he sings so gleefully, like the wife of a knife-thrower in a provincial circus, and I can't imagine a killer—two killers—smiling more prettily. I find myself wishing that you would bite Olivia.

Your loving sister,
Aurelia

I am back, Octavio, your father, Orlando, I suppose remembering myself at fourteen or fifteen, the age you
should be when you receive this letter, all long-limbed
nimbleness, like a boy who might leap over a bull, and, remembering my judgments of Kwant and of Salathiel, fear-
ing your judgments of us. I would like to sound as though I
was not justifying myself here, but something in your
aloofness as you chase kittens out of the choir-loft suggests
to me that you, when you are fifteen and receive this letter,
will despise us, and I find myself feebly thinking, we were
not always such as you see us now, Sir, until I remember
that we were in many ways worse, four sleepwalkers who,
as Oliver says too dramatically, had to sleep in some strange
places in order to be awakened, which is why I am taking
this morning to write to you—with the storm approaching
no one will come in to dictate a letter to me, and you and I
can ride out the storm together up here under the eaves
with the wasps (superb papermakers), and moths, and
with occasional stray cats who, even if wet, are without
self-pity.

I want you to understand your inheritance; by which, in
our more-or-less collective society I do not mean property;
I mean the cumulative events which you inherit by becoming my son. I will tell you how I tried to and failed to destroy the corporation which I was about to inherit. And I
am timing this letter to reach you when you are new to your
youthful powers, with resentments pressing against hopes
and ideals. You may, as my son, be the one who gets to tell
my story, so I want to put some facts on record. You will
receive other letters undoubtedly which will convey to you
enough of the lives we had led until I was twenty. We sat
screened in on the polished veranda at Utterly waiting
until a servant told us that dinner would be at eight, too
little time then to do anything else but reflect upon a

glass of wine. Sometimes we strolled around to the open porch — *open* screen door, *close* screen door — on the other side of the house, overlooking the sea, where the breeze blew the insects away, but the view was so raw that usually we waited, there on the porch overlooking the garden, where we could hear Delphine in the hot kitchen built away from the house for coolness and I suppose safety, and at the same time could hear the maids giggle in the dining room, a clatter of dishes and silverware, and we would sit there conversing about life as a dream, an absurd, complicated, pleasant, and inconsequential dream, confident that dinner wouldn't be served before ten at the earliest, but that we were not responsible for these hours we spent waiting and chatting. We debated responsibilities and even what we could in our innocence call revolution, although we couldn't imagine a revolution (which would have been against ourselves, anyway) that we could individually survive so that I as novelist could chronicle it in a realistic — or would that be naturalistic? — novel, Oliver as poet celebrate it in blood-stained uncivil verse with Flamenco rhythms, Olivia as filmmaker compose it into a film as a worthy homage to Eisenstein, with the theme to be carried forward by variations in camera movement and in focus, while somehow telling the story of the deeds and sufferings of light, and Aurelia as scientist explain it as a moment in a social evolution evoked by its own probability, like a moment of integration in the morphogenesis of an embryo. Our conversings wove into a single unpremeditated meditation on the pretexts of revolution and then unraveled by themselves as we sensed that our exhausted lives were no more substantial than reflections in the hall of mirrors inside the front door of Utterly, the door that opened onto the sea — reflections so intense, immediate, and insubstantial. Oliver and I even placed mirrors in the herb garden beyond the pool to induce a metaphysical frisson. I don't know who we must have been reading at the time. Fragments of the broken mirrors turn up now, amidst the constraints of a design, on the burial mounds in the grove, sometimes indeed inducing a frisson, like the premonition of a close shave with death in a barber shop mirror. The word *basin* always makes me think of someone cutting my throat. Our complexity was too contrived. We knew how to be complicated, we did not know how to be simple. We were able to talk lengthily and excitedly about the weather, because Kwant allowed no one but himself to own a radio, and while he might announce an impending hurricane, he also did enjoy surprises. He used the power of his knowledge of the weather over the Creoles and the Indians who (although many of them came from places where they had owned radios, and although others had their own system of forecasting) listened to Kwant's daily homemade and inspired predictions as though he were in communication with higher powers (which in a sense he was). I am afraid that our incisive fervors were dulled or blunted by the comforts of the veranda, as well as by bad metaphors. White and purple wisteria sheltered and scented the sprawling porches. A squeaking glider, iced drinks (which you may still not have experienced when you read this letter; I forget so much of what we do without, and forget which of my references you might not recognize), and sets of maids —we rarely saw one alone (maids whom Delphine said were pampered) —so many pleasures arrayed about us as we waited. We were young and beautiful friends, enchanting and enchanted (claims which I could illustrate with anecdotes); or if that sounds too free, or too ideal, then let me say that we were bewitched, too self-bewitched to perceive the games that Kwant was playing with us. Aurelia, who traveled back and forth to college and then med-

21

ical school, could make paleontology and biogeography combine pleasantly with the dazed perfume of honeysuckle and bergamot. Oliver knew much of what Aurelia studied, he could even get into a field ahead of her and find the glittering facts, but he preferred, as even he said, expensive information about expensive objects, letting his name be put on mailing lists for catalogues, reading the advertisements when one had handed him a magazine for him to read a book review, he sometimes treating the world as an ultimate giftshop, returning from travels which he described as "in search of lost weather," remarking that all balloons are weather balloons, studiedly poetic, allusive, and to me, too indulgent with his obscurities. I love obscurity in women, but I do not like it in men. I did not always laugh at Oliver's jokes because we looked at words from such different angles. In those days, looking into mirrors and uncertain of the weather, yet always alert, we did read and study, but otherwise we rarely got around to doing anything more strenuous than display our taste in wine while waiting for dinner. We rarely even wrote letters, for writing letters was not yet government. We governed ourselves as benevolent despots, forcing our whims and caprices toward extremes in the hope of an aesthetic illumination or at least excitement, and in a peculiar coincidence or foreshadowing — the event seems to telegraph ahead that important letters are on their way — letters initiated some change, for we were discussing *Romeo and Juliet*, to rescue an evening from boredom and to save the play from what Father Converse had taught us to think about it, to revive it by using it to think with about our lives, that play with its lightning fast adventures in the middle of the starstruck night. Oliver mentioned that Juliet still received letters from desperate lovers. We laughed and agreed that such a claim was useful to attract tourists to

some fake tomb in Verona, but that we didn't even have
tourists (unless we counted Lord and Lady Baltimore, an
old joke I will explain some other time perhaps) on our
backward island governed by our grandfather, we had
neither tourists, television, telephones, or even telescopes
(lest we gaze at Umberland, I suppose), nor did we have a
tragic Juliet (Oliver said that Turner painted her alive and
well and living in Venice), at the most we had zombis, or at
least stories about zombis working the fields at Umberland
in the slow middle of the night, at Umberland, the sugar
plantation, *my* plantation to be as soon as I was twenty-five
years old, almost another island, connected to Primavera
by an isthmus or causeway which was not much more than
a long sand dune which the United States Government
had built when it took over the island during the Second
World War, and which Kwant's laborers had to maintain by
dredging the lagoon on the sea-side, where boats harbor
and anchor, and where the seaplane used to land, the men
carrying buckets of stuff they had dredged from the lagoon to the top of the dune and dumping it, Oliver, Aurelia, and Olivia sometimes fighting off the sea gulls for a
chance to investigate the mud, the three always seeming to
expect the sea to return to them something they had lost,
or to award them some prize they secretly deserved, in fact
the four of us playing obliviously among the oblivious
black men who didn't seem to look for anything to come to
them from the sea, or from those buckets. But we played
on the dune, or isthmus, only near Primavera, always con-
spicuously indifferent to Umberland, the nearby presence,
which none of us had ever visited, not even as far as the
botanic garden planted in front of the high metal fence that
ran across the island and out into the water. We could
see Umberland across the cove, and Kwant occasionally
brought flowers for the house, or interesting specimens of

leaves for us to study, but we knew more about Goethe in the botanic garden at Padua than about Kwant's garden. And in that childhood which was in some ways idyllic — "a good house, a stretch of sea below a window, and a large sloping field" — and in other ways somber, slightly melancholy, we raced down the sloping lawn to swim in the stretch of sea, never seeming to swim toward Umberland, but we approached it nonchalantly, glimpsing (as we rose from the water and pushed hair back from our eyes, as though we didn't know precisely where we had swum to, and why) the exotic trees lined up in obedient rows (usually two of a species together, a "green, yet growing ark," as Oliver quoted aptly), yet though the simple grid was imposed upon them, the trees managed to look recalcitrant, they were unruly even though they were pruned and trimmed — perhaps because they were pruned and trimmed — and some were cut into shapes, Kwant's utopian topiary, but joyless. The maids, and certainly Delphine, the cook, said that the fields beyond the botanic garden were sugar cane fields that were worked at night by zombis who longed for the taste of salt which would enable them to return to their graves. But no one on the island quite had a grave, and we were surrounded by salt water. The maids told their stories without enough enthusiasm to thrill us, and Delphine we knew was from Baltimore, she had been a singer in a tavern ("I know about the walking dead, Honey"), but we responded with the degree of horror that seemed contracted for in those days between the white children and the servants who, I suppose, did not dare to horrify us with stories of ordinary haggard men laboring in the fields by daylight, selling their lives for so much less than they were worth. Why they didn't murder us all in our beds I will never know. And the maids did not dare to horrify us with stories of their own lives, perhaps because they felt themselves spoiled by working in the house. Certainly Delphine told them that they were. Their reticence contributed to our comfort, but perhaps also to their own. I recorded the zombi stories in my notebooks without conviction. I know now from writing their letters for them that they never told us, never entrusted us with, their true beliefs, nor are they likely to now, because with Delenda's new methods of governing, and Kwant's death after his long self-imposed exile at Umberland, their more curious beliefs have deteriorated into common sense; and because they dictate to me as though in a trance, but perhaps affected by knowing who is taking down their words they speak of their experiences and feelings and hopes for the future, but rarely of the old days or of magic, although I seem magically to disappear for them as even a scribe while they dictate, self-absorbed or possessed by their task, until they have finished their rhapsodic dictation, whereupon they look at me as though they have been impolite, wondering what they can do to return to themselves and to make me alive to them again, for they have receded so far from me as I have transcribed their words with my pen— they transformed by inspiration, I transformed into a tool for writing—that I laugh, and touch their hands, and do my conjuring with those who choose to be conjured with. I suppose I have learned enough, or at least gathered enough information, to write that immense novel I was going to write when I was twenty-one and was going to launch myself toward New York under free sail, which would be better than Baltimore where, because of the adventures, or misadventures, which I am about to describe, Kwant consigned me to care for the family business in money and stamps, which I will tell about some other day. This is supposed to be a letter, not a bill of indictment. I know now that I will never write that book—the young man of heroic sensitivity explaining an island to itself—and I only used the idea of writing it to get my way, for what I was not willing to do or to demand for myself I was willing to do or to demand for the book I was going to write, and that willingness to act for the book which was going to write itself through me, along with talk about blood and fire and zombis, and about *Romeo and Juliet*, about stolen bodies, and about the bearing of art upon life and love, or the bearing of life and love upon art, all the talk of the idle young who, I now realize, couldn't have done anything because my grandfather, the grandfather of my sister Aurelia and me, and great-uncle of Oliver, owned the island, and we were unwitting prisoners of our own overwrought style which conveyed our overelaborated meanings, but was too unconstrained for politics. Even Oliver who called the kitchen the *hothouse* knew that our growth had been overprotected so that we would have to grow even more eccentrically if we were to achieve harmony, or at least symmetry. Yes, we delayed action as we read *Romeo and Juliet* aloud—"Prodigious birth of love it is to me / That I must love a loathèd enemy"—here on this island where time passed so slowly that we would look up and suddenly see that it had passed as quickly as an illusion and that we had done nothing with it, we had provided in the present no legacy for the future so that the present was not leavened by intimations of a visionary future, and we were as Olivia said we were, "Low on provisions." Oliver delivered himself of a messy image, that a poet is a midwife who buries his hand alive in language so that he can deliver words that will live in the lives of others—he thought in ill-fitting, clumsy departures from our common sense like that. Oliver would stand in one of the tailored celadon-blue linen suits from his collections of clothes that were never quite pastel, although they could be mistaken for it. One twilight he appeared, or materialized as Olivia said, in a white suit which, when we walked into the brightly electrified library, could be seen to be violet on the verge of invisibility. Olivia, whose throaty voice seemed always to be crossing the threshold into or out of silence, compared Juliet and the accident of her death with the deliberateness of Antigone, buried alive, and Oliver could put his finger on a passage in Henry James because as he said no two pages of a book looked the same to him: " 'Madame de Cintre is buried alive,' cried Newman. 'What are honor or dishonor to her? The door of the tomb is at this moment closing behind her,' " and I added that James should have said, "Madame de Cintre, c'est moi," to Oliver, who as he closed the book said, "The door of the tome is closing behind her," and then he told us of a twentieth-century writer whose ashes were indeed "buried" in a bronze book. We stirred only to fetch books the maids couldn't have found for us; one maid alone could find a book, but two together couldn't, and they stayed together. We stood to adjust a wicker chair the better to enjoy a view of silken cats dimpling the waters of the moonlit pool as they touched at the fish through the unpleasant wire grid which had to be stretched over the pool to protect the fish from the birds. The birds scolded the cats. Olivia said that the grid made us see the world as René Descartes had seen it, and as we chatted, somehow, amidst distractions, we seemed to have decided that Oliver would spend the night in his father's family's mausoleum behind Tornata, and that I would sleep in ours nearer to Utterly. And now, years later, I can't reconstruct our reasoning except that we had nothing more urgent to do. Oliver kept saying that we must die to the world and be born again in an art nouveau mausoleum in order to live as artists, and he added that he and I must be in separate tombs to spare rude talk. Olivia said that she wanted a tomb of her own with "communicating doors," and we laughed our way through jokes about the doors of communicating tombs, as we were able to laugh easily for we had reached permutations of such incomprehensibility to the servants in our luxurious games that they added us to the list of subjects which they dared not talk about, although perhaps their reluctance to gossip about us expressed hatred and contempt, or merely good taste. Perhaps they were bored by us, and were indifferent. You can, I suppose as I look across at you and listen to the growling approach of the storm, go out behind the ruins of the two houses and probe the mausoleums. When I was your age they loomed large in my imagination. You and I have walked past them often, but you do not seem dismayed. On the chosen evening your grandfather Salathiel was perhaps afraid to express fear for us, and he matter of factly made me comfortable for the night with monogrammed sheets, a cotton blanket, and a pillow, although he held on to them for a moment too long when handing them to me, a fraction-of-a-second interlude in which we both might have second thoughts. Oliver and I agreed upon no illumination except the full of the moon: "the most patient brilliance of the moon," as he kept quoting Keats to keep himself precise. Oliver had more to fear than I, for his parents were laid out in the tomb, not long enough to be objects of archeological interest — their shrouds, he said, still quite fashionable. I wonder how old a corpse or mummy must be in order to be declared an artifact? When do we take rings from the fingers of the dead into our museums? My mother was buried in Druid Hill Park Cemetery in Baltimore where she had died at Johns Hopkins Hospital. I pause here at the crossroads of another story I will not tell today.

Well, Octavio, you and I have just spent an hour watching this summer storm come up to shake us here in our cozy loft. I could preserve this storm by describing it to you now, complete with what your mother calls lightning volts. When I was a boy I said to Father Converse that I was going to write an epic about rain, and he said that rain was not an epic subject. When I told Salathiel, he looked at me seriously, he did not say no. My birthday was a few days off. Rain cleared the air like a palinode or like an apologia for dusk. Aurelia, who fell into our childishness for reasons of her own (perhaps to purge us of it, for she was never dishonest but was sometimes therapeutic, willing to administer a placebo, ready to discuss the contradictions or at least problems in manipulating those one loved in behalf of values they might not assent to), accompanied me and helped me to arrange myself in the tomb. She did not look around, although she was preparing to return to medical school at Johns Hopkins later that summer. Perhaps, tactfully, she did not want to take my scene away from me. Oliver paraded off with Olivia, murmuring verses from Webster,

Call for the robin redbreast and the wren,
Since o'er shady groves they hover,
And with leaves and flowers do cover
The friendless bodies of unburied men,

and asking for rhymes to *catafalque* and *conscript*. I quoted silently to myself, "Oh William, we receive but what we give, / And in our lives alone does nature live, / Ours is her wedding garment, ours her shroud," wondering if I believed what the words said, and thinking how much I would be willing to give for an epistemology I could live with. Oliver and I seemed doomed to recapitulate the worst of the Romantic movement, living as we did in that policed landscape, spoiling origins by our search for orig-

inal experience, and imagining as we did that we might still
be on time and might yet dwell enraptured and unin-
formed in an unpoliced nature. But our intentions never
quite interwove with unintentional existence. We knew
that we did not want to go back, to trace the way the others
had come to reach the place at which we found ourselves;
but we did not know where we wanted to go forward. I lay
in that early empty darkness before the full moon arose,
feeling silly in my awareness of such starlight as I could
see through a window, expecting to derange my senses
inspirationally, but merely thinking dry and derivative
thoughts about *Romeo and Juliet* and *Antigone*, about any tal-
ent that I might have buried under dead books, wondering
if as punishment for burying myself alive I should be
buried alive actually, or else for offending some law known
to the police, or to politesse, but not to me, I should become like Creon, uncle of Antigone, the *walking dead* — I
wonder if you will recognize these names, if you will know
any more of them at fifteen than you know now, playing
peek-a-boo with a hard-to-get kitten behind a pile of
blocks, unselfconsciously and conservatively childish for a
change. I didn't want to be in the universe of either Sopho-
cles or Shakespeare, they had different continuities, different discontinuities. I wanted my own universe, at least
my own island, which I hoped I could write into existence.
Something of my own generation. I wanted reciprocities, a
word which perhaps breaks through to me because Olivia
repeatedly broke into our complacencies saying "I want
reparations," even as she had complained through the twilight as she took the other path with Oliver, "I don't have a
tomb of my own," and Oliver replied, "You are better off
than I am, you have no place to bury your affections." I
thought that Oliver heard what he was saying with his
jokes — we all thought he knew what he was talking about

in that manner of his as though he had strolled downstage
to deliver a soliloquy so intimately that the audience would
feel honored — but we were wrong. He spent years trying
to tell himself with images what we thought he already
knew. As he said later, after studying Delenda's delays
(the mass of deferred correspondence accumulating in the
postoffice until we all deferred to the improbable presence
of the future gathering itself in the present, bearing upon
it, bearing down upon it, as though for Delenda reality
were not beyond or behind appearances, but were rather
appearances which had been delayed and must be awaited;
for him the eventful was incomplete without a glimmer of
the eventual), "I caught on to my jokes too quickly to understand them," he collected comic epitaphs but even that
fact told him nothing. Later then, in the darkness, ideas
going to and fro until they had muddied their own space,
unable to see anything horrifying, but adequately horrified by the texture of darkness — lightning just struck
quite close by, Octavio, and you look at me (I wonder what
you think I am doing as I write, you express so little curiosity) as you seem to hear some birds dislodged from their
perches in the trees, and I turn my chair to catch such light
as I can — and although Oliver would say, later, "I will
never be a poet, I was comfortable even in a tomb, I am
disgusting, I didn't even have enough experience for a poetic *conte*," with his emphasis on *conte*, defying us to hear
anything but elegance in his choice of the word which he
wedged into conversations with a straight face while aware
that he heard overtones and undertones of his favorite pun
and also heard our discomfort as we kept our agreement
not to respond to him as he stylized himself, *our* Oliver,
some gain and some loss in that process. Olivia said that he
would not be a poet because he went shopping for images
rather than experiencing them, and demanded more than

nature had to offer. He responded that she demanded
more than human nature had to offer. Well, none of us was
quite at home in the world, and I certainly wasn't at home
in that tomb lying awake among the dead, a silly overgrown lad, an imagination like a bucket that needed
emptying, hoping to induce a sensation so that he could
write stories of life as a melodramatic and somewhat Hispanic dream — undercurrents of German Romanticism —
lived in violent earthenware colors somewhere behind the
surface of a tarnishing and unevenly silvered mirror on a
remote tropical island, but that lightning striking around
us now has more vitality, and the rain has more vivacity,
than had my attempt at an aesthetic illumination, for I felt
groggy, and dozed into anesthetic sleep. I must close the
windows now, but I wait until the last moment because the
loft gets so stuffy and dark, and I can lose myself gazing too
long at the rainy windows rather than light a lamp and use
the precious oil, made from parts of a fish in a process
which I must learn one of these days, or perhaps you will
learn it for us, although I am told of some trees from Umberland which yield oil, copa-iba, but I haven't gone to see
for myself yet. I was, whatever my age, a boy who, if he had
tapped his boyish, adventurous good sense, would have
taken one look around this moribund island and made
plans to leave as soon as he was able. But my imagination
was tied to this island, so that I couldn't strike out on my
own, and I didn't grow up until Delenda arrived in his
canoe, a possibility which of course never occurred to me
as I lay in the dark in that tomb thinking furtive thoughts
about the future, furtive and as the future would prove,
futile and awry. I am glad, Octavio, that you are here to
share this rain with me, oblivious as you seem. I would like
to describe the rain, but I haven't enough wildness to have
important descriptive powers, I am not a great novelist

gone to waste working as a village scribe for voluble, im-
passioned, and illiterate Creoles, and some rather taciturn
Indians, who year by year do seem to cheer up. I suppose
that I have puttered rather than worked with words — this
storm is getting serious, I must think of our fishermen —
and of how the word *our* has changed in my lifetime — although the fishermen are usually in the harbor before
noon, and they know what to expect from a ponderous sky.
All right, I wanted, if not to be Shakespeare (although
what do you write when in your bewilderment you discover that you are not Shakespeare, that luckily he had been
able to write, "Oh how this spring of love resembleth /
Th'uncertain glory of an April day," that he could imagine
structures so large that they constructed real foundations
under themselves as they arose, showing so tenderly what
it would be like to believe in love, while something you
knew seemed to keep you from writing what you knew,
something he hadn't known, although he seemed to have
known everything, and art doesn't listen to excuses) then
all right not Shakespeare but at least to find a way to copy
my experience with words, perhaps the Balzac of the islands, and eventually perhaps of the Caribbean Sea, not
too confident of my philosophy or of my *Weltanschauung*,
unsure of my choice of festivals to attend, but, posthu-
mously, found to be, in spite of some counterrevolutionary
sentiments, the writer who massively foreshadowed the
values of the victorious future, his values compatible with
the latest trends in political theory, so that while I had died
comfortably in my own bed, my writings were preserved
in the amber of historical ironies, rescued by the convo-
lutions of a dialectic. I see that in my fantasies I plot the
trajectories of my life far beyond and long beyond my
death — the delusion of my early momentums — I would do
for my fictional Caribbean Sea what Braudel had done for

the Mediterranean, weaving the history and geography of the islands, with forays onto the mainland, into the story of the growth of a young man's mind, or I would be a slightly domesticated Joseph Conrad, even happy with wife and children, who would prove with images that not only is there something worse than the *nothing* of nihilism, as Conrad had, but that there is also something that is better than nothing, the plot of the novel would tell you so in words that would be worth repeating, something apt that Oliver might quote. Or no, not Oliver, who quoted promiscuously, but Olivia, something Olivia who disdained quotations would, albeit reluctantly, quote because the words were as wild as she was but savingly as dependably sensible as I was, words which would make "familiar objects be as they were not familiar" (Shelley), in a focus so precise that it would "make the visible a little hard to see" (Stevens), and I lay listening for reliable, stable, and persistent words in that crypt, words that would be keys to experience, anticipating and rehearsing, shuffling among my sensitive selves for the best one to spread out like a *tabula rasa* to receive delicate but usable sensations, good raw material for a story, but all that I saw was a scene in which a woman turned from a view through a window, a view which seems to be delayed in the glass, saying in reconciliation, "Oh, I didn't know that was how you saw it. But can you also see my point? Why I think your wait-and-see attitude is a mistake? Why would you have thought that I saw the problem so differently from you?", only a few aspirants leaving clues to her exasperations as she resigned herself to his procrastinations—but that scene seemed remote from me where I lay studying my repertoire of lukewarm fears, and I lay feeling that I had kept an appointment I had secretly made with disappointment, and failure. I could taste the disillusionment as a medicinal flavor in my mouth, and I

saw that I should have anticipated this failure, for I had
sensed that my future depended upon my failures amount-
ing to their own version of success, depended upon some
negative development such as Aurelia explained to me in
the local lizard which once had four legs—called *tetrapod*,
Octavio, you cannot predict the word you will need, so
learn them all—and the lizard progressed or regressed (I
hear an echo of words that I won't need to write for a few
more pages, I can feel them approaching) until the legs
shrank to stumps, short little limbs which it can use for
crawling but which fold back along the body for its serpen-
tine undulations, so perhaps I can regard some of the successful undulations of my life as compensations for the
failures, but they do feel a trifle reptilian, slightly slimy. Yet
I have learned since Delenda arrived that I can alter my
behavior, and in fact I have learned to climb trees, and to
swim farther than I thought I could out to the traps, and
these changes in behavior (I am avoiding mention of behavior toward people) have changed my muscles and my
instincts. I am the embodiment of different powers. And
having you as my son has altered me, the role of father
regulating my growth as a man, with every effect I have
on you affecting me. I begin to think of myself as an attractive middle-aged man, a becomingly receding hairline,
no-nonsense weather-beaten face, unapologetic eyes, an expression of gratitude but never of devotion, and strong
arms with which to hand over the love I feel, and to grasp
the love that flows back to me; superabundancy. (I was
right to plan for a long hard rain, for I have not been interrupted, no one has come in to dictate a letter. I see from the
window, holding you up so that you can see too, that the
yard is flooded, so the dirt floor downstairs will be muddy,
at least along the edges. Raindrops seem as similar as
snowflakes are said to be different, but these raindrops, al-

lowing me time to write you a letter as I watch over you at play, make a discernible difference to our future. More lightning-volts.)

I awoke from somewhere beyond dreaming—perhaps you have read of this episode in your other letters, and know more about how I got there than I do—there, elsewhere, in a dark shed among bodies which breathed and stirred, although no one spoke. I could have said from recent experience that it was as dark as a tomb. Then a barnlike door swung back on rollers and the bodies, four or five, shuffled out. I was pushed and pulled by hands I could not see until I stood in line, and as I went through the door I was armed with a machete. Outside the full moon illumined the scene in silver and black. I followed the body ahead of me, gradually able to discern the outlines, until by the time we reached the rows of sugar cane, no one speaking, I could see everyone quite clearly, but could recognize no one, and I gripped my machete and fell to in line behind a body, and saw the rhythm of it, he chopped only to the left so I chopped only to the right, no one seemed awake or even conscious, but the cane fell noisily, and we chopped and chopped in the moonlight which made the thick cane into palpable darkness, I felt like I was slicing blackness, I the most dangerously armed I had ever been in my life, and a little afraid of myself, uncertain what I would do, yet more afraid to step out of the steps I was following, too horrified, too unhappy to look for a word that would speak for these sensations. I spoke to no one. I couldn't think what I was doing there. I tried to think about salt for zombis, but I couldn't feel voodoo. My inability to think felt wrong, felt cowardly, for it kept me from saying what was wrong or from doing anything but cut sugar cane in the darkness for a few hours, then I obediently, although I didn't know what I was obeying, shuffled back to the barn

like a boy who had been doing a man's work — but what
was a man's work? — and I could see, or did I merely devise? — the silhouette of a black man with a gun as the door
closed behind me. I sat down and listened but heard nothing. (I haven't recorded the interruptions of this storm
which is unfolding the story of its power. The rain angles
its way under the roof, but since the beams and rafters are
exposed I can follow the routes taken by rivulets of water,
and cover up or move any letters that might be dripped on.
The chief cat can open the door to get out of the rain, and
nonchalantly hold it open until they are all inside, maintaining a truce among themselves, even the wilder ones
who, I suppose untouched as kittens, won't let themselves
be touched, trying to look complete and indifferent, rather
more like you than like me, who never discourages ca-
resses. I will learn about this storm in detail later when
women start arriving to have their letters written.) When
from the sounds I judged that I was alone, I stood up. My
hands hurt. I felt lacerations on my arms. Even my feet
hurt. No one moved outside, no one spoke, I was alone. I
ordered myself to pick up the machete I had dropped beside me and I pushed open the door which made un-
attuned, unoiled noises, scratching into the dreaminess of
things. I stood outside, stricken, feeling massacred by
moonlight, and no one, not a sound or word or thought of
common sense to help me, not knowing where I stood out
there on my own, but rather than think I walked to where
we had been cutting cane as though I knew my job. I recognized a green fiberglass shed, obscene in the moonlight,
looking like a color sample from some poisonous photo-
synthesis, a green that only money could have evolved.
Then I hacked at the coarse cane, and hacked, and found a
dull mechanical movement to shape my own unimaginative
space, listening to the blunt and angry percussions of the

falling cane. I worked as though my life depended on it, and then, descending in a devolution entirely into myself, I worked past fatigue, hunger, anger, and blisters, I felt no indignation, I worked until I felt the arrangement of all my senses around the objective and constraining sugar cane, a sensation which was like reaching a thought I had been struggling toward without knowing that I would find it beyond the unequivocal cane, in something outside myself, and then coming entirely out of myself I cut cane on every side of me, I whirled with my machete, I twirled, and then I hurled the machete aimlessly, I assented to my belated and perplexed introduction into labor, and into warfare, and I could feel my thinking, alone there amidst black greens and silver highlights, monstrous shadows and a hard-hitting moon, initiating me into a consensus that others shared but which I had not suspected, they not zombis at all as for more than a moment I had suspected, and I found out later that much of the cane was harvested with a machine (when its engine would start), but right then, without consulting reason or fear or facts, my body seeming not only to be my body but also an anecdotal history of pain, yet evoking a new loyalty to it and a respect for it, I saw the first startling green of dawn, then the violets and yellows, and soon I could see that I was either alone or supposed to think myself alone, hence was free to act as though I was alone, or as though I thought myself alone, and I could tell that this place was Umberland. Yet I knew that I was not deserted, for someone had arranged this performance of guerrilla theater—I was skewered on someone's good intentions—and I learned to read those intentions as I labored that futile night alone in that garden of Persephone—"direfull deadly blacke both leafe and bloom"—cutting shapes of blackness in that graceless underworld, the blood on my hands black to me in allegorical

moonlight, as I looked at my fatuous life, at what I could
see of it, by the criterion of moonlight, and saw my delusions, that I was self-reliant and on my way to self-
illumination. I limped around on a tour of Umberland. The
fields, the outbuildings, nothing very impressive. Even the
black tropical greens were beige and brown as daylight
broke. The rectilinear forms of the sheds were almost
quaint against the curvilinear growths of tree and vine.
A truck, a gasoline pump, everything industrial-shaped
looked frail and temporary, unassimilated by a place to
which it remained unaccommodated, a place where hard-
edged and metallic ideals were mocked as frail illusions by
the corroding salt-sea air, the rust in metal cavities, and the
churlish vines. A waterpump and trough, so I pumped
water and washed and drank. Then I was not tired or discouraged. I was groping for a way not to postpone the
meaning of this event, to understand what was happening
to me as it was happening. I walked leisurely around Umberland, an unprepossessing island when seen in the en-
croachments of daylight, less and less convincing grounds
for the horrifying constructs of the night. In the glaring
light, the fiberglass shed looked fully a delusion, the product of ugly and blundering self-deception. Years later a
hurricane demolished it. I understood Umberland now as I
could not have understood it in the equations in which it
was merely a name that represented money. *My* money.
What I was worth. Now it represented nothing. I had expected a sugar plantation to throb with power, but it
looked futile. Olivia said that Oliver and I, at least in our
youths, could not sufficiently distinguish what was expensive from what was beautiful, that our sight was corrupted
by calculations and appraisals. I admit that I did miscalcu-
late when I thought that I could walk away from this essen-
tially uninteresting place with its few machines, a truck

and a pump, which seemed to anticipate abandonment, although I did freely walk out through the gate, which was open, and through the botanic garden, with its seriatim trees, and across the causeway (isthmus) to Primavera, and I said nothing and explained nothing, and asked no questions, for I hoped to profane nothing, not to lose the rare clarity of knowing what I was seeing as I was seeing it, and then an appointment with my grandfather, Kwant, to discuss money, although he rarely allowed himself to get the drift of a question the answer to which might intersect with his money, or even my money, a meeting at which I explained that I abnegated my inheritance, that when in five years, the summer of 2002, I would be 25 years old, I would take control of my property inherited from my mother and held in trust for me, that when I came into possession of the corporation which owned the land to which I controlled egress, ingress, regress, and progress (and, as Oliver once added, *congress*) — and under my ranting Kwant was reasonably explaining "corporation" to me as a legal fiction, and ownership as a myth, explaining to me as though to their author my responsibilities to the workers and to the economy of Primavera, and the advantages of *limited liability*, a phrase I heard and marked for future reference along with *convertible stocks* which I wrote down in my copy book lest I lose the phrase, along with "discretionary funds," even as I yelled that the moment I owned Umberland Incorporated or Umberland of Limited Liability that I would on my own authority unincorporate, disincorporate, and bloodily dismember that unlimited liability, that limitless liability of incorporation, and Kwant was continuing for our uninterrupted six hours of talking (except for my trips to the bathroom) his patient ironclad explanation that many of the workers were hired to give them work, I could hear him stealing ground from under my

wrath, that some of the money to pay them came from the
sugar quota which the United States had granted Primavera, a quota of 18,000 tons, and that Umberland, Ltd.,
bought the sugar from Poland, yes Poland, at the world
price of $.60 a pound, cheaper than he could produce it
and transport it, and sold it to the United States at the protected price of $.75 a pound, which was charity anyway
because the United States had a surplus of sugar, that the
money to pay the workers came from Polish sugar, and
from the sale of coins and paper money and stamps which
were manufactured in Baltimore, Maryland, an enterprise
I would soon learn more about, and that I might imagine
myself more comfortable without property, but would I
imagine the men who would have no employment, and
who now paid no taxes on their wages, had I thought about
that? And had I noticed by the way that all of us were dependent, even with his restrictions on importations, on
some expensive imported foods, that the people had to eat
something besides beans and corn, that they needed food,
clothing, shelter, and medicines, that they wanted better
and more all the time, just to look in the company store
sometime at the stock, why some of the Indians needed aftershave lotion to wash their statues for a ceremony—the
statues that Oliver said belong in a museum as though they
are too good for the people who made and use them—and
the "Bombay Britches," the British Army surplus shorts
the men insisted on, button fly, pleated front—would I like
to see the receipts? Did I know how much these items
cost? Did I know about the cult of ritual underwear among
the Creole women and what their heavy white cotton
drawers cost? Who did I think would pay for such commodities? How would the medicine man or witch doctor
pay for his fetish objects? Did I think that money grows on
trees? Did I know how much *trees* cost? And did I under-

stand where toilet paper came from, did I appreciate that we had the finest toilet paper money could buy, without floral prints or decorator colors, not like that sandpaper in Mexico City, and did I know what a septic tank was? Did I know how anything works? The plantation could not always pay for itself, we were really only middle class, not wealthy, he paid maids who stood around giggling while there was work to be done, miscellaneous Indians floated up in patched canoes, occasionally with an outboard motor, but didn't work much better than the motors did, or wouldn't work but who had to be cared for—couldn't I use my eyes?—and really anything I owned was worthless without that sugar quota which came to us through good will because he had gone to a military academy in Virginia (he had? when? I couldn't stop to sort out the chronology of his life which seemed to expand or to contract to fit his convenience) with the future Maryland congressman who became the Chairman of the Agricultural Committee of the House of Representatives, a grant, a grace, a favor dependent upon the inertia in a fickle but syrupy Congress, a favor we could only partially repay by lending him, the congressman, free office space and some clerical help during election campaigns, and he (Kwant) was less free to do what he wanted than anyone on the island, he collected silver only so that the maids would have something to do, polishing it, that he spent his days redistributing the wealth, such as it was, about as quickly as he could, which was slow (because if I gave each of them a thousand dollar bonus do you know what that would do to the value of the money they have already labored for and saved, the few who are capable of saving, and do I know what would happen to the value of that thousand dollars?), and he continued to write lines for me to perform in this economic comedy, in this farce of freedom I had thought I would

produce, and he continued did I want him to give the
workers a raise in pay because I wanted a better life for
them such as they wanted for themselves—store-bought
idols instead of make-do fetishes—and I said yes, of
course, I want for them what they want for themselves, and
he said well then, and I said well then what?, and he said
you want more for them, you want for them what they
want for themselves, and I can show you the invoices of
their desires, and you can't raise their pay and improve
their standard of living if you don't have a corporation
earning money, can you? "Do you realize that the poor are
people who have no money? You are discomfited because
your abstract and spangled ideas are not fulfilled, you are
offended by our luxury, a penitent, but are you so insensi-
tive and tyrannical that you would dictate to these people
how they should live because you do, you must understand, want to unemploy these people whom you do not
know, while I am committed to them, when I fire a man
because our economy needs unemployment I fire him
face-to-face, after a dialogue, I knew his father and mother
and I recognize his children and remember their names, all
my relationships are comprehensible, no one's life is delayed by documents stalled in a desk drawer, I don't give
orders and then disappear, I stand my ground in an en-
counter with a man who may not be able to feed his children or clothe his wife, I don't give orders so much as I tell
them what they can see for themselves from the condition
of the fields or of the machinery needs to be done, and who
are you to impose your ideas on people who are only statis-
tics to you unless you perhaps remember the Indian lad
who was a servant-boy to you when you and Oliver broke
your legs falling out of a tree, and for sometime—could it
have been a year?—after you had mended. And wasn't he
glad to earn the money? Or perhaps you remember the

names of the maids who fetch you ice or wine or a book, and I said but you *rule* them, you make money from their labor, and he said my job is ruling them, and justice is each man doing his job to the best of his ability, and you are talking about matters you are not acquainted with, which is like chewing gum, a comparison which so bewildered me that I surrendered and did his Diktat for him, saying to myself that I was impotent, helpless, even despotic, able to lament but too unimaginative to know how to do good without doing incalculable, inconceivable harm, and whoever had arranged my education there in the cane fields had not known enough to teach me anything either, I would be a disappointment to them for I owed both my sweet-and-sour educations, in the sugar cane and in Kwant's office, to them, but I could not repay them except by keeping from them the whole story, or what I knew of it, which was that I did not know enough to act correctly, for I did not know how I would provide food, clothing, and shelter, aftershave lotion and toilet paper and ceremonial drawers, I was merely a bureaucrat among philosophers, and only after Kwant had fled to take refuge at Umberland, and my incorporation provided no more work and certainly no money for the men, women, and children, only then did the unimaginable happen, they provided food, clothing, and shelter for themselves without my help, and as everyone thrived they rescued me from my delusions about my power to do good, for I had not been powerless, I had been worse, unimaginative, unable to think inventively about the predicament, too horrified into imprecise thought to construct alternatives, and I could think of no response to the pleasure Kwant took in showing me to be in the wrong, he swelled up and reckless with the thrill of picturing me to myself caught in my own traps, he, my grandfather, my escort into the impasse, saying to abysmal me as he stood up for the first time during our interview, "Money is the blood of men, and who has none walks dead among the living." Let me see where I am now. During that night at Umberland I learned enough to want to know no more. Yet I would be further schooled, not only by studying at Johns Hopkins College, but in a second-floor office overlooking Charles Street in downtown Baltimore, with a view of an old Cathedral. I suppose Proust could have *used* the view. More of that another day, perhaps. You are asleep on the floor, Octavio, and I am tired from the effort of writing this letter to you as I see you a decade hence, and as I imagine us as you will see us then, there in the year 25. I am writing, I know, to defend myself against what I imagine to be your judgment of us, and I suppose that I write this letter to turn myself in. Yet I have changed so much several times since these events that I might be judged as I am now, not as I was, the island simpleton. We were born into different worlds, and you in yours are so clear and silent in your sullen lucidity that you sometimes frighten me. Yet I don't know why, for you enjoy the songs I sing to you, and here you are, merely a boy asleep on the floor of a choir loft converted into a scriptorium of sorts. What can you do to me? I will write again soon, a letter to be delivered sooner.

Your loving father,
Orlando

Orlando was too hard on himself, Octavio, and stopped his letter at a low point. Olivia's letter will complement his:

Primaverde—Hoken-Ahau 7th—Year 21

Dear Octavio,
I have received this morning a letter from Orlando, written five years ago, in which he tells me how he has written to you about his night at Umberland. I think of you when you

will read this letter, and I begin to write, as though from far away, "It is not for me to tell you this. . . ." But then I see you playing with bricks from the foundation of Outterly, and I check the falsification of this Kwantian language ("in any event," "on the other hand," "the former," "the latter," "the fact of the matter is,") and start again. I know from Delphine, who has told me what she knows, how Orlando was spirited to Umberland and why. I will write only of what I saw, and I didn't see much of Orlando after that for Kwant spirited him off to Baltimore to attend college and to learn the business about stamps and money. Oliver left to tour the world, calling it a business trip because he was going to Edinburgh where the trust funds that supported him were managed in what he described as clean cut and tweedy Dickensian quarters, even though he had not seen them yet. He would eat lumpy porridge and would buy sweaters from the Royal Scottish Society for the Self-Improvement of Gentlewomen, he was searching for hand-knit sweaters in shrimp, colonial brick, celery green, and porridge, he had reduced the Romantic Quest to a shopping list, and could be tiresome about the Firth of Forth. He had as usual memorized maps so that he would be knowingly familiar with his route from the hotel, "actually a small inn where wool traders have been staying for centuries," he knew, I often thought in those days, too much about the wonders of the world before he had ever seen them, knew too much or was acquainted with too many facts to be discomposed by surprise. I did not travel much, but when I did, I preferred to be astonished, and indeed I could be stunned into momentary self-annihilations by the Washington Monument in Mount Vernon Place in Baltimore, or the Shot Tower, as well as the Eiffel Tower, and I tried to find my way only after I had lost my way several times among the sourceless beauties. Aurelia was studying medicine at Johns Hopkins Medical School. She returned from medical school after completing her internship in surgery, and with Oliver, Orlando, and me, planned a picnic to celebrate our reunion, Orlando's approaching twenty-fifth birthday, our second wedding anniversary, and his defiance of Kwant, for Orlando, although biting his lips too hard, said that he was tempted to disincorporate regardless of the consequences on his birthday. I was at the beginning of another unsuccessful pregnancy. I thought that Orlando intended something marvelous, without my appreciating what it was, for he and I did not suffer or enjoy the same incorporations. I rarely bit my tongue, but he did frequently. We thought that we were all wonderful, we four getting to know each other again, we felt ourselves to be the completion of the island, the reunion of its pupils schooled in exquisite self-awareness, and we still thought, in spite of the warnings to Orlando, that we knew what we were doing. Now I know that to know what we were doing we would have to have known as only gods can know, we would have to have known the consequences of our actions, and so, in our quiet way, we had a violent pride, a classical pride which began as the opposite of but ended the same as a classical despair. So we strolled through the botanic garden which Kwant had arranged as though he were arbiter of trees, Oliver guiding us as though he was familiar with the island, although he was following cues in Orlando's eyes, and with the help of a few maids, a set of four, who seemed unimpressed or unintimidated by Umberland, we strung Chinese lanterns, and after the maids left, we sat, Oliver, Orlando, Aurelia, and I, on an enormous concrete block, apparently once the base of a radar tower built expensively by the United States perhaps sixty years before, after Pearl Harbor had been attacked. An obliging hurricane had

washed the tower away, apparently. The moon rose before
the sun set, and in the convergence of double light we ate
our picnic on this uncomfortable cement island, Orlando
said that he felt a little as though he were in downtown Baltimore, or picnicing across from the steel mills at Sparrows
Point, or on the parking lot of a supermarket in Highland-
town. But the cement had washed away leaving pebbles as
though on a beach, and images flickered on my screen, the
invading guerrillas wading ashore to establish a beach-
head. However at my fingertips vines were curling over the
edges of the concrete platform, Oliver said that the word
tendrils might already be a sufficient poem, and undernour-
ished weeds bloomed jauntily in the moonlit space, some of
the blossoms getting ready to close for the evening, and we
danced to an antique phonograph (Kwant's from Paris,
circa 1939), we danced until we felt that we had defeated
something dour, austere, and extortionate in the landscape, this place with its pitiless additions of sheds and
outbuildings, additions somehow wrongly added to a bad
beginning, with each wrong addition wrongly implying
that one other addition, the right one, would correct the
wrong relationships, but it didn't, or it wouldn't, it never
does. Or does it for the artist who knows how to use a
false start, but for few others? Orlando explained his predicament, he had tutored himself in corporation law and
economics, and had studied the rather anomalous position of Primavera under international law, and we reck-
lessly decided (although Oliver had his canny—or was it
uncanny?—Scottish trust, and Aurelia had finished and
paid for her medical training, although she wanted to
buy equipment for the island infirmary, and would need
scientific books and journals, and fees for the expensive
information retrievals—the computer searches—which
were her idea of luxurious self-indulgence—the Romantic

Quest duly electrified in analog or digital, and even I had money in a fishy bank at Grand Cayman because I didn't want Kwant to know of the sums Ginevra and then Salathiel funnelled to me to guarantee my independence, my infundibulated funds which Salathiel increased after my marriage to his son, so we decided, while wondering for the first time in our lives where our next meal would come from, although we had never known in any useful sense where our other meals had come from, and in fact our next meal was in the picnic basket, chicken fried in whole wheat batter, bread of stone-ground flour, and several bottles of a companionable champagne, not to mention much which represented Delphine getting rid of leftovers, we decided to take the risks of losing the sugar quota and affecting the men and women in ways we couldn't predict and which they might not have chosen for themselves — I said that we had not even the right to wish for them what they wished for themselves — we would not be able to continue buying our own flowers from the Indian women who brought them to the veranda to sell them, and for all we knew our presumptuous act, which was our attempt not to presume, would hurt the sugar beet farmers in Poland and in turn whoever depended upon them, although they must have learned the uses of adversity by this time, and we must and we would take the chance, for we did mean well, and we were conquering the morbid atmosphere at Umberland with our jolly buoyant mood, we ate and drank from the wicker basket — Oliver said that we were having a perverse luncheon at Tintagel — he never could join the world as it is (it was now dark night), as it would have been without his free associations, and while he might say a mere conflict between his *Lebenswelt* and my *Lebenswelt*, he would decorate his sentences with words like *Lebenswelt*, he was educated too far beyond his experience for my comfort, and I still dislike having shadowy allusions painted onto *my* experience, someone else watercoloring over my woodblock print, or handpainting my movie film, or interpreting my dreams. The sum of decorations is not architecture, I would have said to Oliver, except that I was at that moment seeing what I took to be an unusual collection of what they felt to be my all too usual oscillating oblongs of light, I don't know what I was or am supposed to do about the way I see, I see according to my lights, and we lay on our backs to watch meteorites burn against the atmosphere as they frictioned into sparkling trajectories of light, none of us evasive enough to make a wish, Oliver saying, "The sky tonight is like something Olivia sees, isn't it Olivia?," yet tenderly, a tendril of his attention reaching across to touch me, for we were seeing it together, and they knew that I did have common sense about the senses we had in common, and we were in our cooperations constructing a vivid mental feeling which we could almost give a name to it was so tangible, an *esprit de corps* arising in celebration of the disincorporation, so that we knew we were seeing and hearing the same sights and sounds as we looked at the stars in their silent distances, epochs away from us, and then Oliver, perhaps embarrassed to be grown so together with us, began tossing pebbles at the lanterns, putting them out, and spouting silly reminiscences about how nothing had happened to him in that crypt, that he had slept unmolested by morbidity, which he thought was outrageous of him when he should have found his thoughts and feelings outraged by such proximity to the dark elucidations of death, yet if ever a man lived who did not know how to die a little in a crypt he was that Oliver, Oliver of the Anachronisms, preparing himself for poetic movements which hadn't shown any movement in decades. When the clouds occluded the moon, he stood, all swashbuckling silhouette against the sky, quoting from one of our old plays, *The Northern Lasse*, "Would you have foughi by candlelight?", and Orlando remembering the cue responding, "Sir, I dare do't by Daylight, Moonlight, Starlight," and Oliver returning, "Owle-light?", and he hooted, but then instead of amplifying his silliness with an anthology of references to owls, he did join us as we lay inviting the invasions of moonlight, Orlando lying on his side looking westward to the sea, Aurelia holding her finger up to the tendril of a vine that was venturing across the pockmarked concrete, Oliver and I leaning against Orlando, looking eastward to the ocean, when Orlando, who did not see things in the dark, said that the sky to the west was brightening, that the sun was going to rise in the west to confound our eyes, while Aurelia commented, laconically, that the universe itself was our only clock, and that as she measured its movements, allowing for the continuous creation of matter (I could hear her enjoying an opportunity to mention one of her favorite theories), the hour was still too early for the sun to be visible (she would not say *sunrise* as though she were addressing an assembly of pre-Copernicans and must inure them to the trepidations of the earth), and Oliver was saying, "Perhaps twilight has lost its way," as he turned slowly to see what they were talking about, and then I heard cold sobriety in his voice as he whispered, "The combat is upon us," and so I turned also, and indeed the sky to the west had opened the width of a razor's blood-stained edge and for a moment, turning, Orlando's hand on my thigh, Aurelia's hand touching my hand, and Oliver kneeling shoulder to shoulder beside me, I thought that this collection of the four of us could pounce, could leap right through to the other side and beyond, such inappropriate thoughts spring open like trapdoors in front of us in those desolate moments when one event has ended and another event has not yet begun, but even as I saw the width of the opening in the sky widening, and its edges blur into violet, the light bled up into the blackness of the sky, and not certain what I was seeing, I looked to Orlando who, still a gentleman, stared into the darkness at the light as though he dared it to approach the ladies, and when he flinched I glimpsed back in time to see a scalpel of light knife into the sky and carve out a vase-shape in the violet light, and damn Oliver who could not be quiet but who quoted, "For black blooms, and it is purple," and I was trusting Aurelia to provide a scientific explanation, something comforting about physics, perhaps with a colorful name like firestorm, for if we could give objective names to this event perhaps it would not pertain to subjective us, four young people with good intentions, but she said, unscientifically, that the sky is " 'streaming like an open vein'," and I knew we were perilously close to myth, yet she added that the chemistry of the fire was peculiar, *nuée ardente et inconnue*, and Orlando said, "The continent is on fire. America is on fire," and as a series of explosions strafed the sky he incanted, "Monterey, Tampico, Vera Cruz, Coatzacoalcos, Villahermosa, Canterel, 'And all being is flaming suffering'." We watched, seeing only that which enabled us to see, the long low horizon of fire, and we feared so that we undressed and waded into the water, at first attempting to be playful, then solemnly as we subsided farther into the water, squatting or kneeling until only our eyes were above the water, a mood as of sad Roman soldiers witnessing the irreversible destruction of Rome from afar, *Roma summus amor* destroying itself, and we breathed above the gentle waters in the lagoon as in the west fire, white fire, bloomed upon mountains of red horror, a cold-blooded fire, not beautiful but sublime, like an unlimited source of ferocity, the western sky become the ground of inferences we did not know how to make. We saw fires which might have been distant islands, but we were certain only that we were seeing light without knowing what we were seeing. Nor have we ever learned what happened, ever seen a ship or plane, our story uneasy because of our uncertainty about whether or not we were alone, and about how to plan on being taken by surprise someday. And when the sun did tint the sky in the east, we looked back and forth between the two luminous phenomena, the visible extremes, and as we stood in the water, now without any impulse to playfulness, yet looking to and fro, we watched the gradual eastern sunlight dilute the western lights, we watched the long blue flame disappear into ordinary daylight, and then we noticed floating toward us a boat, a canoe, with a hint of dolphins coy in the water behind it, Orlando and I swam out and looked in, and looked at each other awestruck until I screamed "Aurelia," for she would know what to do about the body of the dead Indian decked with herbs and flowers, and Aurelia and Oliver swam out, we helped them aboard the canoe, and Aurelia—I suddenly became aware that she was naked, that the five of us were naked—Aurelia touched his pulse, she put her ear to his chest, and she whispered to herself aloud, "Code or no code?", which we knew from her hospital sketches was hospital code for the decision whether or not to revive a patient whose heart has stopped, I suppose that "no code" was the decision not to call an emergency team over the intercom with their code number. As one voice we said "Code" and she said, "I think he's in a coma or a trance, perhaps sedated, perhaps dead, I feel vital signs but I can't judge brain activity," so as Oliver threw flowers and clay pots overboard, except for one shell-shaped cup the Indian held in his hands, which I reached in and took to save from Oliver's helpful excitement, we maneuvered them into shallow water and tied the canoe to a stake, and Aurelia breathed into him, beat on his chest, and worked his arms to and fro until he awoke, less surprised than we were, apparently, and healthy enough, since by evening he had taken over the island because, as he put it, his face was the countenance of that year (which was later called the year 1, but I don't think we ever had the year from zero to one, I have worn down my fingers trying to figure this out, and when we switched calendars we lost most of our anniversaries, and I lost track of time, which has always seemed to me to change unreliably anyway, so I liked his slightly ramshackle calendar with its *chaykin*, the five unlucky days, dog days, which had to be fitted onto the eighteen months of twenty days each in order to add up to a year. And since I didn't know my birthday—Salathiel hadn't even asked them my name—I set it in Chay Kin, which I think means "the festival is lost," and I observed and sometimes celebrated my birthday then until I grew wiser and decided to forget about my birthday and some other annual anniversaries of grief, other annual images of pain. Delenda also called them "the nameless days," which again I thought suited me because while not nameless I didn't know the name I had been born into before I was called Olivia, but I am certain that I would recognize that name were I ever to hear it; I'm certain that I haven't heard it yet.) Delenda, as he revived, looked at each of us full faced and in profile (and he would do so often across the years), reading our faces as the names of years, or as pictures of ideas, in some Mayan hieroglyphics of his own, I suppose, apparently recognizing us from somewhere among his prophesies, which was disturbing but flattering. He made me feel that I looked right because I fulfilled some image. I was grateful then, although I am doubtful now about that process, he seemed so often elsewhere in time. I will not describe our gaiety as Oliver and Orlando beached the canoe. Somehow propriety required that Aurelia and I help him out of the canoe, where by now he was standing in the middle, and onto the shore — I don't know where we learned the etiquette of emergencies — I, wondering what he would think of us, aware of my breasts, I'd like to know what Aurelia was aware of, the two of us carrying an inexplicable naked Indian between us, his effort to walk impeding us, and Oliver laughing as he quoted, "Testiculus habet et bene pendentes," I'd like to know what he was thinking, and we four, immediately upon becoming *we five*, smiled with each other in what I felt as a primal sympathy, we sat down on the sand among the vines that crawled along the beach which ended in the "tangled bank" of underbrush, and he held each of us by the chin again and looked and looked until he said, "No, I am not the countenance of the year, I am the face of the next thirteen years, I will need that long to prepare for my next death." He spoke to us: "After that, you are on your own. You will be judged by the difference between what you did, and what you might have done, to help." I did not like the parts of his speech I could not understand, about the face of the day and countenance of the year, but he liked me, and I enjoyed that. He said more, and in those few minutes we learned as much about him, as many facts about his past, at least, as we would ever learn, but we also learned the essential, that we loved him, which meant that we believed him (believed *him*, but not his cultivated ideas concealed in images of time). He did not then or later explain the funereal canoe, he would only mutter something about the face of the day as his face — which I think indirectly influenced some of my movie scripts — and I didn't ask many questions because I didn't want to encourage obscurity. So he came to us from the sea which had seemed almost to be on fire. Finding him was like finding an idea we hadn't known we had been looking for until we found

it. We forgot the rest of the world, indeed the loss of the
world, in our excitement. Weeks later someone commented
that the seaplane had never returned—and the battery
radio in Kwant's office picked up nothing, which might or
might not mean anything—and my small supply of movie
film was useless without electricity, which we suddenly
lacked because we seemed to have agreed to abandon
Kwant's little power plant without ever discussing it. In fact
the fire or whatever it was seemed somehow to have made a
movie of its own on some of my film, but a monotonous one
which Oliver examined attentively, very witty I suppose,
admiring the semblance of actuality and the honest use of
the medium which called attention to its physicality and
materialty in a triumphant vindication of anti-illusionism.
Well, I could be literal when I wanted to be, and I had
never thought of the art I wanted to make as illusions, although I was not at all sure that I was opposed to them. I
doubt that I ever understood the concept of illusion, then
or now. I continued to write my screenplays because I had
begun to and because Delenda encouraged me to. That
sounds unfair because Orlando also encouraged me, and
helped me to write a play, *Aboveboard*, but that is another
story. I thought that someday I would adapt it for the
screen. Anyway Delenda Nascendi Kinh was the name he
usually told us, perhaps the invention of a prescient priest
who knew that Delenda was going to get out of his hands. I
could describe for you, and if you like you can ask questions when you receive this letter, the flowers and the pots.
The memory of the pots is interesting as we begin to make
our own indigenous pottery, and none too soon I would
judge from the number of shards fitted into patterns in the
grove. I could also describe with minute particularity, in
what Orlando calls my "unscrupulous detail," the ellipse
of green lights which shone above him, which yet kept

slipping off into a parabola of purple. Oliver later dived for the pots and the artifacts, as he called them, he couldn't believe that he had thrown them overboard. But that was long after the canoe had, I suppose, drifted away in a storm, and Oliver dived even though Kwant and Converse were roaming somewhere about Umberland. Oliver intended to identify where Delenda had drifted from, but he found nothing rummaging around in the water except some barnacled wood which had been gnawed by bark beetles, and which he gave to Delphine. Oliver knew better than to ask me the names of flowers, although I remember asters, anemone, and eucalyptus lining the floor of the canoe, any of which might have come from anywhere. Another canoe arrived a few days later, filled with Indians carrying their own geraniums, orange trees, and many beans and gourds, but they are another story, and besides, you have played among them. If they knew about Delenda, they weren't telling. We laughed so much, we five, finding our clothes, giving Delenda the damask tablecloth from the wicker basket to drape over himself—we ate the last of the food and had quite a little party—and then crossing the causeway Oliver said solemnly, "Where four are, there five shall be," which in spite of sounding sentimentally archaic didn't feel like a quotation. I could tell you so much more if only I knew what is important. When we came to the fork in the path I ran toward Utterly to fetch more clothes, for we were being covered with a dusty ash, and also to look for Salathiel, and I heard Delenda, who had learned much from a sentence or two during our interviews at the beach: "Take me to Kwant." He asked to be directed, yet he seemed to be returning into his own country by a different path.

Our love, Octavio,
Olivia

I have returned, Octavio, thinking of you. The other hand-writing you occasionally read here is from one, or many, of the children practicing writing against the day when they must begin writing letters for themselves. And to help me with the task of copying. I now calculate that you were, when you left (I suppose in Delenda's canoe), about the age at which we would have started to encourage you to write letters of your own, to build up your interest in the future. We find the letters a pleasure, and someday when this young girl has not taken over my pen to help me, perhaps I will be moved to try to explain why. Meanwhile Aurelia writes you a letter which I have caught just in time, for booklice have been nibbling it, and I must reconstruct a word here and there, the way I did so many years ago contemplating medieval manuscripts, and peering at the place in the manuscript of *Beowulf* which might suggest that a faithful woman was keening over his corpse, the choice of one word following from the conjectured meaning of the whole poem. Where I can't read Aurelia's letter, I try to read her mind, or I walk over to the Infirmary (or send a child) to ask her. Occasionally her guess is only as good as mine.

The Infirmary—Chin-Uch 18th—Year 22

Dear Octavio,

I am certain that stories, some now legends, have reached you about my grandfather, Kwant, and about how Delenda opposed him. I can tell you part that you might not know because as a doctor I took over the medical records in Kwant's office, and I learned about Kwant from documents what Delenda apparently somehow inferred. He was good at guessing. At least his action implied that he knew, the event makes more sense if he knew, but he could not have known. Implication is a problem, as when behavior of an embryo implies foreknowledge of its environment after birth. The eyes are implications (*contain* implications?). The eyes imply light and something to be seen. So much I would have enjoyed teaching you, so much we might have talked over together, or with my other students. But I am, according to your mother, supposed to be doing history here, not science. Not yet. Primavera was owned by Kwant, who inherited it, an island which had been orphaned, in a period of decolonization and devolution, and which his mother had bought after the First World War, when she collected islands. Kwant declared Primavera (including Umberland) a sovereign nation, a bluff which real nations simply ignored. Umberland was owned by Orlando, but it was held in a trust controlled by Kwant. I am not certain that *owned* is the word. Kwant was governing the islands, but I don't know what was governing Kwant. Some people seem always to have been here, others arrived as immigrants, or were rescued from shipwrecks, and even a small colony of blind slaves lived at the farther end of Umberland years ago, slaves in everything but name. I interpret from documents here that they had an eye disease contracted in gold mines. They seem to have kept to themselves and to have died out. Sometimes refugees from voodoo on the islands to our west arrived, unfortunately bringing with them an infection of magical thinking; they walked, in their fears, as though they were wearing restraining jackets, and as they walked they might dodge a phantom, for they peopled the island with ghostly enemies. Olivia worked brilliantly to free these people; she had a knack for finding continuous physical tasks or acts for them to perform, and their own actions would arise like a suspension bridge enabling them to cross over their abyssal fears. These were among the people who gathered often in the plaza, standing around in their make-shift groups,

scarcely tribes, but banding together to watch Kwant perform. Kwant had endurance beyond other men. He rarely
left a room during a meeting, he always stayed visible
throughout a festival. He impressed the Indians and Creoles so that whatever their rituals or dances, Kwant became
the center. He never danced. He would sit in the square in
front of his small office building, which you know as my
infirmary, the building built of stones said to be ballast
tossed overboard from early ships that harbored here. I
doubt these legends, but also I know that the stones are not
indigenous. Your mother says that they are from the same
ethnic group, however, which is probably more to the point
than my geology. The "natives" would feed Kwant diuret-
ics, theobromine, stuff disguised as love offerings, I think
even an extract from the Calabar bean, although I haven't
confirmed that, the *ordeal bean*, I think it was called, and
they would suggest that he had to drink the cacoa, food of
the gods, or they would be insulted, and in their amused
hatred and expressionless anticipation of their own failure
they would feed him something to cause diarrhea—why
were so many of their rituals ordeals? Oliver says that their
ordeals are their metaphors for their lives, but one can
think of one's life as an ordeal without needing metaphorical ordeals, which seems to me supererogatory. Kwant
would smile complacently, looking like a treasurer of a sol-
vent society, and he would share their offerings with them,
he would extract or exact promises from them, or negotiate
with them for compromises, and he would stall them as
they became uneasy, for since they dared not refuse their
own offerings they would soon be sick or would excuse
themselves, one group embarrassed because their code
forbade them to have a bowel movement after noon, so that
they would be glancing at the position of the sun while
Kwant sat impassively, his eye measuring the movement of

shadows, he never gloating but drily commenting on the excellence of the brew, returning to the official papers on the table beside him, adjudicating a dispute, even napping without leaving his chair during the siesta he took early so that he would be awake during the general siesta, checking invoices and taking inventory of the people napping here and there in the shade. He was a man who took a pleasure in people that was not the pleasure they took in themselves, or the pleasure they sought to give. He sat — "President Ironblatter" in the musical comedy Olivia was always threatening to write — humorless in khaki army fatigue clothes, reading over the score as he rehearsed his orchestration of our self-defeats.

I resuscitated Delenda in the canoe which was decorated as though for a marriage. He was decked in flowers like a bridegroom. Butterflies hovered about him, their shadows fluttering across his face, precise little symbols of a high romance. Even then the ash had started to fall, the wind was rising, results of the "fire" which others might have described. Delenda revived. Then I revived. Then we wrapped an ivory-white cloth around his waist, and he immediately looked correct in it. He had a command of inanimate objects so that if he put a feather in his hair, or in mine, it not only stayed where it was put, it also completed the proof of a theorem, making an idea self-evident. I was beside myself with joy walking beside him across the causeway toward the square. He emerged from the copse of trees which contains the burial mounds (the section Oliver rather insensitively calls the Moratorium), near the gazebo at the far end from Kwant's office. I could see at the other end of the plaza, which rains had eroded into a canoe-shape more than a square, to where Kwant was holding audience with groups of Creoles standing about, and sullen Indians sitting on their heels in the ashen dust thickening about their feet. Delenda walked like a prototype, oblivious of Kwant, his hand touching mine, but not holding it ("Being-present-at-hand-side-by-side" became intelligible for a moment), walking as though his path just happened to intersect with Kwant. Delenda, who as I later learned could think with his feet, was tracking a quarry quite steadily, while I felt like I was trying to walk from the stern of the canoe to the bow. Delenda was squinting, but not from harsh light, for sun and moon would have been about even in the opposite skies, and the air was hazy with moist dust. Squinting Delenda walked toward Kwant. The Indians seemed not to recognize Delenda as an acquaintance yet they showed signs of recognition. They must write letters for themselves from their own point of view. They seemed to me to be smiling their consent propitiously. Kwant smiled, although smiles were not becoming to him. He touched his khaki sleeve to his forehead, wiping away the gritty grey sweat, or smearing it. I ran up, I caught up with Delenda who touched my hand as with one gesture he ripped from Kwant his loose-fitting khaki shirt, pulling along with it, as I could see although I was glancing around for Kwant's soldiers, a colostomy bag, and as Kwant rose along with the shirt Delenda grabbed the khaki pants and tore them off him, yet without disturbing the urine-collection device strapped to his leg in his peculiar self-bondage, and I could see in the eyes of the Indians and of Kwant's guards as they arrived to help him the completion of *their* theorem, Q.E.D. Delenda sat down laughing in Kwant's chair as Kwant, urine dribbling down his ankle onto the ashen dust of the plaza, ran past us into the trees. Later I learned that he continued his retreat across the causeway to Umberland, and that, according to Delphine, he would not accept my medical care. That was the first time I saw Indians laugh, although within a few days Delenda had them laughing even at themselves. They had been worried at seeing day in the night the prior evening, and now as it seemed to them seeing night in the day. Delenda, as he stood up and climbed onto the table, got them to agree to a distinction between day, and the light they had seen in the sky at night, and to the distinction between night, and the dusky daylight we were standing in. "Filthy weather," I heard Oliver say. Delenda showed them the open blossoms of flowers which closed their blooms at night, and pointed to birds which would have been roosting in the dark of night. He said, illogically to me but conclusively to them, "I stand in the middle of the canoe," pointing to the table, the desk, he was standing on. He squinted, the Indians laughed, so I laughed a little too.

We were reluctant to surrender our ideas of Kwant's power. I suppose we had been more infatuated than we knew. He had frequently sent small packages by way of the mails, *correspondencia urgente*, to Switzerland. We had assumed, if we thought about it, that the packages contained money, although if we thought about it, little money circulated on the island—the laborers kept an account going at the company store, and usually were in debt to it. I learn from Kwant's papers, which I suppose Salathiel in some sense inherited, but in which he displays no interest, that Kwant had long before been to Switzerland for medical treatments; that he had had trouble with his bowels is suggested by his notations on an early medical history, for next to "Evacuation of bowels" he had written, "It is like giving birth to razor blades." While in Switzerland he had undergone elective surgery for an artificial opening to be constructed into the colon through his side. He wore the colostomy bag, and periodically he mailed one of the bags to Switzerland where it was tested for parasites, typhoid, cholera, urobilinogen, stool fat, protein content, and the percentage of nitrogen. I found reports for tests on poly-nuclear leukocytes, Shigellosis, and Salmonellosis. The reports were all negative. I felt, reading the reports, that Kwant's love had turned around upon his own self-enfolded intestines. He had had himself torn open, how-ever incisively and septically, so that he could keep himself empty, yet see himself as overflowing, so lost in love of his own labyrinth of guts was he. He had forms of self-knowledge denied to most people, for he learned regularly that he did not have porphyria, one of Oliver's favorite dis-eases, a disease of the royal family with which Oliver, more expert than I, practiced childish deflations, as he used to tell, and perhaps will tell again, unseemly stories about the royal family submitting its stools for medical tests. Al-though he jokes about their being born to the purple, I think he found their cooperation with science admirable, while Orlando might still tediously be asking what *royal* could possibly mean. Olivia could answer that: "It means stand back."

I learned about Kwant's regimen for health, about how he buried other of the biodegradable colostomy bags near trees in his botanic garden, deploying, with his own hands, his manure about his favorite trees. His office contained, and still contains, a large incubator. He would begin to in-cubate a clutch of about twenty-one eggs, and at the end of the first day he would eat the first egg raw, at the end of the second day the second egg, and so on, as the embryos de-veloped, until at a certain point the eggs would be handed over to Delphine to be used in cooking. I can see from notes and recipes that we were all eating eggs prepared from recipes in a cookbook called *The Fountain of Youth*. I have never told Olivia or Oliver, I don't want to listen to any of their jokes. At college I first comprehended music by performing experiments on the development of the embryonic chicken heart. I now regret those experiments. I can't imagine what I could have been thinking of.

The Indians and Creoles and everyone else were gathered in the square, the plaza, after Kwant left. I looked and looked at Delenda. I gazed. I had made a difficult private journey upstream for many years, and now in a few hours I was swept downstream toward that man. Or, closer to the truth, I was swimming downstream toward him. I found myself backing away along the path to Otterly because I did not want to let him out of my sight. I had to become a doctor in order to learn that what I had most wanted to become was a paleobiologist. I wanted to explain the evolution of eyesight. I haven't yet. I felt, when I looked at Delenda, the way I felt when I could feel myself approaching the discovery of a problem, or the discovery of the solution of a problem. Emancipation was at hand. So much of this was negative. I eliminated false emanations, and dwelled in what remained. Now I felt as though I had been acting correctly, that even my mistakes had helped me to prepare myself as though I knew he would be here. My past now served the purpose of bringing me to where I was, which was remarkably close to where I wanted to be. I had felt uneasy about returning from medical studies to participate in the self-indulgences of life on this island, although I would be able to do good here. That evening was the end of my philanthropy, for before nightfall I loved but one man. Later, in good time, loving him was a philanthropic education. The rest of the world might have consumed itself in flames that night, but I, however selfishly, felt the completion of my equations in the middle of that canoe. Delenda floated toward our shore a corpse but disembarked my self-evident bridegroom.

Your loving aunt,
Aurelia

And Oliver writes on a lovely piece of paper in which or through which I feel that I can see the words of poems, but when I peer closely they are not there, or are not legible.

Tornata, among the ruins—Hul-Ol 7th—Year 23

Dear Octavio,

This morning we were straightening out some problems that have arisen because letters have crossed in the mails. Letters from two or three years ago, arriving before letters written six years ago, look quite different when the earlier letter arrives. Delenda, who has stood in my memory so often where he once stood above me on the cliff where the house was, pointed to Primavera—I took his gesture to mean the whole island—and said "canoe" but he also pointed to an envelope into which he was placing a letter and said "canoe" and the image caught up so many ideas (it concentrated attention on both island and canoe, or on both envelope and canoe), that it did not distract attention from objects, it made them radiant with meaning. Old letters from Aurelia and from Olivia—both tell me that they are writing to you, and both tell me slightly different facts about Delenda's arrival. Aurelia enclosed a letter from Olivia: "Dear Aurelia, You might as well attempt to trace the evolution of laughter as the evolution of eyesight. With love and laughter, Olivia." Which started me trying to understand the evolution of laughter, but I tire of attempts at understanding. Aurelia persists. The letters criss-crossing in time, and at odds over the facts, have required me to remember precisely, and to remember I begin with the traces of laughter which remain as efficacious in the present, twenty-odd years afterward, as the ash which is visible in the unusual growth of trees the following year: when we cut down a tree for pulp, even we amateur dendrochronologists can find the widened intervals of the years one, two, and three. The ash which Kwant seemed determined to ignore, as he seemed to ignore any evidence he had no power over or did not understand. Which any amateur chronologist looking at a cross-section of me would recognize in spurts of intellectual or emotional growth, those wavering widened rings, as I acquired knowledge Kwant had no power over and developed some powers he did not understand. I suppose he was unable to explain to the Indians what was happening in the west, for they claimed to be worried that night would be prolonged indefinitely, and the men seemed to be saying that they would have to make love until the long-delayed dawn came, but as so often their fears seemed hypothetical, not actual, for they were not making love, they were merely talking as though they were creatures in a myth who would, were night to continue, be required to continue love-making. They didn't seem to divide the hypothetical from the categorical at the same border the rest of us did. Or most of us. Some of us. They could tell that they knew as much as Kwant did about the flames in the sky and the ash, and that was not much, especially since radios, teletypes, and one walkie-talkie set intended to deceive his militia into a feeling of transcendence, were the most advanced means of communication he allowed on the island, and they were silent. (Someday I must write an ode in praise of Kwant, our *miles gloriosus*, for as a dictator he forbade much that I would have forbidden myself had I held the power, as sometimes in my more vulgar fantasies I have. Kwant disallowed plastic, chewing gum, bulkheads, newspapers, floral-print fabrics, and as he announced one night dramatically, "semioticians." "I will have no semioticians on this island." Olivia muttered that we had all better start packing, but we knew he didn't intend us when he cursed, "autotelic bastards!" Whatever his motives, however condescending, he usually left the

Indians alone, satisfied that, whatever their rituals might imply about the spirits, they knew they were dependent upon his power. I suggested that his coat of arms should bear the motto, "Nothing alien is human to me," and although Olivia laughed, she suggested that I renounce the cleverness of complete reversals if I wished to be clever and attempt three-quarter turns or fractional pivots and poignant puns. She made fists like a boxer and while ducking and weaving punched me on the shoulder, and when she saw that I was seeing her as a prizefighter she said, "Yes, like this, without contempt.") That evening in the plaza Kwant and the Indians were bluffing each other, yet the Indians seemed to have experienced something like the ash that was descending upon them, or at least to have legends in which they had, ancestrally, experienced something like the ash, and they complained that dawn had not come, that night had covered day, which was typical of the way they alarmed themselves by exaggerating facts to fit their pessimistic theories. On the southern part of the island, and across the isthmus at Umberland, wind-blown ash sawed leaves from trees and sandpapered the bark, but no more than two hundred yards away we were spared the pumice of the wind. Primavera, turned temporarily grey overnight, emerged from the rain the next day scrubbed clean, brilliant reds and greens and yellows, our island restored to an underpainting of primary colors, our world looking soap-and-water clean in the primitive light. This was a few days later, when Delenda was telling us about volcanoes, about adventures in *tierra blanca* after eruptions, and about Volcan Ilopango, which made him sound quite old since he had such information about the ancient past. Yet he was not trying to mystify us. I suppose he was thirty years of age and had gone to a mission school. Aurelia thought that he must have studied geology, but he always said that he knew no more about the firestorm than we did. Neither the Indians nor Delenda nor the Creoles seemed to be acknowledging the rain of ash as they stood around in it. When the square was filled with people (as a former colonialist and more or less retired capitalist I can tell you that the natives "have instant communication among themselves," something in addition to the drums which were announcing our arrival), Delenda stood up and looked out over the crowd. He threw up his hands in a gesture of helpless pleasure or happiness, then he sat down hard in Kwant's chair, which broke under him. He laughed, the implacable Indians laughed, Delenda tossed pieces of the chair to left and right and wildly in the air above the crowd, and those who caught pieces laughed and tossed them indifferently into the bushes. He stood upon the table Kwant used as a desk, shuffling his bare feet among papers, the story of our lives according to Kwant, and wrapping his tablecloth around him tightly, he began. He told us the laws, which he said were not laws, merely his will, and not even his will, but his hope for us, with a few additional details he would work out later. Each of us must write a letter to someone every day, preferably to be delivered in the future, possibly quite far in the future, even five or ten years hence. This little suggestion of his made changes which are still changing the meaning of the suggestion. I think I understand now that this rule of letters was his modernization or adaptation of something viable and communicable in his Mayan heritage. He continued that the letters were to be kept somewhere—Delenda looks around him—and the postmaster will deliver them. "You, you," the people shout, and "No, no," he answers, squinting, which impresses the Indians (we had a tribe I called the Semiotic Indians until Kwant left and the pun lost its point, and we could refer to the bean-cult people who arrived shortly after Delenda as the Seminal Indians with no disrespect and with some justice). We are to live, Delenda continues, looking around, taking in everything, although we could not know what he was seeing (later he said that he was merely seeing the possibilities we could not see because we were too familiar with the place), to live so that we would be prepared to receive the letters waiting for us, to be in the right mood for them. Some of the Creoles were so used to pretending fecklessness in our presence that they claimed not to know what a letter was, but when they admitted to understanding what Delenda was requiring, they joked with each other, pointing to one fellow, a red-headed clown, who they said would never be in condition to write a letter. Delenda grasped their point. "Orlando," he said, "the village scribe, will write your letters for you while you are learning to write," and we knew that he wasn't joking as he continued, "He will write your letters on paper which Oliver will make, as he teaches you how to make paper, when he isn't teaching children to read, and to write," and so the scene unfolded in good humor, as scenes around Delenda tended to, as though it had been tightly furled and had only to unwind. I had made paper for years, and Delenda had me caught in both actuality and fantasy. In actuality I had learned to make my own paper to use for my poems and for letters. When I corresponded with prisoners in American jails I enclosed blank paper as a gift for them, because in fantasy I would be in a prison house writing poems and a diary on paper smuggled in to me, and my writing would be smuggled out. How was that done? My fantasy was skimpy on some details because the accounts I had read were vague. But I did think, between the actual and the fantastic, that the prisoner who could make his own paper could make his own freedom. When Converse set us exercises in writing

letters from famous people in history, I would compose
mine as from prison on contraband paper. I wrote "The
Prison Letters of Giordano Bruno," verse epistles, and I
suppose that if I can confess to them, I can confess to anything. Hadn't Ludwig Wittgenstein finished writing the
Tractatus Logico-Philosophicus in the prison camp at Monte
Cassino? I think so. As Delenda spoke, suggesting work
details, we felt as though we were coming offstage. We listened. Orlando looked into my eyes. I could see him remembering our amateurish conversations about politics
and government and economics. "The truest government
is self-government," he said to me in his tone that I called
the prosaic undercut; the tone meant that he was touched
by emotions whose power felt threatening. Orlando's
words were perhaps an old saw, something sententious and
tautological and non-verifiable, words we were to have
copied unthinkingly into our copybooks at Converse's dictation when we were studying rhetoric, suffering repression of our laughter (and Converse said that our laughter
was repression of our knowledge of evil), and contemplating safe and easy revolution. I could feel Orlando and me
folding up and putting away the last of the implications
Kwant had brought from Europe as we unfolded for ourselves the implications enveloped in Delenda's epistolary
politics. I smiled as I remembered the self-disciplines
which arose spontaneously when, for example, as a child, I
was posing languidly in a doorway at Tornata, at the other
end of Primavera, in the house that is a story in itself, when
Olivia dashing past would call out, "Mail came, I put a letter for you on the table in the hall," and I would warily
conform to some standard of decorum I had set for myself, stomach tucked in, shoulders back, but casual, and
I would march (if one can march with nonchalance, and
with dignity), to Utterly, thrilled with self-importance (and

terrified lest it be merely an advertisement), the imagined letter glowing with a pale but distinct aura, then I would pick up the letter, and if not feigning indifference then feigning something else, I was usually feigning something, I would glide out of the complications of that mirrored foyer to find a place appropriate to open it—the porch above the sea, the morning room, the glider on the veranda where others would be certain to see me reading my letter, the letter that had come addressed to me, that feast for my eyes. I do not know what I was longing for from a letter, but I was longing for it. Not the note Olivia once elaborately sent me—she had sent it to Baltimore to be mailed from there—which read, "Flee! All is discovered." What possible messages made me so curious about the mail? I have always thought that I deserved more mail, better, longer, more detailed and more loving letters, with a little more interest shown in my life than was usually apparent. I did not like letters that were talking only to themselves. I receive beautiful letters, but I can say that the letter I have been waiting for—what an exciting gamble to pick up one's mail—has not yet arrived. Perhaps it is in the mail. Maybe tomorrow. By the 10th of the month at the latest—isn't that when bills used to be due?

You may remember, Octavio, when you were no more than three years old, writing letters which you dictated to us at any hour. Once I came upon you crying. "Who would you like to write a letter to now?", I asked, and you brightened as you solemnly dictated in your boyish babble as I doodled words for you with my pen, the feather from some bird as solemn as you. Sometimes I think that I wouldn't turn and live with animals, wouldn't go back to nature, it seems so sad. You did not understand at first why you did not receive many letters, so we began writing to you frequently, and soon you were receiving letters, although not perhaps the ones that you were waiting for, those phantom messages to you which I suppose haunted the letters we were writing.

You learned our holidays, our truancies from the chronological order of the letters, the occasions when a few people might receive a letter early, with unexpected and not always pleasant complications. Olivia was angry when a letter forgiving me some peccadillo arrived, as she put it, before her forgiveness arrived: sometimes she undermined experience with her own hypotheses. Our island, through the letters, became a converse domain. Primavera seemed, or seems, to be on its way to becoming a land of truth, or at least an island which rules itself as truth rules itself. That evening of the ashes Delenda looked around the square and pointed to the Church of the Renunciation, pale yellow in the twilight. "Our postoffice," he said. At that moment—and ever after we seemed less to have moments than events—our sometime tutor, Father Converse, stepped out of the crowd, and Delenda jumped briskly from the table. The Indians were making moves that Orlando and I knew signalled the warm-up for one of their tireless monotonous dances—dances that were like staring at an anaconda for an afternoon. But on this occasion they were to dance out of ritual toward history. I wondered how they would dance on the ashes. Delenda held up his hands for silence. "I am tired," he said, and I stopped breathing. "I am going to sleep," he said, and I put a hand over my eyes. I stopped moving as I gasped with disillusionment. Then slowly I taught myself to believe that he was tired, merely a tired man. I thought of a line of poetry from Dylan Thomas: "Man be my metaphor." I looked at him and saw that he was tired. I could feel how I did not want to see him plainly, as in any sense an equal, not a hero. I had been seeing him as a criticism of me, please let him not be an equal lest I have to answer him as an equal, responsibly, man to man. I caught myself wanting him to be taller than I was, but he wasn't. I made an effort and I saw that he was not mysteriously more than he appeared to be, and that he was not ironically appearing to be less than he was. He was an exhausted Indian, with the face of a man who was all present and accounted for. He looked, in my eyes, beyond beautiful and ugly, like a face on a pre-Columbian pot, a happy expression, but one familiar with terror. I grew up, however belatedly, like a tree bursting through the roof of a greenhouse, like a boy outgrowing fairy stories, comic books, and even *Kidnapped*. Delenda walked to Converse and said, holding him roughly by the cassock, and glaring into his eyes, "Are you a priest?" Converse looked appalled. I thought, of course, as so often with what Delenda said, I had thought something like that the whole time, he led us to ideas we could have reached if we had thought for ourselves. "No," Converse said, "I am not a priest." With that, saying, "I had not expected truth," Delenda ripped the drip-dry cassock in two in a single swift gesture which included unwrapping the tablecloth from around his loins and wrapping it around Converse, whom I had never thought to ask, with all my flirtatious questions, once asking him if spiders had orgasms, what he wore under that anachronistic cassock which Kwant required him to wear as appropriate to the scenery of the island, and as an embroidery upon his own power. So much of what Kwant did (and we followed him too far) located meaning outside the actual, that the actual seemed meaningless and insufficient. Why did we go along with methods which had so much contempt for us, and for which we held contempt? Why did Kwant want to control what other people did? None of us transcended the picturesque. "Goodbye," said Delenda, master of surfaces, to the pockmarked back of Con-

verse as Delenda sauntered onto the path to Utterly while
Converse dwindled toward Umberland, Callipygian Delenda, Converse of the almost impeccable retreat, almost
perfected through years of tutoring Olivia and me, experienced discalced recusant recalcitrants, letting him teach
us only what we wanted to learn. Perhaps Aurelia will
write to you sometime how she led our exhausted Mayan
Indian — the man who would not be king — to bed and joyous slumber. Orlando and I briefly danced a scarf dance,
give and take, take and give, but he and I knew that Olivia
awaited him, so letting go of my apricot-colored scarf, he
waved — happily "it wasn't a gesture but an emotion" — and
ran toward Utterly. I stayed and danced farther into myself, into my own powers, until I reached the people I was
dancing with, and felt akin. So. That was how it was going
to be: papermaking. My luxurious and spendthrift avoca-
tion, making handmade paper (which I often took longer
to make than I took to write the poems the paper was
meant for), was going to be practical after all. I would be
useful. Productive. I thought to myself, so incompletely
did I understand the changes which had begun so rapidly,
that, well, I would open a little shop on the island. For a
moment I felt around me the aura of some down-at-heel
deposed royalty selling tasteful stationery to support himself in exile after a revolution, and I would be a better man,
a gentleman, even noble, because in adversity noble is as
noble does. I looked forward to being technological. I
would have the right, as I was seeing it then, to some of my
tiresome mannerisms, because I would be earning my own
way. Then I thought, perhaps I shall not be tiresome after
all, that many of my self-loathings were affectations, protective colorations. If I were working, I would be a little
further beyond reproach than I had ever been. So many
errors, yet even then the errors felt like misleading clues to

the truth, to some truth at least as durable as a tree. I would like to have written a poem that would live as long as a tree. But I had been thinking alone (I thought) about my poems. Delenda's gestures completed my gestures, and some of my gestures completed his gestures, as one person's gestures can complete another person's, and such completion elevates the gestures into an emotion. I knew the difference between the way I governed myself in Edinburgh and the way I governed myself in Paris, or Baltimore, or Rio de Janeiro. Yet I hadn't noticed that I was governing myself. Delenda's revolution showed me to myself as I had never acknowledged myself: responsible, self-governing. Then the darkness began, sometimes, to let its hair down, to tell about itself.

Love and history,
Oliver

Oh, Octavio, handling Oliver's handmade paper I can almost feel that I touch his hand. But any meditation I might write now on hands would be a diversion from the confession that I can feel coming. I did not know, when Delenda appointed me postmaster, how much he knew about letters in general, or how much he knew about my connections with letters. I remember now when Delphine first wanted to mail a piece of driftwood scribbled by bark beetles or perhaps seaworms into a semblance of writing. I demurred, officially, although I had taken on an office which had no official rules. I was the source of my own officiousness, and amazed I was to find out how much of it I had within me. I don't know what inspired me to tell other people what a letter must be in order to be a letter. But of course I knew what a letter was. A letter was found waiting for one on the table in the hall. If it accompanied other mail, bills and advertisements, then the decision arose whether to seize immediate pleasures, opening the letter first, or to delay the gratification. To open the unpleasant, impersonal, possibly degrading mail first was to risk spoiling later pleasures. Once the greeting from a computer, "Thank you for being a good customer," so pleased me, made me feel so happy, that I was embarrassed for minutes afterward, and guiltily reminded myself that I was a "good customer" because I had been a "bad son," paying a bill when I received it instead of following Kwant's instructions to pay it a few days late. I had to learn to harden myself against "Dear Occupant," "Dear Sir or Madam," and once, a miracle of energetic, improbable misinformation, "Dear Mr. Prince." I studied the solicitous mail closely for professional reasons, with a professional eye, watching myself to see if I were being seduced, and if so, how. That profession I will explain soon enough. The real letter, which so many others imitated but which they could not fully deprive of meaning, was the letter waiting in the mirrored foyer, or, in Baltimore, handed to one by the mailman looking up from stuffing letters in mailboxes, smiling with recognition, as one, as I, happened to arrive in the lobby just after the mailman arrived, oh happy synchrony, oh well-rigged recognition. That real letter had been written with any degree of passion or friendliness, but still it participated in a criterion idea of a letter. Dear Sir. My Dear Salathiel. Darling—. It was read in the morning room, with coffee, then folded along the creases where it was already correctly folded ("Really, Salathiel, only a secretary folds a letter *that* way . . ."), reinserted in the envelope, then envelope and letter studied over for hidden meanings—choice of stamp, postmark, inkblots, return address or no return address, and my favorite, an error in the apartment number or street number in Baltimore, an opportunity to use my skills as a Freudian numerologist— and the letter and its meanings which hovered beyond the letter were reread as one stood beside the bay window at Utterly thoughtfully overlooking the sea. I would absent-mindedly tap my cheek with the envelope, then accept a distraction and turn toward the day. Apparently forgotten on an endtable among the ferns, the letter lay untouched, unread even by the most well-meaning and curious family and friends. The maid put it on one's desk where its flame flickered, guttered, and sometimes went out. Or a brief neutral excerpt might be read aloud to the others later, to appease their curiosity — "Is Oliver well? Where has he got to? He's *doing* the Lake District. What does one *do* when one *does* the Lake District?" — to console them for their depriva-tion, their unsatisfied craving to possess everything that you were and that came to you, but the compensation was con-descending, they knew it, they were only being polite, al-lowing one to share part of the letter so that one should not feel cruel and selfish. *Perhaps* they were. Occasionally a whole letter might be handed over on a sunny day. None of them had received a letter, and one's own was lukewarm, or chatty, skimpy in its details, so in a gesture which could pass for largesse, and which was completed by no one else's ges-ture, I would pass a letter at breakfast as I rose to help my-self to more eggs from the sideboard, sharing the letter as though to say "I love and trust you more than I love and trust this exasperating correspondent, see, I have no secrets from you. Love me. Share with me. Love me more than you have shown that you love me." Yet more than once I read letters I was not supposed to read, always aware that I was breaking a powerful taboo and would suffer for it. Now of course I open your letters when they are deteriorating, not knowing what else to do with them. And taboos change. I think now in truth that manners are much improved. Few of us are left burning with curiosity about the contents of a letter. Many of us, having read our letter, pass it around.

Salathiel to Octavio

The letters of Delphine: I was remembering Delphine and myself through veils of chagrin. I learned how authoritarian I was, with no foundation for my authority. No reason to reject peculiar *billets-doux.* "Sermons in stones, and books in babbling brooks," Oliver quoted to me. I never learned to like the supposed letters, the indecipherable stones inscribed with slightly addled lines. They hang around useful as paperweights until their appointed time of delivery, and people seem happy to receive them. They add them to the graves. I feel confident enough to turn away only what smells bad or attracts insects. Which some of the paper does anyway. I like mail that I can hang neatly, higher than rats and eager people can reach, arranged in proper order. Olivia, our resident Delphinologist, seems always satisfied that she can read Delphine's missives. Delphine did have an eye for an eloquently worm-eaten piece of bark, I could appreciate that, and of course Oliver remarked helpfully that the ancient Mayans had sometimes covered their codex — their *codices,* I can find nothing to erase with — with the bark of the amate tree. "See *caudex,*" he said. Oliver once made paper out of banana chips — we ate it — and Olivia mailed what looked to me like collages, sometimes with an inaccessible space, so many trapezoids locked in visual combat. And the Indians: until they got the hang of dictating so that Orlando or anyone who was handy could write their words phonetically, and then in our gradual hodge-podge lingua-franca, the Indians might drop a literal line, a piece of string, quipu, the *Knotenschriften* I had studied once in anthropology, but which I could not *read.* Even Orlando, who was not given to symbol or emblem, to embol or symblem, once mailed a net to Olivia, whose comment when it arrived was that it had arrived not a moment too soon, that it was precisely what she needed. I learned to admit that an object wasn't a letter simply because I couldn't have read it, although I remain uncertain how meaning resides in so many alien forms. I will admit that they make me stop to think, that they slow down the delivery of the mail as sometimes darkness overtakes me still mulling over a dried starfish, or picturing myself as I might have walked, more than fifty years ago, from the foyer into the morning room, carrying a conch shell addressed to me, reading it over my breakfast coffee, holding it as I stood gazing at the sea through the bay window, absently touching it to my cheek, pressing it against my ear, hearing the resonance of the island noises that correspond with the natural pitch of the acoustic-chamber seashell. Now our people do, by fiat, declare almost anything a letter. But if anything is, or everything is, then nothing is. Mailing a conch shell is a trifle too pantheistic for my taste. Yet I must say that I suppose I know what they mean, these messages thrown like bottled letters into the sea.

So much for fancy, now for facts. When Delenda appointed me postmaster I feared he guessed my secret (everyone knew what I did, but who knew what it meant to me?). I worked intermittently for Kwant at the stamp and money office in Baltimore. I could confess nothing of this history if it had not been brought to an end when I encountered my cousin Ginevra there for the first time as an adult. Later we married. She had memorable collarbones and I remember them. I have around here letters from Orlando which mention his stint in Baltimore. They are pale compared with the letters I could write. Primavera was supported in part by seigniorage, the difference between the cost of the paper and printing and minting of our money and our stamps, and the price we sold them for. I had to oversee the printing of money, which was sold to wholesale suppliers of stamp-and-coin collection shops, along with a few bills printed with attractive errors, for these had an inflated value because of their scarcity. We released our supply slowly, inconspicuously, to our "preferred" collectors, those we thought would not sell their collections at auction, because when our stamps or coins came up at auction we had to buy enough of them to establish impressive prices for the annual published lists of current auction prices. I had to oversee the printing of stamps, and I even sat cancelling the stamps. C.T.O., we called them, cancelled to order. I cancelled the stamps at the edge so that I didn't spoil the picture. We did a series of the flora and fauna (usually insects) of the island. We did a series I liked of the same scene at different times of day, and we did any commemorative as long as the subject was collectible. We did American presidents and we did astronauts. And once a series of great actresses. I was twenty-five when we married. Kwant was not displeased with that. I felt rather free. I toured as far as I could travel in one day, to Hershey, Pennsylvania, to the Luray Caverns, to the Delaware Water Gap, to Gettysburg, to Ocean City, Maryland. I was reluctant to spend the night anywhere except the apartment which Kwant owned, and which seemed to impose a curfew on me, even as a married man. Scrounging around in Kwant's office for paper to give the children, for them to mash up, I uncovered a letter that I wrote for the Primavera Collector's Society, Ltd. Primavera was not in the usual stamp albums because it was so small, and was not recognized as a sovereign nation. It wasn't even in the United Nations. We benefitted by selling our own albums. De luxe, as we said: "Custom-crafted for you—your name will be stamped in gold on the front cover." These memories are painful. I had forgotten my crimes against the art of writing letters. I will record this specimen here as my penance for having written it. On the envelope a machine with a built-in bias pasted stamps crookedly so that they would appear to have been put on by hand. At the top of the letter a machine has printed a note in ink, in my handwriting, so that it looks as though I added it as a "personal" afterthought: "I have just returned from a meeting with the President of Primavera. His Excellency has authorized this history-making exclusive for just the first 20,000 United States Collectors who reply." Special printer's ink would smudge if someone rubbed it with a moistened finger to test if it was written with ink. If punishments fit crimes, I suppose we should have had our hands cut off for our abuse of hands: simulated handwriting, imitation handicrafts, bogus handiwork, the businessman's handclasp. What was I?, the handyman of the second-hand and the hand-me-down experience. What did they expect to receive from my hands? They received something, my letters touched them, I received touchingly simple, sincere, "warm" responses. People wrote to me about the pleasures they received from their purchases. Their letters were better than I deserved. But my letter awaits us:

Dear Friend,
I have secured a fantastic coup for you.

If you are one of the first 20,000 persons who reply, you can profit, at the original issue price — before the inevitable law of supply and demand can work its action in the marketplace.

For, by exclusive agreement with the Honorable Ferdinand di Pyreneos, we are exclusive distributors for the first Primavera Postage Series in history to be MADE WITH 23-KARAT GOLD.

The lush island of Primavera, which even Christopher Columbus failed to discover, has long been famed for the exquisite beauty of its rare stamps.

Gold is also rare, and each official Government of Primavera stamp is proof-minted upon a large 3.24 square inch surface of real 23-karat gold. Gold is a collectible too, I don't need to tell you. The stamps represent the rare flowers of Primavera in the botanic garden of the President. They are exquisite gems of the engraver's art, brimming with detail and high sculptured relief. Indeed, from the tiniest detail of a flower to the replica of the official portrait of the President in the corner of each stamp, the dramatic designs are raised *in bold relief* from the surface of the gold.

While there can be no guarantee whatever that past price increases can be expected to hold true for the future, it is also possible that they may be even better. The price of gold has increased while our artists have been at work on these stamps, but we are absorbing the loss.

You and your children will have a remarkable and lively introduction to the flora of Primavera, immortalized in golden pictures. For with each stamp is a "flyleaf" with an entertaining, accurate, and educational story of that stamp.

The cost for each proof-finished stamp, produced upon a large surface of real 23-karat gold, is just $29.50 each. As legal postage of the nation of Primavera, each stamp is bonded to special philatelic material with a gummed backing for durability through the mails *and* as a collectible. Your stamps will be sent conveniently at the rate of one gold stamp per month.

The letter went on, Octavio, my prolix offense against the language, I as the prodigal son poisoning the arts of letters and of friendship, misusing the prolificacies of language, and yes, I am ashamed. I must plead, in extenuation of my epistolary abuses, that the letter was not original with me, that it was the descendent of some ur-solicitation that Kwant must have composed many years before. But with the advances in technology I was able to add another original touch, a postscript in my own handwriting: "It occurs to me that in my enthusiasm to explain why I consider these stamps to be such an exceptional combination of values, I neglected the *main reason* it is such a collector's treasure. For as any collector will tell you, it is the *history* and *beauty* of a stamp series which gives the deepest and most genuine sat-

isfaction. Any price increase—and the works have tradi-
tionally gone up in price—while surely to be appreciated,
will be just a confirmation of your basic sense of values."
This last paragraph was my own invention. I feel a pain in
my heart when I read it. I could scream in anguish because I
helped to injure the language in America by using it to con-
fuse values. I did my part in the Age of Manipulation. And
of course the golden stamps sold out. I distributed the
money among Kwant's accounts, as I was instructed to. And
paid bills with checks drawn on banks as far away from the
creditor as possible, so that the check would take longer to
clear. Although sometimes I mailed a check early to have
something to mail, to feel in touch with that larger consciousness, the U.S. mails. And the stamps were, to tell the
truth thoroughly, a good investment. They appreciated in
value, or perhaps the word is salability. I was asked often,
usually by myself, why I returned to Primavera, why, when
I was in America, I did not simply escape from Kwant. Of
course he was my father, as well as our dictator, but my
deepest reason in Baltimore, where I learned to give deepest reasons, was, as Ginevra and I realized, that we preferred to be in Primavera, for in Baltimore no one actually
listened to us, they seemed to be thinking about something
other than what they were doing, and in their distracted
hospitality no one was interested enough in what we were
doing to oppose our wills. Their tolerance felt like indifference. Few could attend long enough to understand that our
family had as it were assembled from Germany, Austria,
Switzerland, France, and Liechtenstein and had transposed
itself into the Hispanic mode. They stretched their anglo-
philia to cover us. No one seemed to care that I was not
merely an heir, that I had published several essays: "The
Meaning of *Beowulf*," "The Meaning of *Sir Gawain and the
Green Knight*," "The Meaning of *Tom Jones*," "The Meaning

of *Middlemarch*," and "The Romantic Quest and the Meaning of the Available." I did not press the point because I was writing to find out what I meant by *meaning*, and I was not eager to be asked precisely what I meant. My meanings were not quite available to me, at least not available as a product I could have sold them on. They had identified me as a harmless unidentifiable exotic who might be useful someday, and all their courtesy and generosity and gracious smiles, dinners at the Kennel Club, invitations to the Bachelor's Cotillion, the same smiling black man at every other party gracefully scrambling eggs at midnight for the young couples, I passed him once on Eutaw Street and half-recognized him as an old acquaintance but couldn't place him until a block past the point at which he looked at me without recognition when I greeted him Hello, although he had smiled and said Yessir to me many times, then I punched my fist into my hand as I stumbled along Mulberry Street on the way back to the office. And every season another new debutante with the same old longshoreman's foul mouth, each season a granddaughter of a president, or someone kin to the Bonapartes, or the parents who had entertained the Duke and Duchess and denied that they had paid them a fee for attending parties. And the field-hockey heroine harnessed in her first formal dress, making a reluctant clumsy curtsey like a new way for a goalie to make a save. People so generalized, they were a temptation to believe in archetypes. When I circulated among the other young men I was too alien to be a rival to them in the marriage market, although I was hypothetically eligible because I was said to be rich, and after I was married I was safely out of circulation. They were all quiet spoken because they were going to marry well, so well engaged that they did not need to be noisily engaged. Each of them made a good first marriage. Later—in how many cases? enough to generalize? how feeling for them fades at the farther reaches of induction—they discovered that their father's business which they had entered was boring or "lacked nobility." The father died upon being so found out. The son met a woman other than his wife, who was looking around wanting to want something. He borrowed money from his bewildered widowed mother who was loving life more than she had in years. The *post obit* loans financed his divorce, paid the tuition of the children at Roland Park Country Day School, and furnished the apartment he took with his new wife, supplemented with some quite good things from the attic of his mother's house (so much too large for her now) in Guilford. Then he mismanaged his mother's finances and the gun, which was always kept loaded so that no one would mistakenly play around with a gun thinking that it was unloaded—the gun would be discovered as though it had been planted in his life as the concealed beginning of a story which, as soon as he recognized the gun, he realized he had found an ending for. That is how the end of a story determines its beginning. The gun had belonged to his father. The blast, the noise, was a mocking serenade, a solo chivaree; it was like breaking a suitable engagement. One man had asked an acquaintance to lend him a shotgun to shoot mockingbirds which were keeping him awake: thus did they make known the agony of their lives through images.

How do I compare with them? I sold them our paper money and our stamps, myself a collectible of sorts, but suspiciously unenthusiastic sitting on a shooting stick at the hunt cup races in Green Spring Valley or at the cockfights on My Lady's Manor. The money and stamps increased in value, and eventually I returned to Primavera willingly with my more willinger bride, who had after all grown up here, sequestered in Tornata. I am writing you this long letter trying not to think as Goethe thought, that the best I know is not for boys. Perhaps by the time you read this you will no longer be a boy. I thought all night about Kwant's intentions in sending me to Baltimore, and I suppose about my intentions in allowing Orlando in turn to be sent by him. But intentions are overwhelmed by events. Purposes are served. In some ways Kwant was like a father to my children, while I was like a grandfather to them. Aurelia seems to see everything as serving a purpose in a purposeless world. I'm not sure. I had something that I wanted to say back there in Baltimore about energy as a function of things being out of place. I was planning a book on art, with urbanely concealed social criticism, a book to be entitled *Out of Place,* with a theme, illustrated with examples, of different energies created by the bearing of parts upon each other. I was thinking about falling into place, about import, about boundaries. Not that I was clear, but I would become clear, and I was not demonstrably wrong, as they clearly were wrong in their impatience and inattention. So Baltimore was a playpen to me, a city of petty constraints, and I preferred to witness Kwant's experiment — "Time is money, money is energy, the sugar is our money, and money is our blood," he would proclaim. I preferred to take my chances as a slightly awkward word in the sentence he was trying to compose, hoping that as a part, slightly out of place, with a bearing upon the other parts, that I could subvert or dominate or at least sway his meanings. I was mistaken. He provided the context, and everything I did merely bore upon his context and derived its meaning from it. I learned the hard way about importance, about import, about how meaning is carried into events, about miscarriages of justice and mismarriages to existence. But Baltimore was not so bad. By chance, if chance explains anything, one of the windfall letters I have picked up this morning is from Orlando, remembering guiltily his penance in Baltimore, the simultaneous crime and self-punishment of writing those letters to collectors. His self-recriminations over those honey-tongued solicitations are so like mine that I will confine myself to quoting one paragraph written for an issue of silver stamps. The postscript, in his simulated and smudgeable handwriting, reads: "One of our collectors in Utah recently wrote to me, 'I was displaying my collection to friends and other collectors in Salt Lake City. I was offered $450 then and there for the Silver Primavera Collection of Tropical Trees, and then offered $500. But no-siree-bob, I naturally refused the offer. That along with future albums will go to my grandson. Someday.' The original price of Silver Trees was $245, including postage and insurance." How could I have spared Orlando? Why should I have spared him? How could I have known enough to have known what was good for him? I knew the offense of sitting in an office writing dishonest letters to collectors, the "you" letters as they were called because we wrote to them from their point of view, telling them what they were going to feel and think and do, prompting them to do what we wanted them to do by reading their greedy minds for them: "You must be wondering, as the value of your money is eroded by governmental policies, where you can put it to protect it. It must have occurred to you that what the rich buy increases in value, while so much of what you buy deteriorates. You have been selected by a computer which chose only 10,000 names from a list of 250,000 submitted to it, as one of the people who will understand the value of our prospectus. We can't tell you the names of the wealthy people who preserve the value of their money by buying our coins, but. . . ." I did not know enough to choose a world for my son; I saw no place to preserve him, no place to put him to

protect his value. Aurelia wanted to study medicine; Oliver
was peculiarly safe. I had to want Orlando to be prepared
to survive or to succeed in a contemptible and disgusting
society. That American style we learned—we taught ourselves—that self-fouling language in which one spoke of a
"personal friend," and in which we found ourselves per-
suaded by a sales pitch which was remarkably like our
own—I ordered bulbs, iris and lilies, from my address in
Baltimore for the garden at Primavera, and forever after
received announcements of flowers that would grace my
garden at the address in Baltimore, and I would look
around at the apartment which the computer had described as a "garden" and laugh, and order more bulbs. I
did not like Baltimore but I loved it, and not only did I
learn there to think with images, as the apartment became
an imaginary garden, I also learned that there are bad images, and bad thinking with images. Our prose there, in
that place, explains something of our prose on Primavera
as we all, in slightly different ways, tried to distance ourselves from that utilitarian and mercantile prose which
used the gestures and language of friendship to sell products, objects without a natural pitch, which corresponded
to nothing in the environment, and which lacked resonance. The language of commercial factors. Orlando as
folklorist collecting and using an expression such as "No-
siree-bob" (assuming he wrote the letter; perhaps he merely copied it), was desperate and self-defeating. He had
arrived too late for pawky proverbs (I lack a convincing word for what I want to say here: he was too late for
authentic, genuine, or even *true* speech, and for me even to use
the debased words is to hear Olivia saying, "Please pass me
the mouthwash."), and his transcriptions of the actual
made us remember that there must be an ideal. Merely to
transcribe what people actually said in Baltimore was an

act of unintentional irony. Orlando clipped quotations from the newspaper—"A promise. A promise is for how long? Only until the sun sets."—always sentimental about peasants, ever expecting a working-class hero to breathe life into the language which had suffered a seizure as it was being taken over by a conglomerate. I have quoted part of his letter—"these unique stamps hold great promise for the future"—and of course I pick up many other letters by chance, some as they happen to fall from packets where they are hanging. But if that letter of Orlando's had not had a bearing upon the others transcribed here, I would not have copied it. It fell into place. Perhaps I give the name chance to a choice I have not yet chosen. "Chance flowers into choice," a poet had written. I am trying to understand what Orlando had written in the same letter about probability: "I judged, from that night in the canefield, that I knew once and for all time, in a single melancholy induction, what it would be like laboring for the profit of others. Aurelia and I spent hours vexed by the question of how we knew what we thought we knew. For me to judge that each occasion of laboring would resemble this occasion, I had to assume that the whole context was not going to change. Because if it did change, those changes would change the meaning of labor within that context. So I assumed knowledge about the future when I assumed that each experience of labor would be like that. I assumed continuity. We each seemed to have our continuities which we took for granted, but few of us had the same continuities. Olivia points out the false continuities which we take for granted, and even the falsities in her own film scripts as we rehearse them with her, and she promises herself to focus abruptly on different planes, which seems truth to her but an evasion to me (not merely because she has neither film nor electricity). And I could not figure out how to write a story in which the beginning would confront the reader directly, without being falsified by its continuity with the middle, and with the end. Yet my guess about laboring, that any future occasions would resemble that one occasion, has an animal certainty about it. Perhaps animals can be certain but wrong. I will think more about this, Salathiel. I would like to feel that appearances are trustworthy, but I am aware of my own deceptions and self-deceptions, protecting Olivia, and the price I pay for that, and protecting myself, and the price I pay for that. I'd like to live a little more unprotected; I suppose that life is a continuous process of detheatricalization; or I mean that it should be. I am trying to explain myself in terms that I can understand." I wonder, Octavio, if I haven't introduced false continuities of my own. Olivia once said that no other continuities exist, but in the logic of love, Olivia is Olivia, and as years pass she finds her honest transitions. As a method of thinking, I will *choose* among the letters which *chance* to be on my desk. Here is Oliver:

Tornata—Pom 20th—Year 9

Dear Aurelia,

If I must write a letter today, let it be a letter to you, for I can still look upon you as capable of objectivity. I feel sometimes, this moment for example, that I have spent a lifetime conquering emotions, and then erecting quotations above them as trophies: ". . . his youthful face clouded yet by the pain of a conquered emotion." Yet somehow I don't get to do with my conquests whatever conquerors get to do. Or perhaps not a conqueror, but camp follower of my own emotions, they always bivouacked a little ahead of me. At least no conquests that I have lived to enjoy. I have been cheated out of being a poet because, although I administer last minute discriminations of taste and seem finicky, I am not willing to be disgusted, or for that matter, to be disgusting, and thus and there and thence I am idle and talkative, but not a poet disgusted into rhapsody, one whose every ode sublates a palinode. Now Flypaper Kwant is disgusting, I think, but he is not an epic or lyric subject. Salathiel never seems disgusted, rarely discouraged. But then he is no poet. You and Olivia are disgusted often. I think of the tree Kwant grew in his botanic garden (he said "botanical"), a gamhem tree, from Sumatra. It has a soft bark, an enormous trunk, and a soft, pulpy interior. In Sumatra, at least according to legend— and who am I to bury a legend?—the people bury the bodies of suicides in the tree, which soon heals over the incision. In moments of despair I think of being buried in that tree (it still flourishes among Kwant's alphabetically shanghaied trees, not far from a mulberry you kept up a secret acquaintance with when we were forbidden to go to Umberland). And then without worrying about your point of view, I have hospitably included you, Olivia, and Orlando in my suicide, so I write of the four of us buried in the tree,

> Ourselves inside ourselves,
> And who will ever know we've died
> Consumating suicide,
> While time runs rings around us?
> A quartet quoting Tennyson:
> "So fold thyself, my dearest thou,
> And slip into my bosom and be lost in me."

Now drifting into quotation, and quoting myself, almost disgusts me, but I merely feel disquiet. Yet I had a recent disquieting experience which seems like a hint to me that I am approaching my poetry (which is none too soon since I am about thirty-three and approaching thirty-four). I remembered the gamhem tree in my search for materials to use in making paper. Not wanting to give Kwant or Converse any provocation, I shadowed into the shadows of the botanic garden at evening, and quietly cut a hole in the tree. I was able to reach in, to scoop out the soft pulp, and then as I reached in farther with my hand, I seized a hand in mine, crunching its bones in its last handshake, and I thought to myself, about lend a hand, and take a hand, and about tempestuous sea-changes, I had a sensation which reminded me of the time I stepped on something soft while swimming in the lagoon, and pulled up a rubber glove, I had a clear sight of you wearing surgical gloves, and then I thought about the bones, well, as well them as anything else, and I added that handful to my bucket and scooped myself on home. I can't say that the experience disgusted me. I felt thrilled, and educated. The experience was as transparent as an image which conveys a clear idea, bringing me discernibly closer to my truth. I fear, I think I fear, that it delighted me. I won't need to tell you, Aurelia, about the materials that make up the paper I am writing on. You know me well enough to know. You knew me well enough to bring me the paper press as a present from Baltimore so many years ago, so long ago that the actual number of years is lost in Delenda's transpositions. I wish my poems had such power, the power of the truth that I feel in trees, even in the trees Kwant misappropriated for his imperial quincunx orchard. I don't think you care about poetry, unless you care about Erasmus Darwin, *The Loves of the Plants*. But you care about me, so you care about poetry for my sake. Somehow, I feel rather aimless today. Do you remember, Aurelia, the "complimentary closing" Cézanne was inclined to use in so many of his letters? "I touch your hand." I am moved—touched—by that simple expression. How did he become so unsophisticated? I can feel, beyond my

tender feelings, some movement of the macabre in my imagination, some constrained movement like a tree propped
up and tied down with stakes to shape it against its grain.
Perhaps my largest evasion: avoiding the energy in horror.
I have been too inadequately horrified to love adequately,
and I suppose I write to you because you know for certain
when something disgusts you.

In our rapport,
Oliver

This is the next day, Octavio. I don't take time to look back
and to read over what I have written. Have I said that each
piece of paper I handle is now a story? Much of this paper
was made by Oliver who had studied papermaking when
it was almost obsolete as a craft. I could not detect irony
when he presented blank sheets of paper to friends. But
that was later. We would give him firewood or beer or a
fish, even fruit which he could as easily have gathered for
himself. I gave him gaudy stocks and bonds and paper
money, neither of us acknowledging the parody of commerce, or the travesty of the medieval court, I as the lord
dispensing patronage to the wandering minstrel, or the *scop*
in *Beowulf*, the poet with his *topoi*. The old papermoney became mere paper, and the paper became moneypaper, a
medium of exchange. As I write to you, occasionally I recognize flicks and flecks of the purple, silver, or gold-
colored money of my childhood and early manhood; and
even of the lovely white-on-white dollars that I designed
when I was a social success in Baltimore. The dollars were
a success too, following me through Guilford, Homeland,
and Roland Park, and out to the Green Spring Valley Inn,
where I would be invited by fathers who had bought the
money so that their wives could appraise me for their
daughters. I won a prize from a numismatic society in Ne-
vada for my white-on-white. Not much of the money

reached the island. Aurelia found some in Kwant's old office, but most of the money was shipped directly from the
printer in Baltimore or Philadelphia to the wholesalers.
Oliver had seen the money on sale in a shop in Paris, and
tried to buy some of the older bills, which were quite
scarce, with some of the new bills, but without success. I
see shreds and patches of the stock that belonged to me,
for I seemed to have owned Arvidco, Ltd., a corporation,
although Kwant had not told me much about it. I was trying to live, according to Olivia's genial characterization, as
an ambassador without portfolio. Kwant said that Arvidco
manufactured pins, to keep me in pin money. Another letter arrived for you today from Oliver. I will store it in the
incubator, for the paper is in excellent condition. You will
be able to read in this paper how Oliver taught so many to
make paper with almost anything. Perhaps you remember
the delight with which you used to help him. He taught us
all to work with what he called "the available means," a
phrase Olivia in her grove is still declaring a tautology, she
and I agreeing in our quest for the anti-Romantic, or
post-Romantic, that the quest motif had been inflated in
importance, and had displaced—this is her list which we
are still sorting through—restoration, replacement, rehab-
ilitation, reconstruction, reproduction, renovation, renew-
al, revival, resuscitation, reanimation, reorganization, res-
titution, relief, retrieval, reclamation, recovery, and conva-
lescence—we are still waiting for the word to emanate
from the experience, we stout critics of emanations, and
when it does we will net it. A letter from her lies emanat-
ing upon my desk: I will insert it here:

Nowhere—Chay Kin—Year 26

Dear Salathiel,
I want you to understand how far from grateful I am for my
various inheritances from our mutual past, for what have I

received but obstacles, and what have you bought in buying me but trouble for yourself?, although I know that you
meant well, I am impaled on your good intentions. I am
willing for varying lengths of time to think of myself as
crazy, I live with that word until I realize that I see a sky
that had been vermillion ovoids patched on a slanted parallelogram of light, that I see what I see, and I see it feelingly,
and that I am not crazy, although somewhat crazed. People
like Orlando, who think that they are the operational definitions of sanity, are maddening. I am not crazy. I was not
crazy, I was unhappy, but when I was or am unhappy I
can't think, can't think my way out of the unhappiness
(I don't quarrel with Ginevra's "Count your blessings"
worked in needlepoint for my bedroom when I was a child,
but my blessings always looked bloody to me, haunted by
human or perhaps I mean to say inhuman sacrifices, and
she had stitched the word in such red intensity that one
had to invent the word *hemography* [or so Oliver said] to
convey the quantity of emotion in such needlework), and
would sometimes be too unhappy to consider my responsibility to what Oliver (with my self-betraying complicity)
was amused to call my "yellow logarithms," what Aurelia
once suggested were compensations although for what she
did not say, or did not dare to say, and certainly I never felt
compensated or recompensed, and I am too exacting to accept sublimations and displacements and ersatz experiences — you all know my lists — although I have heard myself shout that I do want reparations, which I never explained, and could not have explained until I learned for
myself by agonized and appalled gazing at my feelings that
I was unhappy, plainly and simply unhappy, walking in
circles as though I were tied to a stake, and then I might do
something a wee bit destructive as though to call attention
to the surface of my unhappiness, an unhappiness caused

by my involuntary impoverishment, I feel poor in some way that I could or should feel rich (I love Delenda for getting us to write these letters because I never would have thought, without my obligation to write every day, of writing my daily grievances, and by the time you receive this letter you will understand that my mood has passed, you will be understanding of my pain, and I might not remember myself what I have written here, although you can be assured that somewhere my flesh remembers there in the future where you are reading this letter. I love these letters because I know I am going to make a mistake and write something that I will regret, so I do it and have done with it, and that frees me to do what I like for the rest of the day as my mind hums with postscripts, some abusive, some loving). I have been unnaturally impoverished and I know, with the logic of my impoverished feelings as I seek redress of my grievances, that you were too tentative, too cowardly, that you gave money to save me rather than confront those two people (who were they? where had they come from? where were they going? events on this island are not that mysterious, they are merely kept hidden sometimes), and I feel like some new image of the human condition inserted in a spectrum that begins abortion, stillborn, abandoned, adopted, only a difference of degree, perhaps, but a difference in kind to me, for an abyss opens between me and my sources, and this is *my* abyss, and this is my condition, not any human condition, I cannot notice the freckles on my breasts without trying to smell my mother's skin, to brush my hand across the stubble of my father's beard. The rest of you know with confidence where you came from, for all the good it does you, and you were too falsely bland or too tolerant to kill your monstrous father who had cut you off at the crossroads, you lacked the artistry of revolutions although you seemed to be a social critic, whatever that might be, diffused in literature, and I can remember you complaining that the Baltimoreans protected themselves from intense experiences of hot and cold, wet and dry, in and out, up and down, that they left their houses filled with labor-saving devices to drive around the beltway to an exercise class, you anatomized their depleted sensualities, citing the evidence that they preferred convenience to truth, mired down in false transcendences, a city of mediocre escape-artists, but you did not spare me intense, inconvenient, and inescapable experience when you allowed Kwant (although I should not refer to him by adorable grandson Oliver's garbled babbled nickname but by his total nomenclature which if I recall is Ferdinand something di Pyrineos, well I can't recall as it turns out, and if I can't recall the whole name which he was given and which he took when they in their migration or exodus in chauffered limousines converged upon the bordertown in the mountains—Port Bou?—the name should have been Germanic anyway, not Hispanic, perhaps von der Pyranäen, although I would allow Orlando and Aurelia to be de la Pyrénées. And if I can't recall his whole name, I can't even recall whether or not I am in the middle of a parenthesis because my thought continues until it reaches my anger that you, to placate him, allowed him [and I suppose to make him feel an interest in me, that he had something invested in me] to name me for Oliver's dead twin sister, which was his way of providing for the future in which he could say to me "You are not Olivia, Olivia was beautiful and good," and my impulse was to kill, but what could I do, I was only a child?, a girl who without being told gathered the impression that her instincts were wrong, quite unsuitable really, but my instincts were merely violent, they were not unreasonable, they were what my organs reasoned for themselves when Father Pasquale or Father

Converse didn't interfere with them with their *educo, educas, educat,* and I am certain now that my instinctual feelings are the reasonings of my body, perhaps of some organ which I have not yet located and do not know the name of, but which I shall be glad to love when I find it. No wonder Goethe went looking for that gland or whatever it was and was pleased to find it because it was the ground of implications which otherwise were groundless and crazy, which is enough to make anyone unhappy. Not a gland but the intermaxillary bone, I ran over to ask Aurelia. Odd how she and Oliver agree on Goethe. I don't care about Goethe or these rag-tags I remember from what I have been taught, or half-taught or have learned, or have half-learned. I seem to be forgetting everything that I knew but never learned. I know that I am capable of uninspired vulgarity, but I am incapable of tolerating the way Converse taught about Goethe, as though he were holding an idea with a pair of tongs. Lukewarm. Converse tried to teach us to be silver-tonged poets to ready us for our silver-tonged lives, but I wouldn't learn, and I pick up and eat with my fingers and with my eyes. At least Kwant was not pusillanimous. I might be fond of him yet, and that would be vulgar. He forbade calculators and anything called a *cassette,* and his sentences, his proclamations, which tended to start, "All women . . . ," "It is true universally," "Always, Olivia, you .˙. ," were an education for me as I scurried to find counterexamples, little irritants. Kwant told us once of a clever Indian who made money selling feathers from birds. "As though he owned them," I said, and he looked at me uncomprehendingly but at least as though I had a threatening point of view. But why must I threaten anyone in order to be taken seriously? I shall repeat stories from my legendary childhood, stories I heard in that house which sometimes seemed to hover between the sky and sea. Ferdinand von der Pyranäen, our Kwant, was taken by his father, when it was still convenient to seem German, to the festivities for the opening of the Autobahn. He was a child, before the dispersal of that dissipated royalty. The open touring cars drove in a double column which proceeded solemnly, militarily, ceremoniously, like a clockwork festival, until by some slipup a truck loaded with crates of live chickens on their way to market—the truck had Proper-Slaughter-Chickens written on its side—pulled in front of the procession from a temporary dirt access road, and when the lost truck driver saw the double column of cars behind him, he speeded up as he turned back onto the shoulder, and Kwant saw as the truck swerved a white chicken squeeze between the bars of its crate, a centrifugal hen, and flap down onto the *Bahn* where it squatted in the middle as the columns of autos proceeded without hesitation or deviation on either side of it, and Kwant in short pants stood up to watch what it would do, or what would happen to it, and saw through the eyes of the terrified chicken toward its heartbeat, but as he turned around to follow with his eyes he was slapped on his bare knees and forced to sit down, to sit up, eyes straight ahead, unable to witness the further adventures of the chicken or the truck, although later, in France, he saw a dog, dead beside the road, the first dead animal he had seen left unburied beside the road, for him the first time someone's pet had been hit by a vehicle and no one had stopped to attend to it or to bury it, and no one stopped *then* to attend to it or to bury it, and those experiences seemed for him part of a spectrum which was visible to me but which for him shaded into something infra- or ultra- perhaps visible to him but unobservable to the rest of us. Am I clear if I say that he had saddled himself with his own world? Now say what you will, Kwant did know how to hold children's interest with an occasional bedtime story, although even as a child I suspected that the logic of his stories was not the same for him as it was for me. The story about the chicken seemed if not his *apologia* then at least his abdication from responsibility for the domesticated disasters of the 20th century. Yet he, and you, and not circumstances, impoverished me, you allowed him to ignore me, but I am poor, not destitute, and I am not unburied beside any road. My conflict is that as I fight my battles I do not always want my side to win. By the way, I didn't not believe you yesterday, Salathiel, when I asked you to look me in the eye and to repeat what you had said: I wanted you to look me in the eye.

Uneasily,
Olivia

Olivia's letters are more frightening to her than they are to me, I think. She is not at all as she seems to fear she is. I wish that I could hold a mirror up to her, and indeed sometimes I show her the letters I receive from her, and then we laugh. "Did I write that?", she asks. *Sometimes* we laugh. Here, and now, a letter to Orlando from Oliver, on its way to be preserved with other letters, but so destroyed by silverfish or bookworms that I had better copy it.

Yaxtin 1st—Postoffice—Year 16

Dear Orlando,

I am sitting downstairs in the postoffice writing this letter so that I will be near you. I am approximately underneath you. You are upstairs where I can hear your footfall but not see you. I am at Salathiel's counter while he is, I think, helping to haul in a net of fish. I think that this is my fortieth birthday, although I am judging this vital statistic by the vital signs of respiration in the trees and vines and bushes I confiscate for the paper which, since it does the work of money, is I suppose fiscal. I would like to revive the word *fisc* to describe the bucket I collect stuff in for my paper-making. A good word, *fisc*, but its teeth don't bite into the object the way the word *bucket* does for me. A fiscal year. I am also judging the date by those Indians who are preparing to celebrate the Day of the Dead, but how do they remember the Day of the Dead? I just walked out and asked them. They remember the Day of the Dead when they look up to find themselves weaving nets, and they know from that what time of year it might be, and then they ask Salathiel to make sure, since he keeps the calendar. Some of them remember the Julian calendar, more or less, and some live by an Indian calendar which is close to Delenda's but not identical with it. They look at the sun and see some fact that escapes my notice. I thought that Delenda's calendar would suit all of the Indians, even the Semifinalists, but apparently not. Well, as Olivia said, time is one of my consuming interests. This introduction is the prologue to my business in writing to you, which is the long unfinished business of myself. We seem unable to escape, however hard we work, the privileged exemptions of oyster-white linen suits, pale silk shirts, screened verandas, or even my facetious membership in the Incorporated Society for Psychical Research, 1 Adam and Eve Mews, London W8 6UQ, in spite of our position as surviving veterans of Delenda's bloodless revolution. You sit upstairs in your loft taking the dictationship of the proletariat, and I look at myself and wonder, what revolution?, for I have continued to thrive as the local abscessed Narcissus, so many of my feelings lost in alliteration. The only revolution I can grasp is that we bury these letters somewhere in the future, and then our chronotropic lives turn toward that future which seems to curve toward us.

But I dally. My birth composed the times before my

birth into a story, and their deaths composed the times before their deaths into another story, and both are stories of
vivid, lucent perishings. Which I have never known how
to mourn. Although I seem to have known how to mourn
the time, or times, beyond my death which I will perish
without seeing. Although I probably am grieving for those
there in the future who will perish without seeing me. I
have been consuming these different times at different
rates of consumption as my cannibalistic present consumes
itself, sometimes chewing more than it has bitten off. You,
Orlando, have not conserved pain as relentlessly as Olivia
and I have. I started a poem, years ago, in my calypso period, during a springtime which lengthened as I shortened
words:

The man goes out,
Starts fight man,
He don't stay home,
And stab him woman.

Later I heard Delphine singing, in her equally inexplicable
calypso period.

Man strut self,
Fight fight man,
Stop hisself
Stab him woman.

I couldn't ascertain whether she had somehow learned of
my poem, and pidgined it with a touch of Baltimore, or
whether I had heard a calypso account of my parents'
deaths and had plagiarized it—yet so theoretical an account. I doubt that Delphine can be accused of having
sung with an island lilt in her voice without awareness that
she was being overheard. I will not contemplate *her* motives. But I write as though from before my private revolu-

tion, as though I had not finally interpreted for myself Delenda's revolution as an imperative to roll events back to
wherever I had hastily buried an emotion and to disinter it
for inspection, and in the spirit of that revolt I returned to
the tomb, mausoleum, house of the dead, I looked at the
bodies of my mother and father there is their *atopia* until I
saw them without any quoted phrase adequate to what I
saw, trying to look without burying those of my affections
which I had just freed from their crypt. Were my affectations embalmed affections? I kept whistling to myself in
the dark of what I was doing to accompany not a *danse macabre* but a dance which like any revolution in the arts has as
its motive freedom of movement. (Each of us seems to
think that another of us thought of this formulation first. I
don't remember.)

Well, Orlando, I was going to let myself off by ending
this letter, but will attempt more. My father, when he was
young, a member of a dueling society, cut his glamorous
face and irritated the wound to form a charming scar. He
threatened my mother with knives. Often. They argued.
He would go out and start fights with men, with socially
inappropriate men, not duelists, but men stronger than he
who would appear to be defeating him but who would (I
feel like a graverobber who finds a tomb within a crypt
within a grave) be restraining him from murder. He won a
peculiar reputation among the men and their women, for
he would misread a scene to mean that a woman was in
some distress, and he would, to her distress, attempt to
rescue her. You are too discreet to mention any of this,
ever, as the men on the island were discreet, and patient,
although when abroad he got himself into trouble. Some of
his rescues (he was saving *someone*, I suppose) were chronicled in songs that you must have recorded in your folklorist phase, and you must know that your discretion is an

improper burial, that too much of my life has been spent at funerals where my friends were discreetly burying impulses, affections, hostilities, desires, and thoughts that might have been painful to me, without my knowing it. Well, now I know it, or at least more of it: my body is a graveyard. One night, after some fiesta, my father returned undefeated from his fight. He was excited, he screamed at the servants, and forgive me if I say this, you have scolded me, told me to commit myself to my images and to work out their implications, but we live on an island of so few images, and I am trying to unfold their implications, he buried his knife in her bosom, only to turn, I gather, for the story has gaps in it, and each gap I find from experience is a guide to treasure buried in my flesh, in time to see the skinny man he had beaten up, a scrappy cocky bantam, who had followed him back to Tornata with a sickle in one hand and a knife in the other, and as he stabbed my father in the heart with his knife, and stabbed him in the groin, my father twisted the sickle, shoving it down his throat until the metal point emerged from his throat in an inverted tracheotomy. Thus they both died from their old wounds. But they live on cryptically in my thoughts. When I looked through the windows in the coffins at the two of them, my two, I mourned them as I also mourned my attempts to hide their deaths from me. Nor have I finished yet.

And now, Orlando, I have returned from completing a task. I moved, I will tell you now in a blunt word or two, the dessicated and moldering corpses of my mother and father from the iron coffins with the glass windows over their faces — someone overestimated or oversold the efficacy of iron as a protection, at least in this climate — strangling my eloquence as I did so, renouncing the words which preceded the feelings, attempting but failing to renounce all words for the occasion, touching the shrouded bodies of those two with whom I felt no connection except with the words ma-ma and da-da, I flinched, but they were linked conjugally, they linked families and they would with a child link generations, so that the place or position for me existed before I did, their *a priori* baby, they were connecting links in the story of my story of my life, so I brought them back if not to life then at least back into life, back into connection, correspondence, and current events. I wanted them out of that mausoleum, and while space in what I regret I used to call the Moratorium is scarce, the bodies do disintegrate or disappear into the growth of the mounds. I didn't see how the formerly poor could deny the formerly rich, we have forgiven ourselves for most of what we used to be. If we are all equal, in that we are all equally correspondents, dispatching and receiving missives, then in a powerful tautology, if we are equal, we are equal, so I, who might have been expected to keep their ashes in an *étui*, I carried their enshrouded bodies, fearful of falling with them, or of falling upon them, and I lay the bodies upon the ground that I had cleared and threw on them the detritus I had swept up in the mausoleum, the family dust. I cut lianas from the trees, thus helping with Olivia's continuing project to hold back the jungle growth—from a distance she looks like a woman going back to nature by battling it to the death—and I began pruning and cleaning up around the other mounds, tossing the stuff onto the growing mounds, *my* growing mounds, I knew what was going into making the heaps, working like an absent-minded caretaker, cutting back undergrowth, widening paths, developing some symmetry between the two mounds so that, after a slight delay, one would see that they were connected by resemblances. I would appropriate from some neighboring mounds an item that would advance a pattern that was emerging on my mounds even as that pattern began to be the foundation for another pattern by requiring correspondences, while my thefts, or borrowings, or no, neither thefts nor borrowings, but changes, created the possibility of new particular patterns on the graves I had robbed of decoration, and created opportunities for a new and temporary, gloriously temporary, overall pattern. Every effect that I was causing was affecting me, and this "reciprocal modification" of cause and effect seemed like a conversation passing through me, like a communication in which the silences were part of the code. And I was going to stifle eloquence, I remembered, so I did, I worked myself into a silence, or at least into a state in which words did not seem very promising, I had found out what my feelings were, people passing through the grove tossed their stuff onto my piles, a gesture of sympathy which I noted for later when I would remember it to console me. Then a child ran through, holding his breath as children do superstitiously among the dead, running past the mounds in a race against breathlessness. He included my parents in his bright-eyed, puff-cheeked escapade, he looked like Aeolus playing truant from a Mercator projection, this wild west wind of a boy threw me a conch shell, I caught it, I held it to my ear for a moment to hear what I had always thought was the echo of my bloodstream but which Aurelia taught me was not, and then turning, I fitted it where it looked as though it belonged among the beloved rubbish of our lives, then turned farther to fit my body into the whirlwind of emotions, I caved in and mourned, and then mourned anew, I broke into the tomb in which they were buried inside me, and then I saw a scene, myself three years old, white linen short pants, a pale grey silk shirt, my beautiful naked father, only a youth, really, I saw with a pang his vulnerable youthfulness, the boyish scar across the high cheek bone, I

could not speak to him, he stood combing the hair of my
beautiful naked mother as she sat looking at them both in
her triptych mirror, skin pinched into a scar from a wound
on her shoulder, and I could not speak to her, I said nothing, I turned away without their noticing the child outside
the shutters in their doorway, and I said nothing to them
there askew in their innocence, I merely knifed them with
my guilty voracious eyes. I saw that scene in which I might
have spoken and had not, and felt a vague guilt, as though
something within me sagged as I tamed myself, while you,
for example, might have felt quivering incitements, intense
impulses. Later, in bed, entering the domain of sleep, I
opened my eyes to see them show themselves to me dressed
in costume for some rude festival, even then an ungovern-
able fête almost completely deteriorated into unceremoni-
ousness, she dressed in his clothes, he in hers, yet she with
her hair down her back like a maiden who walked bare-
footed down from the mountain cottage to the village for
the festival where she might meet the prince, slipping into
her shoes at the edge of the town square, and laughing her
contralto laughter—I think they called it irrepressible
laughter—and he with his blond moustache like the last
sanguine youth in 1914 to become aware of impending war,
and unacquainted with the mixedly metaphorical wars he
was enlisted in, and that night they died, although not before he had added to the quotations he would write on the
walls of the rooms in Tornata Shakespeare's description of
the boar's kiss which killed Adonis: "And nuzzling in his
flank, the loving swine / Sheathed unaware the tusk in his
soft groin." I don't know what I might have heard in my
sleep, I know only what I was not supposed to hear later.
There, under those trees, in that theater of grief, I cried, at
first as I have cried for heroines in novels, or for dying animals, but not ever for people, and then I cried myself to

sleep, woke up, and without thinking about it found that I was walking out of the glade, three or four hours had passed, I had several hours of daylight to look forward to, letters to read or to read over, friends to write letters to, and the hope that this time I would remember where I had buried my parents, there in the mounds, revealingly hidden under dead leaves, not in my flesh and blood and bones, continually unifying.

With fewer specious truncations than usual,
Oliver

The Infirmary—Ho-uinkil 5th—Year 24

Dear Salathiel, Dear Father,
I remember you saying of Ginevra that loving her was like being in love within a painting by Rembrandt, and adding the comment that each painting represents the space of a different love. I wish I could write a letter that would be a space for daughterly love, and for sisterly love, as I write to you about the death of your son, my brother Orlando. I will spin the facts softly into a cocoon of silky remembrances. If *materia medica* survives anywhere, or revives from whatever has happened, the record should show that Orlando died of *diabetes mellitus* and its complications. My diagnosis was never in doubt, but it was confirmed when I unearthed a portfolio of watercolors Olivia, Orlando, Oliver, and I had painted ages ago. The portfolio has been secreted in my office all these years so that no one would appropriate the paper to write letters on, the vellum, art vellum I think we called it, such as I write on now. Few people will touch anything in my office: odd that objects which look to me so objective have an aura about them for other people, unable as they are to conquer these objects—scalpels, surgical scissors, even the magnet with which I removed a sliver of metal from your eye—with subjectivity. I

109

train a few students to see use and function in stable, reliable tools; but very few. When I opened the portfolio I saw that several of the watercolors had been eaten away, not by silverfish, but by the kin of the dead dried ants I found. My memory is not always articulate now, but it caught as in a reticule a scene in which Oliver swam into the playroom with a book of watercolors by, as he enunciated the name, Joseph Mallord William Turner. He showed them to us as we had tea, and he told us how Turner had used beer to wet the powdered pigment sometimes. Oliver, *our* Oliver, in a shirt of celadon blue, our alabaster boy (I begin to sound like Olivia, who once, she said, saw him body forth the lights in a spectrum of music by Mozart), squeamish Oliver told us how Turner had watched Lord and Lady Egremont at Petworth Castle as they made love, and that, he said, was how Turner learned to paint a space to make romantic love in. Constable, he said, would be too picturesque, although when Oliver was flip he apologized for it later with some delicacy, as when he commented compensatingly that the space in Constable's paintings was a space to expatiate with a friend in. To stroll in, amiably. Oliver always made some original addition to his borrowings, if only an innuendo, I think even hoping that you would be flattered to hear a variation on your theme. And with a jolt I remember Orlando's story about making love on a historical bed in the Maryland Historical Society in Baltimore, a room to make historical love in, he said. Oliver strategically told us that Lady Egremont had been cajoled by Turner into sitting astride the corner of a large sheet of watercolor paper onto which he threw dried pigments. Then, on his command, or request, she—and Oliver took the opportunity to seduce our attention with a new word, before which he paused as in a recitation—*micturated.* Hence "The Interior at Petworth Castle." We were as usual too impressed by the story and too grateful for the word we needed for our collection to notice Oliver's goal, for we netted words as though we were filling in the interstitial vacuities between words to make a continuum of language through which no experience could escape unspoken, while simultaneously we were pushing the reciprocities between words and things, as when Oliver pronounced the name of a hue in such an intonation that we were enabled to see it, to see the differences among purple, mauve, violet, with the problem that *things* differed for us, so that Olivia for example sees the equivalent of ultra-violet, as though she always had recently had cataracts removed. Or we were better archeologists of language than grammarians. Oliver told us that when she *peed*, pausing within the word, Turner would drag his brush through the urine and dried pigment. We never doubted the never-quite-to-be-believed Oliver, not publicly because his beauty was so improbable that it was not quite to be believed, yet there it was, so around him, almost anything might be true—a beauty out of the reach of love, which is usually trying to be a synonym for belief. At least you said so once. Oliver showed us reproductions of the watercolors of her pudenda (the last time I'll use that shameful word) as he introduced us to yet another rare Tibetan green tea, a tragic tea, Olivia pronounced it precociously, "a dialectical tea," our rare Oliver tactfully corrected, adding that it was redolent of a land that had once been constructed of ideas, and we were enjoying the construction of one of Oliver's educational instructional tea parties, we were always learning even though Olivia muttered her resignation in whispers of *educamus educatis educant.* Oliver was ahead of us, often ahead of himself, prattling about Tibet as the only land where transcendentals were fully immanent in mountains, as *mountain* was predicable of everything—

mountainous people, mountainous yaks, mountainous tea, mountainous metaphysics, mountainous *Book of Death*, and mountainous mountains — and as I pondered, slowly, at my own pace, what he was doing to the word "mountainous," he raced through an anthology of quotations about mountains but slowed to return to Tibet with the comment that no one was punished there for not knowing what had not been taught, Olivia quietly reciting "First conjugation, second conjugation, third conjugation," she was listening to Oliver but she made few concessions, and she perhaps could tell that Oliver was stalling. Oliver told us how Ruskin burned the watercolors he could recognize as vaginas or fornication in the fireplace, between the firedogs, and perhaps would have burned if he had known the facts, the watercolors of the burning of the Houses of Parliament, the flames reflected in the waters of the Thames, because Turner had used the waters of a convenient washerwoman. Oliver could tint a word like *washerwoman* with other meanings. He told us quickly of uretic watercolors, of fire and water, of men quenching their Freudian fires with their Freudian waters, he spoke of flames in watercolor, of burning sensations, of Turner's burning ambition which prompted him to paint a buoyant phallic buoy in the cold waters of a painting already hanging in a gallery in order to overwhelm the painting hanging next to it — by Constable I believe — and added that when Constable said that Turner painted with "tinted steam" he was on the right track. Before we thought about what was happening, Oliver produced this vellum and with a stream of chatter about his cleverness in making pigments from onion skins and walnut shells and such, he resourcefully explained mordants, keeping us occupied with new words, allowing Olivia's comment that "Mordant" is the name of a brother-in-law in an old play to pass without rejoinder because we were al-

lowing his mountebank performance to succeed. Oliver
was always precise, exquisite, and delightfully educational, or at least informative, ever trying to impress himself
and us with facts, and eager to take us along with him on
his explorations, so soon we four were nude and were
straddling the four corners of the paper, happily splashing
cochineal. I can hear Oliver, who had always prepared his
presentations, whispering the word toward its threshold in
English: *cochenille, cochinella, coccinus.* He was the connois-
seur of ornamental, alluring learning. And thus we painted
our famous "Interior at Otterly," four cherubs of early
adolescence, although I, in truth, as the oldest, was old
enough at least to worry about the effect on the floor, but
also I was interested in our experiment, and Oliver lulled
me with a disquisition on "microcosmic salt"—sodium
ammonium hydrogen phosphate—which was made from
human urine. He taught me to incant $HNaNH_4PO_4$ so
that I opened my eyes to chemistry—which he defined as
the art of pouring—as I closed my eyes to what we were
doing. We painted the firelight with our urine, the firedogs, and the mantle over which we intended the watercolor to hang. And we were solemnly at work—for this was
either art or it was something that might get us into
trouble—when you opened the door and smiled upon our
mayhem. You must have seen that we were being governed
by the dimensions of a sheet of watercolor paper, by pigments, by laws of composition (laws?), and by an idea of a
complete picture which, hanging over the mantle, would
complete the room, the self-restraints in the space gently
restraining us. There, back at our origins, we thought that
we had the right to hope to improve upon humankind, and
we were smart enough to refuse to learn to be as secretive
as might have been practical around Kwant. Oliver, I now
know, thought about the secrets we kept from ourselves,

and would not have agreed with me. Our watercolor
(which I rescued after the fire), even after the ants ate Orlando's part, represents a space that is like the hearth of
childhood. A space in which to be childish together for
what is perhaps the next to the last time. For while Olivia
could say to Oliver on that occasion, "For your information, I'll tell you what most boys have learned too late —
sticky messes are of equal interest to both sexes," Oliver
was already quoting Milton's great image of contempt for
the barbarians as a flood of urine:

> *A multitude, like which the populous north*
> *Pour'd never from her frozen loins, to pass*
> *Rhene or the Danaw, when her barbarous sons*
> *Came like a deluge on the south, and spread*
> *Beneath Gibraltar to the Libyan sands.*

We understood that we had been meditating on contempt,
a concept we were acquainted with because we lived in
Kwant's house. I think that I saw Oliver, never with contempt, but too much as a parody because he preserved a
world I could not believe in and which I could not believe
he would take so seriously. One of us was a barbarian, and
each thought it was the other. He could have understood
any of the sciences as well as I, but he used scientific information as decoration, not as structure; he used the metaphors of science as metaphors in poetry, where they
seemed more like seductions than like make-shift tools to
think with. Of course I never discovered a scientific method of thinking about Oliver, and I feel that I was often
wrong about him. I am frustrated as a scientist because I
think of myself as closer to the truth, or to the methods of
approaching the truth, than most people, yet I cannot get
most of them to see the value of what I see in science. I can
understand that the conclusions of science are no consola-

tion. I have nothing helpful to say about the death of Orlando. But in the methods of the sciences are the comforts, even consolations, of feeling that one is getting closer to truth, however uncomfortable the truth might be. Since Oliver and Orlando are both dead, I no longer live my life as a struggle against death. I have written to you for the pleasure of remembering: "sessions of sweet silent thought." I too can remember and can quote. I am sure that you understood why I was testing your urine and why I suggested some restraints in your diet.

Your loving daughter,
Aurelia

Much-Uch 18th—Year 11

Dear Oliver,

Amusing, even droll of you, to say that as a child I choreographed lightning bugs, when you are the impresario who inveigled me, that evening by the pool in the garden, to hide some, with their luminous abdomens, in the hair triangulating above my thighs, so that when I stripped to immerse myself in the garden pool I glowed, and as you three applauded from the veranda, the applause became rhythmic clapping to which I danced, even Aurelia yielding to the temptation to dance as a temptress, which, I hasten to remind you, you called our "sororal borealis," ever ready to take a chance on hitting upon a meaning. Aurelia was celebrating her success in instituting among the Creoles a new custom of picking up trash around their houses, so that they looked like sets for a movie. But the health-inspector civil-engineer in her was satisfied by the lackadaisical people playing her game, picking up trash, burying garbage; she did not notice that they carried most of the trash into the grove where it became something to be placed carefully upon the mounds, they puzzling over where to add it to the wholes, which already were complete, so that the addition would form a new completion. And the grove has neither top nor bottom, so it can be recomposed from an infinite number of points of view, a kaleidoscope. Do you remember the movie I made of myself among the mounds? I knew, as I occasionally filmed the Creoles, that they had something to show me, but I could not yet see what it was. When Aurelia, who could not see that the mess in their yards was their form of order, even if it did shelter flies and mosquitoes, found what they were doing with the detritus when she saw my movie, she called the process the morphogenesis of the mounds, thereby surprising herself into silence. I think I mean *astonishing* herself. I would not have picked up any trash in those days, and I certainly wouldn't have helped to invade the kitchen midden slopping down the hill from Utterly into the thicket of bushes — Delphine had been throwing her "airmail" from the kitchen window for at least a decade — and I knew that the attitude of the poor Creoles toward the death of a baby was different from what mine would have been — but Kwant seemed to regard infant mortality as an island tradition, so I had to help out with the sanitation to defy him. I learned to stand enraptured holding a piece of junk until inspiration told me where to place it most provocatively. And I was so standing in that instant which is easier for me to remember than an hour or a day or a month, even now that months have only twenty days, when you approached me, on your way to Renunciación, with a letter in your hand, you all foxfire silvery lights shading into cautious but tasteful greys, with flashes of a shade you would know a name for, something near shrimp and salmon, or like old but iridescent blood, and when I turned to see who you saw approaching behind me, you by some sleight-of-hand switched to a sulky grey which slowly became enlivened with stable stripes of yellow and of saffron. My but you do change color-guard quickly. I had not meant to invade your privacy. Have you noticed that the blue-eyed white cat does not listen when I speak to him?

Candidly,
Olivia

The Garden, Outterly—Hoken-Ahau 5th—Year 17

Dear Orlando,

When we sit talking in the garden on the iron chairs fretted with rust, although you never quote the letters of the people who dictate their letters to you, you do seem to know the local gossip, and I see, or more correctly feel, you come near to me and go far from me, I see you as you speak construct a plane at a specific depth, say just past your shoulder, a plane that I focus on as you build your narrative, then you sense that I am not listening but am looking, you don't like that, the plane disintegrates as you make comments on my beautiful red (or is it auburn? or is it russet?) hair, and blue-green eyes, comments which arise as a small oblong plane two feet in front of you and to your surly left, and I see that plane, and when you speak of Aurelia and the composures of her work, a not too silent reproach to me, I suppose, then I distrust my own responses, and I see my suspicion mount between us a plane with translucencies superimposed at cross-purposes, differing thinnesses and differing thicknesses, and differing in precariousness and fragility and surrender, but tough as isinglass, and I think you must be seeing it also so I focus instead on an oblong, relatively opaque but luminescent, lozenge of light, and I ask you how you would define an innocent eye, which you take as a new attack on you, you fear for yourself in my presence, which grieves me until I make mistakes such as closing my eyes just when I might have reached you and touched the mutual light I was hoping to construct with your cooperation. When I try to speak to you of our problems I feel that I am being forced to watch the last few moments of an unspectacular sunset and am obliged to flatter it. Orlando, I live in this emotional aurora. My conviction is that everyone does, if they have not been taught or have not taught themselves otherwise, but when I go to speak of it, up goes the veil of your detachment, and it is ice-blue, with pale blue interiorities, and quite convincing depths of deeper blue I wouldn't dare look into. So I close my eyes. If I speak of this aurora and say, Look, gaze upon your own display, see what hangs here palpably in the air between us until the light speaks daggers, you find a polite phrase to say that I am imagining something. You could not conceive of me as a character in a novel written in the style in which you think. I would be outside, my nose pressed against the unwashed windows whose flawed glass deflects the light. I can't always see my own sight because I distrust it. Your theory of experience, of what can be experienced, is too pure. You are the puritan of empiricism, finding your affirmations in positive facts, but you are violent to me, unbeknownst to yourself, because of your absolutism. Back at the cash-register in Baltimore you learned to shortchange my experience. You seem to take anyone but me verbatim. I have lived into a better world than any I was able to imagine for myself, but I feel that I spoil it with my tiresome unmelodic complaints. To love me is at least to know what it would be like to believe, as I believe, in my experience. Now these dun-colored lights arise to signal that I am guilty again of abusing you. Highlights of puce, like a tapestried sunset bought in a fleamarket near a harbor. Orlando, the composition of planes around you usually balances exasperatingly. Oversimplified. Your symmetry is not symmetrical with my symmetry. We need to lose our balance to find our equilibrium. Or, to say what I am thinking, *you* need to lose your balance, walking as you do upon your stilts. Loving you has been a reform-school education. And moreover while I know the date, I cannot transpose Hoken-Ahau the 5th back into the old days. Today may, unbeknownst to me, be an anniversary, a melancholy anniversary, which I may be celebrating in my own way without knowing it. Today could have been my birthday. I know so little.

Your verboten wife,
Olivia

Mux 17th–24th year–The Cornfield

Dear Octavio,

I hope that you are, wherever you are, well. I feel an urge to write to you to tell you what has happened to Oliver. He is well now, but we had some excitement when his forehead, which always had a small convexity, produced a lump which frightened us. I have planned so many operations in my film scripts that I felt that I must be competent to operate, but I found out that I am not, and anyway my operations are usually on the eyes, so that a cystectomy would be beneath my fantasies. Aurelia, who was unusually silent, although she muttered *dermatoma* and *teratoma*, seemed to think that she knew what she was doing, so she operated and I scrubbed. I thought, knowing as little as I do, carcinoma, but after the operation Aurelia showed us a little sac, like a pouch, that she had removed. Oliver was well enough to watch with mirrors (he wasn't *sick*), which he said was sufficient anesthetic. Aurelia took her scalpel and cut out the sac. Then she took her scalpel and cut open the sac, peeled back the edges, and allowed us glimpses of clots of hair, tiny teeth and a little little tongue, all of which Aurelia whisked away to her microscope. Oh, Octavio, people do need each other. I need Aurelia to explain *derma-toid cyst* to me. She says that Oliver as an embryo had made a false start toward being twins (but he *had* a twin, so I suppose she meant triplets, unless he would have been an identical twin: I didn't ask.) Cells from the other embryo had dwelled all these years in suspended development in his forehead, until they had begun to grow again, and she suggested that the opportunity for growth — the shapes and tensions of the space the cells were in — may have signalled the growth of hair and teeth (if the cells retained their equipotentiality; perhaps, she said, they were cells that were *prepared* to become hair or teeth). She talks of how the taut skin over his skull spelled the growth of that clump as it tried to make sense of the field of forces in which it grew, a tissue of tangled, mangled implications, trying to be logical. Oliver, because I suppose that character is not only fate, it is also violent consistency, throughout the operation spoke of Minerva sprung full-blown from the head of Jupiter, and of Sin sprung full-grown from the head of Satan in *Paradise Lost,* and of Mrs. Grales and Rachel in *A Canticle for Leibowitz* (*A Canticle for Leibowitz*? Where had he had time to read everything? or, why had he remembered? these references such as *Rachel* which were references to other references, an infinite regress because even if one reached the first *Rachel* in recorded memory, one could think of prior Rachels. We debated these methods so often: to be is to refer to; to be is to be referred to; to be is to correspond to; I have never quite agreed with these strings of references and correspondences and coincidences; I don't see the resemblances that Oliver sees, and I suspect him of a philosophy of resemblance which conceals false continuities, thus false consolations or comforts. I haven't had enough time or methods to think about his thinking. I suppose he and I have agreed that symbolic art is more naturalistic than naturalists appreciate. Experience contains symbols: hence symbolism is naturalistic, and naturalism is symbolic. But Oliver *refers* too much.) Aurelia no doubt has searched through the mess in the sac for the proto-eye she perhaps lacks only the courage to imagine, knowing as she does that the eye would develop only because light existed to be seen, but not knowing how the genes which guide development could have information about light in the environment. She should ask me about light in the environment. None of us has quite untied imagination from its moorings. All implications are groundless until they construct the ground under themselves, and that comes later. Orlando is back at his station choosing some seductive stationery. I am busy sitting out here refraining from comment on several subjects, although my behavior lately may be a visible commentary on my admirable restraint. And they do know that they can all expect to hear from me by post in the not too near future. Oliver is thinking about mourning the death of the little creature that grew under his skin. He says that it is the image of an idea he had better think through before he forgets it. I do feel that we have lost some possibility, just as I have lost someone, some possible someone, by never going mad and becoming someone I might have wanted to meet. I have never been mad, only extremely entertaining to others, occasionally to myself, and sometimes extremely irritating to others, occasionally to myself. Oliver means that for him not to think about the cyst is to lose a thought that he might have had, and that he might lose a feeling along with the thought, as I almost lost my thought, this afterthought, and Oliver says that to lose a thought (for we cannot really *lose* a thought) is to bury it alive. His metaphors are more morbid than mine. Orlando, who annually repudiates or abjures metaphor, says that Oliver and I suffer more for others than is helpful or necessary, that we try to rescue from drowning people who are merely swimming. I think he should abjure that metaphor, for I can't see that quality in myself at all. He says that the operation Aurelia performed on Oliver is probably less painful than the operations we perform on his skull with our blunt instruments. "The way you make that first incision . . . ," he drawls. Well, I am glad he has some spunk, glad that Oliver is so perky, and glad (that is almost the word) that I can conclude this letter without commenting on the loss of you, on how I mourn your absence.

Love at whatever distance,
Olivia

Hello, Octavio, I am back. I have been copying away, partly because some funny impatient friends of mine here want the old paper for some recipe they are following, to mix with other shreds to make new paper. I gave them some pieces of paper money Delphine used to mail as letters. Strange to see it back in circulation. Oliver commented that Delenda had abolished prostitution in a single act since, if a person was given a blank sheet of stationery, which is close to currency since we barter with it, then the piece of paper could be construed as a proper gift, not as money or proto-money or ur-money, since it has a use, a value in itself. Indeed, the paper which circulates can be pulled out of circulation at any time that someone decides to write a letter on it. Oliver remembers as a child being given dull or cute stationery as an inexpensive but proper gift, one that threw cold water on a holiday — "They knew how to disappoint children in those days" — although he never received comb-and-brush sets, which Orlando received annually, or manicuring sets, which Olivia received and turned over to Aurelia as equipment for her operating theater. That stationery—I am not certain that I did not give him some myself, but manufactured by the printer who did the white-on-white dollars for me—may be the reason he took up making his own paper years ago, for as soon as he could, he would write his thank-you notes for the commercial paper on a sheet of paper he had made, a sheet of such resplendent beauty that it seemed to glow as it lay on one's desk among lacklustre business letters—an act which might have an edge of sarcasm or irony to it, except that Oliver could try to improve one's taste without much condescension—he could be as objective about bad taste as a doctor about a social disease, and if he hurt anyone's feelings, usually he did it by treating impersonally what most felt to be so personal—"As though one had a constitutional right to bad taste, and should fight for the freedom to be vulgar," he would say. But he took up papermaking for its elegance also, in some theory of the leisure class about the virtue and power and efficacy of handmade goods, and about craft as a meditative, self-constructive discipline. As Oliver was to say, "I like the difference between the way I governed myself when playing solitaire or writing in my diary, and the way I governed myself while making paper or reading a book." Oliver often used in his paper the old paper money Delphine had put into circulation as letters. Now I don't know where Delphine acquired the money, or what message it contained. I cannot read her intentions. I think now that paper money—that all money—was a parody of promises, and eventually deprived promises of their meaning, leaving suspicion, distrust, wrangling, and unbelief. Where men spoke of money, I smelled a rat. Or, perhaps I have it now, money is a promise to more than one person. Money was a promise to two people, and it could not keep both promises. Even if it kept its promise for one, it betrayed its promise for the other, betraying and disappointing. I can remember the pauses in conversations among financiers. One party does not say what it thinks. One party feels cheated. Perhaps I understand now why I divested myself of such large quantities of money—why I gave so much to Orlando, giving him the money—in effect spending it—so that I would not have to distrust his motives. He did not have to worm money out of me. Perhaps I understand now Oliver's occasional gambling binges—that he was punishing money for the promises it had broken; perhaps for the promises people (friends) had broken; perhaps for the promise in people that had been broken. He referred to his gambling losses as "the retribution of the wealth." I always supposed that he knew what he was doing in a casino. Delphine's money might have come from anywhere. When first I was postmaster, she tried to mail a snakeskin, once a dead bat, and I had to announce a rule that nothing living or dead could be considered a letter, but Aurelia would arbitrate since she was always working on definitions of *life*. Delphine concentrated on the pieces of drifted wood which bark beetles had eaten, and once when I objected she merely said, as she turned and walked out, "Have you ever heard of Easter Island?" And I thought of all the writing I cannot read, and yielded. Some of her "letters," long deferred references, still hang from the beams, waiting until their due dates roll around (dates do seem to roll over in Delenda's system; I understand only as much of it as I need to keep the chronology of letters). Others of Delphine's driftwood letters have been delivered, read, passed around for the pleasures of sharing, reread, and then tossed in the stove to cook our meals. (Oliver once showed me in the collected letters of English writers how more of the surviving letters were written in the summer than the winter, and he pictured for me the recipient, seated before an open fire, reading the letter thoughtfully, or musingly, and then, hearing the appetite of the flames, tossing it into the maw of fire. And, as he added, the letter becomes enveloped in flames.) Delphine was of course as a young woman a prostitute in Baltimore. She called herself Taxi, although as a singer she was known as Trinidad. Since I am sure that Converse, to whom the money is usually addressed, is dead—at least he has never picked up any mail—I feel free to add the money to the dead-letter office—my little rag and bone shop into which I toss stuff that people might want to use in making paper—although, uncertain of her meanings, I record the facts for you or for anyone who might be able to interpret them. I am, I fear, too literal for her letters—too much my son's father. I'm always looking for a place to put a stamp, even though we don't use stamps. Or looking for definitions. And now I have come upon a group of letters written by Olivia; they should interest you since she has been your mother. The children and young people, practicing their characters, will copy them for me now. She wrote them all in the same week of nameless days, the week we call Uayeb or Chaykin, which Olivia says is the week in which the year, and time, complain about their aches and pains, her favorite week in her favorite place, for as she says, "Utopia is where I can gripe as much as I please." I am going to take a nap. Sometimes I wish that someone reliable would tuck me into bed and tell me the story of my life.

The Back Lot—Primavera—Chaykin, year 10

Dear Orlando,

I am a film director, and although the accidents of the era have denied me film and other necessary facilities (somehow I blame Kwant, although he runs wild out there, dribbling at Umberland, retreating as our gardens advance upon him, our fusillade of corn and beans), so that I have never had the opportunity to shoot my film, to edit it, and to simplify it, or to discover the surprising clarifications that would emerge from seeing my own raw footage: my movies always contained so much more than I had put into them that I did not know what to believe. I might, were I to complete a long film, discover a coherence that would then, retroactively or retrospectively, correspond with a coherent me. I would be collimated, and anyone who knows me knows how I have longed for collimation. (*My* word: I beat Oliver to it years ago.) I would learn to become what I could see from my films I was. A work of art is like me (I can hear Oliver hooting as he reads this) because it can give no account of its origins. "Before art," I think Freud said, "psychoanalysis lays down its arms." I never lay down my arms, certainly not when confronted with Freud. The space between me and my origins is a black hiatus, and therefore my life has been content too free from form, and perhaps too free with form. Style is the elaboration of a beautiful, rickety, and faulty metaphysic, which most of you men seem to learn too late. Content is merely the accident of the era: *il faut être de son temps. . . .* Objective content is the purest self-expression: it reveals, or it displays, the self conquering the object. Try conquering the emotions which arise when that happens! I cannot look back far enough to see whether I began as style or content, or as their reciprocity. Well, I am unrepentantly myself today, irreproachably obstinate. If I could make a film, the origin of which no concept could explain, and if I could hold attention on the images flashing out of the blackness onto the screen — just do something interesting — then the space between the movie projector and the screen would be only as speciously dark as the space between the origins of my experience and the experience, and as dark as the space between my origins and me. And if then I could accept the void and enjoy the projections, I might live on more friendly terms with my own obscurities, constructing that structure I described to you, the one which retrospectively secures its own foundations, as while I am writing this sentence which seems to come out of nowhere and which is going I don't know where, I can feel it, insecure as it is, strengthening the foundation under itself, and under the prior sentences. Unless of course the whole structure collapses because I am myself under construction. I have written as simply as I can about putting ground under myself. I have even written short sentences, because I am trying to sell you on an idea. What I am trying to say is that I see the limits of my sight; and that not the viewfinder, but the projected imagery itself, would show me, by its interrelations, my tacit and implicit theory of what it is to be, and I will not be stopped from this project—the flight of images through airy nothing—merely because of some black hiatus: the gulf between my desires and their achievement. Merely because I may myself be that black hiatus. Already I have lived too long alone as I searched among the available retaliations. Manqué, manqué, manqué. Men are too easily bored, as they call it, by shrill women. *Their* shrill women.

You have, Orlando, always been auditioning for my films, and at any audition I simply pick the one I cannot take my eyes off. I write now a scene for you to prepare. By the time you receive this letter you will be forty years old. Odd that on this island the men past forty are equally handsome, while the various unaccountable necessities of deceit have variously ravaged or beautified the women so revealingly. That deceit: I love you but I cannot tell you the truth, or the truths, partly because my motive in telling you the truth would lie beyond the truth, in what I would want from you, in word or deed or feeling, for being truthful (and I think I should have been rewarded much more than I have been); and partly because while I tell myself that I want your good and your freedom, I don't like your understanding of what is good for you, I don't like some of what you do with your freedom, because I think that your good is loving me (which would mean preferring my good to yours), and I think that your freedom lies in choosing me and choosing me and choosing me, and any truth I told you would be to manipulate that choice. And if I don't manipulate that choice, the reason is not that I prefer your freedom and your good to mine, the reason is that I am too proud. Anyway, perhaps the men look so handsome because I don't look at them closely. Oliver will play the doctor. You will play Orlando. I will play Olivia. You will not need much rehearsal: I know how you have been acting.

OLIVER: First, before I decide upon the operations I can offer you, I ask each of you to tell me something you desire that you have not told the other.
OLIVIA: Odd, words come immediately to my lips. I want to be envied. [She wears shot-silk yellowy-beige blouse, wheat-colored slacks; she has ash-blond, *ashe-cindre*, hair.] I hadn't known that until you asked the question.
ORLANDO: Odd, I want never to envy. [He wears a linen-white linen suit.]
OLIVIA: You have never told me that.
ORLANDO: I did not want you to know that I envied you.
OLIVIA: You need not have . . . need not have envied.
OLIVER: Who do you think is more powerful, you or your husband?
OLIVIA: He is. We always do what he wants to do, which frequently includes the two of us rescuing me from what I want to do.
ORLANDO: I can't believe that you would say that. Of

course she is more powerful, Doctor. I envy her disobedience of any will but her own, and even her own apparent will sometimes. I see her always as acting, never as reacting.

OLIVIA: Do these questions pertain to the operation?

OLIVER: Yes, of course. I am not curious. Only one more question. Do you think that you are equals?

ORLANDO: No, and that is the problem. She has inexplicable gifts that put her beyond my practical understanding, yet I confess that I think she has done little with them because she constantly changes the subject. And I can rarely resist the temptation to save her from herself, even from the self that I think is truer to itself than I am to myself. More honest. More loyal to its deviations. More shameless.

OLIVIA: Of course I am not equal to him. [Pause.] He is accomplished, resolute, and stern. He is methodical and thoroughgoing, like a gentleman, and he keeps his disorder to himself. I am untrained in these skills. I have little discretion and lack some necessary protective coloration he was born with. Or acquired. Can't you get to the operation?

OLIVER: I can now. Please remember that the operation is elective. Either I elect to do it or I don't. [Close up of Orlando's face, with adjustments of focus.] For the gentleman, one eye is blinded but not removed. The blinded eye remains attractive to others but sightless. When the patient closes his sighted eye, he sees hypnogogic images. These images are experienced as though on a frontal plane, although actually he is seeing behind the blind eye, for the rods and cones in effect look backwards and observe the chorio-capillary circulation immediately behind the retina. They pick up phosphocreatin flashing in the eye muscles, and some lighter and darker areas which are the small sinuses. With both eyes closed, and focus thrown backwards but the images projected as though onto a frontal plane, the patient sees brilliant patterns which coalesce into scintillating images as vivid as dreams. [Focus on Orlando's face shifts until the images resemble this description.] The patient will learn how to use his post-operative vision. I could suggest further sophistications such as catheters of light inserted into the small sinuses, but that perhaps is too contrived . . . a matter for taste to decide, perhaps. [Close-up of Olivia's face, with adjustments of focus.] And for you, Senora, both eyes are blinded, and the visual purple is injected directly with luminescent fluids so that it becomes visible. The movement of the chorio-capillary circulation is perceived from behind the eyes projected onto a frontal plane, but now that plane is beyond the field of *arabesco* lights which the eye sees within itself. Since you have two eyes, the two images within them will be integrated into a single, three-dimensional, almost unthinkable field of light. When the patterns from the choroidal circulation combine with the visible retro-retinal movements and the injected luminescence, the problem of integrating the stereopsis into one multi-planed dissolved view, resolved in a single focus, will, if successfully solved, yield the enchantments of self-illumination.

Studiously,
Olivia

Dear Oliver,
Olivia's face in the scene I sent to you dissolves into your face which must be a local amateur-theater of moods—your features and expression as The Vagabond Players perhaps—enacted with a slight delay between the emotion and its expression. The focal plane is at first a few inches in front of your eyes, but gradually it approaches until the

eyes are in focus, and then it continues past the face until being diffused at infinity. Do not blink. Enlarge your eyes. You and I know that you know how. A voice-over speech: "You will, if we agree upon the terms specified in this paper, be blinded in one eye. Both eyes will be internally illuminated by phosphors injected periodically. You will see the ordinary world through the phosphenes in your good eye, but that view will combine stereoptically with the view of the phosphenes in the other eye, so that what you see of the world through one eye will be highlighted by sparkles of light that flash across the scene. Although one eye is blinded, both eyes will appear blind to others."

My love,
Olivia

(P.S. Oliver, I realize that my characters tend to sound like each other, a combination of my eccentric photophilia with some ragtags of Aurelia's vocabulary. So far the impression I have is of *art nouveau* science; or perhaps *fin de siècle*, although which century is the question. I see that my theme is focus, but I don't claim to know how to focus language yet, and when I had film and made movies in and out of focus, everything that happened visually seemed to me beautiful and true; I had the method that would become my metaphor, and enjoyed the buoyancy of my self-infatuations. Unfortunately all that others saw was my rashness in sharp focus with a shallow depth of field. I might have concealed my rashness, along with my wretchedness, in a hard-edged narrative, but I chose not to. You will notice that *focus* is the latest of my operative metaphors that I am overworking. I will thank you if, by the time you read this letter, you have not quoted the experts on *focus* to me. I can't remember any samples of *focus*. And please, I am not challenging you to think of any. You and I have agreed that we see meanings, not objects; I am working on the meaning of seeing meanings, and studying the tempo of light. In my films, one would have been able to focus on what is out of focus. I don't think you can do that ordinarily. Oliver you have a tendency to look dreamily up and out of the picture, much too romantic, much too *beyond*. Look at the camera.)

Dear Aurelia,
In this short scene I play the doctor, you the patient applying for an operation. This scene is to be sutured to other scenes, the operation leaving raphe-like scars, visually the impression of a ridge rather than a trench. (The curb, not the gutter.) Some moving around that we will work out at the time, depending on circumstances and the available light. You need not act, only react. You walk into the garden, you stride, you shake hands with a male figure who is somewhat obfuscated, you walking that womanly confident non-threatening sensible-shoe I'll-take-over-now walk of yours, striding at your usual correct pace toward the wrought-iron furniture ornamented with clusters of grapes and grape leaves (I remember when Oliver painted them, announcing as his credo as he mixed the paints, "Always put a little more purple in the black.") You look at your watch and then at the sky, you think about efficiency and love, about love and efficiency, you pace a little, then seat yourself in our old lady-like fashion gracefully with your back to the light (no woman ever went wrong with backlighting), then turn your head away while keeping your eye on me. Do not blink or squint. The camera shoots over my head, which sometimes blocks the view. I, obviously reading: "The operation is serious. Both eyes are removed from their sockets and replaced with prosthetic eyes. The nerves from the eyes are carefully protected during the operation, so that you will feel that you have phan-

tom eyes. Because of the random activity in the nerve fibers
within the neuroma, the visual center in your brain will be
stimulated so that you will see lights in a deep space in
front of you." The speech should be ending as you feel that
you cannot keep your eye on me while turning your profile
toward me any longer. For myself, I would like to make a
film of me laying bricks with my eyes closed. Have you
ever noticed, Aurelia, the hull of a ship which beached itself at Tornata — how it gathered the sand under it which
held it firmly in place?

In close-up,
Olivia

Dear Aurelia,
You and Oliver have both quoted to me Goethe's definition
of color as the deeds and sufferings of light. I admit that
something in the statement appeals to me. So I send you
this scene in which you are busy at work splitting lumps of
shale that might contain fossils. The camera shows you full
length and then moves slowly toward your hands, visible at
the center of the frame, as you say to me, "Wovon mann
nicht versprechen kann, darüber muss mann schweigen.
Whereof one cannot promise, thereof one must be silent.
Both eyes are removed, with the nerves and nerve fibers.
When the tissue has healed, the patient should pick up
very little activity beyond the optic tract since the neuroma
is insignificantly small. The patient sees, but sees only the
activity of her own brain with no external stimulus, none of
the logic of the retina, and nothing from the nerves. Her
brain sees its own activities, its own events, or perhaps it
does not *see* so much as it *is* a chamber of dim marbled
forms. She will see the shapes of her marmoreal thoughts
by their own movements."

Photographically,
Olivia

(Dear Aurelia, I do go on and on with my "Continuous Performance" don't I? These scripts do not convey my meaning, Aurelia, in the sense that my meaning will be conveyed by the motions of light, by focus, by movement—by the movements of my freedom as I discover what I believe by discovering the constraints on my freedom of movement. Even as a child, I was never afraid of the dark. It always seemed to me a form of light. I want to educe light from objects into acts and operations. I want to *be* light. I don't see any reason why I can't become what I behold: and I behold light. [You are handsome, Aurelia, and so am I, but these men start to look like clowns retired from the bull ring, with weary latinate eyes which say that they find everything or nothing equally entertaining. Perhaps they are simply out in the sun too long. My love for Orlando is one long deferral of my hatred which is about to arrive just as he arrives on the scene first to save me from myself.] I must discuss with you whether the brain sees the brain, or the mind sees the brain, and whether the mind, in seeing the brain, or in using the brain, would reconstruct it. If the brain develops in the first year or two in ways affected by behavior or experience or language, then identical twins would not have identical brains, would they? And you have mentioned particles of light which can impinge upon the brain directly. What would happen if they impinged upon the visual center? When I picture my brain and try to see an implosion of my seeing, I don't envision much more than endpapers in an old book. That can't be right. I see what you mean when you say that the ultimate account of the brain would still have to account for itself. Are you telling me that the brain cannot think itself? that it is unthinkable? Because if so, you and I know what that means, don't we?)

(Olivia to Delenda)

Inter colles eugeneos—Muc-Uch 6th

Dear Delenda,

Did you anticipate the consequences of your actions? How did you know what would happen? Did you have a theory? Did you plan? Oliver, Aurelia, Orlando, and I did not study political science as such. Converse did not dare to teach us ideas which might be contrary to Kwant's regime. Instead, we read the classics, so he conscientiously taught us Plato and Aristotle, Locke and Hobbes, Rousseau and Marx, and whatever we read with him or with Salathiel, someone was explaining the ideas to us, although I realize now that the explanations were in a tone of impotent or anesthetized indifference or neutrality, with words pronounced as though they were hypotheses, ideas treated as specimens of ideas, a scholastic approach to revolutionary schemes, all so academic, and I fear that I read them rather too much as scenarios for a movie, with me cast in the role of competent primitive mother of the golden age, competing with pigs for acorns, carrying the embers of fire in a fennel-stalk, guiding my aged parents through the beech trees to the beaverdam where I could help them across the river toward the apple trees. I had always thought that when the revolution came I would dissociate myself from the local aristocracy, or local gentry, who after all bought and paid for me, and handed me an allowance, but you have led our revolution and you sit quietly sketching fossils with Aurelia while I still scheme rebellions with political as well as aesthetic implications, insurrections which would make smashing motion pictures. Now that writing letters is the law, or as you would say, merely your suggestion (but what a power of suggestion, then; I wish an anthropologist would arrive and explicate our cult of letter writing; I'd like to know the synchronic structure of this diachrony), and you go around talking with people as though you have all the time in the world, while I still long for the excitements of storming the Bastille, and I long for incitements which might belong in a guerrilla camp in the mountains. I am happy to write letters if that makes you happy, but I can feel thoroughly bourgeois doing it. I think about everything I do now as good or bad material for a letter: how will this event look when I describe it to Oliver? Dare I mention this in a letter? And am I concealing anything from my correspondents? Back in that other time, I was attracted to the state of rude nature, bartering pig tusks or honey according to my whims, emancipated from money and the false equivalences that money creates — every exchange of money satirizes one of the persons in the exchange because the value of the money and the value of the goods or labor are not equal. The solution would have been not to try to make them equal — money was always going to make a fool of someone — *credo, credes, credit* — but to match desires, to line up corresponding needs, or whims. Now a blank sheet of paper looks so promising to me, and every letter that arrives is also promising, and the letters we exchange, quite unequal in length, yet have an equality. The writing paper hasn't the velocity of money — we exchange letters at our own pace. Kwant used to say "Time is money," and I could feel my foot press on an accelerator. Now were anyone to say, "Time is stationery," I would understand how the promise to write letters has slowed down time for that person. Can I say that the letters are like clots in the hemorrhage of time? (Kwant used to complain about our spending as a "hemorrhage of money," and gold has always had an aura of blood for me.) Parts of our future hang, congealed, in the postoffice, and we save some old letters in Kwant's safe (that lad, about thirteen years old, patiently

worked the dials in every combination until it opened, an
act of adolescent rationality I understood). The letters accumulate their own form of interest. Oliver calls it that
"tangled bank" of letters. I wrote a letter yesterday on
paper I recognized that I had bought in Baltimore many
years ago, merely as something to buy, because I hated the
proprietor on sight, arbitrarily, or intuitively, and wanted
to buy something in order to define our relationship (put
him in his place), and to conceal my contempt. And I
counted out the exact change so that I would not have to
take from his lecherous hand anything he took from his
filthy cash register. Ugh. I did not want his money. Now I
notice that if I imagined myself writing a letter to him, I
might be a trifle insincere in tone, but I would also be carefully weighing my words so that I would have fewer to regret, and less sense of loss. I now weigh, against the inherited muddles and halfway measures at the hacienda Utterly, the legacy of letters waiting for me in the postoffice. The
letters rarely contain bad news, since most bad news has
already been announced. I have, I admit, arranged for Orlando to receive a jolt or two, but then he counts on me for
that. I think that I have been writing to say that I am grateful for these changes — who isn't happy to receive letters?
who doesn't want to hear gentle words from an old friend?
who isn't hoping to hear from a secret admirer? As I make
my early morning reconnaissance on the beach, I know
that letters are awaiting my return. And I hate it when they
aren't. Who doesn't hate a day without anything important, or tender, in the mail? Some of the world is now as I
think it should be, and I like that. I have moments of happiness in which I feel that what *is* is what ought to be, and I
thank you for that accomplishment, which feels the way I
feel when I am entirely within a work of art where what *is* is
what someone thought it *ought* to be, if it were going to be,

and be itself. Politics may be the art of the possible, but art is the politics of the possible. (Salathiel knows about this but he hasn't told what he knows yet.) I will not resist (no governor controls *my* speed these days) adding that literacy and letter writing might bring about the embourgeoisification of the Indians, a prolegomenon to any future revolution. I wonder what would happen to me then. I have some trouble supporting a revolution that doesn't want me out of the way.

My partisan love,
Olivia

Batzul—Year 12—The Loft

Dear Delenda,

The letters have reached some point of critical mass in which they seem to have begun a process of their own, self-intensifying, self-satisfying. I feel always my position in relation to the force of these letters accreting in the post-office. People now seem lighter, as the collection of letters grows heavier, and as we store old letters in the safe or in the incubator. I am relieved to know that one of the uncertainties about the future—is there any mail for me?—has been favorably decided: yes, the letter is in the mails and will be delivered on time in four or five years. I am bewildered at the simple liberation from the tyranny of time in the fact that letters from the past are *there*, in the future, the future made quite real, although I also can see that the letters are merely there now, encapsulated in the present, waiting their turn to be delivered. People struggling up the steep stairs into this loft—I have built a partition so that it is an enclosed room, to give them privacy—are friendlier than they were in the old days. They smile less readily, and they treat me better as a workman than they treated me as *young master.* Their angers are more varied than their aloofness was. The women no longer conceal their competence, and I think that several would now agree that they can write for themselves, except that they enjoy dictating to their scribe. The women meet me halfway. It is like making love in a painting by Poussin. It is like doing Gauguin over again, after nature. Today Felice said, as she subscribed her name, and then unwrapped her skirt, "Orlando, write down everything we say." "What I say also?" "Yes, everything." "Why?" "Because I need something to write in a letter tomorrow." "Has writing letters made changes in your life?" "Yes, everyday." "Then those changes are still to be written about." She rewrapped her skirt and ran off with some idea of her own. Her friend and critic Louisa rushed in with her usual ill-concealed curiosity. "I want a letter just like hers," she said, "the same." "But you know I won't tell you what she said. You have to ask her." "I don't want to ask her. I don't need to know everything, just a few hints. I'll guess the rest." "Felice complained that she has nothing to write." "*My* problem. Nothing to write about. *Nothing*. Did you give her something to write about? What a life, you've got to have something worth saying to somebody everyday. Too much writing. I'll bet you gave her something to write about." I try to converse honestly, but I ignore certain inflections and innuendoes. "Yes," I replied, wondering how much of my office I am imitating from Converse, for you never gave me any instructions. "I asked her if she is waiting for letters to arrive. She said that she is. I asked her if the waiting changes her life. She said, yes, it does, she sits around being good waiting for the mail. I said that waiting for the letters makes changes which are still to be written about." "Write me that in a letter and I'll sign it," she said and ran out, knowing however that I won't write a letter except by dictation, and I suppose expecting that I would do what I did, which is to write a letter to her since I would not write one for her, telling her how reading the letters makes changes which are still to be read about.

Perhaps she will return to dictate a letter in her own words later. The letters, Delenda, seem to grow together into a concrete force. I start to feel that to be is to be in correspondence with — I think Oliver or Olivia said that to me, or perhaps I said that to them — and my future begins to be visible as the inheritance of this present in which we, whatever else we have been doing, have also been waiting for letters. Attending to letters. Stretching toward not only tomorrow, but sometime next year. Olivia has walked past me and flicked under my eyes an envelope addressed to me in the year 25. Time becomes more tensile; it achieves the tensile strength of a good poem. I look forward to a letter now the way I look forward to one of the women who knows me; the next one might be a humdinger, I want to open her gently and feel her so near come from so far, the distances varying with the deeds, as reading a letter might stagger me with the absolute immediacy of a force which I can't stand up against, until, returning to the actual and inevitable quotidian from the definitive indeterminacy of her body, I return to my commonplace self and to the commonplace facts, I arise, put the letter away or help her to tie her skirt, ever mulling over the improbable and conventional complimentary closings "Yours truly," "Very truly yours," "Sincerely," "Sincerely yours," "Most sincerely," and looking among them for words you can bear down upon with all your strength and weight, words as ductile, tensile, and flexible as times with you have been.

My kind regards,
Orlando

Tornata—Year 16—Chay Kin

Orlando, Mon Cher, My Brother,
Yes, Orlando, a revolution of unburial. I cannot bear for last night's dream to disappear without a trace, so I write

mentioning it to you there in the year 26 (if we are still alive: dreams do make life seem so insubstantial, and I remember when we pretended we couldn't tell the difference between dreaming and waking, and remembering seemed like dreaming, but now I think we have the differences straight: my life begins to feel less like a rehearsal and more like a performance). If I write the dream, or even mention it, the mention will make a difference, albeit an almost imperceptible one, as delicate as the trace of a butterfly as it swerves upon the wind (you will notice that Aurelia and I have been out in the fields netting analogies again: we don't kill the butterflies, we stare at them, agreeing to meditate on the functions of beautiful indiscernible [well-nigh indiscernible] differences in evolution. So many birds and butterflies that once would only have stopped over on their migrations now have stayed that they make quite a discernible difference: I help Olivia with the guest list, her census of insects [I hear you calling, Vladimir: *insect, incest, nicest*: but I am not answering.] Damn, just now do I see the point of telling you a dream, but that dream is not the point: I do have an ambition to preserve from the generalized perishings more than the wings of dead butterflies and moths to incorporate in my recherché paper. I shall make dilettantes of them all, except the incorrigible Abelardo who can make paper which I can only describe as cynical; in fact he made this paper I am writing on, a white which is more the lethargy of white than any white I deign to recognize; yet it is an achievement in its own way, and he does come to our papermaking sessions voluntarily, so he is, as we used to say, making his statement: and if I have chosen to preserve even the faint memory of a youthful Abelardo then surely I must choose to preserve the impulse with which I awakened from the dream, the impulse to write to you, which will be the meaning of the dream as you experience it there, in that future which is gradually taking such a clear shape that it helps to shape the present which is still somewhat misshapen from the pasts upon which it builds. But at least I have learned to preserve the momentum of a dream by writing a letter to a friend (and cousin: a droll word). When Kwant talked about conservation many of his principles were sound — even lining up the trees two by two, if it didn't seem so prideful, might be admirable: but he acted the admiral of trees, reviewing them with binoculars from the deck of Utterly, impressing the trees into the service of his fantasia. However I think he was right never to open the island to tourists, not wanting, as he said, a nation of bellboys and prostitutes. "A nation of 300 people," Olivia would say, although I don't think we were ever that many. Kwant kept the census in his head; Olivia said he counted people when he had trouble falling asleep. Kwant would look at Olivia with his expression of tolerance for a useful experiment. I can see the appeal of owning an island and of owning the people on it, to have them obey one's will, although I have enough trouble obeying my own will. The four of us, as heirs and heiresses, didn't know what we wanted early enough, snug in our complacencies, or we lacked the courage to admit that we wanted, not only what arose in the midst of us four, but a world like that in common with others. Even Olivia, however outspoken, fumbled her desires. So that we could not have succeeded Kwant as rulers because he had clear, distinct, and indubitable ideas about how other people should live (roughly, in the manner most convenient for him), while we didn't know what to tell other people about how to live; and it hadn't occurred to us that we had no responsibility to tell them, they could have decided for themselves without us, if we hadn't felt that we had some hereditary right to interfere. Salathiel concealed his apostasy in a genial criticism

142

and in his belief that life would someday be governed by art but that he didn't know how to work out the details. He was, everyone said, like a second father to me, but has also been like a second father to his own children (you, cousin), and I am not sure that he didn't allow Kwant to act the role of father. As I said, I am not sure. Salathiel could not figure out how people should spend their time in Utopia, what they would do with their days, and meanwhile everyone, whether suffering in hard labor or floating in idleness, was guardedly sullen, because everyone was serving Kwant's purposes, the Unseen Hand of Primavera and Umberland. We were born into a world in which every object and person was put in a position in relation to the tasks of money (I had to *work* at wasting it, believe me: shopping was exhausting; I paid a terrible price to exact the proper tribute to my money from vassals and trolls behind counters [until Olivia's great improvisation for contralto bassoon on a word I had given her, *counterlove*, although I had not heard in the word the meanings she heard, and I dared not quote to her the lines of verse because she would have turned them against me: "He could cry out on life, that what it wants / Is not its own love back in copy speech, / But counter-love, original response." Not with shoe-horns or crowbars could we get the same meanings into the word *original*. All our meanings were too desperately individual as we pursued self-fulfillment—or did we call it self-expression?—we manipulated the books of life, shrewdly looking for a place to put our money where it would be safe. I traveled, which you thought was silly, but I was looking for a place for the four of us where *we* would be safe. Yet I never found a place where the topic was not money. We four would be together, yes, but sometimes we were not so much together as merely equidistant from the language of *net gross*. We were born in an enclosure. We seemed to know where the borders were, but were unable to cross them; or we found them closed, like the couple I met in Gary, Indiana, when I stepped off the train for a minute to look at the most discouraging sunrise I had ever seen, when the woman with instant American intimacy said to me, "We traveled a thousand miles to a Fountain of Youth, but it was closed for repairs." Try recollecting that emotion in tranquillity. Why did we always think that they handled these things much better in France?

Now at least Delenda wants us to think for ourselves, which would suit me if I were sure of myself or of my methods of thinking. Without waiting for surety I begin this letter, after that dream, when I feel strong enough to enter the space on the other side of my usual thoughts. So, overcoming my resistance to narration, I will reenter in the middle where I was when I wrote to you another day, when I thought that I had completed my reburials.

If I said that I had forgotten where they had interred my sister Olivia I would not believe myself, yet I had "forgotten." The mausoleum connected to Utterly (how? action-at-a-distance?) contained an iron casket shaped like a boat, moored to a marble base. The ship-shaped second-hand coffin, the peculiar conceit of another era, was used for my dead twin sister. Waste not, want not. I tried to remember how I had forgotten her. We were eighteen months old. Eighteen months. A year and a half might sound better. I remember her presence. I thought that she belonged in the grove. So I slightly trespassed; at least I entered your mausoleum, and I wrenched the little ship from its marble dock and I carried it into the grove, and I set it down in the aisle, the space between the mounds under which her mother and father lie, and I will not describe my grief, or the restoration of feeling, how I came to feel more intact, more comprehensive, because I became curious about the green moss which grew on the casket, it had felt so dry, and I touched it. The moss was green wax, artful, so that the coffin was sealed like what? a bottle of wine? a letter? The two famous contrary emotions arose in me: fear and desire. I was afraid of the darkness inside, yet I desired to behold a marvel. And you who know me will know how quickly I worked open the lid, but you will not know, thinking as you have that the corpse of my sister has been a guest in your family's crypt, that the coffin was empty; or if not empty, that it contained a child's clothes and a few toys, only a few things, really, but uncountable, unaccountable. I had never been so close to the inconclusive. The words I could think of, the ones I search for with some *give* to them, gave way under me as I ran toward Salathiel and reached him breathless, gasping the name Olivia. I frightened Salathiel until I could say, "My sister, my sister," and I suppose he saw the green wax under my nails, my disarray, for then he quickly told me the story, that my father had taken Olivia and me sailing, against everyone's rules, without life-jackets, but only in the cove or lagoon but far enough beyond the breakers so that when Olivia fell overboard she was able to disappear, simply disappear, Salathiel repeated as though he had been there, and I who had been there remembered nothing about it, the event had disappeared, simply disappeared, but I peer now at the word *disappear* to see its effect upon events. They told my mother that the body was unsuitable for viewing and rushed a ceremony with the available infant's coffin near Utterly. If you had feelings about the corpse of my sister the night you spent in the tomb, you were mistaken. I think now that I might become Olivia—she is always, always on my mind—and think that I would have become Olivia, except that your parents bought that infant girl and then more or less presented her to my grandmother to be brought up with me as more or less a cousin to you and Aurelia, but then my parents were dead, my grandmother was edged in black, and Delphine, who became Olivia's nurse, wouldn't live at Tornata because she said that she wouldn't live in a house with poetry written all over the walls. I feel peculiarly cheated that the emotions I felt when I was carrying the coffin were wrong, or misplaced or irrelevant to the contents. I am not trying now to find my sister Olivia. I am trying to *found* her. When I have founded her, I will know how to bury her. She can never be too late for her own funeral. I have, of late, recovered her presence conclusively. I am sorry not to know her also as a person.

In brotherly love,
Oliver

The next letter is in dreadful condition. While the children have been helping me, and commenting on the letters they copy, they have been studying the art of epistolography — it comes back to me now from an exhibition of Sumerian literary letters, the letters students wrote as an historical royal correspondence, the play of letters to and fro among the kings of Ur, Isin, and Larsa. One of the letters was written by the daughter of a vanquished king to the last king of Larsa. (That perspective: who knew he was the last king of Larsa? Surely he didn't. But the students composing letters to him later, during the Amorite dynasty, surely knew, and wrote from the point of view of the woman asking to be restored to her priesthood. One would write so differently to the next-to-the-last king.) I liked those letters because in them all true omens were false; that is, the literary letters describing omens which predicted the future successfully were composed long after the event, while any letter with predictions belied by events could be assumed to be a real letter with real predictions. The prediction which proved false proves itself a true prediction. The letters Alulim received at Eridu probably must be adjudged inauthentic, although at least they were written on clay tablets so that they survive better than this non-cuneiform non-clay paper tablet does, fretted by insects. Eridu was founded by Enoch, the son of Cain, which I would mention to Abelardo, but no one here makes quite the same associations that I do, which can leave me melancholy, an elegiac island memorialist, the last or next to the last person on Primavera quoting Genesis 4:17. I do try to ignore the history of religion, the barbarous history, but I feel like a barbarian when I do so. Abelardo, whose eyes are somewhat better than mine, will write out Oliver's letter as we have reconstructed its contents.

Tornata—Chin-Uch 9th—Year 22nd

Dear Orlando,

I am at Tornata, in the scrap of old garden, where I have left no stone unturned this week. Somehow writing into the future like this sends me back to our communal past, to our childhood which Salathiel enjoyed more than we did, perhaps because children are born social critics, since to watch the adults in the actual world is necessarily to think of an ideal which is a criticism of that actuality. But we were happy. Today, looking at the vivid, almost *risqué* hue of this paper I recently made, I remembered Converse teaching us a poem and reaching the words "crimson joy," which I thought were excellent, "thy bed of crimson joy," until Aurelia said, "He means the vagina," and I cringed, although I could have listed Cunegonde, quaint, Peter Quince, the Widow Quinn, and I had shown Converse how to pronounce *and* as *'n* when reading aloud Malvolio's speech about Olivia's letter in *12th Night:* "By my life this is my Ladies hand: these bee her very C's, her U's, 'n her T's,

and thus makes shee her great P's . . . ," but now to dispute
Converse and Aurelia I countered, "Crimson is a color
made of mashed worms," and Aurelia said, "Yes, she had
an inflammation made by worms of a sort," and Converse,
so antiphonal, chanted, "The invisible worm that flies in
the night," and explicit Orlando softly whispered "syph-
ilis," I felt surrounded, Converse continued with examples
from his memory, his tell-tale memory, citing a woman in
Nabokov's *Ada* who refers to a rival woman as "Miss Con-
dor," he of whom Olivia said he did not read life, he proof-
read life, scribbling proofreader's marks in the margins of
brooks (". . . and books in babbling brooks") as well as
books, the man for whom all music was program music. I
keep writing because I want to get good value from this
paper, which cost me much labor in lifting up stones. If we
were still twelve years old huddled under the porch giggling I would tell you that it is made from something seriously disgusting, although it feels amusingly unsanitary to
me. But if any bookworms devour this letter, they are close
to cannibalism. I am about to attempt paper of a sickly
rose.

Serio ludere,
Oliver

Orlando had pinned another letter to that one; rust has
stained the letters in the corner. I remove the pin. I remember reading this letter when Orlando received it, our
happiness, our delight for Oliver. This young woman, Yolanda, will copy it for me; it is in good condition but quoting it here seems apt.

Hol-Ol 5th—Year 23—The Versorium

Dear Orlando,
I arose tonight like a flame from the middle of the banked
fires of midnight, awakened from the riptide of a dream

into astonishment at the quick insight that I had not outlived my ambition to be a poet, I had merely misplaced it,
for I have realized enough of my ambition, without knowing it, to be satisfied. I don't mean the stale easy ideas about
silence that we held when we were young, *mon cher*, when
you were Flaubert, and I was Mallarmé, when we sought a
form that implied only a purer form, and thought that art
should not try to *say* anything, which was fortunate since
we had nothing to say. Our art would be a *mariage blanc* to
existence, reflecting the *nuit blanche* that our lives were to
be; but as Olivia helpfully pointed out, our whites were
tattle-tale grey. I see now that my cryptic little poems sub-
tracted something from experience, like a body of engineers draining wetlands. My true feelings inhere in this
paper which holds the mood in which I made it the way
water in the cove holds light above itself long after the sun
is out of sight. The paper I have made as gifts to you or
Olivia or Aurelia has collected my thoughts and feelings
for me so that I can see what they are. I can't guess what
anyone else sees in my paper, but few saw anything in my
self-entangled verse anyway, and most saw nothing at all. I
think Delenda knew when I used the bark of the *amate*
tree — *ficus petiolaris* — that I was paying homage to the Mayan codex. Aurelia responded to paper made with the
fleshy pink pulp of a yew growing across at Umberland,
and she even guessed the mulberry tree as the source of
one set of papers, evoking from me elaborate information
about the silk route, the white mulberry, and the silkworm
with its "silent advance" from China to Savoy. I have saved
much that would have perished, and have invented a few
ways of stating feelings which didn't exist in quite the same
way until they were stated. I begin to see the paper as a
dictionary of my thoughts and emotions and experiences.
Of course the first volume of my poems, untitled, is scat-
tered beyond retrieval, although it did not go unappre-

ciated, and the sheets were used in their own ways to think with. But now I declare by fiat what I sensed this afternoon in the satisfaction I was feeling while lifting some paper from the drying rack: my paper is my poetry. They hang there, among the letters no one will ever read the whole of, but satisfyingly there, *among*, taking their place, mothering images and fathering ideas, as every letter and every poem rewrites our futures, the ever-more-legible ramifications. It is like seeing oneself climb a monkey puzzle tree.

Like some outcast counterspy, I was squishing along through the marsh at the far end of L'Ombreland, part of my continuing quest for plants whose pith I can use for paper, and as I trudged through mud and morasse the meaning of the words, "The sedge is withered from the lake," hit me as I stooped to cut the sedge. I accepted that "And no birds sing" meant a break in poetic inspiration, but now from my experience I had produced an interpretation of withered sedge: no materials were available to be made into paper—they were out of papyrus—so that the silent or unevoked poet was as unable to write his words as he was unable to speak them. While I had solved for myself the torments in the division of labor, for I unite in myself paper-maker and poet. I feel very self-employed. I entitle my first volume, *The Uncollected Poems.* I don't want to threaten you but I could write a history of the relations between poetry and the means of production of paper, couldn't I? I could. And I could reread all of philosophy listening for mentions of paper, hearing new undertones in the old words of Descartes: "I am here, seated by the fire, attired in a dressing gown, having this paper in my hand. . . ." How you admired that, Orlando, as properly transparent prose. I try to write to you lucidly, but the passage seems to me almost unbearably symbolic. Is the indubitable alone the lovable? And now I must include, if not agonize over, the influence of Kwant upon my work, for I have been affected (deflected, inflected, flected) by his choice of trees to collect and to colonize in his botanic garden. See Ben Jonson's *Underwoods, Forrest,* and *Timber.* And *ut pictura poesis.* In another world I would be the curator of a show of the paper painters had bought but had found too beautiful, too self-sufficient or too expressive, to use: and I would find poems in the portfolios of Turner, Cézanne, Matisse, and perhaps even Picasso. And I can peer into the statement the Buddha makes to Monkey: "As a matter of fact, it is such blank scrolls as these that are the true scriptures. But I quite see that the people of China are too foolish and ignorant to believe this, so there is nothing for it but to give them copies with some writing on." Now to think whether or not this letter is worth the paper it is written on.

Undoubtedly,
Oliver

Chay Kin—Year 13

Dear Delenda,

I see the aura of eclipse and abandonment above you. May I be of help? Should I say farewell? You make me almost ready to promise to behave, if I thought it would make a difference to you. I am living as though I were waiting for a love letter. I don't know why I sound so hypothetical. I am, categorically, waiting for a love letter; nor can I think of a better categorical imperative: you must live as though you were about to receive a *billet-doux.*

I was almost disarmed, waiting here in the grove for the body which has been lying all night in the postoffice for burial this morning, but everyone was drunk and is still drunk, so I sit as I sat all night until the flash of green in the east signalled the dawn of what I gather from the position of the sun (which I see through a hole in the foliage cut by some Indians who seem determined to keep us oriented) is the winter solstice, give or take a day. I sit in this ascending cascade of light—which Converse might once have called a caratheodory of light, bless him, always teaching me something, at least you put a stop to him and his free-floating zeal. And have, willy nilly, put a stop to some of my impulses as I hesitate, remembering the letter I long for, now that I have learned to distinguish longing from dread, the letter which might be in the mails, somewhat delayed, not at all what I had expected, but so much better, so much more, that I fold my hands in my lap and keep my options open, happy provincial anarchist that I am, really only an amateur at vengeance, as I suspect my friends have long noticed. When you leave the grove, when you walk out of the theater of lights, I do hear myself saying, "Goodbye, Flute." Shall we agree that I am grateful and am writing to thank you because I will be better able to face what I do when I read about it in the future than I would have been had I merely remembered it.

In gratitude,
Olivia

Uayeb 8th—Year 14—The Beach, the Cove

Dear Octavio,
While I write seeking understanding, I write to you who seem least likely to understand, since you witnessed nothing of what I am about to describe. Perhaps I am defiant and feel no need to justify myself; sometimes I am. Today I am uncertain. Let me say that I killed Delenda at his request, I killed my Mayan *makina*. I remember at Johns Hopkins working at my table in the biological laboratory where I sat studying the classical problem that when the eye of a tadpole is removed, the hindlimbs grow malformed

152

in the frog. The professor leaned over my shoulder and said, "How is your cemetery today?" I was so overwrought that I wept, thinking the while about the evolution of tears. Only later in life would I sob hard enough to suspect that gasping for breath would expel air from the lungs and force one to breathe deeply, encouraging survival. The professor then told me a story about a caterpillar, perhaps knowing that I hated facetious stories about animals or insects. He told me how the caterpillar, beginning with its tail, ate itself up to the head until "nothing was left but its sorrow." He said *his* sorrow. I wept more. I felt no temptation to weep for Delenda. *"Ne sorga,"* Beowulf says: "Do not sorrow."

Delenda always wanted to learn what I knew. Sometimes I thought he was keeping me busy, keeping me from asking him questions about himself. Perhaps he was not interested in his history. And at least he kept me learning about my work. I felt certain that he had been educated by missionaries, yet he undercut certainty with his inconsistencies. He mentioned the Usumacinta River and Chiapas in a special tone, but I did not inquire. He knew so much, but talking with anyone, he did not seem to know what they had to tell him. I never felt repetitive, although repetition-and-time was the one of his obscure subjects he did try to teach me. Delenda might be in a hurry, but he could and would change pace in a moment. He behaved as though each person's time was as valuable as his own (which I suppose it was, and is), and he left no one until most rhythms were synchronized with his, or his with theirs. Kwant treated time as though it unwound from a clock. Delenda treated time as though every day were a reunion, greeting the face of a day like the physiognomy of a friend, to be recognized. As Olivia said, Kwant had a botanic garden at Umberland and a zoologic garden at Primavera; his gestures, his ill-grace, and his footing commented on his power. Delenda had forgotten that he had power.

Delenda was curious when he learned that I could read so much information about time and tide in the fossils, and by looking at a shell could tell that it was let us say two hundred thousand years old, or one hundred thousand years old. I am afraid that I enjoyed amazing him with my scanty information about dendrochronology—I had spread myself too thin, followed too many interests, and was expert in nothing when I met him. He listened to my sketch of the history of the Greenwich Observatory with excitement, even passion, almost recognition. Teaching him facts was like introducing him to a friend: I turned to myself astonished at the pleasure I took in my knowledge. He explained to me that the faces carved in the stelae (I had seen many in the anthropological museum in Mexico City), faces he would draw in the sand on this beach when he strolled with me here in the evening, were pictures of the names of years, or months. I would explain to him as well as I could time and space and causality, I sensed that he had heard what I said before, although my physics was peculiar because I couldn't accept the usual understandings of *mass*, and my history of theories of time included William Kingdom Clifford, while my local critic Oliver said that I should include Lewis Carroll, or Gilbert and Sullivan, while I was tracing my sources. With Delenda I learned the problems of exposition as I tried to introduce him to the facts of the case while moving the narrative forward. He was fascinated that I made every fact bear upon a problem and did not emphasize the accumulated solutions to problems. Talking with him would be like talking with another scientist for me, although Olivia said that our conversations sounded to her like a meeting between the

Inchworm and the Centimeter in the Nut-and-Bolt Shop of the heart. Delenda's theories did seem open to experiment or criticism or verification, and even to disproof, or at least I thought so, and we sat on this beach exploring thought-experiments about time. I tried to figure out for myself how I could measure his velocity without altering his position, or how I could locate his position without altering his velocity, but I couldn't find a solution except one in which I had to be two people. Delenda was sad sometimes as though an inertia inhered in the very system of his beliefs, as though the work he had put into believing as he believed were a higher form of idleness. I am afraid he learned from me about unavailable energy, and began to see the limits of a theory he could have changed only with an illumination which did not occur. I am glad now that I have begun this letter, and I have had to pause to watch the wind so active in the vines tangled along the shore, my "tangled bank" the others decided to see as beautiful for my sake. I watch the progress of some seagrass I will teach you about in a few years. It flourishes in shifting sands. When the grass grows so thick that the sand ceases to shift, then the grass dies back, but then the sand begins to shift again, the grass recovers and thickens, and then the sand ceases to shift again. The wind in the leaves of dry vines touching the dry sand as they probe beyond the tangled bank. Delenda told me about a day which could also be called Etznab (*also:* but what else was it called? had I forgotten the names of days?), a day for the god of flint knives, a day for bleeding (I took him to mean human sacrifice), a day for restoring good health. He said that the word for *invisible* in his language is *night-and-wind*, and I knew that he was getting at something. This twilight wind this evening, however, is forthright and visible in the movement of the vines which it seems to help as they feel their way with sensitive, attentive, tentative tendrils, "as they sport along the shore," Oliver used to say. Delenda did not think that time defined from the perspective of an observer in the spatio-temporal continuum would conflict with time as a sequence of infinite movements of the faces of days. I suppose the theories didn't touch at any point. But he said once, "I have read about this succession on one of the stelae. In the pictures, infinity foresees its surrender to the finite. Actually, eternity says that it will lie concealed along the coastline of an island." Delenda knew that he was talking only to himself when he made statements about the eternal. But he seemed satisfied that he knew what he meant, even if I didn't. Aurelia Nullifidean, Oliver called me. Delenda said that he would be governed by the powers of the months until his birthday when he would have been with us thirteen years. He designed a ceremony. I was to help him, and I helped him. I had always known that he was not mine, that I would have to let him go. I let him go. I think that so much that I believe is true, or that I know it in the way truths are going to be known when truths are known, but what I know has few implications for how to live from day to day, and fewer implications for how to die. Delenda seemed to know something that had a bearing on what I knew, but I couldn't catch it, I couldn't make a scientific study of him, or of us. I thought that my methods of study should derive from the objects of study. But how to study Delenda, the master of so many methods of his own? I silenced myself with lies about cultural relativity. I would like to describe this last scene with him to make it visible there on your horizon. I dislike emphasizing what I did not understand and could not (cannot, will not) accept. Perhaps I should write to you about nights in bed with Delenda, for that I accepted unquestioningly. His flesh was home to me. For his ritual Delenda positioned Olivia, with white

flowers, in the north-east corner of a quadrant he imagined
on the beach; Oliver to the north-west, dressed in black;
Orlando with red flowers at the south-east; and I with yellow flowers, and draped in yellow cloth, at the south-west
corner; all of us decked with four-petalled flowers. Delenda lay across a table with his head hanging over one end
and his feet hanging over the other. He chanted to himself,
convincingly remote, deep in his Mayan language which
began to seem like another space. I became convincingly
aloof in English. Then his singing became familiar, I recognized a song he often sang in bed in the interim, an hour
or more, between lying down and turning toward me. He
sang, as he had taught it to me in part, saying that the
whole song had given an anthropologist writer's cramp:

> *Will the sun be able to shine the sky into dawn?*
> *Will people be able to walk?*
> *Will they remember how to stand?*
> *Because the others have carried away*
> *The black ink and the red ink, our painted books*
> *What will people do?*
> *Will the earth continue to support the city?*
> *How will we find our balance?*
> *Will anyone tell us what to do?*
> *Who will be our guide?*
> *How will we weigh corn in the marketplace?*
> *How will we measure the land?*
> *Where is the mould in which we shape the law?*
> *Is there a place to start?*
> *What fire will show itself as our light?*

Delenda's feet were bound, and his hands were tied behind him. His stomach rose, naked and vulnerable. Invol-
untarily I glanced at my medical bag. Delenda sang. I was
growing entranced. I was practiced in being enchanted by

him. I knew that he was capable of chanting for hours until he was ready. Sometimes he sang to me so long before touching me with love that I forgot about him, I would be feeling smooth waves taking wrinkles out of the dry sandy beach, until he would astonish me with a touch that began at the beginning of myself and constructed me into forces which shaped themselves to the contours of his forces, and we lost all constraint in our submission to the self-constraints of love. But with him concealed in song my thoughts wandered from him. I knew that these monotonous songs could last indefinitely. I saw Delphine approach me, Delphine at seventy or eighty, she claimed not to know, and now, like that untouchable wild cat born under Utterly, the one that crawled into my lap only when it was sick and dying, Delphine asked for my help. She thought that she was going into labor. I had palpated a tumor years before, when I forced her to let me examine her. I assumed that she was finally feeling pain associated with that. Delenda called me to him. "Help her," he said. "Lithopedion." I don't want his knowledge to be a mystery. He used to read my medical books in the Infirmary, and he had a way of remembering what he would need. Our facilities were as poor one place as another, so we lay Delphine on a blanket where the grass and vines become beach. I had operated with lasers, I had trained in cryosurgery, and had learned simpler techniques only as I had needed them on the island. I hoped to ease Delphine's dying, but she insisted that she was in labor. The hard lump I could touch in her distended belly felt like death, not like a baby. I sterilized my hands, using the last of the alcohol, calculating that our bootleggers could distill more from the stray sugar cane that grows wildly about Umberland. I was using the last of everything in the supplies Kwant had left in his office, the legacy of his long love affair with his innards, the

legacy although he still roamed alive at Umberland. Since
Delphine was contracting, or trying to contract—I wondered about her history of childbirth, if she had borne
children, where they might be, I saw like a photograph a
naked black woman kneeling on a table in a room filled
with medical students. Then I inserted my fingers and felt
a stony thing, and I slowly worked out of her rigid pelvis,
feet first, the tiny calcareous male fetus, for a moment more
stony phallus than fetus, which I suppose had died at
about the seventh month as it turned for its descent. The
seventh month, but generations ago, at least forty years. It
was like touching aborted contempt, or utter negation. I
was about to put a finger to the calcified eyes when Delenda called, "Aurelia." I had forgotten about him and the
pain which was going to be needlessly self-inflicted on him
by my hands. I hated the violence of obscurity, the gratui-
tous mystification. His tireless chanting had lulled me like
a noise that absorbs all other noises, and until it stopped I
did not realize I had been dwelling in it. He smiled, he
laughed, but his glee matched nothing I could feel. It could
have been only for himself and for something that was beyond me. We had always met each other halfway, but perhaps only part of us had met completely. I had thought and
felt differently, and had interpreted his words in my own
way when he taught me that zero in his mathematics was
completion, not nothing or void or nought or nil or va-
cancy, or the point at which value vanishes. Delenda whispered to me. I did not show my unhappiness, I merely became professional as my love ruptured from my belief. I
returned to Delphine to care for her, although now she
slept quietly, or wanted me to think that she slept quietly.
"Do not sorrow" indeed. I walked to where Delenda lay
outstretched on the table, his stomach taut, the skin tensile. He had instructed me, explaining that he would take

all infections with him. I took my scalpel and incised the skin as though I were performing a laparotomy. Under the circumstances in an odd sense I could not make a mistake, yet I knew that I was lost somewhere in a tangle of promises, pledges, and a Hippocratic oath. From his point of view, I was not doing any harm. Olivia helped. No anesthetic, no asepsis. I could, if I had had the skill, have read the future in his entrails. I suppose I did. When I signalled Orlando, he brought me, not the tiny canoe Delenda had carved and provided for this ceremony, but Delphine's stony fetus which I buried in the abdomen, Delenda chanting, Olivia in an ecstasy of comprehension I could not share, Orlando sullen and I could feel *brotherly*, signalling disapproval in spite of himself, and Oliver pale, serious, and ready. I clumsily sutured the body of my beloved until it was the coffin of the fetus. He continued to bleed, as I could see, and was bleeding internally, as I could also see. I had a terrible thought, looking at him, that he was too damaged anyway to be worth saving, a cold indifferent thought that I would have to get myself another one. It was not *my* thought. Delenda looked at me with that fraction of himself which still pertained to me and he nodded. I did not know what to do except to perform the tasks he had requested me to perform. I felt the tragedy that we had not understood each other's definitions of zero, but I thought that I had improvised the operation rather well. Doctors don't like to admit that they might add to pain, but now pain seemed in some way to be the point, enabling him to make connections among eras. The plane of his experience, the amiable decisiveness on which I had been able to focus, now opened up to depths or to recesses, to something beyond that plane; I had been thinking that for him as well as for me green advanced visually, but now I could see that for him green receded infinitely, while for me it

160

advanced, so damn green, the foreground of my experience
had a hole in it, and I could not see him as I saw him and
peer into that hole at the same time, and in an anathema of
my own I chanted in an improvisation which showed I had
studied under a master, for in my solo I chanted Damn
transcendentals and damn emanations, damn upward displacements and damn downward displacements, damn
sublimations, damn mysteries and damn all mystics, damn
the *ding-an-sich*, damn unobservables and unverifiabilities,
damn *halo* even if it derives from the Greek for threshing
floor, damn skyhooks, damn the devil's vaudeville, damn
trompe l'oeil, damn all damnations and anathemas, damn everything that is more than is the case, damn emotion in ex-
cess of the facts as they appear, damn all that one cannot
speak of and must be silent about, damn all discrepancies
between appearance and reality, and between promise and
fulfilment, and damn concepts without percepts, for they
are worse than empty, they are almost empty, and damn
percepts without concepts, for they are worse than blind,
they are almost blind, and damn deep structures, liberal
theologians, defense mechanisms, damn mediations and
damn myths that think themselves in men and damn language that says itself through us without our knowledge,
damn whirling dervishes and faith healers, damn the spiritual regenerations and damn the human condition, and
whether or not Delenda heard me I was not to know. Olivia kissed his forehead, Orlando gripped his hands, tied as
they still were. Oliver looked aghast but smiling at Delenda, his hand fluttering for a moment before settling on Delenda's shoulder, and he controlled himself with a solemn
quotation, *nu se herewisa hleahtor alegde, gamen ond gleodream,*
and courteously translated in case his fellow students had
forgotten the lament, "now that our captain has laid aside
his laughter, his games, and the glee-dream," and I found it

easier to know what Oliver was feeling than to know what I was feeling, still seething anathemas. I touched my fingers to the pulsing vein in his neck until, for a moment I could feel us sharing, I wanted for him whatever this was that he wanted for himself, and I heard the last words I was to hear from him, "too pure . . . less pure," and we looked up at the caracara birds floating in the sheaths of early evening light. Green, pale but unmistakable, in the prelude to sunset. Our last green sky together. A pause in the chanting which continued behind me as I walked away knowing better than to turn around and face the horror of my assent to his will. I could not have forced him to live without destroying him. Either he destroyed himself, or I destroyed him. I felt the tragedy that we had defined life so differently. Never since have I been able to feel life as the struggle against death. That evening on the beach I failed, I made some terrible error of ethical relativity, I didn't know that I knew an absolute in the light of which what he was doing was wrong, dying in response to the dictates of some archaic moribund absolute which I don't think he had been born to but which he had deliberately revived or reconstructed, his need to fulfill some prophecy greater than his need of a future with me. Why should I have been separated from someone I loved? Too many have been forced to part; no one should voluntarily abandon the beloved. *And I was his beloved.* His system was too perfect for the actual world. I should have forced him to my beliefs. My tolerance only declares me a lukewarm nihilist. I will find my old notebooks and refresh my memory: what was I learning to believe before I loved that man, my believable Delenda, my beloved?

As we walked away, Orlando said, "If no one needs me, I would like to look at Ocean." And so we stood with him as he was about to pick up a new thread in his life; as I knotted mine. I know that I did not kill Delenda, that to say that I did is to indulge myself in an oversimplified version of cause and effect which he would have hated. He was a variable to which, for a while, I got to assign the value. Or to think I did. He remains a variable to which I now assign a different value. *Delenda est.*

My love,
Aurelia

Late Autumn—The Beach—Lumberland—Year 23

Dear Octavio,
The sunset begins. *This* sunset begins. "Morning and evening are like promises kept." I sit here at the farther edge of the isthmus where the beach is building up sand. What is the opposite of sand? I wonder where the sand comes from. Eighty or more years ago the United States Government built up the beaches of Primavera and Umberland. We do behave strangely when we think of defending ourselves. I suppose that rocks are threshed into sand by the ocean. Occasionally I find pot shards, and nowadays I leave them as I find them, unless they would fit into the grove. Sand seems to me more dependable, more permanent, than rocks. Was Wordsworth correct to call the poet "the rock of defence for human nature?" The United States Army Corps of Engineers dumped sand, not rocks, to defend our coastline. I sit here on the reliable sand to take my memories from the beach, to write on this paper which makes me feel like a rich uncle writing to his favorite nephew, courting the lad who is being nice to him for his money. One learned, in that other world, to make the most of cynicism. I am beyond that now, for at last I have (after feathers and butterfly wings, after some of Kwant's old funny money from Baltimore, and much foreign moolah I kept as souvenirs of my travels) found my material for

paper: I have devised a successful method of making paper, weaving it almost, then pressing it, out of the leaves of trees. At last I can publish my feuilleton, and perhaps attempt my *Leaves of Grass*, in folio. But beneath these facetious words I hope that you see and read the poem in the palimpsest of this paper, a poem of the lament that is the melody of leaves, but a lament ameliorated by my delight that I have at last constructed a piece of paper which quotes the great tradition of poetry in an original, peculiar way. My paper is almost never an ideal. I, destroyer and preserver, have produced paper which produces consciousness of leaves. The paper I produce is producing me. Educing me. That is my poem, the poem of conscript leaves. I could wish I were named Boisfeuillet. I am growing leaves in the sea now, cultivating the grasses, an oceanic gardener. The paper I make from sea-grass will be a new object of knowledge. That new object of knowledge will produce a new theory for its comprehension or illumination. My sea-bloom paper will be a new way of thinking about the new reality which it is, tasting of salt, feeling of sand.

I have come here to sit and to remember, from what I called the "night Octavio was borne," the ocean, for I was ignoring Delenda by watching one wave at a time, looking now eastward to the ocean, now westward to the sea, and counting. Delenda's songs had a timelessness that was boring unless you entered into it. I liked to enter the songs by going about my business and later noticing that I was within the melody. I was trying to count, to see if waves do come in groups of nine in life as they are said to do in literature. With my memory I found it difficult to be original because I remembered so many origins. Now I remembered Joyce's sentence which we once diagrammed with Converse, I do believe the last children anywhere in the world to be dia-

gramming sentences. We have fixed Converse's wagon, I
suppose. "They serpented towards his feet, curling, un-
furling many crests, every ninth, breaking, plashing, from
afar, from farther out, waves and waves." We had noted the
use of nine units in the sentence about nine waves. Was the
sentence imitating the movement of the waves? And that
plashing was rather *art nouveau*. I had written *plethora* once,
which amused Olivia unaccountably, and they all mocked
me for *myriad, calliope,* and even *gazebo,* although we had a
gazebo, so that the name wasn't at all exotic. We seemed
not always to hear the same meanings in the same sounds:
plashing versus *splashing.* I was always listening to sounds,
listening for sounds that would carry import. I would or I
might seem trivial, a boulevardier, handy-dandy but a fop,
and every word might be trivial unless perhaps I proved to
be right about something I couldn't quite discern there in
the distance beyond the breakers. And there, in the distance as I was counting waves from shore to ocean depths, I
did discern a raft, with a figure on it, and as I saw that it
was drifting toward the breakers I turned and noticed
Delphine not looking where she was going because she
was looking where I was looking, and turning back I saw
that the figure was Kwant, our Ferdinand, on a raft fash-
ioned from the wreck of an old hull beached at Umberland. Looking at Delphine I saw beyond her to the flames
so that I thought she had come to tell us of the fire, but
even as I realized that Utterly was on fire—I seemed to
know immediately that Converse had "let the red rooster
loose" in the house (as perhaps he had in my parents' house
so long before)—I saw that whatever she had come to tell
us was forgotten as she saw Kwant with her far-sighted old
eyes, and I thought that in recognizing the peculiar ideo-
gram of his naked body that she read an unwelcome message, unpleasant, cacographic Kwant, but she held her side

in an image of a woman astonished by agony. I watched Kwant across the furrowed plains of the ocean as the sun, descending behind us, obliterated the western horizon. He looked too white. Then one enormous anomalous wave, I suppose a ninth, raised Kwant in his drifting hull, and, overturning him, wrapped him in the winding cloth of waters, incendiary in the sunset, burying him alive in the ocean, our bitter version of the old Venetian ceremony, the Wedding of the Doge and the Sea. *Sic semper tyrannus:* that man had usurped the trees. When we left Delenda to die alone I explained to Orlando what I had seen happening to Kwant. We did not take time to think of Utterly burning. I know that Olivia will write to you of what she saw next, but I want to be sure that you see what I saw—although I could not quite know what I was seeing—as I bear witness that we stood in the water focusing beyond Kwant and thinking of Delphine and Delenda, tasting grains of sand in the salty water I splashed on my face and tasted on my lips, then hurled into the ocean the maddeningly uninformative seashell cup from which Orlando had given Delenda a sip of water, I saw the cup drink and then disappear into the ocean from which it drank, quite swallowed up, then something plashed, and I saw the dolphin familiar to us as Mirador swimming toward shore with another dolphin, the two of them with nudges sea-shepherding something ahead of them in the water, something my eyes could not get a purchase on, I was dizzy for a moment, reviving as I stumbled and fell into the shallow water, recovering too late to see whatever it was that Orlando saw as he reached the sandbar uttering a sharp shrill cry of anguish and hope, plowing against the waves toward Mirador, that immediate man, determined to be your father, the father of his immediate son.

All my avuncular love,
Oliver

(Olivia to Octavio)

Mux 16th–Year 23

Dear Octavio,

Before I write you a letter, there's something I want to say to you about the death of Delenda. I saw a quadrant of light with greens at the center, varying greens which vied with the white above the greens, the yellow beneath, the red, or reds, to the left, which felt like east to me, and the black to the west. Several blacks. I watched the lights palpate, the colors pulsing, vaporizing, oscillating, and the white, yellow, red, and black condensing toward the green, a green now so palpable in its possession of the light that it cast shadows, that beseeching green, like amaranthus at twilight. Since Delenda was dying, I waited for the colors to yield to black, but in a reprise the yellow spread out over the green as the green expanded over it and up into the white, and the green swallowed the red even as the red was bleeding into the white and yellow, while the black reached beyond blackness to yield itself to the enigmatic green which retracted into a sphere of light which, as it dispersed, made invisibility visible for a moment. I will testify to what I witnessed: Delenda Kinh died, his quadruntal colors nullified into vacant light surrounding a persuasive green. I felt as though I were putting on a mended stocking in a rented room.

I would like to write to you so that the parts would combine, would bear upon each other in this letter the way parts of this event bore upon each other. Everything seemed to be happening at once so that I now know that Utterly was burning on its cliff as Kwant was upending into the Atlantic Ocean to our east, while Delenda was I suppose dying for reasons of his own a few yards away across the isthmus on the sands of the Caribbean Sea. I saw what Delenda saw, straining upward on his table, that Kwant on his raft walked north to south yet stayed in one place as the raft under him floated south to north, I saw comprehension or recognition in his eyes, although I do not know what he was affirming with that glance which contained, as I saw it, a flicker of regret, and I could guess for myself that Kwant, as he adjusted the sail, was navigating toward his beloved España, probably hoping to land there in 1939 when he was about seven years old. When I saw that pitiful parchment baby I guessed from Delphine's stories to me that Kwant was the father, but only a few years ago did I receive from Delphine a letter in which she described her exploits across the years in leaving food for Kwant and Converse, whom we had thought of as foraging. She also described her sewing. At Umberland years ago the Creoles maintained a chapel for the Blessed Isabel, who Oliver said would be the patron saint of inflation, having helped to make gold so available that myths of the golden age could no longer compete. But apparently Kwant had told stories about Queen Isabelle of Spain, including one in which she vowed not to change her underwear for nine days. (Thereupon Oliver christened the color of our church, Renunciación, "Isabella yella.") The Creole women would not change their underwear for a nine-day period of devotions, after which they would hang the underwear in the shrine of Santa Isabel (they promoted her to sainthood themselves), would hang their tough linen drawers, or their innocent cotton underwear, and my dear nurse Delphine (whose lithographic baby could be deciphered as the half-uncle of Aurelia and Orlando, half-brother to Salathiel, and was sewn by Aurelia into Delenda as into a shroud), she labored for Kwant, piecing the old drawers into that quilted sail which looked to me, in comparison with the sunset and the firelight, to be a deeply modulated saffron yellow, and I thought how the sight of the saffron triangles patched into a crazy-quilt sail resembled the part of my sight, my vision, that I had never adequately shared with anyone, so that throughout my childhood I was willing to forget about it and simply said Oh skip it when someone was disagreeably refusing to hear what I was saying I saw, yet I remain loyal to it, the terrorist who will not negotiate a truce, but then unconditional surrender was never one of my conditions. That evening few of us saw what the others were seeing because we were looking in different directions. While Aurelia and Orlando tended to Delenda, Delphine awakened and spoke to me. She had told Kwant about Delenda's plans. She had been so large when she had been my nurse, she loomed as an immense screen on which I projected my images as I told myself the story of my life—or was it the scenario of my life?—and now I was pained to see that she was so much smaller than I was, and had been so for many many years. Now, like an actress who can appear larger than she is, she roused herself to smile her roustabout smile, then suddenly she was dead. Obeying her words, I carried her alone, and apparently unseen (as the others walked into the water toward where Kwant was drowning unreachably beyond the breakers), along the path winding up the cliff to Utterly. I lay her body in the small brick kitchen and I threw into it, mourning as she had taught me to mourn, flaming boards I wrested from the burning house. Her kitchen burned ferociously, fiercely, in triangles of somber blue flame. I do not know how much you know, Octavio, or how much you will know when you receive this letter. When I think of you I see light in a color I can't quite remember the name of, a color that scintillates beyond yellow, orange, and pink. Perhaps I have never seen that color, or perhaps I have never heard its name. In writing to you I have restrained myself, I have constrained myself, and perhaps have compromised some truth. After all, I am your mother. Too much happened that night which ended so happily for me, yet even the quietest and most neutral statement of facts displays the horror: I burned the body of the dead family cook in the outdoor kitchen behind Utterly.

Your loving mother,
Olivia

The Loft—Mux 16th—Year 23

Dear Octavio,

I don't know whether I arrive early or late with this news, with these facts which once made such an impression upon me, although now I am more interested in facts than in my impressions. You will have heard, I know from talking with the others, how Aurelia followed the instructions of her dying lover and husband, Delenda. I gave him a drink from the cup which he had brought with him, and which he had said, laughing, was for begging water. Later he must have died, and his body must have been spirited away by the Indians, to be buried in one of the trees with which they mark the solstice. Delphine died, and Kwant drowned. As Utterly continued to burn. I am certain that I heard Delenda's last word to us, "purity," but Oliver heard "party," Aurelia heard something else, so none of us is sure what we heard. Nor is it likely that he had a revelation that he would have kept from us until the last minute. I heard him tell Aurelia once that as he had been compelled to come to this island, he was now compelled to go on, but I couldn't decide whether she was listening or not. I suppose that since Delenda arrived we have lived in anarchy, anarchy except for the regular delivery of the mails, the improbable, novel, informative mail. When Delenda first issued his decree, or suggestion, we were foolish. We, who had nothing to do with our time, or little to do with it, usually found ourselves too busy to write. I could write a book about my reluctance to write thank-you notes for the gifts, and for the implications given along with the gifts, from that tawdry world. After Delenda's epistolary revolution, we enjoyed separating from each other in order to go off alone to fire a letter into the future which was becoming more and more precise, as for each of us, the four of us, the future was unknown but a precise unknown, and the existence of the letters told us that we would have something to be grateful for, as indeed letters turned out to be the gift I could write a thank-you note for most readily. When Delenda told me to make an office in Renunciación where people might privately dictate letters, I was indignant, for I suspected a punishment that might, like elliptical billiard balls, fit the crime, some crime of mine that had never been defined. But I was also thrilled and gratified. I thought that I would temporarily put aside my ambition — I, the *vox populi* — to write an immense realistic novel, a novel that no matter who succeeded in the battles of history would be treasured by the victors, a novel that would be worth reading under the dome of the sky. I would not be ambiguous, but by letting facts speak for themselves, and tacitly implying an ideal, I would be on the side of history, and I saw myself as they saw me looking back upon me as I foreshadowed them. But after the fires in the western sky I had to wonder who would ever read it, so I could postpone my ambition, put aside my human comedy, while I temporarily took dictation as a village scribe, incidentally picking up local lore. I could collect more of the rich and pawky proverbs of the folk, I thought, as I had begun collecting them as a child. I knew little more than could be learned sitting in a mahogany glider on a veranda, looking at reflections in the glossily varnished floor of golden oak, and watching lightning bugs which Aurelia was collecting for her studies of the implications between phosphorescence and eyesight, while Olivia defined Aurelia's reluctance to see that seeing is believing is loving. Later Aurelia would be giving Olivia lessons. I think back now to my evening at Umberland cutting cane, when I learned enough to know that I could not bear to know much more, the ugly discrepancy between a man working for himself at his own pace, and a man laboring for others by their clock and buying corn by their measure with their scrip. I began to suspect that one theme of that evening was to make me see the words I had been transcribing into my notebooks, as though to say to me, "If you want our lives, you shall have our life," so I have never used the "field" notes I have collected, and have rarely quoted the Indians or the Creoles, unless writing letters at their dictation is quoting. So I began with trepidation mixed with pride my career as the scribe, to the amusement of Olivia and Oliver, and for lo these many years I have sat taking dictation from a rainbow of people some of whom dictated not so much to me as at me, especially the aggrieved who had labored at Umberland and who took months or years to work off their grievances. Slaved at Umberland, and not free to kill themselves because they loved their families. Oliver used to dress up and come in to dictate a letter for a lark, and Delphine, looking me in the eye, spoke her fond and comforting letters to Olivia and even letters to me which I was not to receive for several years. Delphine, of course, could read and write as well as I could. She was born on Pennsylvania Avenue in Baltimore and had sung in bars on "The Block," yet she explained once—I cannot write you all of these stories at once, and when you were old enough to hear them, you had gone off seeking an explanation elsewhere—that cooking satisfied her, that the intensity of cooking pleased her more than music or sex could, and she could do it at her own pace. Balzac must have had more time than I have had. I must rest now for a few minutes.

I stopped writing this letter, Octavio, to walk outside

through the plaza, to think about the idea that has just occurred to me, and to write to you about it here in the cool of
the evening. I can see now that I have *written* the letters,
even if only in the sense of having written down the words,
and I wonder, knowing how indirectly Delenda worked, if
I have not by writing letters for whomever and whenever,
and even wherever, surpassed the ambition I had to write a
great novel, one as profound as it was popular, and have
fulfilled the best part of my ambition as this island has
voiced itself and pictured itself through my pen. Looking
at the clusters of letters hanging about the walls like chili
peppers drying in the shed, I see that I have written a book
beyond the book I could have composed of my imaginings.
And I have written it without being as unhappy as I feared
I would have to be to write an important book. I have discovered my definition of the imagination as a place where
beautiful women dictate words which are like an emanation of the place, and better than the penman could have
conjured up on his own, women who then (sometimes)
reach to touch him on the lips, as though to explore his silence. And even if I, and I alone, have read that epistolary
novel quite the way in which I wrote it, that perhaps would
have been true of anything I might have written, and is
true of other authors. You will read part of my novel, Octavio, if you read any of the letters preserved in the safe or
in the incubator. In fact, you are reading part of it now, in
this letter, in which I can announce the approach of the
denouement. Oliver has done his work well, and few
people need me to write their letters for them anymore. So
if you will excuse the belated self-satisfaction of a hard-
working man, I hereby and in this moment and in this sentence retire from my post, and I declare this letter the last
chapter of my book, the story to which so many lives have
contributed—so many lives, each of them a story—a story
known only in fragments but which, especially in those

parts saved for posterity by Octavio, the writer's son, ranks
as a masterwork of modern naturalism ("but not, I fear, for
the general reading public"), although in form this post-
industrial novel returns to the origins of the English novel
in Richardson and in Fielding. The story not merely records the native customs and idioms in a style which fulfills
its name, *secretarial realism,* a style which is *au pied de la lettre,*
almost literally literal. But the style also fully implies the
narrative which, with discontinuities which are true to our
lived discontinuities, chronicles the provincial tragedies
and comedies which evolved on an island cut off from the
modern world. Here we read a moving "meditation on the
foundation of identity, the mysteries of parentage and dying, a record of loving, disillusionment, the sustaining importance of tenderness," etc. These tragedies and comedies are absorbed in a larger story, for while an episode
may be tragic — they do not know enough to act, yet act
they must, so they act wrongly or badly, aware that they
might die at any moment, that their time is irrevocable, irreversible, irrecoverable — or an episode may be comic, for
sometimes they are ridiculous buffoons who make a farce
of their lives by overestimating or underestimating the
strength of life itself, yet their burlesque, even as it seems
an act in their *vaudeville flottant,* rises to comedy as the sometimes silly people raise themselves to comic seriousness,
somewhere 'twixt earnest and game, by writing letters
which so provide for the future that they create probabilities in the present that guide them into that future where
the letters await them. They did try to live as though they
were about to receive the important letter they had been
waiting for with confidence and excitement. Shall we call
their story a *romance?* Their author thinks of himself as the
next-to-the-last romantic. Perhaps you are to be the last.

I have not forgotten you, Octavio, as I have meditated on

the movement of the letters as they circulate among the people. I have one other discovery to record, one other memory. Your mother, Olivia, had carried the body of Delphine to the kitchen at Utterly in order to cremate her. Aurelia seemed to be thinking. Oliver and I waded into the water so that I could, in a freely improvised emotion of my own, launch the diminutive canoe Delenda had carved onto the waves. I watched the waves and thought of how to describe them should I want to record the scene. If words could preserve waves, then these inspired secretarial words of Flaubert which I recalled from an ancient dictation lesson were beyond perishing: "Les vagues battent contre les murs où quand il est marée basse déferlent à leur pied sur le sable." *Déferlent.* They unfurled. I looked up to confirm the words which experience would, I knew, verify, and I saw the waves unfurl upon the sand, I saw why Oliver preferred sand to rocks, for if we were merely writing our names in sand, it was nevertheless the *same* sand, then Oliver cried out an electric lyric cry as I ran through the waves toward Mirador and the other dolphin who between them were keeping a baby afloat, like a newborn dolphin, and I found strength which felt equivalent to valor and reached out to unfurl you from the husky whispering waves, you fell into place in my arms, everything looked valiant to me, and Mirador and Oliver seemed to join in lyric electric laughter. Looking at you, salt water in my eyes, I saw you enveloped in a primal light. I carried you, I bore you in my arms, Aurelia and Oliver now hinged to my sides, toward your mother who stood griefstricken, waiting and weeping above the cliffs at Utterly.

Your loving father,
Orlando

II. coherence

Well, dear Octavio, I have been trying, in several senses, to correspond with the facts, as Orlando would have wanted me to, while doing justice to Olivia, as he would have wanted me to. I was going to end this letter with you being borne ashore, our observable boy, extemporaneous son, perennial grandson, but Olivia has died. Her body will be laid out here in the postoffice tonight, in what has become an informal meeting hall. I regret that you did not know her these last two years. She was severe with us, even harsh, and usually rash; but we had learned to count on her for that, and she was dependable. She was happier of late. From among many letters — I can recognize the paper she made for herself, erratic rhomboids, capricious quadrilateral lugsails, fibrous and translucent, overlapping planes of the transparent and planes of the opaque, for her paper is the outward and visible sign of the outward and visible light on which she focused her gaze — I have chosen two to copy here. I hope for more help from these children and young people who seem always to be about, for I feel myself weakening, and I do not resist. Olivia, by the way, built an excellent house for herself. She arranged sticks and branches as a horizontal warp, and then trained vines upward as the woof. Her woven house was comfortable, there at the edge of the grove. I still sleep here, under my desk. In our last conversation Olivia told me that we must have had so many possessions back then, back there in Utterly, so that we could be hospitable, but that we should have seen through the hospitality, should have looked into it, since for each hospitality we extended to guests, an oppression was extended to the uninvited populace. I suppose that we lived as though we were expecting to entertain, but few guests ever came to Primavera. And I can see that the preparations we made — the overcrowded larder, the varieties of cheese, the choices of wine, as though each taste had its own chromatic scale, and each semi-tone had to be represented — were to kill certain feelings. Kwant chose among liqueurs after dinner like a virtuoso of poisons who appeared to be lengthening the evening while actually he was shortening one's days. "I am happy with the hospitality of the postoffice myself," Olivia said, and indeed, enough fruit and vegetables are brought here and left on tables for the taking, or cooked up by someone with nothing else to do, that we usually have a meal in progress, something simmering, and a pot of stock sits always brooding on the back of the stove. The women are preparing food now for the wake, if that is what I must call it. Already the table usually covered with stationery has been cleared and covered with bowls of fruit. Octavio, what Olivia *ought* to have done was perilously close to what she *ought not* to have done; she lived imperatively. And now she ought not to have died. I was not prepared for this. I was not finished telling her what to do for her own good, and she loved me for that.

Chaykin 5th—Year 24—The Grove

Dear Aurelia,

I hope that you are alive to receive this letter. I have few such hopes for myself. Most of the letters I write now are only in my head, addressed to Orlando, whom I used to try to make feel bad about himself so that he would try to make me feel good. I am growing tired of explaining myself to others; I want people around me, but no questions. I have been imagining a letter to you throughout Chay Kin, and even I can't gauge whether I was deluded, self-deluded, or working with an image. I will assume that I was working with an image. I have seen you help some of our friends who

(Olivia to Aurelia)

want tattoos removed lest they turn up in death dressed in
the wrong spiritual clothes, preferring to appear dressed in
scars, which illustrate their lives more adequately than the
tattoos do. Remember, when we were children, how Oliver
would trace letters on my forehead and then tell me that I
had *guilt* written all over me. We would all take off my shirt
to see if it was written on my back. Looking at my skin, or
my absence of skin, I was going to ask you to put your scalpel where your mouth is and to help me, for I felt that in
some dreadful atavism or regression or devolution, that in
some dreadful throwback of evolution, that my nerves had
become a form of skin. I think it could happen: the ecto-
derm of the embryo shapes itself into the skin, but also into
the nerves, so nerves are a form of skin. You always said
that I was more logical than biological, and Oliver would
add that *illogical* is also logical. I wanted you to perform an
exploratory operation — I would have helped you — so that
you would see for yourself the layers of skin growing inside
me, skin wound around and around inside me like a sandpaper shroud. You have told me that I am overly sensitive,
and I am trying to explain: I get gooseflesh behind my eyes
when I look at Orlando's burial mound in the grove. You
helped so many, and I often helped you to help them, and I
was writing to you for help, but since I began I am starting
to remember the night we acted for that tribe of exogamous
Indians who floated up in the excitement after Delenda's arrival, providentially bringing the corn which they were de-
voted to, and a cultish mystique about beans, and how you
played the doctor in their ceremony, I will quote myself at
length before I forget my cares: "My eyes are skin, Aurelia:
I can see your eyes but I do not see them seeing mine. I can
feel my eyes seeing, painfully, yet I remember when my eye
felt itself being seen and seeing, pleasing and being pleased,
as once my vagina felt and gave feeling, pleasing as it was

181

pleased, delighting and delighted. Orlando had a well-defined narrow waist, but what does a narrow waist define? I have been pleased to be looked at with desire and with love. I look at that word, *pleasing*, as I write to ask you *please*. The words are overlapping. Please, Aurelia, the skin grows inside me and turns back on itself, with less and less space to grow in, stiffening like a bloodied cerecloth. Now that my visible skin is peeling, peeling, leaving my flesh exposed, some terrible reversal of skin and nerves is obvious. You need only transplant skin that grows inside me to the surface where I need to it protect me. Such transplants are simple. I would not reject my own skin. Aurelia, I grow like an abrasive, self-usurping onion. The cilia grow into each other and mat together when I sweat. I exude, and moisture congeals coldly around my empty bones swathed in that clammy epidermis. I am angry that I should have to die like this, ugly with my red and ecru complexion." I look now at my delusion: it seems to me more precise than actuality; experience is more blurry than dreams.

But those Indians whom Oliver called the cult that came to cultivate our garden. They were our most concrete philosophers, although I have come to see that their seamless sequence of physical acts which successfully grows beans, which seemed to support some insupportable metaphysics, was less a system of ontology or even cosmology than it was a seasoned, weather-beaten etiquette, verging on politics, and they were governed by their needs, which entailed being governed by the needs of the bean-plants, the Indians and the beans ruling each other by turns. They arrived in shabby fiberglass canoes. They were not allowed to marry each other, and in the absence of another intact tribe, they elided everyone else on the island into a single tribe, which gave us an oddly pleasant feeling of comradeship, even kinship. It was like being converted to a cult which had no doctrines, and we were freed to regard each other as a group, equal to each other as aliens to that tribe. We hadn't thought of ourselves as a team like that in a peculiar game, with brides and grooms carried to and fro like flowery footballs. They told us that their tribe was one man, and that he would give birth to a baby girl which would be given to the other tribe, us, to be cared for. This formula in their logic translated into the fact that one of their women was going to marry a man she met on Primavera. One of us. They built that hut out of wattles and lianas, quite useful that turned out to be as a lesson, *utile et dulce,* in architecture, for the rest of us as we gradually went eclectically native, and they delightedly improvised, in the absence of a shaman who might either have officiated at the ceremony or more probably spoiled it with criticisms of their use of the available materials, which included you and me, troubleshooters dressed in top hats and cutaways which elicited both terror and giggles from the mischievous Creoles. Oliver jested at our uterine routine from Uterly Castle, and said that we were the first hysterical conversion symptoms he had ever seen walking, dressed up, and ready to strut. He warned me that a mediator is always negated, but I didn't understand mediation, and anyway I was no longer Olivia and was not yet or not quite anyone else. I swaggered—we had cigars and moustaches—I felt like the stage manager of a dream, dressed more for a burial than for a birth, closer to obituary than to obstetrics. You and I picked up the girl as she emerged from the hut carrying wind-flowers. The men, who seemed as vague on the anatomical details of this birth as they were decisive in their architectural impromptu, and drunk on rum, took her from our arms and carried her wrapped in a cloth. I, improbably dependable throughout, dependably saw diamonds of newly minted white light diapering the sky as you and I, lifting her from the arms of the men, handed her to the groom, who in their system was I think also a woman — Oliver said that he hadn't the courage to dream what this confraternity of people soberly enacted in their unembarrassed lives. And then that bean tribe, which as the creative man had just given birth to a daughter, lapsed into what seemed to be a postpartum depression, they seemingly merely glum with their rum, although I realized later that they were sad because no one else would be likely to marry into their particular symbolic logic. Yet in the intervening years I have seen that logic alter to accommodate the facts of life on Primavera. Oliver lambasted us all some more, lamenting that he had been born among unimaginative commercial shopkeepers, moneychangers who compartmentalized their dreams and their desires, limiting the meaning of *futures* to the dimensions of a marketplace of commodities sold for eventual delivery. I didn't think that I was guilty of quite that, and I was glad when Orlando threatened to arrange a marriage for Oliver, a threat which made him pause for thought. You, Aurelia, gave us one of your semi-annual lectures on cultural relativity to stop our joking, forgetting that you were standing there in top hat and cutaway like an Austro-Hungarian professor delivering his habilitation in rare habiliment. I think that when you saw yourself gesture with a cigar in your hand that you laughed, seeing your self off-balance, but then of course you were able to render your absurdity into a "formative disequilibrium," you gave us a lecture on the origins and history of shaving legs and underarm hair, telling us about a woman who cut her hair with a blade and cured the hair from under her arms like tobacco, and then gave it to the men to smoke, to poison them, to put them out of their misery, and that she was the first woman in history to shave her legs, to take a razor to her legs, and who in hell, you asked, was the first man to take a razor to his face, to

touch his flesh with flint or with metal, and what had he
been thinking of? You and I wore moustaches for that wedding, and now I am growing quite a witchy one myself, and
I sit here looking at my legs, quite available in my version of
a lava-lava, and see the hair and the skin just about where
they belong. But still I feel cut by the sarcasms of time, and
I will say so. Through the "porthole" the Indians keep
trimmed in the trees for me, so that I can see the sky, I see
residual clouds, tinted by the sunset, bodying forth the largesse and grandeur of an island evening. When we were
children, pretending, and feeling the pang of pretending to
be what we knew we somehow were, I spoke my line in the
play Orlando wrote, "I have a cousin in Tibet," and Oliver,
who was usually being Branwell drunk or Branwell sober,
said soberly, with the correct diplomacy between childhood
nations, "I should think so." His tact was that of a colleague,
and Orlando touchingly wrote it into his collaborative
script. How kind you all have been to me. I hope that I have
not been too much of a trial, or too much of a punishment,
for you. I am quite well, Aurelia, romantically un-self-
deluded, and I release myself on my own recognizance. I no
longer take the lure of suffering. Do you remember when I
learned that General Henry Shrapnel had invented *shrapnel*.
I was appalled. Oliver annotated the fact as the logic of the
Romantic movement: "one *death* within us and abroad."

Ever impetuous,

Olivia

Year 25—October 8th—Pasta Verde and Penumbraland, Ink

Dear Aurelia,

I resolve, after this letter, to write no more letters than are
necessary to maintain the look of plenitude in the postoffice.
Our futures are well provided for, and I have other work to
do as the overseer of the undertakings. I carry enough stuff

back and forth from the postoffice to feel that I am doing my duty in the realm of messages. I used to walk up there at night and sit alone in the vast empty room looking at the letters as I could see the bundles hanging above my head in the dusky light, and filed around the walls like sheaves of wheat. I meditated on that future which Delenda objectified for us as a power transcending the present, so that we would look at ourselves as we would be seeing ourselves at some future moment. Was I oversensitive to feel a veiled reprimand? Was he merely someone else telling me that I was likely to misbehave? Of course I was likely to misbehave. I am likely now, thinking of writing no more letters. I was fortunate that Delenda arrived as I was tiring of making up my own rules, tiring of proving my independence. But I am getting to be able to see myself as I will be when I am an old lady. And perhaps receiving no letters because I haven't been writing any. They might even withhold the letters already addressed to me, but I don't think Salathiel would do that. I must continue to circle around this problem. I have always found it difficult to tell the difference between my abandoning other people and their deserting me. Now the postoffice seems busy day and night, and I let myself be drawn into the happiness there. But I am not unhappy on my own. I have thought through the problem I had with my skin, that painful but precise illusion. I was reading, or misreading, the dermatoglyphics of my hands, when I realized what I was doing with my hands, and forgot to feel sorry for myself. You have said that in evolution what can be eventually will be, that the voluble helix will attempt to say as much as it can, and will seek a place to say it in. I have listened to you, although I cannot have been much help. In a variation on your theme, I am now turning toward doing what I can do. I have spent too much of my life complaining, and then complaining about my complaining, which seems wasteful. Some of the evidence against me hangs preserved in the batches of letters yellowing and drying like the salty feathered seabirds Delphine used to hang in the kitchen, where peppers, onions, potatoes, and herbs were kept for future use hanging above her head, and out of our reach. We could scent the pies lifted above our heads. Yes, I remember. Yet I can't remember when I last cooked anything, although I carry herbs and berries from the mounds up to the postoffice. Sometimes I eat down here with those who come to mourn or to think. I don't know how or when I fell into the role of caretaker, even undertaker, picnicking serenely among the "dumb heaps." This ink I made from berries that ripen among the mounds. Paper I often scavenge and retrieve like some old seabird feeding in the wakes of fishing boats. People give me paper, and I write very small now. Whatever the truth of long ago, I have been converted from that sometimes insufferable woman (if such I was, for I always not-too-secretly thought that I was charming, more honest than tactless, and a little unappreciated), converted into a woman who, perhaps fulfilling Delenda's intuition, can do very little wrong, for I have found an art that I hadn't thought of as an art, one for which the garland of the muses, plucked from burial mounds, might well be mine. Here among the graves, where I can do no wrong, and as I continue to work without a working definition of *nature*, and *life*, whatever I do as I prepare the mounds with the lifeless stones and underbrush I have cleared away, then overlay that with living vines which I disentangle from the surrounding context and weave into a covering, whatever I do completes a pattern only to emerge as the pretext for a more comprehensive pattern which will be formed by the miscellaneous contributions of the mourners. They do, after all, know the dignity of whatever they have come to bury, or to mourn anew. They add decorations to my decorations until the sum of decorations intensifies into architecture which combines with the heliotropic grove of trees and vines. In this funerary grove, "the grove of death," nothing is out of place for very long; or perhaps everything is out of place and therefore has energy. Even the umbrella fixed open on the top of Oliver's mound will be answered or echoed by another shape; perhaps an old target will surface from somewhere and be ceremoniously dumped upon a mound, showing us that we know more than one way to section a circle. I do think about what I am doing, but I do so by listening to see what needs to be done, because everything, as it falls into place, creates another place for things to fall into. I am not complacent, Aurelia, but I acknowledge the limits of my powers. I try, when I sit with those who have brought their dead down from the postoffice in the morning, to sit with them until the dying and the death have fallen into place, until the death belongs to the deceased like a characteristic possession. Dead, yet still oddly incomplete, because the death also belongs to us. Nothing is what it is and not also a reference to other references also. Death may be our most abstract reference. A thing is what it is and also refers us to another thing. We collate references: *refero, referre, retuli, relatus. Confero, conferre, contuli, collatus.* One might think of conjugal love. We decorate the mounds with references. Any errors we make in a pattern will be seen by someone else as an opportunity, we seize opportunities to improvise our designs, not hurrying to complete the incompletable burial of our unburiable beloved so unthinkably dead. We teach ourselves and each other to bear the unbearable. Our lives were so often so haphazardous. I, for example, never saw myself as I would have been seen by my mother and father, and that has been a loss. People, as difficult as they may be, are not as difficult to live with as phantoms.

So, Aurelia, I am living on the ground floor as caretaker, scavenging in the trash for references, a concierge or housemother or matron, and an inadvertent architect of tombs, my own wattle house as much a cocoon as a house, as I dwell, livingly, among the dead, without nostalgia, engaged in transmogrifications, among which I saw last night, when more things had fallen into place at the end of a long day, the dance of the fireflies, so much other occasional phosphorescence amidst so much growth and decay—life and death have many eerie lights in common—who would have thought that things that fall down would be so glowing?—and so with lights behind my eyes, with candid lustre within my eyes, and with the lights of life and putrefaction before me, I saw appreciatively that, even glancing at the ordinary planes of light which shape the darkness into windows, the circumambient darknesses, I could not, with viewfinder, camera, light-meter, and fast film have caught and conveyed the action of light as I saw it move, oh the insufferable beauty, I would that Oliver were here to quote as he was wont to quote Thoreau, "light is a spherical congeries of pyramids," I could begin to understand his habit of quoting as his method of collating references— perhaps he saw more of what I saw than he was able to prove to me at the time—and I realized that light is what challenged me in films because light was what film betrayed in its lacklustre feignings, that light depended on what was being remembered and the names one recollected and one's ability to be overwhelmed and to swoon in the *adagio* of moonlight, and that even a painting could be better than a movie film because a painting could represent a space to inhabit with someone I loved—we might enter upon an Uccello, a Corot, a Monet—Salathiel may have loved me (taught me to believe) more than I have acknowledged, I do use several of his ideas—and Orlando may have loved me more than I could have accepted after my womb had died—being with Salathiel is like being neighborly in a painting by Breughel—and I rarely feel now like a song sung by the picture of nobody, or like the picture of nothing, in fact very unlike, for the friction of words clashing in unthinkable abrasive tangents to each other has generated more sparks of color behind my eyes than external strokes of Edison's light on sugary silver screens could. Now I see, Primaverally, that my letters, with their burden of so much that I could not bear to think about, and often cannot bear to remember that I have written (and now that my old letters to Orlando are delivered to me, as his widow I must face the logic of my ideas which forms a discombobulated rainbow, with yellows next to unlikely purples, like pumpkin next to pink in a *stil leben*, or rose next to an unripened green in a *nature morte*, an Etruscan rose, so many loanwords I hadn't thought of as a debt I had to pay back with good sense, my clauses freely floating without anchor in the syntax, and I so mistaken in my infatuation with pain, my unenviable intimacy with pain—and oh how I asked for trouble! —yet at least working against myself as an obstacle I created frictional tribulations which tinged my stubborn words with arcs of light penumbrously. I always almost meant something by my words. But my prose stinks of some old patrician unreality, and of my rebellion against some old patrician unreality. I have found my art elsewhere, here at the edge of elsewhere. I have made my movie to my own satisfaction here in this grove, this theater of *Lebens-Tod*, the theater of my task, of my *Leibestod*, where light is always lambently orchestrating the growth of the voluble vines and the ramifications of the trees, where no one tells me that I would be better off doing what they tell me to do, where I seem to be accidentally good, accidentally happy, with qualifications, for example the proviso that when I stumble over the little iron coffin Oliver left in the path I recollect him and his death too vividly, recalling stray fragments of his speech, his reference to Shelley writing that economics was poetry to the degree that it required the "just distribution of the produce which it multiplies," and his handing out as gifts sheets of the paper he had made, speaking in the tones of a soap-box orator about the lyric redistributions of wealth which was only on paper. The last paper he gave me was made from sea-leaves. As I took the paper from his hands, I was remembering, and we seemed simultaneously to recognize its resemblance (uncanny resemblance I would say, except that "canny resemblance" seems to me an empty set) to the *pasta* he had brought back from Dyfed, Gho-chiau, for Delphine to see and on which, as she did with *pasta* shells and *lasagna* and the pie crusts on which she forked words before baking them and roosting them be-yond our reach on a shelf in the kitchen (once inscribing *pidgin* on a meat pie and then making herself unavailable for questioning later, so that we never knew what we were eat-ing), she pricked letters with a fork. All that I ever learned was that Oliver was cultivating "foliage of the ocean" be-yond the eastern reef, trying to stabilize a trellis he had built and had submerged for vines to convolute upon. He washed ashore like so much sargasso. I wade into the cove to find weedy trophies to throw upon his grave. So many years ago he told me his epitaph: "The little Actor cons an-other part." But I keep thinking to myself, "Here lies one who wrote his name on paper," and I mutter quotations to myself—"The sea-blooms and the oozy woods . . ."—as I seem to have inherited his task—although whether I am preserving fragments or fragmenting poems is unclear to me. I try not to regret the incontrovertible merriment which arose in the postoffice the night after Oliver's funeral. They were eating his seaweed paper between bouts of duelling with mugs of rum — but all of it, as you said Oliver would have said, "food for thought."

You could come to live here, Aurelia, and we could look together across that black hiatus at the light and movement, and you could try to explain refractions to me again, or the structure of the rainbow, or why two people looking at the same mirrored surface see different images. And I will tell you that light is the alluvium from the abyss. I do not intend to renounce words which originate among the obscurities: *fero, ferre, tuli, latus.* Rickety, rickety language. Now I look up and I see longitudinal pulses crossing transverse undulations as retributions thresh the light. Enough. You, Aurelia, I would usher you across the threshold so that you could see the growth, in slow motion, of the trees and the vines in the light of my bioscope, see with a pleasure that would be enhanced for me as I held your hand and asked if you were seeing what I was seeing. Asking would suffice, you would not need to answer. Here, in this grove, where nothing stings me except the loss of those we love, I have found the motif and the motive of my aesthetic revolution: freedom of movement . . . freedom of movement within these vaulted trees where I can see time as the measure of the rate at which I am consumed by light. And at last, amidst the echoing greens, I am a woman who keeps a clean house.

Happily,
Olivia

I am here again, Octavio: Salathiel. Salathiel. I am old today, feeling my age, wondering if Olivia knew that she had never left us, although she might have, because she loved us. She had, as she said, the energy of a misplaced person. As old as I am, as hopeless as I feel with Olivia dead, I still respond when I see a sheet of blank paper, something in me quickens, although more and more I see paper as a place to write or to rewrite memories. The letters have taught me too well how the present is modified by thoughts about the future, for the present for me is modified by the thought that I can have very little future remaining to me. Yet I remain curious, and curious about you. Today I have been seeing in memory an occasion when I was not eavesdropping, for they paid little more attention to me than they did to a cat, and I was conscienceless or shameless as a cat overhearing them as they poised for their endeavours. I was deliberately memorizing them, for they were to me less four separate children than a region which I might stroll into, and when I imagined the future I saw it as resembling the region that was created in the midst of them as they happily overlapped each other's edges. I was happiest when Olivia, Oliver, Orlando, and Aurelia had trapped themselves in the seriousness of their play. If one day I found Aurelia the most interesting, then Oliver became interesting because he was next to Aurelia, and Olivia was interesting because she was next to Oliver, and Orlando, who was sometimes dull, was always interesting in a nexus with Olivia. Ginevra used to say, "When you have children, you have nothing else," but she frequently looked into our nest to count them, and I suppose that I found that particular poverty sufficient — the world seemed to belong to them, the future was theirs, and I would sit in our overgrown garden thinking of prolificacy, of fecundity, of thriving. I was so sitting when I heard Oliver and Olivia on the veranda. Oliver had been studying mathematics in that style of his which was as much like shopping for a gift for himself as it was like studying. He would scout ahead even of Aurelia, who was older. Olivia interrupted him with studied spontaneity. Olivia: "I think I'll go there by myself for a few days." Oliver: "Where?" Olivia: "Tornata. To stay with your grandmother." They could make Tornata seem very near, or very far. Oliver:

"Why?" Olivia: "She may be lonely." Oliver: "Then take Orlando too. More for her to talk with." Olivia: "No, he and I would talk to each other. And when he's there she treats me like a grandchild." Oliver: "But you'll have none of us to talk with." Olivia: "Yes, I will, I'll talk to myselves." Oliver: "But even that's only two. You'll be bored." Olivia: "I have many more than two." Oliver: "How? I count only one, really." Olivia: "No, no, many more than that. I talk to myself in the future, to me tomorrow, or next week, or whenever I please, and then if I remember, when I get there, I speak back to me, I answer." Oliver: "I don't believe you. You're making all this up." Olivia: "I don't care whether you believe me or not. You always think you are better than anyone else." Oliver: "I mean I don't believe you can divide yourself like that." Olivia: "But of course I can. Who would stop me?" Oliver: "But how many of you are there?" Olivia: "I don't know. As many as I wish. I don't count everything. Grandmother thinks that counting is vulgar." Oliver: "Is there one of you a year from now that you can talk to?" Olivia: "Of course. How could there not be?" Oliver: "Talk to her." Olivia: "I'll tell her what I think of impertinent boys, and about Oliver who looks as though he never has to grow into his clothes, and I'll ask her if he is behaving himself any better." Oliver: "Ask her if *she* is behaving any better. Tell me how many of you there are." Olivia: "What are you getting at, Oliver? I can talk to me tomorrow at 3 and remind me what I am supposed to be doing. Lessons, probably. What is so difficult about that?" Oliver: "Don't be so self-pitying and proud, Olivia. If there's you at 3 and you at 5, is there a you at 3:15, and 3:10, and at 3:01?" Olivia: "What are you getting at? I don't like you when you're getting at something." Oliver: "I'm asking if you count seconds and half-seconds. I'm asking if you divide yourself infinitely." Olivia: "I don't exactly understand infinitely. I suppose that I take more than a second talking and listening, so I don't divide into tiny bits." Oliver: "But suppose you have as many Olivias as you have future instants. Infinite Olivias. Think of that." Olivia: "I don't want to think of that. I told you I don't know about infinity. Converse didn't teach infinity to us yet, you know that." Oliver: "It's in the book, Olivia. Infinity is endlessness, limitlessness. If you had something that was always increasing and you couldn't reach the end of it, like time or space maybe, I'm not sure." Olivia: "But so many selves seems different to me. I don't trust what you're doing. What do you have that's infinite?" Oliver: "I suppose I could have numbers, like a trillion times a trillion, but beyond that, without end. Infinite numbers." Olivia: "Here comes Aurelia. She'll spoil everything." Aurelia: "What are you playing?" Olivia: "We're not playing anything." Aurelia: "All right, Olivia, Father Pasquale told you not to be so haughty." Olivia: "Well, I have something you don't have. Oliver's just showed it to me. Infinite. I have me, and he has the numbers, and you don't have anything." Aurelia: "I think you're being mean. You'd better let me have something infinite." Oliver: "You can have all the numbers that are half my numbers." Aurelia: "No, that's not fair. Half isn't as much. It's not, is it, Olivia?" Oliver: "Half is twice as much, Aurelia. Each number has two halves. You'd have twice as many halves as I would have whole numbers. I think." Aurelia: "No, no, I don't think you're being fair. I'll take the numbers that are twice your numbers. Two times." Oliver: "You can have all of them. I don't want them any more. Which is larger, Olivia, an infinite number of pairs of shoes, or an infinite number of pairs of socks?" Olivia: "I don't have to answer that. Your grandmother says that it's vulgar to mention socks." Aurelia: "Do you have something better than infinity, Oliver? You have a peculiar look, like you're hiding something." Oliver: "I gave you what you wanted. I'll just take the infinity of infinities." Olivia: "I'll bet there is no such thing. I'll bet you Oliver is making this up." Aurelia: "Anyway, I already have the infinite numbers, you gave them to me. They can't be yours." Oliver: "I'll let you have something you'd rather have. I'll trade." Aurelia: "What will you give me?" Oliver: "The infinity of finite things. The infinite number of things that aren't infinite." Aurelia: "I like that better. It's what I wanted the whole time, the finite number of things that aren't infinite. What does Olivia have?" Olivia seemed to speak from a threshold: "I'll just have whatever is left over when you two finish." Aurelia: "What else is there? Is there anything else? I don't trust her, Oliver. She's not fair." Oliver: "I'm not sure. I think she's taking everything that doesn't exist." Olivia: "All I want are the things that have been thought but don't exist, and all that's yet unthought of." Oliver: "You have to give me an example." Aurelia: "She means like purple unicorns. She can take them, for all I care. Uh oh, here comes Whoosits. What's left for Look-who's-here?" Oliver: "We have a present for you, Orlando. The set of all empty sets." Orlando: "You three have a funny look. I'll bet there's no set of empty sets. It's something you made up." Oliver: "There is if I say there is. And if you did your lessons, you would know. We've been divvying up everything." Orlando: "What do I get?" Oliver: "I have this really odd gift, really peculiar, for finding presents that suit people. You can have the alphabet, Orlando. It will suit you to a T." Orlando: "I don't want it. It's leftover because no one wants it. It sounds like more lessons to me." Oliver: "No, you'll like it, really you will. The letters are next to each other, not like numbers." Orlando: "Numbers are next to each other." Oliver: "Not really. Between one and two, there's one and a half, and between one and a half and two, there is an infinity of other numbers,

and then an infinity between them. An infinity of infinities."
Orlando: "I don't exactly understand infinity. But letters
don't mean anything." Oliver: "But they do, they do. B is
beta, house, and G is *gamina*, camel, all the letters have a
story." "If no one has ever thought of that, Oliver, then it's
mine," Olivia said, I think cleverly escaping the infinite
which would have been as unbecoming to her as it was becoming to Oliver, who succeeded in making the others
happy with what they had, although still suspicious that he
had more than they. I never heard whether or not Orlando
knew what Olivia had been given, or had taken, for herself.
He would remain faithful to the alphabet, but never certain
that he should not envy Oliver, who carried the infinite as a
flattering accessory which matched his eyes, but just as
someone somewhere in these letters has said that Oliver's
beauty was beyond belief, the infinite put beauty beyond
probability for him, beyond calculations, so far beyond belief that it was almost faith, until Oliver gave himself leave
to love the improbable and astonishing, not-quite-to-be-
believed paper that he made with his own hands, decisive
and complete in itself, green and salty lyrics, fathomable
odes, oceanic pastorals. Olivia tormented Converse with
her experience of the yellow logarithm, but she knew in her
own way the colors of squares and parallelograms which
she said were as different from each other as frosted arctic
flowers. She said that no two triangles ever looked the same
to her, and she solved equations with her own colorful
methods, sometimes erroneously, creating a new space of
her own, a space Oliver said he might have to claim as belonging to him since it was from the infinity of wrong solutions. But also, if thought is incapable of thinking itself, then
perhaps thought itself was hers, our lynx-eyed Olivia. Aurelia treated even infinity as though it were finite, sometimes
slightly underestimating experience, until she became in-

finitely indivisible from Delenda, after which she could no longer calculate probabilities, for she had found only probable grounds for her judgments of probability, while with Delenda she saw certainty in the flesh. My stalwarts. I sound lugubrious, Octavio, because I am waiting for your mother's unthinkable funeral to begin. . . .

So much later. Days. Oh, Octavio, geraniums and orange blossoms. I awoke so thoughtless that it was like a new idea. I could smell flowers. We do not pick blossoms any more, we need the fruit, or the birds do; or we need the sight of growth. We do not kill turtles, although we use some eggs. But I smelled orange blossoms. I opened my eyes to look for something to disapprove of. I was startled to see flowers before I could give a name to them: geraniums. For a moment I thought that I was looking at a garish fabric. Kwant had proscribed flowered prints. Then I saw the flowers in deep relief against a woman's shift: orange and pink reds. She leaned over me, and then returned to dancing. I realized that I had been hearing an almost inaudible rhythm of feet dancing on the dirt floor. When had geraniums ever seemed exotic to me? Surely they were out of place? She pressed my feet and asked me if I could feel. Could I? I thought not. I answered no, but I was uncertain. It was like finding oneself not up to using one's freedom in Dublin: "I said softly to myself the word paralysis." I knew she was pressing my foot, but I could not have said what I was feeling. Pain? I didn't know. Merely a marginal awareness of her hands. She pressed my calves and thighs. I knew then who this was. She was Yolanda, who had governed us all for a day with an eggplant casserole. I had been teaching her to organize the letters in that chronological order which changes almost daily since a letter to be delivered in two years might be inserted before one mailed five years ago, but not to be delivered for three more years. I liked it when a letter caught up with another letter which had been waiting for years. The letters move backwards and forwards like a tide. I have been the librarian of time, able to see and to feel with my hands the shape of things to come ever being reshaped. But here she was, feeling the shape of my legs, while I was not feeling equal to the tasks of living. I thought, I will die more *evenly* if she will leave me alone, for a numbness seemed to have reached my heart, but I sensed enough absence of feeling to know that I would have to die soon, that the diseases of old age would be cured. Yolanda rolled me over and pounded and rubbed my back. I thought, Oh, don't bother, I'm not worth the trouble, my legs are going bald, my body is nothing but an accumulation of errors, misinformation stored as warts, freckles, wattles, and other mistakes manifest in hairs on nose and earlobes, with two toes that have been broken for at least twenty years, several knuckles swollen into weather forecasting devices by sprains that are older than she is, my will dismayed to find that it can't control my limbs, and I feeling as bad as I look, so many of my emotions inexpressible in the limited repertoire of faces I can make, one constant self-pitying expression suggesting my eager appetite for food, my dubious prostate, and my exasperation with these fatigues of the flesh. I snore even when I am awake, like something that has crawled from a grotto. I lay there, having banked my fires, determined to resist. I had nothing to live for. But also I had nothing to resist, for I was being ignored. I grew aware of the light patter of feet as Yolanda was dancing again, perhaps forgetful of me, holding geraniums and orange blossoms. I did not want to acknowledge her by moving, but I was lying in an uncomfortable position, and I don't breathe well lying on my stomach. As I lay, I heard her preparing tortillas and beans. Occasionally I heard others come in to help, women and men occasionally talking and whispering, which I interpreted as a conspiracy about me, or at least about my body, lying on a blanket in the corner, the morning after a wake. Although I learned later that it was two mornings after. I could not remember the etiquette for such an occasion. The courtesies of my grandmother, the good manners my mother had taught me, seemed so close to being right. Perhaps virtue could not be taught, perhaps the good could not be defined, but good manners could. I could hear Abelardo touching papers on my desk at the other end of the postoffice. I knew where I was all too well, lying on a blanket in a slight concavity in the dirt floor. But what were good manners now? I would have to think. Across the room, near a woodstove, at least a hundred people must have taken turns eating breakfast. I could hear them as I slept.

I awoke, my pintle swollen hard, mindful of a dream. Footsteps approached me, paused, and then returned the way they had come. I love beautiful women. Is that unfair? I rolled over and leaned on one elbow, rubbing my eyes, pulling the blanket over my embarrassment. Yolanda walked toward me, smiling. I had, I could see, fainted or fallen unconscious when they had brought Olivia's body into the postoffice for the wake. I remembered only the door opening. *There*, Death, *there* was thy sting. *There*, Grave, *there* was thy victory. I had spared myself the mixture of communal grief at her death, and individual rejoicing at being alive. Let them appreciate their lives, I did not object, but I would have grieved at their resurgent joy. I was well out of it. Yolanda must have spent the late night and early morning watching over me. She had, and the next night too. I sat up. A man brought me soup, Raoul or Valentine, or both, but I was not hungry yet. I rose like an old catastrophe, with their help, and they half carried me out of the postoffice and across to Olivia's hut that grows beside the grove of mounds. I rested there for a few days, Yolanda carrying food to me. I could lie and listen to the sounds from the postoffice. Such complicated musics, such complex noise. I had not realized that Olivia had been so close. I had thought of her hut as far away, "over there, beside the grove." I remembered Oliver saying to her, actually quoting a billboard from Belvedere Avenue, "If you lived here, you'd be home now," and Olivia replying, "I do, I am." I lay resting, and by means of sounds I rearranged and mapped the distances. I walked a little among the mounds, I picked berries, and made ink. I tried to think of uses for my corpse, but even I knew that my social conscience was merely feeling sorry for itself. I heard Abelardo's voice grow stronger day by day, until one morning he arrived to deliver a letter to me, and I sensed from the protocol that he has replaced me as postmaster since I have been unable to perform the duties. He doesn't ask me when I am returning to work. Yolanda read the letter to me. And I suppose that my hut beside the mounds seems to them the most convenient place for me to wait: a foyer, a porch, a lounge. I walked more and more, although my walking was a macabre comic dancing. I walked better when I worked, so I cut back vines and threw the trimmings on Olivia's heap. As I go about the tasks, I feel choreographed by her, for in the obvious place for a mulch pile is a mulch pile, which I toss mulch onto; where a rake might conveniently be hung, a rake is hanging. Scissors, trowels, gloves, buckets for berries, boxes of broken glass, shells, trash, junk, discarded items that might be useful in decorating a grave. The last of the painted windows was broken in a party at the postoffice, a fracas; I could hear the smash and was wishing I were there. The next morning bits of colored glass formed on Olivia's grave a pattern of colors she would have been proud to have seen:

when had violet been brought so close to yellow and to pink? It was like being mourned with the *joie de vivre* of Henri Matisse. *Vis vitae.* The grove held more activity than I had imagined, in my office all day, for Olivia had described the entertainment, but I must have thought that she was imagining, for I pictured her sitting here like patience upon a monument, although that was not her style. The grove, I discover, is a busy crossroads. It starts to seem like an annex to the postoffice. This morning I heard sounds from up there, the sonorities of breakfast. No one brought me anything to eat. Other people walked past me. I felt like a stranger, uninvited, unwelcome, uncertain. I was again unable to remember the etiquette appropriate to the occasion. What were the rules for a hungry man? Had I ever learned them? Should I wait until I was asked? I had a basket of inkberries (*ilex glabra*, lest the universal name be forgotten) I could take with me as an offering. And they could gather all the inkberries they needed in a few minutes. I picked up my basket of inkberries. I hadn't learned a procedure for arriving hungry and almost empty-handed and uninvited to a meal that seemed to have been in progress for several days, judging by the clatter I had been hearing. Yet when, without having decided anything, I found that I had arrived, abashed and doubtful of my welcome, at precisely the moment another man arrived, but he young, strong, "socially useful," I felt as I glanced at him that one of us was one too many. I halted as though I had heard a command, and then turned about-face to seek refuge in myself. I stood between me and them. Or was that bad grammar? Did I stand *among* me and them? I pitched. My body pivoted. I and they were not opposites. I was already in the middle. I would have to reach them, to pitch myself forward to them, and to give myself momentum I let myself fall forward as I yawed, expecting to slump into a heap but Yolanda caught me by the hand and forearm, someone else had my other hand and elbow—who? oh, Ruth, with Corinthio, that other man arriving as I arrived, helping her, and as gracefully as a step in the old dance they seated me, they said they had been saving a place for me, breakfast seemed to be becoming lunch, I ate, and after half a bowl of Maria's bean soup, which was more than I had hoped for, I was beginning to hope for so much more. Not for more food. For something else. I was not sure what. I had feared, surreptitiously, that I was so old that I would be death itself to these people; but I can see now, at least today, that I am so *unnecessary* that I represent the freedom of their lives, their freedom from necessity. I asked Abelardo if he would manage the postoffice to allow me to finish this letter. I realized, if not immediately, then later, sitting in this corner writing, that the atmosphere in the postoffice has changed, that it had changed perhaps long before Olivia's death, without my defining the change. I had not noticed that so much activity had grown up around me as I distributed the letters or sat to write to you, with help from Yolanda, Ruth, Ramona, and the others. The work might have gone more quickly if Yolanda (in truth sometimes no better than she ought to be) would have left me alone, for she picks over me and has been picking over me for months, grooming me as though she were looking for something. Or preparing me. My eyebrows looked like an ox yoke, but she trimmed and plucked among them. She was excited when, several pages ago, and how long ago I have forgotten how to figure out, she read the quotation from *Beowulf* that Oliver spoke, and she has encouraged me to quote more in my rusty Old English in my rusty Old Voice; I sound to myself like something left over from a war, emerging from a barrow. I quoted the Latin line Chaucer uses, "mulier est hominis confusio," and then tried to explain to her, although I couldn't explain to myself, why I had quoted it. So I confused myself with the "melancholy pleasures" of my own irony, but I hope for the last time. I did not translate, "woman is the ruin of man," I apologized, and explained that I had made a bad joke. Yolanda returned me to *Beowulf* and to seeing myself seated on the lawn at Johns Hopkins where I first read *Beowulf,* and I wished that my old teachers could be there to hear me using the poem. Yolanda listened raptly to my recitation of such as I could remember. I would have been like Ion, would have translated and explicated, after emerging from the rapture of quotation, but Yolanda doesn't want to hear my translation. (I will teach her the themes of the poem by the way I live, but that will be another story.) Yolanda saw her name here and says to say Hello. The postoffice was always active. In the old days, the rickety loft would be shaking with Orlando up there taking dictation, but now some activity is always going on. With the noise fairly constant, I find that I can concentrate better than I could before, when sounds were intermittent, and I was listening for something.

Octavio, now I am writing on another day. Abelardo will tell me its name. Everyone is writing you a letter. I seem to be writing you a book, and you will wonder, when you read this — for I refuse to imagine you not reading it, I can't imagine you not reading it, I won't imagine the infinite unthinkable ways of not reading my finite and alphabetical book — I think of you as fathers and grandfathers have thought of children who have gone off to be educated and who will return as in a *Bildungsroman* knowing who knows what? Perhaps knowing that the object of their quest had been underfoot at home the whole time. You will wonder how this book which you hold in your hands has come to exist. Writing to you has been a method of thinking about what I have to say that is worth writing. But I am not too strict on myself, and I write some of it whether it seems worth while or not. I never enjoyed photographs unless they were of family or friends. This book has come to exist or is coming to exist because friends bring me ink, or berries and galls for ink, and sheets of paper they have made, completely full of self and entirely unselfconscious, gifts which are partly to feed my fires, because the longer this letter gets the more amused they are, and somehow my writing keeps this party going. But quiet here now. Pens scratching. The accidental expressionism of ink splots. Everyone writes you a letter, with some giggling and some raising of eyebrows and raising of eyes. Sometimes I feel that we are playing a children's party game, but even with the farsighted memory of old age I can't remember any game quite like this one. Everyone intensely quiet now, concentrating on you, but borrowing and lending words in the flotsam and jetsam language we are developing, "lingua franca et jocundissima." While I have been writing to you, my English-American has been becoming a literary language. Who would have thought that I would be learning so many new words that I don't know how to spell? Tears form in my eyes nowadays for no reason, unless seventy-odd years be reason enough, and exhausted glands and tired ducts. I begin to fear that I shall outlive myself. I doubt now that my writing keeps this party going. I see now that I am not the host, as I was wont to be, that I am not responsible, and need not thank anyone for coming, and they need not thank me: oh the obsolete forms of our old arrogance, and the assumptions which seemed to be part of the foundation of our lives, but which are easily removed without weakening the structure. And if not strengthening it, by their removal, then clarifying it. The center of the party moves from person to person. I was happiest as a child among children at a party. The four of them were usually having a party, although I didn't know enough to see it as such at the time, to think of it in those terms. I could wish now for a history of parties such as Oliver would have compiled. I learned so much listening to their lessons with Converse, whose teaching had a perversity I thought was useful. Facts come back to me that I know I never learned from governesses or in school, facts I must have learned by eavesdropping on their lesson about a party the Earl of Salisbury (we were connected to him, our family, through the Salzburg branch) gave (threw?) for James I of England and Christian IV of Denmark, where a guest representing the Queen of Sheba dropped a basket of wine, cakes, and jelly into Christian's lap, knocking him onto the floor, whence he was carried, transported, off to bed, staining the bed with jelly. How else would I know Sir John Harington's description of the women dressed as Faith, Hope, and Charity, Hope too drunk to deliver her speech, Charity bowing awkwardly and then returning to Faith and Hope who were vomiting on the floor? Victory, I seem to remember, had to be led away to the foyer, where she passed out. Oliver liked Harington because, he said, he translated Ariosto, invented the flush toilet, which Oliver called the first translation machine, and wrote while in prison, translating the imposed sufferings of prison into the self-imposed transcending agonies of art. Oliver enraptured us with facts, but such isolated facts that the facts and the isolation seem as obsolete as that arch world is obsolete, so flawed and fragmented, its luminous universals quite extinguished by its filth. When he referred to Amandine Aurore Lucie Dupin, Olivia was ecstatic, but none of us knew that he was referring to George Sand. Fortunately he outlived archness and irony, his jack-a-dandy tone; and he never meant to leave the rest of us behind, he always helped us to catch up with him. I think our party is an improvement over Harington's, although his does prove that if you get history right, burlesque and folly can take care of themselves. I was a man who did too little because I thought that I could do nothing right until I had enough information. I waited too long too often, as Olivia said, "more acted upon than a stage." I do not know how much information would have been enough. Part of me was too proud for the ordinary life I longed for. I was an appreciative observer, however, looking on, oh so *penseroso*, with interest. I saw what Kwant did with power, and I couldn't devise an alternative (since I didn't want power like that) except powerlessness. I tried to work power into equations with love and truth and freedom, but I never proved my theorems satisfactorily to myself. Yet each disproof did precipitate another theorem, another attempted proof; I did not give up. I eavesdropped on children at play as they learned their lessons or played their games, because I thought that they might be learning something, or that they might know something, that I should know. I thought that I might write a critical history of childhood, but now I see that by childhood I meant *party*, that a critical history of parties is what I should have written, inspired as I was once when walking down an unfamiliar street in Baltimore along a quite dowdy block of houses with disheartening facades, I looked into the windows of a townhouse where I saw a room completely prepared for a party, I could see a cut-glass punchbowl, candles lighted on the mantelpiece, and a man and woman, surely the host and hostess, apparently testing the punch in the calm before the first guests arrived. And although I did not know them, I was embarrassed, for me and for them, that I had not been invited, and I hurried past the window lest these people I was not acquainted with see me and wonder, and perhaps regret, in their perplexities, why they had not invited me to their party. I will tell you another day about Aurelia, who spends most of her time under the mulberry tree at Umberland, and about her notebooks and letters. She has sent me some frayed computer printouts from a database service she had used at Johns Hopkins when she toyed with the possibility of using computers to work out the connections among branches of learning. From among her cross-references she sent me two congenial, albeit droll and ancient, references:

PARTIES AND CULTURAL VALUES: A KIBBUTZ EXAMPLE, PSYCHIATRY, WASHINGTON, D.C. 1970, NOV. VOL. 33 (4) 482-493. ISRAEL INTERPERSONAL-INTERACTION CULTURE-ANTHROPOLOGICAL VALUES RECREATION. ANALYZES THE SOCIAL GATHERING KNOWN AS A PARTY AS IT OCCURS IN THE COLLECTIVE SOCIETY OF A KIBBUTZ. THE KIBBUTZ IS, OF NECESSITY, GROUP-ORIENTED HOLDING THE OVERRIDING VALUE OF GROUP EXPERIENCE AS A BASIC TENET, OF ALMOST MYSTIC INTENSITY. SELF-CONTROL AND CONFORMITY ARE BASIC TO THE MAINTAINING OF THE CULTURAL STRUCTURE. SOCIAL GET-TOGETHERS ON AN INFORMAL LEVEL ARE COMPOSED OF PERSONS OF ABOUT THE SAME AGE, WITH CHAIRS ARRANGED IN A CIRCLE, AND CONVERSATIONS OF A GROUP, RATHER THAN PERSONAL, NATURE. THIS IS NOT THE FEAR OF REJECTION OR EXTRUSION KNOWN TO COCKTAIL PARTY ATTENDANTS IN THE UNITED STATES, BUT THERE IS JOKING, SEXUAL HUMOR, AND GROUP REGULATION OF BEHAVIOR LIMITS. THE PARTY IS THUS SEEN AS A SOCIAL MICROCOSM REFLECTING CULTURAL VALUES AND NORMS OF THE SOCIETY AS A WHOLE.

I thought that in spite of the fact that the language sounded to my ears like chalk scraping against a blackboard, and felt to my lips like eating cardboard, that I could recognize some kinship with that party, except that our party seems less to reflect the society than *to be* the society, and is more macrocosm than microcosm. And is *extrusion* the opposite of *intrusion*? The longer I looked at that abstract the less I understood it. The other reference Aurelia sent is in a similar language. My old business letters may have been soliciting and seductive, and they were, but this language sounds as though it lost some profundity in being translated from the humane to the inhumane Humanities.

WILLIAMS, A.F. PSYCHOLOGICAL NEEDS AND SOCIAL DRINKING AMONG COLLEGE STUDENTS, QUARTERLY JOURNAL OF STUDIES ON ALCOHOL. 68, 29, (2-A), 355-363. NEEDS COLLEGE-STUDENTS PERSONALITY ALCOHOL-DRINKING-PATTERNS SOCIAL-BEHAVIOR. 91 COLLEGE-MALES WERE ADMINISTERED THE PARK PROBLEM-DRINKING SCALE AND THE HEILBRIEN NEED SCALES BEFORE A COCKTAIL PARTY, AFTER DRINKING 4 OZ. OF LIQUOR, AND AT THE END OF THE PARTY (AFTER DRINKING AN AVERAGE OF 11 OZ. OF LIQUOR). INHIBITION GENERALLY VANISHED FROM THE SELF-DESCRIPTIONS OF DRINKING, SUBJECTS TENDED TO DESCRIBE THEMSELVES IN TERMS OF ACTIVITY RATHER THAN THOUGHT, AND THEY BECAME INCREASINGLY SELF-CENTERED.

I would call our party collegiate, but I don't think we have that much to drink, and few are unfortunate enough to become self-centered. I suppose that a computer might look among its microdots and retrieve the *Symposium* of Plato, the *locus classicus* of parties, where Socrates teaches Alcibiades that love is a dialectical education, or at least that loving Socrates is; and teaches us all that tragedy and comedy are convivial. Aurelia has so many books entitled *Symposium*; indeed, I have been borrowing concepts from one of them, a symposium on developmental biology, with a lovely essay on the development of the chicken's heart: "Form and Function in the Embryonic Heart." It helps me to imagine the morphology of our party. I suppose that a computer might also be able to return to me Dante's *Convivio*, so pleasant to remember, but not illuminating our particular party, which as far as I can see can be neither created nor destroyed, for the party expands and contracts, but is never less than a party. I see now what was wrong with the parties I knew before, for the perfect party would never end, would never even threaten to end. Our party feeds on the emotions and thoughts it produces, and produces more of them, increasing the available energy. Our party is not a celebration, unless it celebrates its continuance, omnivorously gobbling up birthdays, feasts, anniversaries, and even the days of macabre memory, the death days we commemorate in spite of ourselves, as when one remembers gazing upon a dead infant, and then takes another sip of wine. When I was young we were late for parties, but consistently late. Orlando would quote Thomas Young, "Procrastination is the thief of time," and Oliver would quote Oscar Wilde, "Punctuality is the thief of time." We were not saving time by being late. I can see that we were reluctant to be present, something dreadful floated in the atmosphere, and horror dimpled the surface of each dinner party, a vanity or emptiness, or at least pointlessness. We were not nihilists, fearful of the nothing, because certainly *something* existed, but we sensed that others had made it, and we were helping to make it, worse than nothing: next to nothing. We were not tough, but we were hardened to horror in order to persuade others that we were happy, lest we feel guilt for our unhappiness. But we were merely hardened, not happy, and lights glossed over our countenances. But now I cannot be late, for the party is always going on, and always about to begin again, and the Indians and Creoles, so used to dragging their feet as we did when Kwant was master, are happy to attend with punctilio a party which they cannot be late for, where everyone dances, for none of us drags our feet as we did when Kwant was counting the minutes and measuring the days, and no one is called tarheel. We find ourselves busy and impeccable guests, not straining ourselves to any limits. Something within me always wanted to get up and dance, so I do. On good days. Delenda took one look at me, after Aurelia, our coastguard, brought him to Utterly, and he saw that my peace was unpeace, that I had made the negatives but had not printed the positives, or that I had never caught fire. Delenda, on no authority, I suppose, but like a child reasonably assigning roles in a game, perhaps seeing my smile which was too gentle, too propitiating, the winning smile of a losing man who hoped that wrongs would set themselves right without indecorous disturbances, much less violence, looked at me and appointed me postmaster. Yolanda is asleep across my feet. I have a premonition of death from my legs, for the circulation slows, they grow numb so easily. I must wake Yolanda, and then get her to wake up my feet, which are also asleep. Food is ready, I can smell corn and beans. Which meal this is depends upon who is eating it: one person's breakfast is another person's supper. I will eat and then return to my hut. I've seen the party, I've had several next-to-the-last dances. Now I must make an effort to stand up. I cannot do otherwise, can I?

Good morning, Octavio. A new day. I spent the night dreaming that I was getting away with murder. Murders. I have lost track of days again, but I suspect my motives in doing so. Delenda. He never mentioned that I was Aurelia's father. Certainly he didn't consult me as her father. We never huddled in the brotherhood of men whose affinity as men was greater than their loyalty to the women they were discussing, shrugging their shoulders in manly exasperation and then in manly resignation. He proposed no ceremonies or rituals that I was aware of, he simply moved in. He appointed me the postmaster as though I had spent my life preparing for the job. I was so accustomed to interpreting events as a punishment—as Olivia said, Kwant didn't summon his grandchildren, he subpoenaed them—or to interpreting them as a reward, that I was trying to connect my appointment with my guilt or merit. But Delenda was not so indirect. He was subtle but explicit. We were all excited and afraid. I was glad to have some occupation, so I converted Renunciación into a postoffice, which didn't take much doing. Orlando arranged himself as scribe in the choir loft. He could never keep his fly closed. We never tired of saying, "Where late the sweet birds sang," for silly reasons, for reasons that accreted to the line so that although we repeated it, we never said the same line twice, "Bare ruin'd choirs, where late the sweet birds sang." And Oliver, looking at some of his paper from which he had erased old verses by dipping them in barrels of rainwater, lamented, "bare ruin'd quires," but he was pleased with the effect of faded watercolors. I fear little of my rambling will mean anything to you, Octavio, unless you appreciate that it has meaning for me. I laugh now as I write the line, our old joke, which children and the Creoles, who could scarcely have known Shakespeare, quoted with me. Sometimes I see myself sitting on bubbles of accumulated silliness. And especially now, neither host nor caterer at this rudderless party. The party has become my clock, my only means of measuring the movements of my life. It consumes my interest. Someone is always here to keep it moving, although sometimes it diminishes to a few unlikely embers, two drunken men talking through the night, warming our "unextinguished hearth." We always have someone who doesn't want the party to end so early, for who indeed wants a successful party to end (and who wants to admit that a failing party could not be revived?); and who is it anyway, which Caesar or Kaiser or Tsar, who declared that a party must end? On what authority? We don't want the party to end, so it doesn't. Even now. As I sit writing, several people are asleep. Siesta. But my pen scratching away as I write is the lullaby accompanying their somnolent dance. What you are holding in your hands perplexes me, if it is a book. For whom? Why? I am not sure that I remember. I pause. They awaken. Time for my siesta in the hut.

I am back now the next day, Octavio. I napped in my hut, then returned to the postoffice in time for fish which Juan brought, and bananas, and sugar cane to chew. I thought that this time everyone might have gone home, that the party was indeed over, but Yolanda and a dozen others were quietly cooking, and humming, and I begin to suspect that there is no party, or that this is simply the way we live now, everyday life in modern Primavera. Yolanda says Hello. She says that she has loved me all her life, and that if I didn't live in a hut beside the burial mounds she would marry me. She says, "You don't like me now, but I will grow on you." I do like her now, and she does grow on me. She also keeps me quoting *Beowulf* when her brother is around. I sit listening to her, looking about for objects to prop me up, and trying to stifle some old vanity in me that wants to think she is not teasing. I still desire to be desired. I never saw anything much more beautiful than the sight of desire in a woman's eyes. Ginevra used to say, "Desire makes a man handsome." I wonder if that is true. Hasn't it also made men ugly? So many uncertainties if I go to generalize. I am sure of little except that I am a particular old fool with old imaginings, obsolete desires, antiquated needs; I have seen my day, and should be keeping out of sight, although I don't really believe that. My problem is that everytime I imagine a woman's face, and a moment brimming with responsibility, when I look closely I see Ginevra's features in that face, and my heart splits open in my chest along its Kamasutra seams. I think, when Yolanda falls asleep across my feet or against my legs, that she has indeed grown on me, a concrete imagining. She was unhappy because her brother behaved selfishly and hit someone when he was drunk, so that he might not have been welcome in our eyes for three or four days. We would have been glad to see him then, but he didn't return for a week. He had been fishing off the farthest point beyond Tornata, and waited there several days before he found the courage to do something that would be useful to the party, to make a bench out of driftwood he found there. He returned lean as a carpenter and was quite welcome. This book continues to grow; I'm not sure what to make of it. We did not dance enough, Ginevra and I, I see that now. What could be more urgent than listening to this music? I don't want to remember what seemed so important to us. I forget the grounds of my reluctance to dance on Primavera. We did too little for fear of doing something wrong, or improper. Sometimes I think that in those books of etiquette, and in the implications of the furniture and rugs, and the distance between the parents' bedroom and the child's bedroom, that the only good child was a deadened child. Why as a child was I expected to keep so silent? What did I know that I wasn't supposed to say? Shouldn't being good be good for you? I think that I can understand now that we privileged children were to be silent because we were to be given more than we deserved, more than we needed, and with our silence we paid a price for our inequitable share, not telling anyone, not letting anyone on to glee, delight, or enthusiasm, silent there in our entresol while the noisy poor dirtied themselves behind a cellar door. One might have walked from rug to rug through the house, as from island to island, without making a sound. I was brought up as though the world were an heiress I was going to marry, but I must keep quiet about it, must not noise it abroad, while the poor were being mismatched in overpriced weddings to an impoverished existence. In Baltimore, I mistook the noise of the poor, in my sentimentality, for music, instead of hearing it as their protest against their arranged marriage to inequity. Here, with this music, I am witness to a wedding that matches love with equal love. I am in the midst of the espoused action, and when I feel overwhelmed, I return to my little house to sleep. Which I will do now, sleep beside Olivia's theater of memory, her orchard of the dead.

Morning. I tell myself, Octavio, that I don't have to deserve this. I am using the daily writing of this letter as an excuse to come up here to the postoffice now, to see what is going on while I add a few lines. Something always is going on. No one has spoken about it, at least to me, but we do seem to keep a sentinel of sorts posted in the postoffice. Once I would have thought myself ill-mannered to fall asleep at a party, and I have suffered from the well-preserved memory of such a *faux pas* for fifty years. Now I am not embarrassed to wake up and to find that hours have passed. The texture of time is different from what it was in the old days, even though we were, at Utterly, leisurely, even running the business of money and stamps in Baltimore at our own pace — at a pace, Kwant once complained, that would not keep pace with inflation. But time, even at our most casual, with dinner sometimes as late as eleven (and one unforgettable night, Delphine surpassing herself, at one-thirty, with Kwant quite drunk, forgetting that he hadn't eaten, and I on the veranda with Oliver, Aurelia, Olivia, and Orlando in an evening and night of self-surpassings), time was scheduled in spatial units which we could locate ahead of us. We knew rather closely where we would be at a certain hour, and where we were supposed to be, and we automatically made allowances, and usually felt truant. Now time seems an altogether different medium, as uncountable as hours spent in love-making. I thought of time because when I woke up just now this man, Valentine, was singing. He sings too well to put in an appearance more than once a day, and when he turns up, he is always bearing something for us to eat, almost too many gifts. His singing forms a peculiar island of time in the larger time of the party. Whatever the raw noise when he enters, a buzzing confusion usually, as he begins to sing the buzzing confusion blooms into individual responses to his melody, Valentine seeming to set the pace, yet responding to the responses he evokes, giving back something we have given him, and giving something more, his voice sounding always grateful but never self-congratulatory. His song, or at least his part in the song, expands and contracts, sometimes increasing to join another part in a new neighborhood of sounds, in a ventriloquism which makes each of us feel that we are singing robustly, for even I the listener become quite choral and join in with what is left of a voice (I find my seventies in many ways easier than my sixties), and sometimes decreasing as our newly strengthened voices fill the space as full of sound as an egg when the embryonic heart begins to beat *allegro.* Then his voice separates and finds its own direction, it makes a place for itself, but friendly other apprenticed voices that know the way—Yolanda, Raoul, Eloisa, Francesca, Davido, and Abelardo—follow his voice to that place and enter, and enlarge it, as they accelerate together, so that where time had once been divided into equal and indifferent units, oh so metronomic, as though fifteen minutes of dawn were equivalent to fifteen minutes of sunset, and one read the sun as one might read a meter, now time (in the song we sing at our different paces, the pace we learn from the pacemaker for whom we seem to set the pace) feels like a victory over itself as the song, *our* song, becomes a place of asylum, protecting in dance those who have entered too late to catch a place for their voices in the song, but who move freely within its ministering rhythms, here in our government-house sonata.

Good morning. I have missed a few days, Octavio, writing letters to friends. Yolanda says that I write too much about writing letters. She says Hello. She says that I should write about her, sitting here on her good behavior hoping for a letter, meanwhile enjoying herself with me. I am a pretty good fellow at a party, Octavio. Old men and parties are not what they were when I was a boy, when an old man might have sat rather too close to the fire for a few minutes, and have been uncomfortable, but otherwise have had a splendid time. Yolanda is as silly as I suppose I am, although who am I to judge? Two silly buckets on the deck. To be vain and coy at my age only adde to the romantic comedy that is being enacted about me. I feel well enough to think about dying, and Yolanda has agreed to arrange me down among the mounds, near Olivia, in the deathplace, one among the other ripening silences. What if this life were not, as those four debilitated themselves by thinking when they were adolescents, a dream, but a poem, perhaps a ballad, cumulative, and with repetitions, but with incremental repetitions? And if I were its critic and interpreter? Would that explain anything? I doubt it. Don't a day, and music, *thicken* as they go on? Even what Oliver called our eucalypso music? Or am I merely looking for another controlling metaphor, a consoling image, an idea to make me comfortable with the the painful fact that I am glad to be alive in this joyous comedy when so many I have loved are dead? I could trace the contribution of Ginevra's death to my renovated happiness. If none of them had died, I would not be where I am now, and I am happy here. I do not know what to do except to build toward the happiness of others. But I remain the reluctant heir, grudgingly enriched by the pain and sorrow of others for whom I feel responsible. That may be the proprietary feeling of an old man. I sometimes find myself missing possessions and ownership. But I suppose I was no more responsible for the lives and deaths of the others than I am responsible for the success of this party. Or for the failure of it when it fails. Although even a failed party is a party, and we continue. I am not guilty of the ironies and condescensions of my life. In her own country, Yolanda would have been a princess. In my country, she would have been a maid. I can't see virtue in either one. Nor can I forget the altered distances entirely, I can't forget the assumptions of my role as heir apparent of the island, and can't shed the feeling that I am doing people a favor by being among them. So much to be purged. And Yolanda has her own prior distances which she must overcome. For the truth is, as I am learning, and failed to learn when I studied some anthropology, the Indians are terrible snobs, with all the distances between people prescribed in advance, and no one free to make an original move. I feel their condescension, I see them looking upon me as a parvenu, although they try to hide some of these thoughts. They do lack the strength of numbers, since they are from broken tribes, and they see that they must soften the edges of their sharp distinctions. Some of them even arrived alone, and as Olivia asked, What were they doing, headed due east in a canoe? Aurelia remembered explanations such as puberty rites, and initiations, ostracisms, excommunications. Such an abysmal word, so forlorn, *excommunication.* Were *they* the refuse of those shores? We did not ask questions. The Indians did not, I would say, in the early days, pull their oar at a party. Perhaps Yolanda will explain more of this to you someday. Yes, you, Yolanda, for I know how you will look up at me when I read these words aloud, or how you will touch me on the back if you lean over my shoulder to read what I am writing. I have made arrangements for my funeral, Octavio. I notice that I am tempted to tell people how to mourn and how not to mourn for me, but I have thought of reasons to resist the temptation. Mourning, by some route of memory or of logic, brings me in my memorial logic to Olivia, who once said that she saw better at night without the lights on because otherwise how could she see the darkness? She had a knack for electricity and could make repairs in what she called "the electric" when the rest of us were bewildered. She would help Kwant's garrison of electrician-soldiers with their problematic power-plant, and then walk with her fingers extended toward the maids, saying "bioelectricity, come get your bioelectricity," and the maids would dutifully scream and scatter, giggle and run offstage. Olivia spent her life, she told me, learning how to govern herself by the movements of light. I can see her as I saw her when I came up over the hill to investigate the fire at Utterly. I saw her as she lifted you out of the arms of that triptych Aurelia-Orlando-Oliver, as you, in your black rubber wetsuit, awakened to your task of enlivening with your frisky puppyhood. You were that way when we got you. I remember Olivia later proudly saying, "When you have children, that's all you have," and she laughing that year when she chased after you as you ran out of the grove into what she and I saw with common eyes (in what we also saw was a moment of cooperative attention), as a parallelogram of light across which jumped parabolas of the aboriginal light which tossed and turned in the leaves.

Olati 5th

Dear Octavio, I have been out helping to plant some seedlings, the *leucaena leucocephalia*, a story in itself, a useful tree, for now we use it for paper, firewood, building materials, and we eat the young leaves and the seeds, or grind the dried seeds into flour, or "coffee," and dyes for paper such as I am writing on now. A remarkable tree which seems to evoke our inventiveness. My last clear memory of Oliver shows him standing on tip-toe, plucking the new leaves from a tree, saying to the children, "Look up. 'Thy life's a miracle.' See the available leaves." I think sometimes that his death killed Olivia, for she said that only Oliver had understood her tone, the tone which comprised but also compromised her meaning. I can see her, not daring to look at him for encouragement, but trusting him to help her if she got into trouble as she told us that we didn't know what classical statues had looked like with their painted colors and their moustaches. Moustaches, we exclaimed, knowing how to play our parts. Yes, moustaches, Olivia replied, perhaps too busy keeping her balance to hear the complicity in our tone, for it would have thrown her off balance. "Haven't you heard about the perfect room, practically a vacuum chamber, discovered at Herculaneum? *Years* ago. The statues were painted and had moustaches woven of human hair affixed to them. Statues of women had merkins." She added that the archeologists excavating the room had been buried in a later surprising volcanic eruption, so that the evidence had been lost. Olivia studied the varieties of our doubt as they were visible through the varieties of our collusion, and seemed satisfied with the results. She collected, I wonder if I have told you this, stories about children who had inherited estates while still *in utero*, rich but posthumous kids, as she described them. Her museum of humankind differed from mine. None of my thoughts had ever included *merkin.*

While I have been resting, Yolanda has massaged my hands, and as she rubbed them, I could feel tangible regret and guilt in them, not for anyone I had hurt with my hands, or touched illicitly, as I might have needed to put my hand on the shoulder of someone who didn't need my hand on the shoulder, but regret for those I should have touched because they needed me, or guilt over those whom I desired to touch, yet had not. I felt the restraints and intimidations in my aged hands, and much of the arthritis seemed the memory of unanswered questions of who and when and how and where to touch, and Yolanda took away with her forgiving fingers the stiffness from my hands which have been, without my knowing it, held in angered custody. She takes off manacles. Even now my hands hesitate, for I had not meant to write so much about myself in this letter. I was preparing for my death, however, not for what is happening, or for problems of skin and flesh and touch. Yolanda has pursued me with so many questions of who I am reminded of when I look at her that finally I have realized that she reminds me of no one, and I suspect that she has made her point. This morning I wondered, who is she to herself? From her point of view? Did I want to know? I felt vertigo. I think of the story of an old man and a young woman, of January and May, in Chaucer. But Yolanda has lived by another calendar, and the calendar we use has eighteen months, not twelve, and for Chaucer the world began in March. Should I be explaining any of this to her? I could lecture on the topic of springtime. I wonder, what rights have I in relation to her? I look at the intervals between us, man and woman, old and young, European and Indian, so many totems and taboos prescribing distances between us (among all of us), and prescribing them long long before we ever met. What is our kinship? What are our affinities? We are human, surely we are entitled to huddle together in any darkness, or even any light, for such honest comfort as flesh can yield to flesh. This is a lifeboat, not only an island. I have looked upon Yolanda as upon a daughter, which told me how far to stay away from her, how close to come — so fa-

therly, so bantering, tolerant, and proud. But she is not my
daughter. I think of her as my sister and with the word arrive
the rules of kinship and I think of looking around for a suitable husband for her. Abelardo is too young. I am too old.
But she is not my sister, although I have let myself imagine
some Dickensian twists of plot that could reveal us as sib-
lings, reconciled after loss and danger, to dwell forever in
exciting but chaste proximity. And then I try avuncular. So
near and yet so far, the uncle and the niece, too many cross
purposes. Her childhood language differs so from mine that
she does not count as family precisely what I would count. I
heard me describe myself as a bachelor, but I am a wid-
ower, not a bachelor. And I heard me make a mistake about
my age, although in truth I am not certain what year this
would be, or precisely how old I am. Yolanda examined
closely that Ginevra was my cousin and that we grew up
speaking English, the first in our family to do so, but I with
a tutor sometimes, she with a governess-duenna, so that
living at the far ends of the same island we developed different accents and vocabularies, but not very different. I look
at Yolanda now as once I looked at the geranium flowers,
trying to see them on their own terms as they displayed
themselves, exotic, not as I had seen them in flowerboxes
on Mulberry Street in Baltimore behind the Enoch Pratt
Library, or even in the garden at Utterly. I saw African origins in them in spite of horticultural sophistications. Geraniums were strange again. As is Yolanda. I don't want to be
linked to her with links that existed before we did. We have
inherited no relationships to each other and no rights in
each other. She frightens me, not as an Indian, although
that is scary, but as a variable to which I don't know how
to assign a value. I don't always understand what we are
saying when we speak the language which has evolved so
quickly, too quickly for me to have learned how to write
colloquially. I can't bring myself to write down what she

says as though she spoke a dialect. I am uncertain of my distances in this neology, wary of the word that might misrepresent my meaning. I won't write down the words that I suppose are Mayan: who knows what meanings are lost in transliteration? I suppose that Delphine's seashells and driftwood and stones with significant veins in them were revelations of meaning that were to be read in some analogy to reading words. I think that I can see their resemblance to thoughts. I don't want to be dessicated, starving on attenuated abstractions when I could feast on fervent immediacies. I am not superannuated. But how shall I read a woman like Yolanda?

The next day. I have never been so free before, so unclassified. Ginevra was my beloved cousin who was preserved a mystery from me in our childhoods (and from herself: her grandmother, recreating her mother's girlhood, made Ginevra take baths with her petticoat on). Our family became families to keep us just far enough apart. They created enough discontinuity between us so that we had to invent our own continuum by thinking of little else but each other. Whatever family and circumstance decided for us, language finally decided what we wanted to do. For although I was frequently forgetting her, when we met as young adults in Baltimore, away from the complete family, we knew that we were out of place in the same place, and that we spoke the same language. We knew from our words much of what was going to happen because it was going to happen in those words. We even knew words for each other that no one else knew. The morning of my wedding, the memory may not be irrelevant to the current events of the island, my mother returned from Tornata where she had given her veil to Ginevra, the veil she had worn at her wedding. She said to me, "She is the picture of me the day I married your father." But Yolanda looks like no one I know. She has exhausted my repertoire of resemblances. I am an old man, long ago taken out of the action. Her face, with high cheek bones and clairvoyant eyes, is a theater in which I see enacted the discoveries and reversals of character. I seem now to myself not so much old as impressively archaic. Well, I do continue. But she is no more aboriginal than I, no more celestial. She has her feet on the ground, as when she danced with the geraniums. Yolanda says that being old is an achievement. Is it good for her to think so of my good? Am I to love someone more than I love myself, just when I was getting to like it? *Senex amans, senex amans, senex amans.*

Olati 7th: Yolanda must marry someone who speaks a language different from hers. *Exolinguistic,* she says, a word from my language I don't remember hearing. Her family learned it from their anthropologist, in the old days. Yolanda is descended from an anaconda which gave her tribe its gift of speech. They were born from its mouth. I am fascinated by these stories, but I am old, I owe myself some discretion. Isn't it enough that I must squat to shit among bushes of corn, demurely holding a leaf before my face? And must piss where I think urea will be useful? Sometimes I walk to Kwant's botanic garden to fertilize the trees so that they will continue sprawling beyond his categories, thus I try to be socially useful because I remember Aurelia saying that in the emergency ward they didn't revive heart-attack victims who were not likely to be socially useful. I think that I will go hurry now to visit Aurelia who so rarely visits us. Yesterday I was seeing no obstacles. Today my unaccountable and immeasurable anger seems obstacle enough.

Olati 8th: The customs of Yolanda's people. I disapprove of them, these rituals which tell people what the intervals between them must be. I thought that the party had done away with all that. Aurelia has had much to say about all this. Should I tell Yolanda how myths and rituals have enslaved people? Shall I give her the references Aurelia has given to me, Claude Lévi-Strauss, *Mythologique*, Volume II. I found the volume in the Infirmary and the page number she had given me, and her underlinings and marginal comments. I despise these rituals and totems because they tell me, so abstractly and prior to any awareness of me, how near and how far I must be from others. I am too old to be told where I must stand. I am curious, of course, and pained, because Yolanda has a "right" to her rituals, and like Aurelia, I have no body of beliefs to replace them with, nothing that could offer comparable satisfaction, I suppose. But the rituals don't satisfy *me*, they distort my experience, and the attitude of the Indians now shows itself for what it is, conventional, even bourgeois, when I thought that they were somehow wild. Why should she not be allowed to marry a man who speaks her language? Yolanda said that *bourgeois* means "have a nice trip," which made me doubt for a moment that she understood any language, but then the interpretation might even be profound. I don't know, I would have to be profound myself to judge, and I fear that I am losing my judgment. I no longer know what Yolanda knows, or how she knows it, or what I think of it. In her stories a butterfly is no different from a bird, but she knows all the differences. I suspect her of using discussion of rituals to draw near to me, in violation of tribal distances I am certain, I can judge that much from the attitude of her brother. She explained to me about Raoul's people, and of course I have a heart, of course I responded. They were required by their rules of kinship to marry only someone with a different last name. Somehow, when the Mexican government required them to give their names in the Spanish style, almost everyone was suddenly named Gomez, so that almost no one could marry anyone else in the tribe, and since they were endogomous as well as endolinguistic they could not marry outside the tribe. Some of the men took off for Mexico City to become flower sellers. Raoul set off in the canoe to escape the conflict, and his sputtering outboard motor brought him to Primavera. Only to the degree that experiences here erase the myths does he become free to approach marriage with Louisa. Of course I care, I sympathize. I have told Yolanda my thoughts, perhaps Aurelia's thoughts, about myth as a story which assumes a continuum, a spiritual continuum which spirits can enter and exit from, or metamorphose into and out of, either a transcendental continuum which is outside and above the actual, and deprives it of its tang and bite, and its actual discontinuities. Or, an alternative, an immanent continuum that falsifies the actual by papering over the gaps and contradictions and lapses, the holes in experience. And which extends the continuum into the infra-red and ultra-violet, beyond visible experience, with stories about that extended continuum. The myths, which always seem to me to be about an increase of unavailability, at least when the Indians tell them, nevertheless seem to teach complacency. I might as well be in Baltimore. We had told the stories of our own lives as though there had not been, and were not then, live alternatives. I was more free than I liked to admit. I have told Yolanda that I see rituals as acts by which to gain something available only from one continuum or the other, and that I don't believe that those continuums exist, or should be thought to exist. Damn sky-hooks and damn pie-in-the-sky. Two people looking at a painting by Tiepolo, not at each other. I want to live by local time. Yolanda responds that she is quite local, that here and now she and her people have their ways, and that if she had to wait two years to receive the letter from me which arrived this morning, that she would be happy to wait two years before opening it and reading it. She is closer to me now than my plantation manners would have allowed me, if our proximity were up to me. We have met as guests at the same party, and are doing our best to make it a success. I have no rules for keeping her away. Now, during a party, or helping each other to write letters, waiting for pleasures that we feel reasonably sure are coming to us from the future, we grow supple, illogically but unsystematically close. I write, knowing that Yolanda is likely to read these words (and to read in her own style of reading which will construct her own style of meaning), that I, who was ready to launch myself into ashen and oceanic resolutions, have been preparing myself, whether I admit it to myself or not, for a tangy honeymoon. My life, which has been lived for so long accompanied by an *andante* for unaccompanied violin, becomes accompanied by *allegretto* for unaccompanied cello. Music for unaccompanied old age.

Later, Octavio. Another day. Abelardo keeps track of days. I recognize the season, the angle of sunlight, and my new comforts. This is what has happened to me since last I wrote, perhaps ten days ago. For Yolanda's people—Olivia and Aurelia helped to marry her aunt and uncle, which seems to have wedded some rituals to each other also—the man is creative and gives birth. For a wedding, or for this wedding, the tribe becomes one man, which is at the same time an anaconda riding in a canoe, stretching from bow to stern. That anaconda-man gives birth in the canoe (which I gather is also an island) to the bride through its mouth. She is a language. The bridegroom must speak a different language from the bride, or the language is committing incest (I think; the logic isn't easy for me to reconstruct). I thought that we all were learning English, although I could see our English slipping toward the other languages until we speak one language, but write others. Yolanda speaks correct English when she wants to. Thus a college workshop in Old English dialects enters the story, for in the process of writing out *Beowulf* in East Anglian and in West Anglian, I all but memorized it. I can't speak Old English, but I can recite poems, and I was faced with the choice whether to explain that I was merely reciting a poem, or whether to recite the poetry in a conversational tone, as though I were speaking fluently, with my own innuendoes. Well, they would not have understood "merely reciting a poem," it is an alien concept, so I felt that I had to recite as though I were speaking with a friend. I found a most appreciative audience among her family, sly and slightly devious Indians who couldn't hear enough of *Beowulf*. Sometimes I would feel that I was out there, between myself and them, but then they also seemed to be out there, between themselves and me, all of us in a peculiarly objective ecstasy. I could substitute their names in *Beowulf* so that I seemed discussing current events: "Abelardo mathelode bearn Enrique," Abelard spoke, son of Enrique. Rasping out Old English, I felt like something awakening from a long sleep after an ancient war, like a man crawling out of a grave.

For my wedding, *our* wedding, several friends became a tribe, or rather fratry as Yolanda reminds me to call it. I could hear Oliver who might have whispered *phratry, frater, brother*. These *confrères* were the pregnant man, the pregnant anaconda. I thought that her phratry was going to be the man, but in one of their sudden reversals, like a flock of sea gulls or a school of fish turning simultaneously, they declared my phratry the man. And calling that tribe a phratry seems to change all the terms in ways that I don't understand yet. The process seemed to me, like a snake in the sugar bowl, harmless but distasteful to some instincts. And fascinating. I was the baby, with butterflies in my stomach.

Or at first I was the fetus waiting in Olivia's hut. Sheltered among them, held in their arms, some of them not as sober as they might have been on this island where I sometimes think salt water might ferment, I felt that I was continuing some process that I had begun at birth, or before birth, in that uterine sea in which I angrily urinated, shed skins, and dreamed pompous tumescent dreams in my effort to be born. After so many interruptions and false starts, I had returned to the beginning. But I had not returned anywhere. I was not beginning. I was something that, in the Poet's words, "continues to begin." Everyone touched me, to give and to receive power and pleasure. My friends, now the pregnant male anaconda, carried me, who in the equations of this exolinguistic exogamy was the ambassador-at-large of a different and new language, a diplomatic baby, an infant, who would be born, Yolanda was confident, knowing a new name for her. Wrapped as I was, swaddled, held strongly in the arms of about eighteen eager and tipsy parents, I was handed out of the circle of arms into the arms of the doctor enlisted for the event, not my Aurelia but Raoul, who carried me across in his omnicompetent arms to the waiting outstretched arms of Yolanda's family, not many of them, but enough delight to declare it a quorum. I remembered Olivia as a child saying solemnly to a man who picked her up and held her in his arms, "When you are finished with me, pass me to Salathiel." And I opened my arms to her. Yolanda's brother, who is a sort of justice-of-the-peace for them, carried me into a grass hut erected for the occasion on the site of my grandmother's Chinese chippendale gazebo, where she used to sit in her wheelchair frankly staring at and disapproving of the mixture of people in the plaza. Yolanda unwrapped me. I was lying on flowers, something stern within me, still inflexible, annoyed at the waste. I was embarrassed and unsmiling. Yolanda began to sing from so far within her own language that I realized just how exolinguistic this marriage was, for I couldn't understand her. Within a few minutes—and what were they doing to me, so old a man, so ready to be left alone? I deserved a bawdy raucous charivari for my folly, not harmony—Raoul responded to Yolanda's singing, the others made spaces for themselves within the song, Valentine's voice sang along, making song into a political science, and social study, and I could feel, against my will which twisted itself into a small entangled knot, the bunch of them growing together, and growing away from me, Indians!, and *others*, I felt that I was alone, I had always been alone, alone in my thoughts and intentions, and now I wanted to be alone or to be left alone, I would deprive them of their game with me, and I would deprive them of me, for I was an improbable bridegroom in an ill-informed wedding I had not done enough to foresee and to forestall, although I knew from letters that it was being planned long ago. *Long* ago. As Yolanda held me like a chagrined baby I could not sigh out my resignations. I was choking on renunciations, renunciations of what I had long desired to renounce, I was too old to live with desire, and my old follies, my foolishness, seemed to have taught me nothing, I snorted in disgust with myself, then suddenly I wept, I catalogued my beloved dead whom I did not want to let go of, I remembered Orlando's earnest expression when he asked, "If I couldn't talk when I was born, how did I tell you what my name is?," and Olivia, who could never get beyond the first line of a song she kept trying to write for the tragic musical comedy she was going to film, "I've done more for love than love has done for me," then bursting out with laughter, and Oliver, "I am the only person who ever fell upon the thorns of life and didn't bleed," and I even remembered overhearing Kwant say of me to one of his visiting generals, "The first son is like the first pancake," and I wept. As I wept I became cautious, wary, because I started to see myself, as though from above, searching in my bedroom for something, tearing everything apart, I saw myself as an eight-year-old boy miserable with loss, and then I remembered the blue sailor doll with yellow hair that Kwant had with consummate and gigantic improbability brought to me from Switzerland, a sailor with a red cloth face, which I kept with me apprehensively at night in my bed, until it disappeared, simply disappeared, perhaps as things do, or perhaps because of someone's theory of childhood, and then I howled, for I knew that someone had taken away my permission to be a child, someone had abrogated my childhood by stealing and I seemed to know with certainty *burning* my doll, the sailor, the *matelot* who was me when I would grow up and yet have no grown-up problems, like a sailor or a bartender, as I thought of them with no lives of their own, the doll whose loss was buried in my permission to Oliver, Aurelia, Orlando, and Olivia to sit peeing on their watercolor paper as they painted the fireplace at Utterly, while I hovered over life in my fear that they would resemble me as I lounged too long around half-dead ideas and hastily buried emotions, yes Oliver was on target with his imagery, yet I did have the wit to break through the succession of obstacles to some verve, I had encouraged their vitality in spite of some hopelessness in me, a hopelessness I could see in the fact that I regretted the loss of my precious doll, he would have become an old sailor tending bar in a jolly port town, a comrade, and I regretted, but I had not demanded a new doll—how could I have? I was only a child—yet how could I not have? I used to talk with that doll. What could they have done to me? *I was only a child.* And even my ambition to sign aboard as one of the crew was too modest, laughing with messmates below deck, a red and yellow parrot on my shoulder, thinking mutinies, I could see that I had understood only omnipotence and powerlessness, and too little between them, I realized how afraid I had been of becoming fully enraged as I heard my-self growling, and I thought, Oh, I am an impotent old man making a fool of himself, but even as I was growling in rage I could feel myself giving up the security of impotence — how proud of me to see myself as a hopeless case — and then without transition I gave the dead my permission to be dead, I forgave Ginevra, and then I simply cried and sobbed like the old man I am, sufficiently shameless, ruth-lessly eager to be alive, and to love to overflowing, and so acting my age, then impatient even with myself as I remem-bered the patient brilliance of Yolanda, I loved Yolanda without the precautions grief had taught me, and with "the delight which is in the grief of love," and this woman who was holding me, rocking me in her arms, was Yolanda, I recognized the scent of orange blossoms and geraniums, they probably shouldn't have picked them but I was glad they had, the flicker of light from torches shone through the wattles, the melody of Yolanda crooning, and my tiresome salt tears. So I shrugged off the shell of arrogance and help-lessness as gradually we, at a pace we seemed to have been negotiating for many months, blended my weeping with her singing and her singing with my laughing until I was singing as she unwrapped her loose robe, a lavish floral print, I held her to me, I let her look at me, we were now I supposed of one phratry, and with voices joined in the air like tessel-lating diamonds, lyrics colliding with the thump of drums and the shuffle of the dancers, our selves collected for us by the surrounding sounds, our laughter together included my laughter at the fear of disdainful laughter that had worried me, for I had not taken Yolanda out of the bridal market and did not deserve a chivaree, I could see that, because they had brought me into the market in grooms, without my knowing it until I wanted to. I would have to learn to stop estimating so that I could learn not to ridicule or overestimate or underestimate or coarsen, but to see the world as Albrecht Dürer saw it, with loyal eyes, and there, in our matriculation among flowers and scraps of cloth and leaves, among our conciliations and reciprocities, we adhered in a "flowery battle," moving into nearness. Yolanda, who can speak for herself, spoke for herself, I looked up and named her Hope, and we conferred, two active objects arriving safely at another border and crossing alive, with our collateral love intact, adhering to each other as closely as words adhere to thoughts and thoughts adhere to things.

Hoken-Agau 10th

Hello, Octavio. Good morning. The party continues. It continues to continue to continue. The party veered, for a few days, into a celebration of our wedding, an escapade of social sympathies, but now I think we celebrate the party, itself a rather complicated self-activating old object which is what it is in that it is always changing, always surpassing itself toward being more itself than it has been before. I have not stepped into the same party twice. I suppose that we are the party that we are attending, yet it seems other than us, more than us. Our morality seems to be to do what we can to keep the party going. No one is ever first to arrive, and no one is ever last to leave. Only a few outstay their welcome. The children enter with their smiling mouths and light-struck eyes, with the legitimate and stern demands to have a good time. I always hated not being invited to a party, even if I knew that I wouldn't want to go to it. I didn't like costume parties, but I didn't like not being invited even more. I liked the small envelopes in the mail that I could guess contained invitations. I would still like them. I enjoyed the parties of my social class in Baltimore just enough to know how much more I would have enjoyed some other party. I feared that everyone elsewhere was having more fun at an ideal party to which I had not been invited. Oliver and Olivia went to parties with the Creoles, but I couldn't even attend the parties of the servants without chilling them, for they saw themselves as they imagined I was seeing them, and became subdued. Somehow being at this party of ours is like being forgiven so convincingly that I yield to the good humor and forgive myself. I see the effect of my grandmother sitting in her gazebo looking for trouble. Now I wonder about her motives, about her atrophied longings: did she become what she beheld? I admit to myself my desire to be invited to all of the parties ever given anywhere, I want to be a welcome guest, and I behave now so that I won't ever be unwelcome. I am at a party, Octavio, where I do not have to try to be myself all the time. I once put in a false appearance for a whole day without doing any harm. But I have a rough guide to conduct: whatever makes me welcome seems likely to be good. I think that I am never more myself now than when I do not have to work to prove that I am sincere. I think that none of us feels so obliged to be so true to oneself that we would injure anyone. The party sets standards of its own, and I am at my best when I do not strain to satisfy them. Thus I say, to give my answer to an old question, that virtue can be taught, and other laws of self-governance, if one can learn to live worthily waiting for letters, and can learn to enliven a party as a good guest should. This morning we are having a letter writing bee, I suppose a celebration of the day.

I see from the letter I received today that the date must be Muc-Uch the fourteenth. We have been clearing the cornfields of weeds, and working a little on the houses. I have forgotten to write here for two months. I have not forgotten you, but I have other responsibilities, other pleasures. My memory has been taking other trails. And I wanted to write to friends here who so look forward to receiving letters. I don't receive many these days, because they were thinking that I was so old that it wouldn't be worth writing to me in the future. But here I am, and now they write to me again. This morning we laughed at old letters that were read aloud. Many of the letters go back ten or fifteen years, and we are beginning to compile a library of the best. Our classics. Others we use for various necessities of life. And the paper itself is always interesting, always informative, bringing to the surface of the present some scent of yesterdays. The party goes on and on and on. Yolanda and I, when I remembered what I had been intending to do, strolled up the cliff to Utterly. I think that I stroll like an ambulatory disaster, but no one else seems to notice. Odd, my eyes still look young, when even the glass eyes that the woman anthropologist traded to the Indians for their myths fifty or more years ago begin to look like antiques. When I look at one of those eyes (for they still turn up in the mail, usually as startling and timely messages from Delphine, who did have a flair for correspondences), I seem to see the past. I can hear Olivia saying, "When the anthropologist arrives, the gods depart."

The place, Utterly, is useless I think. It looked condemned to me, but then I can scarcely bear to look at it. It makes me feel my dislocations and displacements. Except for bricks from the foundation, which have circulated like a separate currency among the children, I think that no one has wanted any part of it. I salvaged nothing but some clothes from the wreckage of the fire, whatever Aurelia brought to me, but I never went back, perhaps because I regarded it as the sepulchre of Converse, who I assume burned to death in the fire he set, although some searched and found no body. Yolanda suggests that he swam out after Kwant, but that may be part of the legend that was told among the Indians. Perhaps the absence of a body scared people away from Utterly. I suppose no one knows quite who any of it could be said to belong to, and I for one don't want to discuss the concept of belonging to. The east wing has capsized, and through a gap where it pulled away from the central body of the house we could see old things. I know that books were salvaged, because across the years, in someone's lap, or on a shelf of Aurelia's growing library in the Infirmary, I have seen their old favorites. I remember Oliver with Joseph Conrad's novel, *The Heart of Darkness*, and with an old anthology of Romantic poetry Orlando had studied at Johns Hopkins, faded and frayed, but smelling of Oliver's favorite glue. He had visited Cambridge University long before Oxford because he preferred the scent of Cambridge University Press books, and when they started arriving odorless, he noted that as another symptom of the decline of the West. His paper was usually redolent. Aurelia carried and still carries about with her, and reads aloud from, Lamarck and Darwin and Piaget, *Behavior and Evolution.* She writes me scientific letters in the great tradition of science as a community bonded by friendly communications. I can answer only paternally. Orlando read his way through Joseph Needham, *Science and Civilization in China*, Lévi-Strauss, Braudel, and the complete, collected, uniform editions of Balzac, Zola, Flaubert, Dickens, and even James. I had seen the books floating about, but had never asked myself where they were coming from. Olivia appropriated Oliver's complete edition of Doris Lessing, and was usually reading *The Four-Gated City.* I could recognize a book she had read by its broken spine. I saw them all with the collected poems of Wallace Stevens, and they all saw me. I recollected where books had been coming from when I looked into the house, which must have had a mile of shelves. I can't remember reading much myself since Delenda died, although as postmaster I was often the first to whom someone would show a letter. So many of the books, so many of the fictions, were about money, as I realize that so much of this letter is about money, or about its absence, that I wonder how many of the books would speak to us now. I was always ambivalent about the *bookseller*, as the *Rubáiyát* was about the wineseller: what could he buy that is half as dear as what he sells? I thought that I would bring something from Utterly to the party. We all enjoy something new and different, even an object brought back from the grove, where it was a decoration, and restored to use. I helped Yolanda through a window and then stood waiting while she looked around. I took inventory of the house as I remembered it, but I couldn't focus with certainty on the year in which it burned, on the particular furnishings of that era, because I remembered so many successive eras and modes. Objects had a way of disappearing into the attic, and then making a come-back years later. As I pictured the rooms I realized that I had been seeing kitchen implements from Utterly being used at the postoffice, that I had seen curtains adapted as clothes, probably even as a bridal gown, for suddenly I could place Yolanda's robe as Olivia's bedroom curtains, the flowered-print fabric returned to the garden as I saw it often draped over Yolanda's figure as she kneeled digging in the soil. I could see that we did not own anything, although we had objects that we were loyal to. Anything taken from Utterly was merely on loan, and was cared for as something borrowed. Well, I too was ready to borrow. As Yolanda handed me some books, I felt oddly able to scan the contents, I recognized more than I would have said that I could actually remember, I could retrieve the feeling or mood of a book, its dominant tone, although I couldn't have passed a quiz on its details. And I thought that nowhere in the studies of government, the court memoirs, the treatises on politics, or the biographies of heroes, could I find an image of the way we live now, dwelling in the guardianship of the party while waiting for letters that have been in our future since some time, often a long time, in our past.

Yolanda handed me, and how odd they looked, three lamps. I had forgotten the importance of electricity until I touched a lamp. And you, Octavio, as far as I know, have never known it. I cannot say how puny electric light now seemed to me in contrast with the forces that illuminate our lives. Kwant's little power plant behind his office, operated by his small militia, is now something of a brewery, operated by some of the same militia, now retired. I remembered the lamps well, although like myself now that I dwell in an atmosphere more than a place, I cannot locate them in a particular time. They seemed always to have been there, correct enough for lamps, which never did look as though they belonged in the rooms, always ungainly, each a new failure of imagination and design. No ugly means of illumination before Edison, and few beautiful ones after him. These lamps must have come with my father from Germany or Switzerland. My fingers seem to have grown to fit this feather pen with which I write to you. Yolanda must massage them again. She seems to me almost able to speak with the memories embodied in their sinews and tendons. Yolanda climbed out of the window and carefully took the lamps which were piled in my arms. The lamps had been converted to electricity from three vases: a vase of gold, I suppose gold leaf; a vase of *sang de boeuf*, antique Korean; and a vase which I had to look at slowly for a long time before I could remember the name of its color, *peachblow*, and a very active old object it is. I seemed to remember that Kwant had had the bases electrified in Brussels. I felt, looking without any particular theory at the lustre of the peachblossom, as I have felt writing to you when so much of what happens on this island seems to bear upon this letter and so feels fraught with meaning, even as the letter in turn bears upon what happens, a growing catalyst. Yolanda and Raoul removed the bolts from the bottoms of the lamps and unscrewed the electrical adapters, Raoul with my nodded assent pocketing the metal pieces which will come in handy. I could see in his eyes that now that he had some metal parts, he had some work to do. I was glad that he could give them purpose; it was close enough to giving them meaning. I looked at the three vases, the gold, the bull's-blood, and the peachbloom, and felt that I was confronted with a choice. Which of the vases was the image of our lives? The gold and the *sang de boeuf* were pretty, but would only have amused us at our party. We have no shortage of entertainment, listening to each other, listening for each other. As I picked up the peachblow vase I was satisfied that its surface rendered our position in this field of ancient forces. The vase seemed to counter-illuminate the light that shone upon it. I could see for the first time that I had loved material things, but money had spoiled that, money aloof there in its transcendence had made me suspicious of people — "The buyer needs a hundred eyes, the seller not one" — and what is almost as bad, suspicious of objects, so that was the point I had missed in my ambivalent materialism, for money was the enemy of my materialism and worldliness, and without money I could love my wordly possessions (whatever was on more or less permanent loan to me, for here and in Baltimore we had confused the *ding-an-sich* with market value, I had taught my children the value of money, but in seeking to rise above money I had concealed from myself my longing for ideas to materialize as images, as objects I could see and touch.) I would send them all back to ransack Utterly. I can tell that Raoul has been waiting for some word from me, that he has been thinking about the usefulness of Utterly, while I have ignored it. Money: I bought Olivia from those two because I would not have been comfortable doing anything else. My purpose was to save the child, not to acquire her. So yes, I have sought comfort, and I can hear Olivia's scorn, "How dreadful for you that money made you uncomfortable." Yet Olivia herself might have thought more clearly, for she rejected as bourgeois so much that was comfortable, but she was not ascetic, and she generously gave comfort as an upholsterer of our graves, leaving it to light to provide such consolation as it could. The vase joined us here in early evening at our quiet candle-light letter-writing party, the convivial Chinese jar of compassionate peachblossom glazes as it fires once again in the kiln of our affinities, in its roundness shaping infinite reversals, borrowing light from the candles, and then lending it to our eyes, which repay it with interest. The vase, which is not mine to give, I offer as my open-letter to the party, as a thank-you note or progress report. It makes the space in the room feel flexible and powerful as it joins us in our silence this evening with, alas, the body of Matthew, who drowned this morning, a loss which has made a discernible difference in the mood which constrains us now, the waste of his young life, the unnecessary perishing, the wreckage. It might so easily have been otherwise. My statements are so commonplace, yet that is all that we have, a common place. We mutter and repeat our mutterings, blurring our thoughts, grieving that life is lived in lurid transience. I think that I see, in the translucencies of my old age, that while "it might have been otherwise," we could not have done much to make it otherwise. We do not know enough. Accidents do happen. We grieve and we regret as though, were the past to return, we might make some other choice. But our only choice now, although not this early in the evening, is whether to assent or not to assent to the death, and we will finally have no choice but to assent, although we suffer the awareness of the possibilities that died with him, we will agree on the worthlessness of life, and then on the *almost* worthlessness of life, and we will resign ourselves to what has happened with some music, tearful embraces, vows to love those whom we love even more than we have loved them, and to show the love. Yolanda is working among other cooks in the lean-to erected outside a window to get the hot stoves out of the postoffice. Every one of us grants access to a quality we might not be acquainted with if we didn't have that person. And now we don't have Matthew, one of our opportunities. And if we were helpless to prevent his death, well, later we will be helpless to prevent satisfactions from returning, awkwardly enhanced by their proximity to death. I must rest now to prepare to take the measure of our grief, for I plan to sit up all night with the body of Matthew. Farewell, Matthew. We are forlorn. Already friends gather for your wake-party. What can we do with your death but *use* it? We do not understand each other's jokes, always, but we do understand each other's griefs, always.

Huc-Uinkil 16th

Some weeks later, Octavio, and the party continues beating like a heart. Admittedly it sometimes slumbers, sometimes fades into dullness. I have not written that it is always fun. But it is always here. Everything we do now bears upon the party. In the old days, those who did not have to labor—aristocrats, criminals, madmen, artists, and usually children — were envied, as they stood equidistant from a full day's toil. But they paid for their dispensation by being self-enfolded or self-divided, or both; by the late twentieth century, to be an artist and to be ruined seemed synonymous, and however useful the artist might have been as an example of another method of production, another approach to the uses of time, the artist was not an adequate image of human life. But I have found the image in the guests sharing the food and objects which have been lent to them. Whatever I do now has more or less to do with the party, and signifies accordingly. The party puts a strain on all events so that they are graded toward it. Like saltimbanques, we slide and tumble toward the party. The party itself becomes our axiomatic metaphor, perhaps indefinable, the term in which the master words, time, space, causality, utility, and even love are to be redefined. The party is the frame around us, creating a space in which former distances do not hold, where guests, and oneself, turn out not to be as bad or as boring as one had feared, and nothing stays quite in the place one had thought it was supposed to be in. I had never understood how *society* existed apart from the individuals who made up the society. I have forgotten how we defined society as it is. But now I have learned a definition of society as it ought to be: a party. Occasionally we have unruly behavior, especially after Ximax produces some of his powerhouse punch which I have called *phlogiston.* Last week Miguel climbed into the rafters, knocking down some letters (which Abelardo gracefully declared a windfall and delivered out of chronological order, causing some enthusiastic consternation), and then he fell onto some people who were dancing, although in truth he dived onto them, and he punched Ximax, who was trying to help him up, in the mouth, hurting his hand rather badly. A few more punches were thrown, and then he stopped. We haven't a person among us who would stop at nothing. He didn't test his welcome for several days. I thought that his isolation, his self-imposed isolation, only defined the earlier isolation when he acted among us on a passion so peculiar to him that he could not have talked about it and thought it over with any of us. What he did, he did entirely on his own, which was a mistake. He wrenched himself from the party, leaving a few men feeling invigorated, kissing their knuckles, and was on his own somewhere beyond Tornata. We have few punishments except cold shoulders. I don't know what we would do in the face of evil. How would we handle a murderer? Put him out to labor for an eight-hour day? Banish him to Umberland? But we garden there. We will suffer these problems someday, undoubtedly, especially if the party so diminishes that people do not care, or prefer to sorrow alone, wrapped up in themselves. I suppose that a crime is an act that damages the party. Certainly evil could and would destroy it. We must learn how to defend it. Some mild altercations have enhanced the party, as when Esmeralda ran in distressed and crying, and we stepped up the pace of our pleasures in each other to surround her with safe love. The party is an organ of forgiveness, always changing, but stable, and self-perpetuating, our solution to the problem of the continuum, our happy symbolic logic only incidentally shaped by the logic of family or of language, as the party invents or discovers shapes peculiar to itself, and as it grows larger it strengthens its own foundation.

The first of the month, Octavio. Once I would have been paying bills. I have remembered to write to you again. A letter arrived today from Delphine, an envelope of seeds, another of her runic inscriptions on my days. I see now

why I am bothered by her messages, for I try to focus on
the seeds, and to focus on the meaning, and I can't get them
together on the same plane. Looking at the seeds, I remember the patented hybrid fruits and vegetables Kwant
would order for the garden, and then in violation of some
law he would pirate seeds or take cuttings from the trees.
Once he arrived with peaches, and after we ate the fruit, he
planted the pits, and later had gardeners graft branches
onto sturdier stock, or make the dwarf trees which gave
him a suspect pleasure. He had trained fifteen gardeners,
which turned out to be providential for us. "Sweet are the
uses of adversity." Oliver might have quoted that, and
often did. How the potential of a seed could be controlled
or owned by a corporation I couldn't imagine. I "don't exactly understand" potential. Perhaps Aurelia can explain it
to me. Sometimes I think that I know what potential is,
when I experience something that it seems to name. What
Delphine intended by her message I can't imagine. She
would have mailed a lightning bolt if she could have figured out a way, or if I would have let her, because she loved
these communications, saying that the worst part of being
a whore without a heart of gold in Baltimore was that, "We
lost touch with each other. Not everybody has phones or
wants people to know their address. Every other insurance
man is a cop. You never got a census of my family. We did
lose each other, we were careless that way, and what I like
on this island is that we do all keep in touch." Which, she
explained, was why when she played the numbers she bet
the number of a house which had a funeral crepe hanging
on the door, flowers and a purple ribbon. As usual she
made a connection I couldn't see. Of course we will try to
use the old seeds, to see what we get, and that will be a
meaning. For years useful plants sprouted on the hillside
where she threw garbage from the kitchen window; she

said it was her way of feeding birds, and it did work. I think now of the pleasures I found in the catalogues of flowers, fruits, and vegetables, how I acquiesced in the rude uprooting of plants from their homelands into Kwant's imperialistic botanic garden. Now I can't decide whether we should be grateful to him or not, since the purposes served are so different from his intentions. Anyway with books which Miguel has quarried from Utterly we are learning more uses of plants and trees. We now derive oil from the copaiba tree, *Copaifera langsdorfii*, and we are germinating more seeds for more trees. The oil from the tree burns in lamps, heals cuts, and binds the scent of flowers into a perfume that so distinguishes the body that I cannot voice my objections to picking flowers. I look around when I stand amidst the uncomfortable trees which Kwant had begged or stolen for his collection, and I understand the differences: for twenty-five years, no one has said to another, "I have my life to live and you have yours," no one on this island has sold anything to anyone else, for twenty-five years I have not looked upon anything that was for sale, and no objects have betrayed my hopes. In Baltimore the occasions and sweet qualities of life—flirtations, seductions, weddings, births, the first day of school, a child making friends in a new neighborhood, a family reunion, the student home from college—every image of friendship, affection, trust, and love that money could not buy had been used to sell products which promised relief from the self-inflicted tortures of that society: and I had used the semblance of a friendly letter to peddle golden stamps. Now no voice, no gesture, no glance that is used for love is used for salesmanship. I can hear words of praise such as "great" and "best" and "wonderful" without checking my wallet as though a pickpocket were about. (I do not have a wallet, Octavio.) I almost trust metaphors again, and lose my suspicions of symbolism. I could even enjoy the way it slows my thinking to the pace of a meditation, a truancy from nature and from naturalism while I contemplate a knot in a board, or a string, or a narrative. I can see that someday I might lower my resistance to ritual and myth, although the story of our party still seems to me sufficient. Even the gods might be too important to be left to the godly. Hadn't Oliver quoted in a letter to me the line from Christopher Smart, "For I bless God for the Postmaster General & for all conveyances of letters under his care. . . ." Anyone for allegory? Father Pasquale once sermonized on "Be not unduly righteous." I could live with a text like that. "Be not righteous over much, neither make thyself over wise: why shouldest thou destroy thyself?"

Chan-Uinkil 6th

Be not unduly wicked is a verse turned by Abelardo who has delivered to me the notebooks Aurelia used to write in. She mailed them to me. They have been waiting among the dirt-daubers in the rafters. Aurelia outlined the course of study and of research at her ideal university. The curriculum was to begin with mathematics and logic, and they indeed continue throughout. But after the introduction of mathematico-logic comes physics, arranged in a double history, from the origin of the cosmos to the present epoch, and from the origins of physical theory among the pre-Socratics and the ancient Chinese to the modern theories. Her course of study brought in chemistry, again from cosmic origins and from the origins of chemical theory, with cross references, so that from Priestley one is drawn to Shelley, and from Wöhler back to Vico and forward to structuralism. Her university course added geology and meteorology, then a theory of the origins of life. Occasionally she swoops down from her outline to a particular fact, describing the molecular fossils found at Isua, and then returning to the history of theories about the origin of life; and with warnings against the speculations of extra-terrestrial biology. In most of her diagrams of the structure of the university, biology is at the center, and the sciences branch off in different directions, although in spite of the rigid lines of the diagram the sciences fluctuatingly overlap. She has written "Freedom of movement!" with an uncharacteristic exclamation mark. With some variability or uncertainty in the order, she has added biogeography, biohistory, anthropology, paleology, archeology, and historiography, along with the history of each of these. She added, again with the concurrent study of the product of thought and the process of thought, psychology and linguistics. Languages were to be taught from their origins as those are understood, so that in one course the student would begin with Indo-European as it is reconstructed, and would learn the European languages as they arose, and would follow an assimilated word to its original language, and then map that language in relation to the others. Aurelia can't intend that everyone learn Burushaski. Sometimes she is thinking of teaching people, and other times of programming a machine, a computer that would contain so much information about languages that when it translated it would be able to trace a word in one language back to its origins where it split from its cognate words, and then work its way forward in the other language until it found a comparable word. From her notes, she did not know enough to sketch even one example fully. She works over the word *life* as she struggles to define a "living university that could contemplate its own *life*. Bad metaphor? Life as 'freedom of form within form' (Buytendijk). Meaning? Implications for experiment? for observation? for experimental observation? 'I cannot live with you, / That would

247

be life. . . .'" She turns to the word *society* and tries the phrases, "society of atoms, society of molecules, society of cells, society of feelings? emotions? thoughts?," but then she returns to *life* and carefully copies out, as though a key-punch operator were going to read them, lines from the concordance to the poems of Wallace Stevens:

> *Fears of life and fears of death,* [Brave 138-17
> *How good life is, on the basis of propriety,* [Winter B 141-13
> *Life is an old casino in a park.* [Havana 142-9
> *Life is an old casino in a wood.* [Havana 144-11
> *It is curious that the density of life* [Nigger 157-7
> *So that's life, then: things as they are?* [MBG 166-13
> *And that's life, then: things as they are,* [MBG 167-1
> *What is there in life except one's ideas,* [MBG 175-17
> *Good air, good friend, what is there in life?* [MBG 175-18
> *A hawk of life, that latined phrase:* [MBG 178-4
> *Yet life itself, the fulfilment of desire* [Men Fall 188-3
> *Over words that are life's voluble utterance.* [Men Fall 188-20
> *There's no such thing as life; or if there is,* [Parochial 192-4

Aurelia defines places for sociology, economics, political science, and philosophy, "the history and study of," and from philosophy she returns to logic and mathematics which seem, from the frustrated erasures in her notebooks, and the arrows drawn to second thoughts which climb vertically up the margins, to compete with biology as the origin or center of the university. "Question *center*," she writes. "One center? Alternating centers? Brain." She plays with compounds, "biomathematics," "logicobiology," as though a game with permutations of words might yield an idea that would govern the unruly fields of learning. Aurelia's map of learning seems sometimes more complicated than the territory she is mapping. I can see what she is doing, and perhaps overdoing, which is to make every fact or theory have a bearing upon another fact or theory so that it enjoys at least a slight enhancement of significance, and sometimes a large enhancement. She returns to language and carefully traces routes for the study of Inca, Aztec, and Mayan languages, for that road led to Delenda, or toward Delenda. Clearly she knows nothing about those languages, unless a list of endearments in the margin counts as acquaintance. She returns to English for pages of information and quotations from *The American Heritage Dictionary* on *bear*, and *bear arms against, bear out, bear with, bear down, bear up*, and I can see that Oliver helped her with citations from the poets, and I remember talking about *beran*, from Old English, meaning *to carry*, and she races through a list, *forbear, bier, bore, bairn, barrow, burly, burden, birth, birr, bring, Inverness, berceuse*, and then Latin, *ferre, afferent, confer, defer, differ, efferent, -fer, fertile, infer, offer, prefer, proffer, refer, suffer, transfer, vociferate*, and then Greek, *pherein, amphora, anaphora, euphoria, metaphor, periphery, -phore, -phoresis, -phorous*, and *tocopherol*. I notice that Aurelia's university omits lessons in dancing, singing, guitar playing. She and I would teach about the universe in different ways, I suppose. Perhaps she assumes that such liberating disciplines will be taught, or at least learned, among friends, or within the family. I'm not sure that I would register in her university unless I was assured that each one would teach one to dance. I suppose that a university can't be thought of as a party, that the metaphor won't do, and that we couldn't try thinking of a party of atoms, or of the history of chemistry as a party. But if party doesn't illuminate the arts and sciences, perhaps the arts and sciences could illuminate party. I would like a computer to retrieve information on the physics, chemistry, biology, psychology, sociology, economics, politics, logic, mathematics, and philosophy of a party. I would like to read a dissertation entitled, "The Life of the Party." Our party is like arising in the midst of an effortless sonata by Mozart. I try to imagine you, Octavio, as having gone off to college, as Aurelia and Orlando did long ago, and I before them, but I no longer know how to imagine college, and no longer know enough to know what I should hope for you. I hope that you have learned to dance. I know enough to hope that.

Ox-Uinkil 1st

Dear Octavio, I haven't much more to write, because I think that you either know what I am writing here, so that I become a repetitive old man, or that you would not understand what I am writing because you lack comparable (parallel? congruent?) experiences. I doubt that you have heard a sonata by Mozart. Unless you had somewhere enkindled a party, or entered one that was in full fiery flower, how would you understand my words? What haven't I told you? That no one has commanded us to do something for longer than I usually remember? No one dominates the party because people tire. Each of us has for a time governed the party as it forms about the person who represents the mood which is surfacing in it. I wonder if a work of art was ever made during a party? I wonder if a party can be a work of art. I need a history of barn raisings and quilting bees. If I call our society a party, it seems to become one; if I go to call it a work of art, I get the shakes.

Ox-Uinkil 8th. Mail has come. Letters have arrived for you, Octavio. I do not copy many letters now. We put your mail in the old incubator where the bugs can't get at it. My elusive daughter Aurelia's letter to me today has an uncharacteristically shrill superscript: *Evolution is not blind!* I will copy the letter because it seems important to me. Aurelia may be the only person who, hearing her tutor speak of Voltaire, at first understood him to be speaking of Volterra, a scientist, a confusion which evoked from Olivia her discourse on Alessandro Volta, died 1827, which further evoked from Oliver his discourse on Heinrich Wöhler and synthetic urea, the death of William Blake, the end of Romanticism, eliciting Orlando's dry observation that Sir Walter Scott had lived until 1832. Their attempts to set a date for the end of the Romantic period inspired Olivia to write a paper, "From Blaise Pascal to Father Pasquale," satisfying her feeling that the processes of thinking, and of upsetting Father Converse, were one process.

The Outlier—Mux 18th—Year 24

My Dear Father,
I have received today a posthumous letter from Oliver reminding me of when we did a translation exercise for Converse. He gave us Voltaire's sentence, "Travaillons sans raisonner, c'est le seul moyen de rendre la vie supportable," and asked for our translations. As Oliver recalled, Orlando translated with predictable literalness, "Let us work without theorizing (speculating)," while Olivia was gnomically terse, "Empty mind, full stomach." And I, for once letting words mean more than I could be responsible for, translated, "Theorizing is unbearable." Oliver, as he recalled, translated the opening imperative, "Work with asininity." Oliver went on about Keats and negative capability. He and I had long agreed on the importance of Keats, of such a phrase as "beechen green," but I heard my sounds more accurately in Herrick's line, "That liquefaction of her clothes," I felt that I was with Herrick as he chose the word *liquefaction*, and I could feel reverberations and yet equilibrium in a phrase such as *brave vibrations*, "Next, when I cast mine eyes, and see / That brave vibration, each way free, / O, how that glittering taketh me!" I felt the torque

251

in language. I introduced Oliver to Sir John Davies's *Orchestra*, for if he annotated some of my scientific texts with poems, I annotated his books with references to science, but we also reversed poles occasionally, as when I sat him down in the gazebo and read the whole poem aloud to him, including,

> But *logic leadeth reason in a dance,*
> *Reason, the cynosure and bright lodestar*
> *In this world's sea, to avoid the rocks of chance;*
> *For with close following and continuance*
> *One reason doth another so ensue*
> *As, in conclusion, still the dance is true.*

Now I find my reasonings leading me in a dance, and I will record something of theory here, and then suspend theorizing for precise observation. Since Primavera has been so isolated, with some birds and butterflies that would have continued their migrations not continuing them, and others that would have arrived not arriving, the island is a laboratory for studying evolution. The environment of the island may change—even the layer of ash was a noteworthy change, and the alterations in climate, the new hues in the sky. I have been training children to observe and to record. At Umberland a mulberry tree grows with branches that have touched the earth and rooted, forming a cavern occupied by bats with several albinos among them, and more being born each year. I sit for hours among these anomalies, as I have for years. Kwant and a metal fence never kept me from Umberland when I was a girl with a flashlight crawling into a mulberry tree. As the balances on Primavera change, behavior will change, and as behavior changes, some clever opportunistic birds or insects will survive, and gradually the behavior which they have improvised will be genetically determined. I am tempted to try to breed a race of albino bats, to see if their behavior changes, but for now I am content to watch. The genome has as its function the realization of all its possible combinations: the voluble helix has a message and seeks the chance to deliver it. I used to think that what *could be genetically, would be.* Now I see that, from the point of view of the genome, what *can be, must be.* Some of these possible forms imply, or at least require, a different environment, a future environment. A change in behavior causes stress in the interior environment of a creature. This stress is information for the genome about opportunities, it is news of the world, with premonitions of the future. The phenotype, the individual carrying the genotype, will seek a new environment which will evoke new behavior which will cause stress and strain which will inform the genome so that it can attempt the combination which will relieve the strain. When that combination is achieved, the new behavior is then innate. Read our Piaget. The influence which has been neglected in theories of evolution is the future, at least the future as it is forecast in the present by the existence of potentials which are yet to be realized, when the forecast inclines the present toward that forecasted future. The energy for evolution derives from the position of real energy in the present in relation to the imaginary energy of the future. I doubt that I have succeeded in conveying any of this to anyone, my topology and topography of time, or what Oliver called my history of the future. Olivia helpfully found words for me which were a help as I struggled for words. She showed me Nabokov's Van who ". . . sought to express something, which *until* expressed had only a twilight being (or even none at all—nothing but the illusion of the backward shadow of its imminent expression)," and also her own Doris Lessing, those phrases, "the shadow of foreknowledge," "this shadow of the future was in everyone." She read Dickens's *A Christmas Carol* aloud to me, every word, doing the voices.

Primavera and Umberland have become, willy nilly, a novel experiment in eliciting new turns from the voluble helix. I could wish evolution were not so slow. Even human behavior is being recorded (perhaps the letters will help), because changes in the objectively probable future are changing the present as it emerges toward that future. That catastrophe, whatever it was, shook the ground of implications. But that has helped to show that the future builds its past under itself.

Dear Father, I hope that you are touched by a warm hand, that you feel rapport with life, that you find your continuity within the larger discontinuities, and then amidst the even larger continuities.

My speculating love,
Aurelia

The island seems to me, Octavio, less an experiment in evolution, than a laboratory for experiments with the intervals of love. I could record many changes on Primavera, although I doubt that they are changes which would evoke changes in the genotype. My only behavior likely to affect evolution is that I sit out here on safari in the grove bopping rats over the head as they pass by, and Yolanda, who is not squeamish, cooks them into stews. I worry about a deficiency of vitamins, perhaps B-12. The rats, the bats, and the cats are the only mammals on the island other than ourselves (and the cows, which, like the chickens, no one mentions; we have no word for them in our *patois,* and no one ever speaks the old names. I have seen the origins of a taboo). The rats jumped ship, or ships, at different times, and they ferociously worked out a *modus vivendi* with the cats, who ignore them and wash themselves, *molto adagio,* when a rat passes by. I should, I suppose, *travaille sans raisonner*—work without justifications. But I like to think about what I do. Killing the rats makes me feel useful, narrowing the distance between the production and consumption of my food, as when I eat berries from the bush. I am amused when a stew looks to me radiant with sound economy. I may be foolish, but I want Yolanda to have some meat in her diet, although I see that we will soon come to the last of the rats. They will be extinct, but their extinction seems to me no more an unnatural act than their being here at all. I am sure that others survive somewhere in the world. History has never disappointed the rats. Among them prowls one old greybeard whom I will not kill out of sentimentality, confused symbolism, and a soupçon of superstition. I have a fellow-feeling for him, and he seems to look through my eyes toward my heart. I have learned from Aurelia's notes and letters about biohistory, the effects of human history on the geographical distribution of plants and animals: cattle and dung beetles in Australia, bees and horses feral in America, fireants marching through Georgia, geraniums domesticated and imported from Africa, and cats, rats, and dogs transported everywhere, except that we had no dogs because Kwant forbade them. Which was like forbidding us to think certain thoughts. I see these rats as historical rats, as domesticated animals, and I pitilessly bang them over the head in an historical act of unnatural selection. I don't enjoy inflicting pain, but the rats upset the balance of the island, at least of the grove, where they are voracious, avaricious, and necrophagous. I spare the old rat merely because I wish to be spared myself, the silly propitiation of some vague power, contradicting what I think I've believed most of my life; but I am too old for the violence of pure theory, and I have much to want to be spared for, if only to enjoy retiring from my post of ratcatcher. I no longer want to kill, but everything the rats do seems so *intentional* that they make my work easier.

Tzun 10th. Good morning, Octavio. I feel happy as easily as a sailboat makes the day beautiful. And gulls. I don't know how much longer I can write to you. I have been helping Yolanda to make maguey paper. I thought, like Oliver, that a market for paper would grow up, but we have no possible equality of exchange except equally capricious and unreasoned whims. Yet we weigh our preferences and find a balance. We find workable equalities. No one could claim to have made a profit. I remember that man, Biff Dunbar, who had come to buy quantities of our money at wholesale prices. As the depreciation of the American dollar accelerated because of inflation, everyone tried to get rid of the dollar in order to acquire something of "real" value. The money of Primavera seemed a peculiar choice to me, even though it was assumed still to have gold behind it. I don't think that they had confidence in our money, but that they were confident of finding a *bigger fool* when the time came to sell. I was able to watch the Americans depreciate their money (and mine) by racing to exchange it for something "real" before their neighbors could. Inflation became a satire of the society, a criticism of the actual false values in behalf of "timeless" or enduring values — but since that was no more than a safe place to put money, it was self-satirizing, the vulgar culmination of the Romantic Quest. The inflationary process was the self-criticism of capitalism in an attempt to define its essence, or to locate the ideal; it had the incidental benefit for me of requiring that I think about a safe place to put *myself*. Timeless values would be able to shift for themselves.

Biff Dunbar and I bargained — the value of our Prima-

vera money fluctuated as we charged what the market
would bear —and while we had various means of stimulat-
ing or simulating scarcity to increase value, our most successful technique was simply that we were usually late
with our issues. The delay illogically stimulated demand.
And Biff Dunbar said to me that I should think ahead to
what I would have settled for in an hour. I thought. He said
that he knew what he would settle for. That we should
write down the figures and then we were to split the difference. We wrote them down on little folded pieces of paper,
like ballots. I was squinting hard at him. He was finding
some pleasure in this transaction with me very different
from anything I was doing to please him. I thought that the
money was rather handsome, a portrait of Kwant in profile
by an artist I had uncovered, Ray Johnson. But Kwant
hated it and ordered me to unload it fast. So I wrote down
the figure that I knew I should have settled for within an
hour, giving him a bargain, I suppose. We unfolded our
papers. My figure was lower than his —he had been prepared to pay an outrageous sum (for he must have known
what our costs were, paper and printing, what did he think
our money was?)—and he quickly averaged the two figures and then quickly wrote me a check, he was in such a
hurry to be gone, I saw him from my window hail a cab for
a quick getaway up Charles Street, and within this drab
event, just another unsatisfactory compromise of my integ-
rity, I saw not only how I had been averaged with my own
consent, but I saw also that the rapid exchange of money
for "goods" in inflation was a culmination of the increased
pace of exchanges, for money had speeded up transactions,
it had zuckered them, and had not only encouraged standardized commodities, but also a standardized and rapid
pace for the exchange of commodities and money: do not
hold up the line, others are waiting, move along, I don't

have all day. And the extraordinary apology, "I'm just look-ing, thank you." Money had done to so many human en-counters what sugar had done to so much food: it had averaged experiences as sugar had averaged the tastes and made possible a uniform and rapid rate of consumption by leveling differences to a single generalized taste of sweet-ness, depriving foods of their peculiarities and textures, another loss of meaning in a speed-up when meaning de-pended upon delay, as one slowly masticating figured out what the taste was, with the limit of generality, hence falsi-fication, reached in chewing gum which implied regular, generalized, thoughtless mastication. Sweetness was ever the blemish on beauty, making existence too easy to swallow.

Kwant, when he read my report, was pleased with the "deal," although he was less pleased when we looked up to see a yacht in our small harbor, lowering anchor, and low-ering a dinghy, the Dunbars from Baltimore who rowed ashore, Biff and Buffie Dunbar, their son Gilman, their daughter Penney (as Olivia said of Baltimore, get the facts straight and the satire takes care of itself). Gilman liked to say "A penny for your thoughts," and point to her, several times an hour. At last Kwant was going to be paid in his own coin. We had money on the island, but almost no use for it. The laborers were paid, but they bought supplies in the company store behind Kwant's office, where most pur-chases were written in a book and deducted from their pay, so that little cash changed hands. Kwant invited the Dun-bars to dinner while he stalled, for the island had little that could be sold to them. This was the night that Oliver's house, Tornata, became a rental unit. Delphine, born in Baltimore, would appear from the kitchen to say, "Ask them if they want a Taxi," and then she would run away laughing, as though she had set up this joke a decade earlier. Dinner. As Olivia said, dinner was priceless. Biff handled blind trusts, but he was an expert in the history of financial communications. His bank required its executives to take a full month's vacation so that wheels could come full circle without their finger on them. And I should not underestimate him. He was fascinating when he chronicled in detail the history of the value of news about money, and how the need to exchange information about money had caused the development of the mails, carrier pigeons, telegraph, telephone, teletype, satellite. He told us about the sticks of salt used as money in Abyssinia, and wondered how they would "salt away" their money; one knew from the look in Buffie's eyes that she had heard his joke before. He told how *salary* meant the money given to Roman soldiers to buy salt, and Oliver had that look in his eye of the addict trapped at the table by etiquette, without his book of etymologies. Biff knew the Fugger letters, he had read Braudel and was aware of the Johns Hopkins lectures. When I commented on the dangers of sailing so far east, Biff said, "Oh, you have to live at the edge." He told of sighting whales, which they had studied with impressive precision, although Gilman preferred dinosaurs. They donated to Ducks Unlimited, subscribed to the Baltimore Symphony, were members of the Walters Art Gallery and had a family recipe of Buffie's in a cookbook published by the Friends of the gallery. Decent people. He told an anecdote about a British prince who wrote a note to the king, his father, asking for five pounds, and who, upon receiving a note from his father declining to give him the money, and admonishing him to live within his allowance, sold the note to an autograph shop for ten pounds, letting the potent signature of royalty fall into profane hands. Biff said that for the prince, it was like having the mint for a father, and he looked at Gilman pensively. Kwant in a festive mood unexpectedly quoted *King Lear*, "No, they cannot touch me for coining; I am the king himself," but the dinner party recovered. These were not bad people, but they had our money and had come to collect on the promises it made to them. Therefore they were our enemies. We could not then, and I cannot now, find the adequate tone for describing them. And tone underwrites meaning. We lapsed into satire and sounded as snobbish as they did. But satire would have criticized them for betraying an ideal, and what ideals did I know, except to be in the process of inventing a method of thinking about what we were doing? And how could I know that they were not, in their own development, at some necessary stage of that process? How could I know? Given the choice between Kwant and the Baltimores (Olivia called them Mister B. and Mistress B., beating Oliver to an allusion, delighting him), I had, with perhaps shameful self-indulgence, chosen Kwant. The Dunbars seemed, with their League of Women Voters and their tax-deductible liberalism and their drip-dry yachting clothes, perilously lukewarm. Olivia, whom we depended upon to be harsh, from her moral intuition if not from principle, said that they were educated beyond their passions. I don't know. She had said that of Oliver too, and of me. I had no evidence against them, but they seemed to be harmless without being good. Buffie was a problem. Biff had been streamlined by Harvard Business School and by commerce and could expect an appointment in Washington someday. Buffie was dull. She talked about mothballs as though they were a clue to the cosmos. She said "That really is something" until it became a metaphysical principle in an inchoate philosophy. She collected first editions of Maryland writers, and could recite Lizette Woodworth Reese, "When I consider life and its few years." She found Mencken irresponsible because he had sold his wife's collection of patch boxes at auction after her death; Buffie was buying them up as they appeared on the market. She thought that Gerald L. Johnson had been naive, John Barth difficult, Anne Tyler too often misguided, amusing but with some unbecoming ideas. Buffie had been pretty once, or almost pretty, but she had appraisals in her eyes. "I'd just like to sell my furniture at auction sometime, to find out what it's worth." "We're moving into a lovely Colonial house in the Valley as soon as the builders finish it. No one in Baltimore lives in Baltimore anymore." She toyed with the silverware, which Kwant always had spread out like a grandee, as though she contemplated buying it, and looked at the hallmark: "You can't touch this nowadays," she said in a mournful whisper as she fingered it. We anthologized her cruelly: "I was hoping to buy sandals. There are no inexpensive shoe stores in Baltimore." "Oh, you have a cook. Not everyone in Baltimore has a cook anymore." Once she called Orlando *Ronald.* "Biff, were we in Italy this year? Yes, I remember, the Medici Chapel was nice, but all those places could use a few plants." Could it have been Buffie who said, "Her hair was so beautiful you would think it was a wig?" Could Buffie have said, "That Don Giovanni was a veritable Don Juan," or have we glorified her banality in our memory? "They stole the Stone of Scone again. What do they want with it. They couldn't sell it, could they?" "There are plenty of good education programs on television. We subscribe." But she also collected third symphonies, and spoke enthusiastically of the Third Symphony in C Major of William Boyce, which Oliver, who collected facts, had never heard of, or even heard of William Boyce. He was in agony. She hoped when she was old and rich to commission the third symphonies of promising composers so that she "would live in musical history."

The four of them tossed out the names of stores like the names of friends, or like endorsements for themselves: Hennegan-Bates, Stieff, Remingtons, Hopper-McGaws. Weren't some of them long out of business? The Dunbars did nothing that they thought anyone could find fault with. They acted on the proprieties their grandmothers had talked over and had decided and had closed discussion of. Orlando admired Buffie's economy in exposition: "We're quite casual. What I wear on Charles Street my mother wouldn't wear for lunch beside the pool at the Club." Later I commented to Olivia that a woven-wicker purse with seashells glued to the top was not evil, that Olivia harmed herself with such exaggerations. Olivia, unrepentant, called Penney the "lass with the proprietary air," and referred to the evening as the night she learned that *bourgeois* means both redundant *and* tautological. And Orlando said: "I'm right about naturalism. Get the facts straight and symbols take care of themselves."

At the end of dinner, which was about 9 P.M., early for us but late for them, Kwant announced that they were fortunate to have arrived in time for the annual fiesta, peasant market, and *Fasching.* Oliver, Orlando, Olivia, and Aurelia, quick-change comedians, echoed, "Oh yes, the annual festival," and after Oliver led the Dunbars off to Tornata, Kwant muttering, "A nation of bellhops," with a malicious twinkle, if that seems possible, we cohorts conspired quickly and then separated to marshal the Creoles and Indians, and ourselves, to prepare for our first annual Oktoberfest. Olivia, who said that this was not the *Oktober* she had been filming in her mind's eye, dredged up a Swiss embroidered outfit and braided her hair, but we didn't have time for irony. Kwant thought of selling them futures in sugar, but he understood that Biff wasn't on a busman's holiday. Perhaps he had been joking. We took inventory—food, clothing, shelter, sex, entertainment, and curiosity (exotic information, tours of the island, ethnicity, authenticity, all would have their price)—we set what we could in motion, Kwant paid off the astonished workers to prime the pump, as he put it. Father Pasquale began the day with a special mass, taking as his text, Matthew 26:11, "For ye have the poor always with you," Mark 14:7, "For ye have the poor with you always," and John 12:8, "For the poor always ye have with you," Olivia murmuring, "For ye have the rich always with you," "For ye have the rich with you always," "For the rich always ye have with you." Then he took up a special collection for the floor he wanted to build in Renunciación, rather taking advantage of his captive audience, we thought. Kwant, so reduced to muttering that he almost endeared himself to us, mumbled, "Floor! over my dead body," but that easy irony was not to be. Polytropic Oliver allowed us to house-clean our lives of the dubious artifacts he had brought as gifts from airports all over the world. We gave eagerly to a hastily assembled native flea-market, which the "natives" thoroughly enjoyed, and unfortunately what the Dunbars did not buy, the Indians and Creoles did, spreading the infection of eclecticism, so many people walking around carrying objects, so many cultures being misquoted out of context, a pollution of exotica, an eczema, cured now that most of the objects have been placed on the grave-mounds. The collection for the poor got some Primavera money into circulation, and the Baltimores were friendly and generous, looking through their change for collectible coins. They toured the island led by a native guide, and were even shown Umberland, an education which was forbidden to us. They bought samples of native delicacies, and ate them like good sports. Delphine materialized in the plaza selling what she called her "velvet casserole," don't ask the ingredients, which she served in the brown onion-soup bowls. Buffie said, "You can't serve that in these. These are only for onion soup," or rather she started to say that but then seemed to erase the words as she spoke them into Delphine's arctic glare. They ate the young leucaena leaves dipped in pepper sauce, and washed them down with local beer, and Biff joked about opening a chain of leucaena concession stands. We did not know how to make the cherry preserves we make now, or the cherry juice which seems to cure most of my ills, or we could have sold them some. Which feels like an impure thought. As the only guests allowed at the ceremony they enjoyed themselves, they danced almost without condescension, they laughed at themselves, Buffie sang to Biff, "He has the cutest little dinghy in the navy." Haiti and the Barbadoes had been a disappointment, commercialized voodoo. We were unspoiled, really the other end of the rainbow. They never questioned that we had a price on everything. They never questioned anything. By late at night, to the rhythms of what Oliver called apocalypso music, they had given away or spent all their money. The next morning Biff Dunbar told Kwant that he wanted to buy more money. But *spending* was not *collecting*, and *buying* money was not *exchanging* money. I remembered the price he had written down that he had been willing to pay. Kwant knew only what Biff had paid. I stepped forward bellowing a high price as the latest quotation set in Zurich, almost doubling Biff's old offer to me on the theory that he had been trying for a bargain. Biff accepted our price without hesitation; Kwant was overwhelmed. I was afraid that he was going to say that he was proud of me.

Thinking about the Dunbars, Oliver, almost speechless with delight, kept saying "Priceless, priceless." Orlando collected their sayings just as he collected Creole proverbs:

"Of course we know Rutledge Daley. We know everyone in Baltimore." Orlando would giggle and, in spite of his attempts to economize with words, he would add, "She really said that, she did, really." The signals in their lives were clear, but so redundant that they were a new form of noise: the ideograms on the shirt, the epaulets that buttoned and unbuttoned, the labels and insignias, the Ratsey sails and the Roland Park Country Day School, and especially the yachting equipment and clothes Buffie's mother had bought at Abercrombie and Fitch when they (it) declared bankrupt, and she laid in a supply of appropriate clothes for the children, in graded sizes, allowing for their growth. Everything they owned relentlessly semaphored *money, money, money.* These people were not bad, but were they good enough for the universe? They treated the world like a convenient appliance. Allowing for the billions of years since the origins of the cosmos, considering the stars and stellar distances and earthly proximities, remembering kangaroos and beavers, camels, giraffes, coyotes, turtles, and porcupines, or looking at a leaf, and a butterfly upon a leaf, arranging itself in a comfortable relation to the sun, the Dunbars seemed cut off, disconnected, and incongruent with existence. Incoherent lives. They kept adding decorations to a world that had seemed complete without them. They treated the universe like a servant. Their experiences seemed to be a running commentary on money, although clearly they preferred to imply money rather than to be explicit. These people who were not so bad, who said *pier* when they meant *pier,* rather than *dock,* and who made expensive, if not exquisite, discriminations, insulted existence by supplementing it with smug adornments. I must add, passing over our snobbery and disdain, that the festival inspired by the Dunbars contributed to the greatest happiness of the greatest number, for everyone had fun, and the occasion whispered hints of what life might be like although lived in the midst of deception, irony, suspicion, and exploitation. The Dunbars returned in their dinghy, with an honor guard of dolphins, and sailed off in their motorized yacht, a harmless craft which yet embroidered unnecessarily on the precise image of life as being at sea in an open boat in winter, where the exigencies of weather set the rules, and the correct human tasks were obvious, and the purpose was to dwell on the surface supported by the unfathomable depths. The Dunbars gilded the metaphor. Yet off they sailed in *The Seafarer*, to sail from Primavera to the Severn River, a heroic distance, calling through the bullhorn that they would return to Primavera. But they never did. Delenda the cup-bearer floated into our lives. I must rest. I have one item of current events to report, and some news about the future. Then I really must mail this letter.

Tzun 14th. I realized while writing to you a few days ago that I was alone in the grove when I could be and would rather be at the party, so I went there. Remembering the yacht from Baltimore — those Dunbars who needed so much reassurance of their worth that they frightened me — has prompted other memories. Kwant's judgment was that Baltimore, which he let stand for America because it was *between* Washington, D.C. and Philadelphia, and so participated in each, although he never defined precisely what he meant by *participation*, was a city of the dead who had died from a surfeit of entertainment. He stood me once on a street corner and showed me the state-run lottery, the tolerated drugs, the alcoholics sleeping in doorways, the storefront where men sold their blood for money with which to buy cheap wine, the stores where the cheap wine was sold, the soft drinks, candy, fortune tellers, and prostitutes, all the pacifiers of the passive, a visual apologia for his rule on Primavera, I supposed, but surely we were no better, merely better protected. In my imagination I disowned Kwant, and that was that. But nothing was changed by that imagination. I thought of myself as a future "social critic" but in the meanwhile so many events in my life seemed to carry meaning that they were like an allegory, and non-political. One day I thought that I had penetrated the secret, that I had learned how to read my experience, and that the style of reading the meanings in my experience was an elaboration of those meanings, and harmonious. I was encountering images which gave point and purpose to events. One morning I awoke in the apartment of friends with whom I was staying because the apartment Kwant owned was being painted. A note on the breakfast table said that they had to leave early, to help myself to whatever was in the refrigerator for breakfast. I could smell coffee kept hot in an electric pot. The kitchen was neat, almost bare, with yellow walls. I opened the refrigerator and saw nothing in it but narcissi in a vase. I realized only hours later that they were kept in the cold to remain fresh while no one was home, but at the time I saw them only as an offering for my breakfast, and I declined the offer. I trailed my fingers on the refrigerator door as it seemed to have decided to close itself, and I helped myself to coffee, without sugar. I dressed to meet Rutledge at the Baltimore Museum of Art, a show of Surrealist paintings. I did not think that they were a space to love anyone in (a conceit I did not formulate until several years later, when loving Ginevra made me pause for thought). At their best the paintings seemed to represent the style of my experience, however, since I accepted some rather peculiar resemblances as identities. When we walked out of the room of paintings by Salvador Dali, we walked downstairs toward the African statue with the the erection which the museum director, a lady, had once covered with a grass skirt. As we approached, a workman walked toward us pushing a statue on a dolly. Rutledge pointed and said, "See the Dali." We laughed. The statue went floating past us like a message, an image which was the vehicle of an idea we could feel that we had been looking for. I pointed at Rutledge as we approached the African sculpture, and pronounced his last name, Daley, and as we laughed together he said, "I think I'll skirt the issue." The set of words and the set of events seemed to coincide; coincidences seemed like meaning; a set of signs added up to significance, until it seemed inevitable that a guest at a dinner party that evening in Guilford was a lateral descendent of Dolley Madison, herself named Dolley; she was explaining when the ice cream arrived that she had been reading a novel in which a dead cat was kept in a freezer, at which point the pets of the hostess, Siamese cats named Narcissus and Echo, pranced into the room. While she was pretending to be embarrassed at mentioning dead cats in the presence of live ones, our hostess was pleased, because the cats were being exceptionally friendly—"They don't do that with just anyone"—and Dolley detested them. I was connecting Daley, Dali, dolly, and this Dolley, and remembering that Salvador Dali had been satirically renamed Avida Dollars. These words, because they resembled each other, seemed proof of an obscure theorem. Images echoing other images seemed to make meaning available. The world was a dream reconciled with my dreams. It was like being without one's shoes in a painting by Signorelli. I thought that when images met and agreed together that my deepest images and most remote interiorities were objectified. My dreams had conquered the objective world. I would thrive on objective hazard. The pretty woman, Dolley, fit into my bed, not into the curved spaces of my chambered thoughts. In the morning she said, "The next time you want to masturbate, go ahead and masturbate, but leave me out of it." And for that remark I could have loved her, or at least liked her very much, just when I had lost her. I asked her to explain while I stalled for time, and she commented, "You make love as though you close your eyes and think of *my* good," which I thought was inconsistent with the other remark, but I didn't think I should start to argue consistency. After that, I always called her Dorothy. I saw, I suppose thanks to her, the dust I had been throwing in my own eyes, I saw the false excitements of my dull narcissism. When Rutledge telephoned later for a postmortem on the evening, he mentioned that a professor in a lecture commented that *Dalai* in *Dalai Lama* means *ocean,* and I merely responded that I thought I should be packing to return to my dry little island.

On a later day, no reckoning with images, I drove with Rutledge Daley to Washington to look at the painting by Leonardo of Ginevra. Looking at the painting, I thought of course of juniper with its bluish-grey fruit, although I could not get past the distractions of a guard with a pistol and the reflections in the bullet-proof glass. I did not imagine that the same evening I would see my cousin, Ginevra, out of place in an improbable garden in downtown Baltimore. As far as I could remember, I had not thought of her in Washington in connection with the painting, although when I saw her, I saw a connection. In the plentitude of bluish-grey evening, standing against the yew beside a wall covered with Virginia creeper, her body seemed the emanation of a power. I saw, and felt, the congruences between us. Even in the dusk I could see an affinity with the scent of her hair. She looked at me with a droll expression. As clearly as I could see the green of the garden I could see possibility, and an obedience committed in a garden. Amidst the thyme, the mint, and the begonias, under a hydroptic willow which the owners fussed over, there in that country which I despised because the citizens, the owners, mistook the power and energy and fertility of the place for their own virtue, I fell urgently in love with the light and motion of a garden in the evening with dew falling, as that light and motion were bodied forth in Ginevra. Then we were in the library. I put a recording, a symphony by Haydn, on the phonograph, and would have left it at that, but she put on Brahms's Sonata for Cello which I would have thought I was too disillusioned to listen to, but I wasn't. Later that evening another guest with whom I was talking interrupted to say that he wanted to watch a commercial on television because of business, and as I was talking he turned on the set, saying, "This will give you a lift," and as he stood watching and listening to the machine, frowning slightly at the problem presented in the commercial, then smiling as the problem was solved with a product called "Yes," I was watching and listening to him although he was not watching or listening to me. So we left the United States. I am no longer as certain about the beauty of a woman as an emanation. I see it now as an emergent novelty, only partially prepared for, not as a means of communicating with a source. Yet I have susceptibly strolled with Yolanda in the unkempt garden at Utterly. Birds long ago ate the fish from the pond in which mimosa trees now flourish. The mint, the bergamot, and the begonias which I brought here from Baltimore grow and flower in their own wild ways, inventing eccentric Fibonacci series. The nandina which we used to nurse now thrives with no care from a gardener, and the excessive pyracantha almost painfully exceeds beauty. Walking with Yolanda, I feel that I touch, as tangibly as I touch the leaves so perfectly shaped to the available light, the good possibilities. The trees, now governed by sun and wind and rain, and by some virtue of their own, no longer look solitary and transplanted. The peach at last looks Persian once again, the curious peach. And among them Yolanda, who is always something more to me than she is to herself, so decisively beautiful, seems in communion with a future which comes at me now at a different speed from last year's future. I now feel that I have time.

Batzul 16th. Dear Octavio, your memory lives on credit in my heart. I have humored my longing for you, fond old grandfather waiting on a cliff. I am half afraid to look out to sea, lest I catch myself looking for you. Not knowing what or how to think of you, I grow reluctant to think of you at all. Love needs something more available than you have been. But I do have news for you. A few days ago, Batzul the 8th, as we accumulate our own anniversaries. We could hear the party oscillating like a pendulum, to-and-fro, to-and-fro. Yolanda felt chilly, tired after gardening for a few hours at Umberland, so we walked up to the postoffice, almost the only place we keep a fire going, trying to save wood. My feeling, perhaps extravagant, now that the sum of all our instabilities is the stability of the party, and now that all our randomness has added up to persisting, open order, is that we eat and we drink at the flame of the party. People were bringing down parts of Utterly which are being dismantled, boards and such from old partitions. Other parts of the house are being fixed up for shelter. Many stray objects from Utterly are useful here, even the long wooden spoons which chanced to survive the fire. Yolanda and I drank some juice and ate a few cherries. We had brought a casserole earlier, about which no one asked us any questions. I went out to the kitchen and stood chatting and sorting beans. When I returned in half an hour, Yolanda was with the midwife. I don't know, Octavio, where to start when telling a story, for it seems to grow, to sprawl, and then to grow together again. The midwife cleared out the people and began to prepare a pallet on the floor, laying blankets over a slight concavity which unearthed a memory. The people strolled out to the plaza to dance and sing, the party flourishing out there among them. They are, at the moment, a different story, one of the many that sprawl around the story I am telling to you now, as they in their dancing surrounded the postoffice, stopping off at the convenient kitchen for a bite to eat. *Our* party continued in the postoffice where I was on the verge of speaking, almost protesting, because the six feet of earth where the blankets were arranged was familiar to me. Long ago, Father Pasquale was allowed by Kwant because he added local color to his script for the island. Olivia called him Father Unctuous. Unctuous nagged Kwant to install a wooden floor as a memorial to himself. "To cover the ground of inferences," Olivia said. Kwant procrastinated. Unctuous wanted his grave dug in the church so that his body would be safe from heathens. He did not dare ask any of us to help. Indians explained politely that they could not violate the body of their mother, the earth. Oliver added that only Miltonic devils ". . . with impious hands / Rifled the bowels of their mother Earth / For treasures better hid," scandalizing Father Pasquale. The Creoles were used to digging for their gardens, but they did in fact bury their dead above the ground, not in it, and they refused to help. So Unctuous, decrepit as he was (although I realize that he was not nearly as old as I am now, but I seem to have caught my second wind), began to dig his grave, intending to cover it with boards until the time came to bury him, which he assured us all would not be long. In truth, reli-

gion was not much of a success on this island, and if Kwant
hadn't been amused, in a literary way, at his picture of himself as a dictator with power over a whiskey priest, then he
would not have bothered. No one would help Father Pasquale until Aurelia volunteered. She had not even a scientific or historic interest in religion, but she could not resist
digging, and looked upon any hole that was being dug as a
combination of a geological field trip with an archeological
dig. Aurelia has told us, perhaps in letters among those
saved for you now in the enormous old refrigerator at Utterly, where we also keep her daily letters observing the
behavior of the bats, the seagrass, and even the sand-
dunes —just about anything that moves —how the Father
argued with her about the dirt. She was digging and
throwing the dirt to a pile on one side, but he said that they
must make even piles on each side as a sign of the opposites
which death would reconcile. "A secret meaning is buried
in every act," he said to Aurelia, an imperfect audience for
sacramental interpretations. "And while our friends, the
Indians, and our faraway friends in the Orient might see
that *all is one*, we must admit that life is filled with oppositions. My body, lowered between the opposite piles of dirt,
will be a mean between extremes. Contradictories such as
north and south, left and right (he would be facing East),
will become mere contraries, and the contraries will be
reconciled, like the coadunation of thought and thing."
Aurelia, who said that anyone growing up with Olivia and
Oliver would have to study logic in self-defense, commented that she needed time to think whether or not
she was opposed to these oppositions. She listened patiently to the Father's sermon as he took his turn digging the
hard clay packed down as the floor of the uninhibitedly
yellow-ochre church, long a favorite of watercolorists in
our family. Picturesque clumps of grass were already grow-

ing on the roof, and ferns which feed on air, apparently, hung from the eaves. "First," continued Father Pasquale, "I thought that graves could not be dug in this soil, and that therefore they buried the dead under heaps of stones or in trees. Then I found that holes can be dug but that no one will dig them. Now I am returning to my original notion, for judging from the hardness of this soil, holes can't be dug." He continued meditating on the coincidence of opposites, and subtly campaigning for the little wooden floor he permitted himself to look forward to. Aurelia heard him say, "The paths of naturalism lead but to the grave," and responded, "Of course," perhaps not understanding his intent. She recalled him saying that he was merely a grave that people walked on without knowing it, and later I was able to show her the passage in Luke 11:14, "Woe unto you, scribes and Pharisees, hypocrites! for ye are as graves which appear not, and the men that walk over them are not aware of them." When Pasquale took his turn again, with a pick-ax, Aurelia was sifting some of the rather uninteresting dirt through her fingers, and comparing the blisters on her hands as they reconciled the opposition between left and right. She was commenting to herself that the insignificant soil contained no geological secrets when she heard him say, "I marry opposites," and then, as she described it to me, when she looked at a sand dollar she had picked out of the dirt, she saw a vision of herself outstretched on the beach, eye-level with the sand, with the ripples and furrows where the ocean had unfurled, and shifting oppositions in the undulating beach, furls of sand shaping and reshaping themselves to the oceanic forces, sand moving into new but familiar configurations, the oppositions in the swirling sand always different, but always with the *same* differences, and she said to herself, Yes, shifting sands, but always the *same* shifts, and then she heard no more from Father Pasquale and saw that he had slumped over into his labyrinth. She felt for vital signs and knew, certainly with more certainty than most of us would have known, that he was dead, presumably from the excitement and effort of digging his grave. We learned only much later, when Aurelia had emerged onto the veranda after showering, in the cool of the evening, that he had died. She had straightened him out "as well as she could," and had shoveled the dirt back into the hole, alternating between the opposite piles because she thought he would have wanted that. When Oliver who liked ceremonies protested, Aurelia answered him levelly, "He was dead, so I buried him." How disingenuous she was I could not gauge, and I was her father. Oliver seemed puzzled, but he was silent. Now such vines have grown over the yellow-ochre church that it is our green postoffice. Oliver used to call it the Church of the Transgression, in honor of Pasquale, and would say, "Forgive us our trespasses," when others walked over Pasquale unaware.

Thus the women attending Yolanda walked, unaware, and Yolanda lay, unaware, sublimely out of place once more. The labor was mercifully short, and a baby girl was borne out of the labyrinth. I have not solved the problems I set out to solve, yet much of my life recently feels like the successful solution to several problems. Events have moved of themselves in directions that I wanted to go in. Some events have moved like wavering emotions, and some like hightide thoughts. I decided that a woman knows that she gives birth astride a grave, she has heard it often enough: "Elles accouchent à cheval sur une tombe." Even a place, I thought, might be reborn. Yes, the Friar in *Romeo and Juliet* had said, "The earth that's nature's mother is her tomb. / What is her burying grave, that is her womb." Act II, scene iii, I would like to check the spelling in the folio. My happiness is on a crest beneath which unfurls the pain and sorrow we could tell each other about. I could write an anthology of moments of happiness so expansive that happiness reaches into the precincts of grief, and then beyond, into serenity. I looked at our baby. I looked at the wonder of her eyes which had not seen any of our wonders. I looked through her eyes toward her heart. She cried, and my body, in congruence with hers, contracted, then expanded. She cried, and I responded. I wanted to forestall any ceremonies about anacondas or canoes, so with the permission of Yolanda, I named our daughter Renata, my attempt to govern the meanings. Overwhelmed and bewildered by joy, I walked outside in the moonlight for a few minutes to share my tearful delight with the awakened unanimities. I buried the afterbirth, a shell, and a scrap of cloth cut from my trousers as Yolanda had instructed me. The hour was later than I would have thought. The night was fully night, vividly apparent. The large hall mirrors brought down from Utterly, where they might have been broken in the reconstruction, reflected the moon as they leaned against the outside of the postoffice. For a moment I saw them, in Shelley's words, as "mirrors of the gigantic shadows which futurity casts upon the present," and then I saw them as objects, merely objects, supported by my sight of them. At last, almost successfully superficial, and beyond mirage, I touched the glass. It was wet with dew. In a moment of forgetfulness I danced like an old salt, turn and counterturn. Dancing was "some sort of belief," like seeing that the foreground contains as much of the background as I need to know, if I observe attentively. Then I remembered that I was alone when I could be at a party, and getting to know our new guest. I touched the lustrous moonwater with a cloth until it was cool and damp, then walked inside to Yolanda and pressed the cloth of distillations to her brow. I sat next to my wife and touched her hand. I held our exolinguistic infant in my arms and blew lightly in both ears, as Yolanda urged me to. Renata rested from her effort to be born. "But who will she marry?,", I asked. "We all speak one language now, like a crew along a coastline." Yolanda looked at me and smiled. "She will marry anyone she chooses to, like her mother," Yolanda answered me, the answerable woman.

This seems to be a story, Octavio, that had no particular place to start; a story that has changed in the telling, even as the telling has made changes; and a story with no particular place to end. I have tried to tell you of our rapports. I have to go up to the postoffice now, so while I am there I will mail this letter, and check on the progress of the party. The party is our only police, our only policy, our conscience. It rules us with a heroic etiquette. Yolanda and I have moved into a room at Utterly, my childhood home, with Renata. I feel slightly out of place in my old home; my happiness there is tainted by sour thoughts, even though I can enter my father's house now without wishing that I were invisible. My thoughts. I found my definition of thinking long ago amidst the impurities of a tainted philosopher, Martin Heidegger: *moving into nearness.* Our revolutions have brought us the freedom to move into nearness.

What do we need but the freedom to move into nearness? I am starting a letter now, a more adherent letter, to my daughter Renata, my corresponding child. I will write for her how I have made a place for myself in a collective and historical process, our party. The feathers to write with I will find on the beach. A child, useful, shapes and sharpens them for me with his knife which he found in the crawl-space under Utterly. This ink, which is sometimes disgusting, I make from berries that ripen among the mounds. Frequently the ink ferments before I can use it. I must ask for advice. Our island life has been like being in love in a painting by Breughel. It has been like walking barefoot in a painting by Botticelli. And lately, with a baby joining our sandy world, it has been like walking barefoot *on* a painting by Botticelli. But the tasks of life have been easier since I learned what to do and what not to do in order to be a good and welcome guest, and to write letters faithfully, and not to be too true to myself; to avoid violent purity. So I have produced this letter which has produced me. I have been writing, and I am happy to be able to write, to tell you, Octavio, the words I hear in my head as I write, that we are having a party, and have been for some time now, and we want, with words I am trying to deliver alive from my heart, to invite you. You are welcome to join us in our consonance, at any time, to come as you are, to take potluck with us. Feel free to bring a friend, or partner. Don't wait until you are ready. And if all that I have written is clear to you now as an invitation, then I suppose that I have finished writing my letter. The letters that made me happiest as a young man were the invitations to parties which showed me that I had been satisfactory and was welcome among friends. Even parties of somewhat somber merriment. As long as I was remembered (even grateful for looks of recognition at a wake-party). Ah, the remembrances of me that I choose to remember. As you are remembered fondly, Octavio, and can be certain of your welcome in this our republic of letters, where our strongest imperative is that we must treat everyone so that we can enjoy a laugh together later.

> Your glad old outrigger grandfather,
> Salathiel

Yolanda says to say Hello.